HEARTS
of the
MISSING

HEARTS
of the
MISSING

CAROL POTENZA

MINOTAUR BOOKS

NEW YORK

HEARTS OF THE MISSING. Copyright © 2018 by Carol Potenza. All rights reserved. Printed in the United States of America. For information, address St. Martin's Press, 175 Fifth Avenue, New York, N.Y. 10010.

Designed by Omar Chapa

www.minotaurbooks.com

Library of Congress Cataloging-in-Publication Data

Names: Potenza, Carol, author.
Title: Hearts of the missing / Carol Potenza.
Description: First edition. I New York : Minotaur Books, 2018.
Identifiers: LCCN 2018027002 I ISBN 9781250178282 (hardcover) I
    ISBN 9781250178299 (ebook)
Subjects: I GSAFD: Suspense fiction.
Classification: LCC PS3616.O8435 H43 2018 I DDC 813/.6—dc23
LC record available at https://lccn.loc.gov/2018027002

Our books may be purchased in bulk for promotional, educational, or business use. Please contact your local bookseller or the Macmillan Corporate and Premium Sales Department at 1-800-221-7945, extension 5442, or by email at MacmillanSpecialMarkets@macmillan.com.

First Edition: December 2018

10 9 8 7 6 5 4 3 2 1

To my mom. I wish you could have read this. To FLF.
Thanks for the ghost stories.

HEARTS
of the
MISSING

CHAPTER ONE

Tsiba'ashi D'yini Indian Reservation
New Mexico, USA

The harsh scrape, out of place in the quiet of predawn, penetrated the low buzz of the refrigeration motors. Like fingernails on a chalkboard, the sound made the hair on her neck and arms stand on end.

She wasn't alone anymore.

Her eyes narrowed as she peered through the open door of the office and into the cavernous space on the other side. Other than a few emergency lights pooling eerily on the floor, the room was dark, its bulky shelves and racks rising out of the linoleum like misshapen boulders.

Sergeant Nicky Matthews was careful to make no sound as she placed her fingerprint brush on the metal shelf in front of her. She stripped off her latex gloves with quiet efficiency as she rose, dropping them on the floor by her feet. Head cocked to the side, she strained to hear any other sound that would indicate who—or how many—might be just outside the broken plate-glass window of the mini-mart.

She hadn't heard a car pass by since she'd been here, and she'd sent the manager home after he'd let her inside.

Her police unit was parked in plain sight by the gas pumps, illuminated by the fluorescent lights in the metal canopy above it. Those lights formed a harsh bubble of white in the nighttime blackness that surrounded the building. The village store sat alone on a two-lane road, the only place to purchase food and gas for twenty miles in every direction. Porch lights from widely scattered trailers and small houses dotted the landscape, but she'd seen no one when she'd arrived. She'd been inside, processing the scene, for over an hour. If the perps had come back, they must know she was here.

Another stealthy rasp, outside and to the left of the window.

She stiffened, focus shifting, tightening. Her hand slipped to her holster, palm scraping the butt of her Glock 23. Whoever was out there was on the other side of the wall where she stood. She'd trained her phone's camera on that area earlier. The perps had used a bat or crowbar to bash in the large windows, and glass was strewn over the front sidewalk. At least one of them had cut themselves when they climbed inside. There were drops and smears of blood throughout the interior. She'd already gathered some samples for DNA testing, but the bloody smears turned into distinct prints in the office. One of the burglars spent quite a bit of time here, and that was where she'd been concentrating her efforts. But no longer.

Whoever was skulking outside had her full attention.

Nicky stepped forward, avoiding the half dozen sunglasses knocked to the floor during the break-in. She turned her back to the wall, body coiled, and scanned the interior of the store for a change in the vague fluorescent light filtering into the room. Someone peering through the window would throw a shadow.

Her scalp prickled and a flash of heat swept over her skin. She swore she could feel a presence out there.

Waiting for her.

She drew in a slow breath, pulled her weapon, and pointed it down along her leg. Her finger rested across the trigger guard. She sidled closer to the window. Shards of glass littered the floor. The rubber soles of her boots muffled the crunch, but the sound was loud enough to make her wince. She paused, listening.

Seconds ticked by.

Nothing. No sound except the ever-present hum of the glass-doored coolers lining the back wall of the store.

She stayed in the shadows, her sharp gaze sweeping the gravel expanse of the parking lot. Tall, scraggly grass stood unmoving at the edge of the light. There was no wind, no scuttling leaves to explain away the noise.

Another minute passed. The feeling of a presence was fading. Nicky exhaled slowly. Her shoulders relaxed the tiniest bit, even as her expression twisted in faint confusion.

Had she been mistaken?

A movement caught her eye between the gas pumps, and she snapped her head to the right. Her body tensed. At a flash of color, Nicky stepped out of the shadows, not worried about the sound of scattering glass as she tracked the motion of . . .

A skinny brown rez dog wandered around the side of her unit, nose to the ground. Lifting its head, it sniffed the air. It trotted toward an overflowing trash can and rose up on its hind feet, one front paw positioned delicately against the side. Nicky's lips pressed tight. You could count the ribs on that poor animal. Most likely it was a stray, but you never knew. It might belong to anyone in the village.

Relieved she had an answer to the sounds, Nicky holstered her pistol. Suddenly tired, she stretched, arching her back. Outside, the sky was beginning to gray. She checked the clock on the wall above the door. The sun would be up in a few minutes, and it would still take another hour to process the crime scene. Then she was going to canvass the nearest homes, to see if anyone had heard or seen anything. She probably wouldn't be done until hours after her shift was officially over.

Her gaze focused closer, and she stared at the pale oval of her reflection in what was left of the glass window in front of her. Dark brown eyes stared back as she ran her hand over the top of her head and slid her fingers through the smooth, straight black hair of her ponytail. She was mistaken for Native all the time. Not by Indians—but by the non-Indians she encountered on the reservation and at the casino.

She sighed deeply, glanced at the dog one more time, and froze. A wave of unease washed over her, this time prickling up her back. The animal stared at the front of the store, fixated not on the place where she stood, but to the left of the window's edge.

At the place where she'd first heard the noise.

Her hand dropped to her sidearm and Nicky jerked her head around. An old Native woman stared at her through the glass.

No. Not through the glass. In the glass.

The old woman's face was *in the glass*.

Their eyes met, and every nerve in Nicky's body stretched taut. The woman's pupils glowed black, glittering and alive, sharp points embedded within a deeply wrinkled face. An ancient, disembodied face.

Nicky *knew* she was supposed to look away—had been told in no uncertain terms by her traditional friends on the rez—but she couldn't move. She was transfixed.

The sun flashed over the horizon, blinding her.

But not before the woman smiled and turned away. Her long white hair whipped in the light—and she was gone.

Nicky yanked out her gun, hit the front door of the mini-mart hard, and ran outside into the brightness of dawn, skidding on the broken glass. The same scraping sound that had alerted her only a few minutes before grated along her skin.

A flash of white raced away and her arms swung up, the muzzle of her sidearm tracking a rabbit as it zigged and zagged out of the parking lot, across the road, and into the grass next to a trampled dirt path. She caught another movement out of the corner of her eye and her head swiveled to the dog. It cringed and shivered as it stared after the rabbit, before it backed up and loped away through the brush, tail tight between its legs.

Nicky's flesh crawled with goose bumps. Heart thudding, she pointed her weapon to the ground, clutching its diamond-patterned grip so tightly it cut deep into the skin of her palm.

Dammit, dammit, dammit!

Scowling, she slammed her weapon back into its holster.

The old woman was back.

That meant life was about to get complicated—and a lot more dangerous.

CHAPTER TWO

Nicky pressed the switch on her unit's radio. "Two-one-three, Dispatch, away from my vehicle. Available by portable."

"Copy that, Sergeant, and out."

She smoothed her hand across her breast pocket, feeling for her pen and small spiral notebook. The manager of the convenience store had come back half an hour ago to start cleanup. His statement was hand-written in the book and included an assurance that he'd get her the surveillance video.

Even though it was early, the sun was up and bright in a clear sky and the temperature was rising. It would be another warm day on the pueblo. She slipped her wraparound sunglasses over her eyes and closed the hatch of her Tahoe, the evidence she'd collected stowed in the back. The closest homes were a few hundred yards away, across the two-lane blacktop. A good place to start her canvass for witnesses.

And she would head down the dirt path where the rabbit had disappeared. She smirked. Down the rabbit hole, right where the old Indian woman was leading her.

A Fire-Sky Pueblo police unit sailed over a short rise up the road and the sound of classic rock swelled in the air. It swerved, tires crunching on the loose gravel of the mini-mart's parking lot, and stopped next to her. Officer Manny Valentine grinned as the Rolling Stones blasted in all directions.

Great.

She stood silently, trying to keep the contempt for her fellow officer off her face.

"Hey, Matthews. Didn't know you picked up this mess." He leaned out the window and his grin morphed into a sneer. "Isn't this below a *sergeant's* pay grade?" He gave her a sleazy up-and-down that made Nicky want to put a bullet in his crotch. "You should make it a point to let your *friends* know what kind of work they have you doing."

Her fingers twitched. Maybe between his eyes instead, but she doubted it would change his personality much.

"I'm off for a well-deserved rest. I'll be seeing Captain before I head home. Anything you want me to tell him? After all, I'm his good buddy."

The *and you're not* hung in the air, unsaid.

"Watch yourself, now." He peeled out, kicking up dirt and gravel that hit her in the legs and chest. A tiny piece of rock stung her cheek, but she didn't flinch.

Ass.

She stepped onto the blacktop, determined to focus on the case. Thinking about her job right now would be counterproductive, an unnecessary distraction. Besides, Captain was watching her like a hawk for any little screwup. She wouldn't give him the satisfaction.

The dirt track on the other side of the road was well traveled. It snaked between two posts of a barbed-wire fence, the wire cut and looped back. Still dangerous if you weren't careful. A dusty footprint headed away from the store, its tread pattern the same as one stamped in blood at the mini-mart. Nicky dropped a black-and-white ruler next to it, and with her cell phone snapped a half dozen pictures at different angles. The same imprint continued for several steps before she lost the trail.

An old single-wide mobile home was parked a couple hundred feet away. It was the closest to the crime scene and also the closest to the path. She'd start there.

Her gaze swept the field around her as she crunched through the dried grass, searching for evidence or signs of . . . what? The rabbit?

Exasperated, she stepped over the line of rocks that edged the rutted driveway to the trailer. A dented metallic-green *ranfla*, its paint faded and peeling, was parked under a listing shelter, red tape in place of one of the taillights. Broken pots, half filled with dirt and plants dead since the last century, were scattered around the cinder-block steps leading to the front door. The ground was scratched up around an area where part of the trailer's skirt was missing. It looked like something pretty big lived underneath.

Nicky knocked on the door. Faded blue curtains twitched behind dirty windows. Her hand slipped to her sidearm. Just in case.

The door creaked open, its sound accompanied by a hacking cough coming from a thin, hunched man standing at the threshold. The smell of stale beer wafted over her. His arm came up to shield his eyes from the sun, a frown on his face. Nicky put his age at about forty.

"Hey," he said in a raspy voice. He dropped his arm to hack into his sleeve.

"Good morning, sir. I'm Sergeant Monique Matthews from the Tsiba'ashi D'yini Pueblo police," she said, using the Keresan name of the pueblo. "There was a break-in early this morning—about three-thirty—at the Fire-Sky Mini-Mart across the road. Did you hear or see anything suspicious?"

The guy rubbed his hand over his jaw and yawned. His face was haggard and pale, his black hair standing on end. Bloodshot eyes squinted at her. They topped heavy dark circles in the skin beneath them.

"Uh. Wait. I can't see. Let me get my glasses."

He stepped behind the door. Nicky tensed in case he bolted, but relaxed again when he returned with thick black-rimmed glasses perched on his face. The lenses made his eyes even smaller but—surprisingly—his face younger. She readjusted his age closer to thirty.

"Nah. I didn't see or hear anything. I was too drunk last night. Asleep until you knocked."

"May I have your name, sir?" She took out her notepad and pen.

"Howard Kie. Hey. You know you have blood on your face?"

The gravel flung up by Valentine's unit.

"Mr. Kie, were you here all night?"

"Nah. Came home about two-thirty this morning. So, does Billy

Oliver still work at the police department? He was a classmate of mine." His eyes slid away from her.

Nicky didn't know anyone with that name. "No, sir. Where were you before you came home?"

"At a bar. Over in Whyler." A tiny town outside the reservation's border. The pueblo was dry, but there were plenty of enterprising merchants just across the line that could quench a thirst for alcohol.

"So, you been at the police department long?" His glance skittered back to her face and the sun's glare flashed off his glasses. "Do you investigate, like, murders and missing persons and stuff?"

It was the third time he'd tried to change the subject. Perps changed the subject.

"Five years." She tilted her head and smiled. "Mr. Kie, may I come inside so we can talk? I'd like to get some more information from you, and I see the sun's in your eyes."

If anything, he paled even more and took a step back. "Nah, nah. I'm fine."

Damn. She was losing him.

Her gaze dropped to his feet. He was wearing dusty cloth sneakers.

"Could I see the bottom of your shoes?" If the tread was even close to what she'd seen at the mini-mart, she'd have probable cause for a search warrant.

He blinked rapidly. "Uh, sure. Sure." He wiggled off a shoe and handed it to her. She flipped it over.

Not the same tread. She gave it back to him and extracted one of her cards from her vest.

"Here's my phone number and email. If you remember anything, please don't hesitate to call."

He brought her card up close to his face, then peeked over it, brows puckered.

She turned to leave and stopped. She had to know.

"Mr. Kie? One more thing. Does anyone around the area raise rabbits? In particular, white rabbits?"

His jaw went slack. "What? You saw a *white* rabbit?" he asked, voice rising. "Where?"

Nicky cleared her throat. "This morning, at the store. It ran in this direction."

"*Dza*. Nah. No white rabbits. Never," he said, shaking his head so hard he had to put a hand up to catch his glasses.

"Well, thank you for your time. Please give me a call if you remember anything."

She left, following the driveway out to a dirt road that led to the next house.

As she walked away, Howard swallowed both fear and excitement.

Maybe, just maybe, this cop would listen to him. Maybe he could make her understand that terrible things were happening on the pueblo. Maybe.

After all, she'd seen the white rabbit.

CHAPTER THREE

Nicky dropped into the chair at her desk, blew out a sigh, and wiped a hand across her mouth. One finger slid up her cheek to probe the tiny nick from the gravel. From a drawer in her desk, she grabbed a towelette and tore the packet open. The sharp scent of lemons was reviving, as was the sting of the alcohol against the cut. She stared at the red stain before throwing the wipe in the wastebasket. There wasn't much blood, but she'd make sure Valentine would regret his little drag race next time he was on her roster.

She started up her computer and logged into the Case Investigator Database. With her notebook open on her desk, she cataloged the burglary's evidence, the results of her canvass, and wrote up the Initial Notification Report for her lieutenant. The low hum of voices mixed with tapping keyboards and periodic rings of cell phones were a soothing background of white noise.

Savannah Analla, the public safety director's assistant, thunked half a dozen thick file folders onto the desk.

"Hey. Weren't you off shift like three hours ago? Stop trying to solve the world's problems. Go home and get some rest."

Nicky yawned and rubbed her burning eyes. She waved at the computer. "I hate it when criminals think they're smarter than us. It's like—"

"A puzzle you have to solve to prove them wrong. I know. And that's why you're the best cop in this one-horse, two-bit town, *Tex*." Savannah grinned, the slight gap between her front teeth giving her expression a girlish charm. "When's Montoya back from vacation?"

"Tomorrow, so only one more night in uniform." Nicky brushed at a spot of dirt on the dark blue material of her slacks. "I like taking these shifts. Patrol officers tend to have a lot more positive interaction with the community. I miss that."

"But not the goats," Savannah said with a wink. "You still owe me for saving you that day."

On her second morning of work at Fire-Sky, Nicky was sent to the parking lot of the police department to negotiate Family Meeting reparations for a petty crime. Completely out of her element, she'd held the horns of a bad-tempered goat while trying desperately to calm the feuding parties as a phalanx of uniformed officers laughed on the front steps. Savannah had marched outside, snapped out something in Keres, and divided the goats and people. Then she'd torn the watching officers a new one and took Nicky to the break room for the worst cup of coffee she'd ever had in her life.

They'd been best friends ever since.

Savannah leaned her hip against the edge of the desk. Her dark brown eyes gleamed behind old-fashioned gold-wire spectacles that somehow complemented the bangs and asymmetric bob of her straight black hair. Even though Savannah was 100 percent Fire-Sky Indian ("Check the tribal register. According to my ancestry, I'm frickin' related to the Earth Mothers"), she was the most nontraditional member of the tribe Nicky knew. Still, Savannah had helped her navigate some tricky cultural situations in the last few years. Her friend's sharp-edged skepticism anchored her firmly to reality when things got out of hand.

Nicky sucked in a slow breath as she pictured the old woman's face in the glass the night before. Those "things" had reared their head again. Literally.

"So, I'll see you Friday, right? I bought the prettiest steaks—to grill this time, not to burn." Savannah's grin widened in her round face, warm cinnamon-brown skin crinkling at the corners of her eyes.

"Yeah, about that. Is, um, Ryan coming?"

In contrast to Savannah, Ryan Bernal was the most traditional

Native she knew. He was also a lieutenant in the pueblo's Fire, EMS, and Rescue Department. With Savannah's friendship had come Ryan's, even though her two friends had a connection Nicky didn't quite understand and Savannah refused to explain. But Ryan was smart and easygoing and he and Nicky had meshed. The three of them had developed a close-knit relationship over the last five years. They knew all of each other's secrets—well, almost.

Savannah's smile faded and her face took on a neutral expression even as a tinge of red highlighted her cheeks. "I never invite him, but that doesn't mean he won't show up anyway," she replied, scooping up the files.

Ryan's interest in—and patience with—Savannah bordered on legendary. But there was nothing going on between the two of them, or at least hadn't been since Nicky had known them.

"I, um . . . I need to speak to him. And you. About something that happened last night. Well, more like early this morning." Nicky's gaze held Savannah's until her friend's face screwed into a scowl.

"Not again." Savannah kept her voice low, but it didn't mask the snapping irritation.

Nicky winced internally. She was about to get another scathing lecture on the correlation between shift-work sleep disorder and hallucination, when the atmosphere of the room shifted.

Heads turned and voices quieted as Nicky's lieutenant, Gavin Pinkett, strode to the center of the room, a frown marring his expression.

"Listen up, folks. Rail Runner's called in a train-*cyclists*—plural—collision on the Fire-Sky right-of-way. OMI's already been contacted. I need four officers and agents to respond and walk the track for recovery, and another couple to head up to the train and take statements. It's stopped on Cochiti land. State and Cochiti PD are en route."

"Hey, Lieutenant. Are they ours?"

The quiet question from across the room rang like a bell in the taut silence. Nicky glanced at Savannah, worried about how she was taking the news.

"Preliminary info says no." Pinkett cleared his throat, his gaze running over the faces around him, finally settling on Nicky. His attention started her heart pounding. She scooped up the keys to her unit and stood, but he gestured for her to stay in place when his assistant approached him with a pink slip of paper. The day-shift sergeant followed one step behind her.

"Talk to you later," Nicky whispered, mouth suddenly dry. Savannah, wide-eyed, faded away from her desk, files hugged close to her chest.

The volume of noise increased as personnel shifted to finish tasks and arrange to head out to the collision field. Nicky's fists clenched, keys to her unit biting into her palm, and waited for Lieutenant Pinkett. As a federal investigator and Bureau of Indian Affairs–trained agent, she'd taken the lead in four of the last five train-pedestrian encounters. She was also the appointed liaison with OMI—the Office of Medical Investigators—because, in the past, there had been . . . problems . . . with OMI's lack of cultural sensitivity. The pueblo was still rebuilding trust with them.

"If we're short-handed, I'll call in off-duty personnel," Pinkett said to the desk sergeant, before he once again focused on Nicky. He walked over to stand by her desk, but wouldn't look at her. She tensed.

"Is the INR done for the mini-mart break-in?"

"Yes, sir," she said. "I can leave immediately—"

Pinkett interrupted her. "Cheryl brought me witness corroboration. The two individuals weren't members of the pueblo." He waved the note from his secretary.

The reservation had seen an upswing of suicide-by-train in the past few years. Still, she knew from experience that the way a train mangled and tore apart bodies made identification difficult. Until a hand was collected for fingerprints, or a head was scanned for dental records, no one could make a determination of origin.

"I'm putting Gallegos in charge. He needs the experience," Pinkett said.

There was a rasping sound as he slid his palm back and forth over the stubbled growth of hair on his scalp. He shifted, cleared his throat, and glanced at her from the corner of his eye.

Nicky held her breath. His body language put her on high alert.

"Besides, you've already worked your sixteen today." He cleared his throat again. "And you're out of overtime this month. Captain's orders. Sorry," he said, voice gruff.

Her stomach twisted. This was the first time she'd been so deliberately and directly frozen out of a case by Captain Richards.

"Look, Lieutenant, you know I have the most experience. If you're short-handed at the site, you can justify, you can—can—" Mortified by the edge of desperation in her voice, she clamped her mouth shut. Pinkett stared at her, lips tight.

"No. He's looking for a reason to jump down your throat and I don't want any part of that. I'll call in another one of the night-shift officers." He paused as if to say something else, but instead pressed his lips into a hard line and walked away.

Anger and something akin to panic swirled in Nicky's head. She tossed her keys on the desktop and raised her hand to press back frustrated tears, knowing she shouldn't—*couldn't*—show any weakness.

The pad of her thumb brushed against the nick on her cheek.

She blinked away the moisture and squared her shoulders.

"Hey, Lieutenant. Who are you going to call in?"

Pinkett halted and swiveled back toward her. Though his expression was neutral, she recognized the shadow in his eyes for exactly what it was: guilt for barring her from this investigation. She wasn't above taking advantage of it.

"You've worked these scenes before, Matthews. Saying this one's gonna be messy is an understatement. Double the gore. Got any recommendations?"

Her mother would counsel forgiveness.

But her mother wasn't here. Nicky smiled grimly.

"Yeah. Valentine. Definitely Valentine."

CHAPTER FOUR

"Nicky? Do you want another beer?"

Ice crunched as Ryan rummaged around in the cooler at the edge of the patio. The smoke from hickory wood chips in the grill perfumed the air, slipping in through the screen door.

"I'm good," she called. "I've got to drive home after dinner."

"You can stay here tonight," Savannah said, voice crisp. She finished rough-chopping the zucchini, and scooped up the chunks to mix into a bowl with onions, squash, celery, mushrooms, and tomatoes, then tossed them in marinade. She peeked over the top of her glasses when the screen door slid open and Ryan walked in. "Is the grill hot enough?"

"A few more minutes." He twisted off the cap to his Pellegrino and slid onto the barstool next to Nicky, taking a long drink before clunking it down on the wooden surface, both elbows following.

"Coaster." Savannah pushed a thick cork circle in his direction. She dumped the veggies into a grill basket.

Nicky picked up a piece of jewelry from the velvet-lined tray in front of her. She held it up to the light, awed by Ryan's artistry. Inlaid turquoise, coral, and amber flashed with each movement of her hand.

"My God, Ryan, these are gorgeous," she said and smiled at the trace of pride hidden deep in his hazel eyes. She laid down the pendant she'd been admiring and scooped up the matching earrings. The intricate mixture of stone flickered and licked in the light, just like the flames they were modeled after. Ryan had set the stones in gold instead of silver, enhancing the richness of the amber's glow.

"I'll give you fifty bucks for the set. Cash," Nicky offered, brushing back her hair to dangle an earring next to her face. "Okay, twenty-five. But that's my final offer."

Savannah snorted as she picked up the stuffed basket and headed out to the patio. The changes to Ryan's face were subtle. While his expression was serene, even placid, his lips twitched and he cocked an eyebrow at her. In any other person, that would be a belly laugh.

"Sorry, Nicky. I'm putting these on consignment at a gallery in Santa Fe. I couldn't afford the gold when I bought it. I'll make you some in silver." His brow furrowed. "But amber won't work as well with silver. Maybe opal," he muttered as he contemplated the pieces of jewelry.

Nicky shook her head, grinning. Friday nights at Savannah's never disappointed. They'd become a cherished ritual in her life, providing a much-needed venue to relax, or vent about their jobs, or do nothing more than eat and watch a movie.

Her smile faded.

Or discuss strange visions of ancient spirits embedded in glass, and fleeing white rabbits.

But not until everyone had eaten.

Savannah's yell of, "Steaks!" had Nicky hopping off her barstool and opening the fridge. She pulled out a plastic-wrap-covered pan containing three beautifully marbled rib eyes. Ryan sketched on a little pad of paper as Nicky carried the meat outside for the grill.

She handed Savannah the pan of steaks.

Hopefully food would have a mellowing effect before their talk tonight.

Her stomach jumped nervously. Especially on Savannah.

They sat on the backyard patio, triangulated around a low wrought-iron, tile-topped table. Under-cabinet lights glowed through the kitchen window, barely penetrating the inky darkness around them. The sharp medicinal scent of citronella blended seamlessly with the warm night.

Savannah's glasses glinted with the reflection of the candle's flame, and its golden light warmed the skin of her face.

"Do you think she was trying to frighten you?" Ryan asked.

Nicky tipped her head to the side, rolling Ryan's question around in her mind. She was glad it was dark. It made it easier to talk about what she'd seen.

"No. I mean, I didn't get the vibe she was there to scare me."

"That's because *she* wasn't really *there* at all," Savannah said with exaggerated diction, an edge to her voice. "Jeez, Nicky, it was dark, you were alone, and you heard a weird noise, so it freaked you out." Savannah sat forward in her captain's chair, ticking off her argument points on her fingers. "You'd been on nights since last Saturday, logged at least three to four hours of overtime each day on a twelve-hour shift. And before that, you'd come off of a long week with that arson in Salida, right? Oh! And the semi-truck fatality on the highway last Monday. Wasn't that a sixteen-hour day?" Sitting back with a huff, she frowned. "None of what you saw was real. There's another explanation." She waved her hand. "Maybe it was the reflection of a face on a magazine cover. You probably saw one of the Kardashians in the glass."

"Probably." Nicky's lips pressed into a slight smile as she hunched back in her chair. She propped her feet up on the table in front of her and continued to peel the label off the beer she'd been nursing since dinner.

"This is, what, the third time you've seen the ancient one, right?" Ryan's voice was low, almost hypnotic. "Did you look away like I told you?"

Nicky took a swig of her beer and grimaced. Too warm. She tucked it under her chair and glanced at Ryan before smoothing her top over her lap.

"Not this time."

"How long did you stare?"

It could have been for a few seconds or a few minutes. Time had seemed to stop.

"Not long, I think. It was like she wanted to tell me something, like she wanted my attention." She shook her head. That wasn't right, but how did she explain the unexplainable?

A breeze swept through the patio, dancing over Nicky's arms and up her neck to toss errant strands of hair across her face. The warm wind should have been soothing, but she suddenly felt a shimmering unease. Gooseflesh peppered her skin and a chill crawled down her spine.

"A flash of light from the rising sun hit the glass and she was gone," Nicky said.

"That doesn't surprise me," Ryan said. "The Sky gods interfered because you didn't look away. They were probably jealous and wanted to distract you."

"*Seriously*, Ryan? Jealous *Sky gods*?" Savannah propped her feet on the table, too, her slim brown calves flexing as she tucked her short dress underneath her backside.

Nicky waited for Ryan's response, but when she looked at him, he was riveted on Savannah's smooth, exposed skin. His eyes seemed to burn from within as his gaze slowly traveled over her body, lingering on her chest and neck. How was Savannah not scalded by it?

When he saw Nicky studying him, Ryan dropped his eyes and shrugged. "Okay. It could have been Fire gods, since the sun's light was involved," he conceded. Savannah frowned.

"Who is she, Ryan? And what's the rabbit all about? Is the old lady a shape-shifter or something?" Nicky asked.

"*We* are not shape-shifters. Tene—Navajos—are shape-shifters. And why are you asking him? He's frickin' Jicarilla Apache! And *Swedish*, for God's sake." Savannah's righteous indignation cut through Nicky's unease. She bit her lip to stop a smile.

"I was raised here, though. It's like having dual citizenship. Both tribal cultures are ingrained in me," Ryan countered calmly. "We are more than our blood, Savannah."

It was an old argument between them. Nicky knew well enough to keep out of it.

He turned his shoulder away from Savannah's now-rigid form. "I think the ancient one is Wind Mother, Ánâ-ya Cáci. She is spoken of as an old woman in Tsiba'ashi D'yini stories, and she's mostly playful. You know, like Loki."

"Mixing up your metaphorical gods, Ryan? Your Viking is showing,"

Savannah said sourly. "Even though *she's* not anything—except for maybe Kim Kardashian—if she *were*, she'd be *Ázáipə Ćíci*, a Water Shadow or Water Soul." She turned to Nicky, eyes intent. "You've only ever seen her through or inside glass, right?" she rapped out.

It was like an interrogation. At Nicky's cautious "Yes," Savannah continued, "Which is analogous to water. And you linked the last two times you saw her to saving someone, right? First, the kid in the arroyo, second, the family who drove into the irrigation canal. Both water rescues."

"You are forgetting about the rabbit," Ryan reminded her quietly.

"Stop it," Savannah said. "The rabbit was just a rabbit, and none of this means anything. It's *not real*. No vision, no omen. No *nothing*." She rubbed her hands over the bare skin of her arms. "Don't you understand?" she said, her voice pleading. "All this gibberish about spirits and visions . . . it makes us look stupid, naive. Like children who believe in Santa Claus and the Easter Bunny. Indians have enough trouble being taken seriously as it is."

Silence fell as tension stretched between them. The breeze was back, lifting the hairs on Nicky's arms. She rubbed them down, even as the wind swirled around her head and wrapped her hair across her throat. She gathered it in her hand to flip over her shoulder, and blinked, taken aback.

Ryan stared at her, then looked up at the wind chimes dangling from the patio trellis. She followed his gaze.

"I believe there is more to this world than our minds recognize." There was an odd catch to his voice, a hint of uncertainty. Nicky's brows knit, puzzled by his statement.

"So you say, Ryan. But you've never seen a vision or a face or a ghost, have you?" Savannah said.

"I don't know," he replied simply. "Ghosts, spirits, visions could be all around us, but appear as a man in a crowd or a bird in a tree. They might be standing right beside you, but because they're so . . . familiar, you never think to ask someone else if they are *really* there, you know?" He gestured to Nicky with his chin. "But if a spirit visits you and lets you *see* them—*know* them—that's an honor, even a privilege."

Savannah glared at him for the beat of a few seconds before she levered herself up and marched to the screen door. She slid it open, and closed it behind her with a snap. Light from the kitchen shattered the darkness and made Nicky blink as her eyes adjusted.

It was her friend's way of ending the conversation, but Nicky had more questions. She dropped her feet to the cement, leaned forward, and wrapped her arms around her middle.

"The rabbit, Ryan. What about the rabbit?" She kept her voice low out of respect for Savannah.

"It represents the underworld. And in Fire-Sky culture, white represents death."

The wind picked up again, scratching dried leaves across the cement. Nicky shivered. "So . . ."

"So, I don't think you will be saving the living this time. The running rabbit symbolizes a restless spirit. Whoever Wind Mother wants you to rescue is either already dead or will be soon." His voice was strangely adamant.

Dead? A sudden coldness filled her. She didn't want to believe him. It was her job to *protect* the pueblo and its people, even at the risk of her own life. But deep inside, she knew what he said held truth.

She needed the answer to one more question.

"How do you know she's Wind Mother? Anaya . . . Ca?"

"Ánâ-ya Cáci. Because she has been here with you all evening. Haven't you noticed, Nicky? The breeze running through the patio tonight hasn't touched Savannah or me. Only you."

As if to prove his point, a brisk gust of wind snuffed out the candle and swept over her, making her hair drift off her back and snake up and around her head. Ryan's hair lay flat against his skull. Startled, she jerked her eyes up. The wind chimes hanging from the overhead pergola stayed still and silent, as they had all night.

The hair on her neck prickled. She let out a slow, shaky breath, trying to maintain calm, but knowing, *knowing* . . .

And as if her stark acceptance of Ryan's statement were an acknowledgment of the ancient one's message, the wind stopped.

"But . . . I don't understand, Ryan. Why me?" she whispered, her voice thready, thin. She was not an Indian. She was an outsider.

Ryan shook his head but said nothing.

The screen door scraped open and her thoughts scattered in a thousand directions.

Savannah stepped outside, still scowling.

"Anyone want dessert? I have pie."

CHAPTER FIVE

The scratching went around and around in his head, like a child twirling in circles with a sharp stick, a garland of wavy lines inside his skull.

Then the kid fell down.

Thump.

Howard Kie gasped and sat straight up in his bed, sheets tangled around his legs and feet. He held his head and whimpered, kicking frantically, struggling so hard he fell to the floor with a thud. Only by crawling and twisting did he manage to free himself. He lay there, sucking in air, his face pressed into the grimy rug.

A sour wash from his stomach coated his throat. He groaned and rolled onto his back, arms stretched wide. For several breaths, he stayed still. His brain throbbed. Bad dream and hangover. He needed a drink. And to pee.

Howard wobbled to his feet and squinted at the digital clock on the bedside table before fumbling for his glasses. One thirty-six. He stared out the window. Dark outside, so still night.

His full bladder made him change the order of his needs. He brightened. Unless he'd left a beer by the sink in the toilet. That would be perfect. But no lights. His head was splitting in two. Light would make it explode. He massaged the heel of his hand against his temple as he hopped across the room to the toilet, grit and goathead thorns poking into his bare feet.

The beer cans in the bathroom were empty. Disappointed, he zipped his jeans and flushed the toilet, wincing at the sound.

Howard rubbed his throat to press back his nausea and stumbled into the kitchen. The dim refrigerator bulb pierced his head, so he closed his eyes as he blindly grabbed a beer. He popped the top and sat down in a chair next to his computer, downing half the can in one long gulp. He sniffed and sat there. Breathing and drinking. He might have dozed.

What sounded like tearing paper made his head jerk up. Startled out of his stupor, he gazed blearily around the darkened room.

The sound came again, building then fading. And again. The hair stood up on his neck. His eyes widened and rolled downward.

They were there. Again. Right there. *Under the trailer.*

The sound was persistent, repeating, but now it was like claws across metal. The floor vibrated through the soles of his feet and chills peppered his skin. Did they know he was here? Knees like water, he raised one foot then the other off the floor, wincing at the creak of his chair.

This was what woke him, he was sure of it. They lived under the trailer, but had crawled in his head. They were calling him, chasing him.

Warning him.

Mouth suddenly dry, he grabbed for his beer, but his hand trembled so hard, he almost knocked the can off the table. He snatched at it again and held it over his tongue, desperate to shake out the last few drops. Anything. The scratching grew louder. Like they were trying to dig up through the floor.

He stared down, eyes frozen open until they burned. His feet tucked tight to his butt, toes curled, arms squeezed around his legs. He didn't want to put anything down on the floor because it moved, flowed, lived. *It crawled with bugs.*

His breaths came faster. He'd forgotten to sweep. Head back, he rocked, strangling on a whimper. *No, no, no.* He should have swept.

Thump. The floor buckled upward. Howard whimpered and turned on his computer. He wanted, needed the light now. The blue and green glow of the monitor flickered weakly, and the bugs streamed darkly to the corners of the room.

Thump. The floor bulged again.

Thump-thump, thump-thump. Merging with his own racing heart, drumming in his ears.

A heartbeat. Heartbeat. He closed his eyes again and moaned. He'd forgotten. They were here to remind him, to set him back on track.

He gritted his teeth. He could do this. He could!

With a surge of terrified courage, he slammed his feet to the dirty floor.

"*Heem'e!* I hear you!"

His voice was high and shrill, like a little girl's. Echoing off the walls and through the floor. In his head.

He banged across the room, reeling on the undulating carpet, arms held out for balance at first. Then he settled, bringing his knees high, and moved, stiffly, gracefully, in an ancient dance he'd thought he'd forgotten generations ago. Each foot pounded the floor, slamming it smooth again as he chanted the dead away. Sang to reassure them he understood.

That he would have—*should have*—been a Sky Clan war chief. From Naha'ya. From the Day Before Yesterday and from the Beginning. If only for the beer.

Then, he could have stopped them, could have helped. And the spirits wouldn't track him. Wouldn't live under his trailer or in his life. And the missing wouldn't haunt him.

Howard stopped, his head spinning. But his mind was clear enough about two things. One, he needed another beer. And two, he needed to see if Sandra had responded. He had to ask her about contacting that cop.

He cocked an ear for the sounds below his trailer. Silence. He breathed a sigh. The dance had done it. They would leave him alone, at least for now.

Until the beer makes me forget something else. With a shiver, he walked around the trailer and switched on every light.

He placed the rest of the six-pack on the table along with a half-empty bag of Flamin' Hot Fritos, and sat down at his computer to log in. Howard smiled. His trailer might be one step from the trash dump, but it had a blazingly fast Internet connection. The cell tower on the hill above his neighborhood was the best deal the pueblo ever cut with whatever cell company owned it.

His instant message popped up on the screen.

Howard leave me alone.

Sandra had replied. He tapped, *No names. They know I know and are watching everything I do. Are you awake?*

He grabbed a handful of Fritos, shoved them in his mouth, and waited.

Nothing.

Sandstorm. You are Sandstorm. I am Acid Rain.

The cursor blinked ten times as he munched, waiting. Those were great names.

She didn't respond.

I want to tell that cop who saw the white rabbit. I'll use code. She won't know who you are. I'm doing it now, he threatened.

No!!! Remember what happened last time? Leave it, Howard. It will be over in a week. It will be done in a week!!!

Howard smiled and popped another beer. She was up.

Use Acid Rain. And Sandstorm. They are very good aliases. I think the cop could help. She saw a white rabbit.

Is she a white cop? She won't care. No whites care. No one cares.

But she saw a WHITE rabbit!!! He tapped urgently and sent the message quickly, trying to impress Sandra on the significance of the cop's vision.

DON'T CONTACT HER!!! Not yet. After next week. Maybe. When I'm famous. I have one more thing to do. Then it will be over.

Howard frowned as he wiped his hand on his jeans. What thing? *OK. Until next week. Are you here or in Albuquerque? Will you come see me? I'll sweep.*

He waited. There was no return message.

She was gone.

Howard chewed the inside corner of his lip. Sandra said not to contact the cop, but the sound under his trailer told him something different. He didn't want them coming back.

The card the cop gave him was in his wallet. He scuttled to his bedroom and grabbed it, then sat back down in his chair. His hands hovered over the keyboard.

No one had listened before. He'd tried and they'd laughed at him, or dismissed him. Or threatened him. So many were lost in the last two years. More than ever. If only he'd become a war chief, he could have stopped them.

His tongue worked at the Fritos in his teeth. The cop was a sign. He would leave a hint and see how she responded—cryptic symbols that succinctly described the danger. Then he would sweep *and* vacuum in case Sandra came.

His fingers itched as he put in the cop's official email address:

MMatthews@fire_skypueblo-nsn.gov
Sgt. Matthews:
You Have to Help Them.

Acid Rain

Howard smiled. That was a very good alias. He hit send and sat back. Sandra didn't understand, that was all. Maybe he would go see her. She sometimes came home on the weekend.

He dislodged a piece of corn chip from his teeth and moved it around his mouth with his tongue. When she did, he'd make her understand.

Make. Her.

After all, the cop saw a white rabbit.

CHAPTER SIX

"Matthews."

Manny Valentine's voice barely penetrated Nicky's concentration. She moved the cursor over the play line of the surveillance tape and drew it backward, rewinding exactly one minute. The man with the bat made a feeble swing at the plate-glass window of the mini-mart. But it was the second guy she focused on, the one doubled over in laughter. She clicked pause and zoomed to his head. His ski mask had ridden up on his neck and there was a tattoo. Her best clue so far in last week's burglary.

"Sergeant Matthews." Valentine's voice was sharper now.

Nicky suppressed a sigh. "What do you need, Officer?"

She adjusted the focus. It looked like . . . part of a hand? The bottom half was cut off by the guy's collar. She jotted a note on the pad of paper in front of her.

"Some old lady and a kid are here requesting to speak to you. They want to file a missing persons report."

Nicky flashed Valentine a glance and settled deeper into her chair. "I'm busy. Give it to whoever's next in line."

"The kid specifically requested you. Says he knows you. Name's Squire Concho."

Nicky pushed her chair back and stood. She leaned forward and clicked the mouse to drop down the video on her computer, then pivoted directly into Valentine's chest. Her lips thinned as she met his slitted eyes.

"I hear I have *you* to thank for my overtime assignment on the train-pedestrian last week," he said.

Nicky eyed him coolly, but inside, her gut burned at his challenge.

"And I hear *you* contaminated the scene." He'd puked the remains of his breakfast when he found a partial torso and head stuck in a stand of chamisa.

His face blazed red.

"If you'll excuse me, Officer Valentine." Nicky took a half step closer and tilted her head up, staring him down. He was so close she could smell coffee on his breath.

Seconds stretched, but he finally broke eye contact. He smirked and stepped aside.

As she brushed by him, he bent in and said in a low voice, "Captain's watching all the time, Sergeant. He has eyes wherever you are."

Clenching her teeth, she strode toward the secure door that led into the waiting area. She'd never understood how the drip of Chinese water torture worked until Captain and his department cronies started a campaign for her resignation. Every day they picked and pushed. Mistakes were amplified into crises. Decisions were questioned. She'd held strong so far, and had her own support within the department and with the Feds. But she could feel her facade starting to crack around the edges. Sometimes sleep was elusive.

Nicky gathered the paperwork from the clerk, read over the brief summary, and opened the door.

"Juanita Benami and Squire Concho?"

Squire scowled when he heard his name. His clothes were baggy and his long black hair was parted in the middle and fell to screen his face. She'd scooped him up for truancy a couple of times, and had brought him in once for tagging and shoplifting. His future trajectory wasn't good, but there was something about him that made her want to try hard to reach him. Not give up on him, because then he'd give up on himself.

Nicky caught fleeting emotion in his eyes—fear, worry?—before he stood to help the ancient Native grandmother—*dya'au*—who sat next to him.

Ms. Benami was so short, Squire practically lifted the old woman off the chair to set her on her feet, and he did this with such gentleness and care. He hunched down to her height, murmured, and gestured at Nicky. The old lady nodded and tucked her hand into his arm. They shuffled across the room, Squire matching her slow, deliberate steps.

She was dressed in a rusty-black skirt that fell to her ankles, her shoulders covered with a colorful shawl. Crabbed fingers thick with silver rings held the edges together. Her hair was a mixture of black and white, coiled and wrapped in an elaborate bun so large Nicky didn't know how she held up her head. Maybe the bun was counterbalanced by the heavy turquoise-and-silver earrings dangling from stretched and creased earlobes. She wore half a dozen necklaces, including a squash-blossom, probably worth more than Nicky's annual salary.

The woman's only concession to modernity was her black athletic shoes. Nicky recognized them because her grandmother once had a pair: SAS EZ Straps with Velcro fastenings made for arthritic hands.

Still, the old woman came dressed in all of her wealth. It was a statement to the seriousness of the visit.

"Ms. Benami, Squire, if you'll follow me," Nicky said politely.

They walked into the bright room that served to accommodate a maze of desks, police officers, staff, and the hum of sounds that populated the day shift. Embedded along one wall were a series of interview rooms. She ushered them to an empty one with a half-glass wall facing the busy department, and held the door for them. When they passed through the threshold, she pulled it closed and turned with a smile that froze on her lips. Grandmother Benami was staring up into her face.

Nicky's heart beat thickly as the vision in the glass flashed in her mind. The old woman before her was hauntingly similar, skin folded and wrinkled, her mouth a pursed, lipless line under an aquiline nose. Her eyebrows were thick, straight, and white. But her eyes weren't the clear, sharp black of the face in the glass. Age and exposure to the harsh New Mexico sun had clouded the irises blue-gray with cataracts.

Out of respect, Nicky looked away. You did not meet an elder's eyes for longer than a few seconds.

Juanita Benami spoke to Squire in Keres, lifting her chin at Nicky.

Squire gave a long-suffering sigh. "Grandmother wants to hold your hand."

Nicky jerked her gaze to him. "What?"

"Give her your hand. Please. Otherwise we'll stand here all day." His voice was still high-pitched, a child's.

Nicky hesitated. She'd been warned by some of the traditional cops about getting "witched." While Navajos would collect loose hair and wind it into charms, *'iińzhįįd*, for sympathetic magic or curses, in pueblo cultures—Fire-Sky included—witches used sharp objects to poke through the skin, injecting evil or sickness into the hearts of their victims.

Squire rolled his eyes. "She won't witch you, okay?"

Nicky held out her hand, faintly ashamed at her thoughts.

The old woman took her fingers in a warm, strong grip, and stared into Nicky's face with narrowed eyes before she frowned and grunted. With hobbled steps, she pulled Nicky farther into the room, before she dropped her hand and climbed onto a chair. Nicky settled across from her and Squire and noted a second contemporary touch. Juanita Benami had a beautiful set of even white dentures.

"Now"—Nicky rubbed her palms together under the table, a little unnerved by the hand-holding—"you've come in about someone missing?"

Squire answered. "My cousin, Sandra Deering. She's a student at the University of New Mexico. She said she was coming home over the weekend, but we never saw her. I mean, her car's here, at Grandmother's house, so she did come home, I guess." He squirmed in his seat under Nicky's gaze. "She's not answering her phone, and . . ."

Nicky raised her eyebrows, her expression softening. "And?"

"It's weird. She's deleted her Facebook, Snapchat, and Twitter," he finished.

"Could she have gotten a ride back to Albuquerque and not told you?"

Squire shrugged. He dropped his gaze, index finger making circles on the table. His grandmother looked back and forth between the two of them as they spoke, her mouth pressed thin.

"Has something like this happened before? Where she's been out of contact with her family for a few days? How old is Sandra?" Nicky asked.

"I don't know. Like twenty-seven or -eight." Lip curled, Squire shot her a glare. "Look, I know what you're thinking, and she's not like my mom. She goes to school. She's going to graduate this summer, in May. She doesn't use anymore."

Nicky let him vent, absorbing the information. His cousin's past drug habit came as no surprise. Like many other communities, the reservation hadn't escaped the scourge of drug and alcohol addiction. It resulted in a substantial transient population that came and went as they followed their next high. Sometimes they'd only be gone days. A week, maybe. But for a few, months or years would pass before they showed up at home again. Squire's mother had been missing for over a year now, but had disappeared for weeks or months on end before that. Nicky suspected Sandra Deering had fallen into that same common pattern.

"I'll need some more information from you before we move forward." She pushed to her feet to retrieve the proper forms, mentally adjusting her day to fit in phone calls and hospital checks.

Juanita Benami tapped the table with one of her silver rings, the sound loud and hollow. "*Dza*. Nah." She stared hard at Nicky with milky eyes, turned to her grandson, and spoke rapidly in Keres.

Squire hissed back at her a couple of times as she spoke, his face red. Then he stilled and all color leached out of his skin. When Ms. Benami finally stopped speaking, he was quiet until the old lady pinched his arm and tipped her head toward Nicky.

"*Baabaa* says you must find her—all of her—or she will be lost. She says a witch holds her now, and will inject her with evil and take her heart and her soul." The boy bit his lip hard and stared at his grandmother through the curtain of his hair. "*Dza, Baabaa, dza*." His voice shook.

Juanita cupped his cheek for a moment, her thumb moving back and forth, and shook her head. Her hand dropped back in her lap.

Squire's eyes were glazed with tears. "She says she chose you because you are visited, have visions, and you have . . . what?" He ducked his head near his grandmother and she spoke in his ear. "You are the only one here who has *tee'e huwana'ani*—faraway eyes—although she says you only have this much." He held up his index finger, his thumb measuring the last joint. "She felt it when she held your hand. But she said you have other resources only cops have that will guide you."

Nicky's mind spun. Though she didn't spread it around, she'd never hidden that she'd seen visions, so Juanita Benami could have learned that from anyone. But Nicky didn't understand what it meant to this investigation.

"Anything else?" she asked.

Squire sat up straighter, frowning now. At least he didn't look like he was going to cry anymore.

"I don't understand half of what she says sometimes, and I really don't get this part. She says you must look for—" Brows knit, he continued slowly. "You must find the missing blood money."

The last three words dropped like stones into a well.

Nicky logged off the Rocky Mountain Information Network and sat back in her desk chair.

Nothing. But that wasn't unusual so early in an investigation.

According to RMIN, Sandra Deering wasn't in jail, hadn't checked into a motel in the region under her name, and hadn't been admitted to any hospital or emergency room in an eight-state area or part of Canada. But she'd still have to confirm the woman wasn't using an alias, and she'd need to send her driver's license picture statewide with a BOLO. Especially to Albuquerque entities.

She'd also called Albuquerque OMI to make sure the woman wasn't dead, and she'd checked the National Crime Information Center. Sandra hadn't had any recent vehicle stops or interactions with the police.

In fact, records from the Fire-Sky Police Department indicated Sandra hadn't been arrested since her early twenties. Those arrests had been all drug- and alcohol-related, including contributing to the delinquency of a minor and a couple of loud party calls. She'd found no other arrests outside the reservation.

A call to the University of New Mexico confirmed Sandra was registered as a student and had filed to graduate in May with a journalism degree. They'd emailed Nicky her semester list of classes, along with the names and phone numbers of her professors. But by the time she'd called a couple of them, it was late and there'd been no answer. Sandra had a class at nine-thirty tomorrow morning. Nicky would swing by campus and see if she showed. She also needed to contact UNM housing about Sandra's on-campus apartment.

Nicky clicked on a separate screen, and the NCIC initial entry report popped up. She finished filling out the form before she signed and submitted it.

Sandra Deering was officially a missing person.

Standing, she arched her back and looked around the common room area. Most of the day-shift personnel were gone. The noise level had dropped, and the sky outside the west-facing windows still held a hint of gold at the horizon. A few of the swing-shift patrol officers typed out reports or held phones to their ears. Her stomach growled and she picked up her cell to check the time. Five past seven. No wonder she was hungry.

Only a couple more things to check, then she'd stop by Savannah's house and eat before she drove back to her place in Bernalillo.

Nicky stepped into the small reference library and headed straight for the shelf containing the tribal registry and Certificates of Blood. She pulled those resources out and plopped them onto the table. Fire-Sky High School yearbooks were slotted tightly together along the back wall, and it took her a few moments to find the correct year and wiggle it out. A stylized phoenix etched in reds, oranges, and yellows graced the front cover. She traced her finger over the raised edge of a feather. This image and Ryan's fire jewelry had a lot in common.

She settled into an uncomfortable chair, flipped to the yearbook's index, then turned to the single page entry referenced.

Sandra Deering stared out at her, frozen young in her senior portrait, a polite smile dressing her lips. It was a much better picture than her driver's license. Which one really looked like her, though? In the yearbook, her dark reddish hair fell in waves around her shoulders, and the smattering of freckles across her nose wasn't completely covered by her makeup.

There weren't many students in Sandra's senior class, so Nicky read over the names as possible resources for questioning. She quickly found a fresh-faced Savannah Ts'itsi Analla, round gold glasses perched on a pert nose, a huge smile on her lips, and braces covering her teeth. Nicky grinned. She'd make a copy and tease Savannah about it tonight.

As she scanned the rest of the class, she jotted down a couple more names before her finger settled on a picture of a young man. Brown eyes made small by thick black-rimmed glasses, a long narrow face, hair sticking up over one ear. No smile. He actually looked out of it, even a little scared. And his face was familiar. She found his name.

Howard Kie. The weird guy from the mini-mart canvass last week. She'd asked him about the white rabbit.

Rabbits. Nicky jerked in sudden realization. Could Howard Kie be Acid Rain? She'd received a couple of bizarre emails over the weekend. One of them appeared threatening, with an image of knives and hearts, the second containing a GIF of hopping bunnies—*white* bunnies. She grabbed her phone and dashed off an email to her FBI contact in the Cyber Division, forwarding the odd messages and asking him to check them out.

She closed the yearbook and opened the Tsiba'ashi D'yini Pueblo Tribal Registry. It wasn't the actual book; that was at the Fire-Sky Cultural Center under lock and key. This one was a meticulously made copy that gave the impression of age. Glossy black-and-white photos were interspersed with the actual ancestral lineage and registrant pages. The pueblo secretary's office kept the book up-to-date, and new revisions were issued each year recognizing births, deaths, and changes in tribal membership qualifications. There was a searchable online database, but Nicky loved the history chronicled in the pages before her. When she'd first come to work at the pueblo five years ago, she'd been so moved by it, she'd done her own genealogy, even going so far as to submit her DNA for analysis.

The index sent her to Sandra Deering's family entry. Part of the Hummingbird Clan, Sandra's mother had been one-half Tsiba'ashi D'yini, while her father was one-eighth Navajo, so she was considered a regular tribal member because she had at least one-quarter Fire-Sky blood. Nicky flipped to her Certificate of Indian Blood. Sandra had been registered as an infant. There wasn't much more. No siblings. Mother and father both deceased.

She closed the CIB catalog and pressed her hand on its cover as she pushed up from the chair, ready to put everything away and head to Savannah's house. Nicky paused and looked at her hand. She splayed her fingers. Funny, the cover felt almost . . . warm. Suddenly curious, she sat down again, opened the book randomly, and found herself staring at Savannah's Certificate of Indian Blood. A prickle of unease slipped down her neck.

Sliding her chair closer, she leaned in to read the document. Like Sandra, Savannah had been registered as an infant. Nicky pulled the tribal registry back in front of her. Savannah's family pages were impressive. Her friend always joked she was related to the Ancient Earth Mother Twins. As Nicky traced her genealogy, she realized Savannah wasn't far off. Her ancestors were recorded for over ten generations, leading back to the start of the book 250 years earlier. Nicky turned the pages, following the ancestral tree. The year and seasons of birth were recorded along with the age and cause of death: lung fever, blood poisoning, consumption, childbed. So many had died young. The causes of death changed over the years to stroke, heart disease, cancer. Even KIA—killed in action—Great War and World War II, Korea, Vietnam. A few people were listed as either *perdido*—lost—or *se fue*—gone—with no date of death. She frowned, not understanding the difference.

Occupations were written beside some names, in Spanish for earlier dates, then, starting about a hundred years ago, in English and Keresan, the native language of the pueblo. Weavers and warriors, teachers and truck drivers. Clans were inscribed. Savannah was from an elemental clan ancestry—Ts'itsi, or Water—practically Fire-Sky royalty. A symbol next to her name denoted she was full-blooded, also a rarity in the pueblo, whose regular and natural membership was around six thousand people.

Nicky's finger touched the name typed above Savannah's. Santiago,

Savannah's brother, had died at age eighteen. Savannah had been sixteen years old. Her gaze drifted to his cause of death and she furrowed her brow.

The cell phone on the table buzzed and a text message flashed on the screen. It was Savannah.

It's late. Stop whatever you're doing and come over.

Nicky grimaced. She felt like she'd been caught snooping.

Give me ten, she texted and closed the books in front of her.

She sat for a moment, rubbing her finger across her lips. Although Savannah rarely spoke about it, Nicky knew Santiago Analla's cause of death. *Suicide: train-pedestrian.*

But it was what had been scribed below that had caught her attention.

In tiny letters, someone had written and underlined the word *Witched.*

CHAPTER SEVEN

Nicky slipped into the darkened lecture hall about ten minutes before class ended, catching the last few slides of a talk on the integration of photojournalism in investigative reporting. The images that flashed on the screen were dramatic and poignant, and she sat, riveted. It said a lot about the professor's ability to reach the students.

She waited until the people sitting in front of her filed down the steps before she followed. A couple of students slowed, giving Nicky curious looks. The university required her to wear her shield around her neck along with the visitor's pass. Even though she was in plain clothes, it was tantamount to having *cop* scrawled across her forehead.

The instructor stood behind the media cabinet, answering end-of-lecture questions. Cynthia Fredrickson was hyper-slim, dressed in gray slacks and a purple blouse, and decorated with a chunky turquoise necklace, bracelet, and earrings. She was late fortyish in age and well preserved, her straight ash-blond hair and makeup enhancing a face Nicky was pretty sure anchored the evening news in Albuquerque a decade or so ago. When the last student left, Nicky stepped forward.

"Excuse me, Ms. Fredrickson? I'm Sergeant Monique Matthews, a special agent with the Tsiba'ashi D'yini Pueblo. Could I speak to you about one of your students, Sandra Deering?"

Fredrickson ran a quick glance over her, too. Her eyes narrowed as she pointedly glared at the bulge under Nicky's jacket, and her rose-tinted lips pinched tight.

"It's *Dr*. Fredrickson. You called last night and left a message."

Nicky smiled placidly at the chilly response. "Yes, ma'am. And this morning, but you weren't available. The department secretary was kind enough to give me an appointment after your nine-thirty class. I hope that's convenient."

With a practiced motion, Dr. Fredrickson pushed her laptop into a worn leather satchel stuffed with yellow legal pads, picked up the bag, and jerked hard a couple of times. The overflow slid down into the pocket and she zipped the compartment closed.

"I don't appreciate your weapon, Ms. Matthews. This is a gun-free campus. You should have left it in your car," she said, a snap in her voice.

"I'm required to carry my weapon while on duty. Even on university grounds, ma'am," Nicky replied. She kept her expression neutral, polite. The woman's stance was one she encountered more and more.

Dr. Fredrickson frowned and swung the satchel's strap over her shoulder. She turned her back to Nicky and walked out of the classroom, her low-heeled shoes clicking against the tile with each quick step. Undeterred by the woman's hostility, Nicky followed her down a brightly lit corridor filled with students hurrying to their next class. Fredrickson turned left into the Journalism Department's suite of offices and unlocked a door tagged with her nameplate. The space was pleasant and tidy except for stacks of used legal pads piled under a large window. Bookshelves flanked a desk that anchored a colorful area rug, and there were numerous framed broadcasting awards hung around the room. A few of them showed a much younger Cynthia Fredrickson with the KOB Eyewitness 4 logo.

"I have thirty minutes before office hours start." Still frowning, she waved to an empty chair across from her. "What can I do for you, Ms. Matthews?"

Nicky pressed her lips into a smile and laid her business card on the desk. She pulled a small notepad and pen from her shoulder bag.

"Special Agent Matthews," Nicky said. "Sandra Deering has been missing since Saturday. When was the last time you saw her?"

"She was in class a week ago Friday." Dr. Fredrickson sat back in her chair. "But I wasn't all that worried. These students tend to be absent quite a bit."

"Has she missed class before?"

"Yes, earlier in the semester. But I have no attendance policy. The only thing I ask is they must be in class for the final presentations. Sandra's is next week."

"Did you receive any emails or phone calls that might explain her absence?"

"No."

"Did she sit with anyone? Have any friends in the class?"

"A couple of the other women, but not consistently. I don't know about friends."

Nicky made a noncommittal noise. She had the class list and could question the other students if necessary. "When was the last time you spoke to Sandra?"

"About two weeks ago. I meet with all the students at least three times during the semester to make sure their projects are progressing. She was very excited about her work." Dr. Fredrickson bit her lip, thin brows creased. For the first time in the interview, she looked concerned. "She's graduating in May and wanted to use this presentation as part of her job applications."

"What was her final presentation about?"

"It was an investigative news piece she said she'd been working on since last summer, but she was very cagey about it. Secretive. Said the story was so big, she was afraid someone might steal it from her." Fredrickson waved her hand dismissively. "They all think they're going to be the next Hunter Thompson or Woodward and Bernstein. When I pressed her for details, she told me her project was so hot, it could put me in danger. I dismissed it at the time as overly dramatic, but now . . . Do you think it might have to do with the reason she's missing?"

Nicky made a notation before she asked, "Do you have any information about her presentation? Did she have to turn in a synopsis or rough draft?"

"I don't require either of those, but if I remember correctly, when we sat down within the first couple weeks of class she gave me a few details. I'd have to check my notes. I'm not sure . . ." She hauled her satchel to her lap and tugged out a handful of yellow pads.

"Thank you. Also, if you have any emails from Sandra, could I get copies?"

Dr. Fredrickson sighed and dropped the pads on her desk before logging in to her desktop computer.

"Ma'am? Can you explain to me what you meant by 'these students tend to be absent a lot'? Which students?"

"You know. Native Americans. I mean, I'm very sympathetic because I'm part Cherokee and I do everything I can to mentor and help them. But, well, in all honesty, very few end up graduating because they're academically and culturally unprepared to live on the 'outside.'" She lifted her hand from the keyboard and made air quotes. "Their heritage is so closely linked to the natural world, it can be overwhelming here. In many ways, they're like children, and, of course, whites have painfully exploited them, both historically and contemporarily. The chauvinistic discrimination and systematic abuse by government has led directly to—Huh." Lines appeared between her brows. She bent over the keyboard and typed quickly. "That's odd. I can't find any of Sandra's emails."

"Excuse me?"

"I searched for Sandra's name in my email—inbox and sent messages—but they're not here."

Nicky walked around the desk so she could see the screen and she made a mental note to speak to campus IT.

"Could you have deleted them?"

"Of course not. University policy is to keep all student correspondence. Here. See?" She typed in a name. "This is another student in my class and I have all of his emails."

"You said you might have notes from a meeting with Sandra? Could you look for those?"

Fredrickson sighed again. "I was, until you asked me for the emails." She yanked the yellow pads forward and riffled through them. "Here we go. There's not much, but I did write down a tentative title for her project. Would you like a copy of this, too?"

"Please. What was the title?"

"Uh, let's see. Oh. Here it is. 'The Hearts of the Missing Still Beat.' Actually, that was my title. Sandra proposed one that wasn't as effective," she said in a dismissive tone. "Although she refused to show me any statistics, she was adamant the number of her tribe members declared missing in the last two years had increased significantly over the previous years. And she had a specific word she insisted on using when she talked about them."

"A specific word?" Nicky was filled by a gnawing sense of dread.

"Yes. I wrote it down. Uh . . ." She moved her finger down the page. "Here. She said these people weren't missing. They were *perdido*. Lost."

The University of New Mexico Residential Life and Student Housing wouldn't release details on the comings and goings of an adult student without a warrant. The same occurred at IT when Nicky asked about emails, but that didn't surprise her. She'd have to approach the FBI and get them to go before a federal district court judge since she was out of her jurisdiction.

The inside of her unit was hot by the time she finished. She started her truck, cranked the air conditioner to high, and merged onto Central heading for the freeway. The information she'd discovered at UNM was confounding. A woman excited about graduating and applying for jobs didn't sit well with the complete wipe of her social media sites.

Her stomach grumbled. She'd already passed the Tramway exit and decided to head to Bernalillo, grab lunch at home, then go back to the police station for more paperwork and phone calls.

The Bluetooth buzzed in her car.

"I got your text." It was Ryan, his voice groggy.

"Hey. You awake?" she asked.

"Sort of. Nights suck. What's up?"

"Ryan, I messed up. This missing person case I'm working on? The woman graduated the same year as Savannah, so I asked her about it at dinner last night." She blew out a long breath. "Not good. She was really upset. Told me to talk to you and politely asked me to leave."

Ryan stayed silent for what seemed like forever.

"Who, Nicky?"

"Sandra Deering. Since they were in the same class in high school, I thought . . ."

"Shit."

Nicky swallowed. Ryan never cursed, even mildly.

"I didn't know." She could hear the pleading note in her voice. "I wouldn't be so cruel, you know that."

"Did Savannah go to work today?"

"Yeah. But I haven't seen her. I was at UNM this morning as part of the case. Will you meet with me? Tell me what happened?"

"Does it have anything to do with Sandra going missing?"

"I don't know. I doubt it." She paused, hesitant. "Ryan, I've never asked about what . . . what happened when her brother committed suicide. I didn't realize there was a connection to Sandra."

"Savannah told you to talk to me about it? That's a step forward, at least," he mumbled. "Do you want to do this now?"

"No. Tonight? When's your next shift?"

"Not till tomorrow morning. Come over to my place after work. I'll cook. And if we're feeling brave later, we can walk to Savannah's."

There was another long pause.

"Ryan, is it bad?" she asked.

"Yeah. But not in the way you think."

CHAPTER EIGHT

Nicky turned onto the road that led to Ryan's duplex. He lived in a new housing development about a mile from the reservation's second largest village, Little Aquita. Built with casino profits and BIA housing grants, it consisted of a couple dozen single-family homes scattered randomly in among piñon and chamisa. Most of the houses were stark, without artificial landscaping to soften utilitarian lines, their only differences in paint color, flat or peaked roofs, or whether there was a carport attached. Children played under yellow streetlights flickering on with the coming night, watched over by grandmothers sitting on long front porches. A few kids stopped what they were doing and stared as Nicky drove her unmarked Tahoe down the street.

She parked her unit on the gravel pad next to Ryan's battered red truck. The sky glowed from the setting sun, small, streaky clouds lit pink from behind. A warm evening breeze enveloped her as she climbed out of her vehicle. With a tired sigh, she shrugged off of her dark blue blazer and draped it across the back of the driver's seat. Her shoulder harness followed. She massaged the crick in her neck before she slotted her service weapon in her bag.

A flash of gleaming orange light—known as a fire-sky—caught her eye as the sun finally dropped below the horizon, outlining the extinct volcano that was at the heart of Fire-Sky culture. Rimmed golden in the waning light, Scalding Peak was the most sacred place on the pueblo, many areas off-limits except to the war chiefs of the elemental clans. Flat on top where the caldera had collapsed, its forested slopes fell smoothly downward on one side, while the other side was a jumble of jagged rocks, deep crevasses, and ancient lava flows riddled with caves. It was a constant struggle for the pueblo conservation officers to keep non-Native extreme climbers out of that area.

The side door off the kitchen opened and Ryan stepped out.

"Nice view, huh?" There was a smile in his voice. "I got lucky when they assigned me this place. Close to work. Close to Savannah." He lifted his chin toward Savannah's home down the street. Light glowed through her front window.

"Yeah." Nicky strolled over to Ryan, not yet ready to leave the peace of the evening and go inside. "Have you talked to her?"

He drew in a deep breath of the sage-scented air. His face relaxed, cares seeming to flow off his body.

"Nah."

Ryan stuffed his hands in his back pockets, and Nicky looked him over appreciatively. He was tall and lanky, but padded with ropy muscles outlined by a thin, faded T-shirt and well-worn jeans. The planes of his face were sharp, his nose aquiline, lips thin. His dark features mirrored every photo she'd seen of Apache warriors from the past, incongruous with his hazel eyes and long golden brown hair. But somehow the whole package worked.

She'd met him five years ago when she first was hired, but there'd never been any spark of attraction between them. Maybe it was because she'd been entangled in the end of a failed relationship at the time. Or maybe because he was focused on one woman only. One who called him a friend but held him at arm's length: Savannah.

Would their talk tonight about Sandra Deering answer some of the questions she'd never asked about Savannah and Ryan's connection? Nicky sighed inwardly. She was afraid it might.

Sunset brought an almost instant drop in temperature and she rubbed her arms. The high desert of New Mexico was like that in April, especially when there was snow left on the mountains.

"Ready to eat?" Ryan asked as he ambled back to the house.

Nicky followed him into the warm kitchen, fragrant with baking food. Ryan wasn't a cook. Most likely she was smelling fish sticks or chicken nuggets, all out of the freezer aisle in the grocery. On the counter, a green salad filled a ceramic bowl glazed with Native black-and-white patterns. Next to it sat a small bottle of Pellegrino. Ryan never drank anything else. Or at least she'd never seen him drink anything else.

The timer buzzed and he grabbed an oven mitt.

"There's water in the fridge. Or coffee."

She grabbed another Pellegrino while he slid a cookie sheet out of the oven. Fish sticks and french fries.

Plates full, they settled into padded kitchen chairs at the table.

Ryan dipped his fish in catsup and took a bite.

"So, what's this about Sandra Deering?" he asked.

"Do you know Juanita Benami?" At his nod, she continued. "She and her grandchild, Squire Concho, came in a couple days ago and reported her missing. Sandra's a student at UNM, graduating in May with a journalism degree. Apparently she came home sometime last Friday night or Saturday morning. Her car was at the grandmother's house, but they never saw her. She didn't answer her phone, and when Squire checked her social media—Facebook, Twitter, Snapchat, email—they'd all been erased. I haven't been able to find her in any of the police databases, either." She took a bite of salad.

"The social media wipe is disturbing," he said.

Nicky hummed an affirmative and continued to eat. It was a classic sign of a suicidal individual on the reservation. They would first commit Internet suicide, then within a few hours or days . . .

"I spoke with one of her professors. She said Sandra was excited about graduating and had a big presentation to give next week. Apparently it was about an increase in the number of Fire-Sky Tribe members reported missing over the last two years. Except Sandra wouldn't give her any details because it might put her in danger." Ryan's brows rose. "I know. That gave me pause."

"Did you check the missing person reports?" he asked.

"This afternoon. There might be a slight uptick, but nothing dramatic. When I reviewed the numbers going back a few years, there was no statistical difference between now and then." She swirled a fry in her residual salad dressing. "And I don't know how Sandra found out any of this. There are no official requests for that information. It's not easy to retrieve, either."

"Maybe she had other sources."

"Maybe." Nicky finished her last fish stick and shook her head when Ryan offered her more. "That professor at UNM? She's required by the university to keep all email correspondence from her students. She was going to give me a printout of Sandra's emails for the semester, and, in her media wipe, somehow Sandra erased them, too, I guess. I filed a warrant today for Sandra's emails archived in the UNM database, and for her swipe card usage at UNM housing." She stared at Ryan. "The tribe was paying a hundred percent of her tuition, room, and board."

"Wow. That's definitely not the Sandra Deering I knew from high school." Ryan was rummaging through his freezer. He took out a sleeve of Girl Scout Cookies.

At her smirk, he said sheepishly, "It's all I have for dessert. Why do you think I'm always over at Savannah's for dinner?"

He peeled open the cellophane and snapped off a frozen cookie. Nicky did the same. They munched quietly.

"This case is really bothering me, Ryan." She hesitated. "There's more I need to tell you, but I want to know what your connection is to Sandra. And why Savannah was so upset."

He shrugged again. It was such an Indian gesture Nicky had almost forgotten how evocative the motion could be.

"She'll forgive you by tomorrow, you know. It's Savannah's way."

She bit into another cookie and waited.

Ryan settled his elbows on the table and stared out the large picture window in the breakfast nook at the dusky sky.

"Sandra Deering was Santiago Analla's—Savannah's brother's—high school girlfriend that last year. My senior year. You already know Savannah was in the same class as Sandra. There was a bunch of us that ran together. Not Savannah. She was such a goodie two-shoes." His face softened, then his lips quirked up on one side. "We weren't." Ryan looked her in the eyes. "Alcohol, pot, shoplifting, tagging. Fights. Sex.

Teenage stuff. We'd ditch school and hang out. We had a spot in the culvert by Peetra Road, under the train tracks. We thought we were so cool."

Ryan stood and turned off the ceiling lights, leaving the hanging lamp above the table as the only source of illumination. He scrubbed a hand over his face and stared out the window above the sink.

Nicky sat quietly and watched him. He rarely spoke so much at one time.

"Savannah tried to get Santiago away from us. She came to the culvert once, in her mom's car. I think that was the only time she's ever broken the law, 'cause I know she was too young to drive. She screamed at us, told us we were wasting our lives, our blood."

Nicky's brows knit. Wasting their blood?

"Especially Santiago. Did you know he'd been selected as a cacique? A Tsiba'ashi D'yini tribal priest. He would have been a traditional leader of his people. A chief. It's more than that, but it's hard to describe in English," he said, giving her a faint smile. "You can't turn that down. It's not like a job, you know? It's a state of being."

Ryan's expression became distant. The light above pooled around him, softening his features. Only the blinking of his eyes and the movement of his lips broke the stillness of his body.

"Santiago would laugh about it, saying he'd make sure things changed on the reservation when he was chief. He'd build casinos and make everyone rich with the distribution checks. He'd decree beer could be sold on the pueblo and abolish the drinking age. Stupid stuff that mattered to us at the time. But if you really looked at him, looked in his eyes, you could tell he was terrified." Ryan scratched the side of his face. "He got really drunk one night and told me he didn't want it, afraid he'd let his People down. Then he let slip he'd been chosen to be cacique because men in his family had 'faraway eyes.'"

Nicky's gaze sharpened. It was the same phrase Squire's grandmother had used.

"He said he had visions of the ancient ones, and special powers. Like how he could tell if someone would catch us if we shoplifted. I didn't believe him, until it happened. A bunch of our gang got arrested for swarming a mini-mart. Santiago got me out, just in time."

Nicky nodded. Sandra had a couple of shoplifting arrests from high school.

"So, we started, I don't know, testing him. Daring him to do things."

Dinner settled like a cold stone in her belly.

"We were all scared, you know? Graduation was coming up fast and we couldn't see any type of future. We were all such stupid fuckups."

Her eyes widened at his language and he gave her a somber half smile. It was the second time she'd ever heard him curse, both times that day.

"It's the only description that really fits. But there was special pressure on him. Santiago wasn't a leader. He was a follower, and to be a cacique, you had to be a leader. I think sometimes it haunted his every waking minute."

"You were there? The night he—" Nicky stopped.

"Yeah." Ryan grimaced. "That night, we met at the culvert. We were all supposed to bring something to get high on. I'd really scored. A litter of kittens had been born out in the shed behind my house, and my mom told me to take them to the shelter." He looked at her, his eyes empty, desolate. "I stole a vial of ketamine and some needles from a vet's bag. You know what ketamine does?"

"Yes," she said. Normally used as an anesthetic, if abused it was a powerful hallucinogen.

"We'd never injected drugs before. Never. Just pot. Coke if we could score it. I filled up a syringe and we decided on one mil each. But when Santiago got the needle, he used all the rest. I don't know how much. I loaded another needle, and the next thing I know, we were all dancing around on the railroad tracks." Ryan's lips were white. He took a quick drink.

"Except Santiago. He stood between the rails, his arms out, palms up. Head tipped back. He began to chant in Keresan. Even as high as everyone was, we recognized the 'Song of the Dead.' He looked at us then, and I swear his eyes glowed. He told us a train was coming and we needed to get off the tracks. It wasn't but a couple seconds later we could feel the vibrations. And did that sober us up. We all ran off the tracks, except Sandra and Santiago. She was giggling and trying to catch the rabbit she said was running around her feet. Hallucinations." Ryan pressed his lips into a pained smile. "Someone grabbed her and I yelled at Santiago to come, but he said the ancient ones were all around him, as a shield against harm. He would prove to us his power by stepping off the tracks at just the right time.

"The conductor had seen us by then. The spotlight from the front of the train was blinding. Brighter than anything I'd ever seen. Like looking into the sun. You could hear the brakes, the horn blowing. But Santiago didn't move."

Ryan's eyes closed, like he couldn't watch the scene he was describing.

"The train was coming fast. It was so loud, and we were all scream-ing at him to jump away from the tracks. And, in what seemed like the last second, Santiago stepped off. He'd done it. He'd saved himself. But Sandra jerked away, ran onto the tracks in front of the train. I don't know how . . ." His voice choked and tears shimmered on his cheeks. Her own eyes burned at his pain. At Savannah's pain. "I don't know how he did it, but one minute we knew she would die, the next, Santiago had pushed her away. And disappeared."

He wiped his face with the back of his hand and looked at Nicky. "And we ran. We all ran away. And we let them call it a suicide."

Nicky pressed a hand over her mouth. The Ryan she knew was so very different than the boy in the story.

"What happened?" she whispered.

"I left the rez. I told everyone it was because I wanted to go, but that was a lie. You know my father—*step*father—is a cacique? He's a very powerful man on the pueblo. He knew I was jealous of Santiago because I wanted to be a cacique, too, and I couldn't because I wasn't Fire-Sky, because of my blood. I think my dad suspected I played some part in San-tiago's death. Maybe someone talked. I don't know. After the funeral, he and my mom told me to leave the pueblo. They banished me from their home, *my* home." His jaw bunched. "It was . . . I felt so lost. Like I . . . I had no place."

"What about your mom's family?"

"That's where I ended up. My father—stepfather—bought me a bus ticket to the Jicarilla Reservation up north. They made jewelry, so they taught me. I liked it, but I was restless, undisciplined. They decided it would be best for me to join the Marines." He chuckled without humor. "God, I hated it at first. But it saved me. I got my GED, went through basic in San Diego. The Marines straightened me out and sent me to Fire School." He smiled. "I finished my five years' active duty, and applied for a job here. I was ready to come back and face my past." His smile faded. "I contacted Savannah and her family and told them about that night, about how Santiago was a hero. How it was my fault. She forgave me immediately." He looked at Nicky, his gaze steady and soft. "I think that's the moment I fell in love with her."

"But that doesn't make sense, Ryan. If she forgave you, why . . . ?" Nicky didn't know how to finish her statement without being hurtful.

The sadness was back in his eyes. But deeper—much deeper—she could see a hardness, a cynicism and anger that was so out of place she wondered if she really knew Ryan at all.

"Why aren't we together? Why doesn't she love me? That's easy. I'm not acceptable in Savannah's world because I'm not Tsiba'ashi D'yini. For her, it's all about blood. *Everything* in Savannah's world is about blood."

Nicky stared at him, openmouthed. It wasn't true. His bitterness was blinding him.

She stood, her chair skidding back. "No. I don't believe you."

Ryan watched calmly. He was back to being the man she thought she knew.

Snatching up their plates, Nicky marched to the sink. She opened cabinets and drawers, found Tupperware to hold the leftovers. With jerky movements, she washed and put up the dishes, trying to gather her scattered thoughts, trying to put everything Ryan had said together in her head.

But it didn't make sense. Nothing made sense. And something inside her was twisting, pushing, screaming for her to understand that somehow, in some way, this conversation was brutally important.

All the while, Ryan sat motionless, his eyes deep in shadow. Waiting.

Finally, when she couldn't stand the silence any longer, she braced her arms on the edge of the sink and stared through the kitchen window into the night. The breeze had kicked up, and the branches on the chamisa swayed gracefully in the light of the moon. Wind Mother. Ánâ-ya Cáci.

Nicky shivered. Would she ever think about the wind the same way?

She shook the thought away, and what she wanted to say suddenly burst from her lips.

"Savannah is the most nontraditional Indian I've met. She is *not* the person you describe. She would never be so cruel. I *know* she's dated black guys, white guys, Hispanic guys. Indians, non-Indians. But you think she rejects you because of *blood*?" She flipped around. "I know she loves her culture, but you make her out to be some type of elitist, racist even."

"No." The frown on his face was deep. "You *want* her to be the way *you* see her. But it's an illusion. To Savannah—to many Indians—their ancestry, their DNA defines them. It colors their most important actions and decisions. It has nothing to do with traditional or nontraditional practices. It is much more elemental than that."

Ryan's jaw flexed, muscles bunching as his teeth clamped tight. He jumped to his feet and snapped off the light over the table, leaving Nicky in darkness.

"You said you had other things you needed to talk about. If you still want to stay, I'll be in the living room." He paused in the doorway, his neck and shoulders stiff. "If not, I understand."

Nicky stood for a long moment in the dark kitchen. Nothing had really changed, except her perceptions. Savannah was still her friend, as was Ryan. And it was funny that he didn't think Savannah loved him when it was heartbreakingly obvious she did. Savannah had never told her outright she loved Ryan, but Nicky knew by Savannah's body language, by the expression on her face when he was near her. Maybe Ryan was too close, couldn't see because he'd already made up his mind about Savannah. Maybe. But unless Savannah had lied to Ryan about her forgiveness for the night of her brother's death, there had to be some other very important reason she rejected him.

She stilled, her chest tight. Although it had taken years to break through, she'd found such acceptance here on the pueblo. Sometimes it felt more like her home than any other place in the world. Her friends more like her family than her mother ever had been. Was it really about ancestry and DNA? That Ryan was not Fire-Sky? If that was true, it made Nicky even more of an outsider in Savannah's world. Was she afraid to open her heart and mind to the real reason Savannah and Ryan weren't together?

Her lips quirked into a wry smile. Because, if this job had taught her anything, it was that she needed to be open-minded.

Nicky grabbed two more bottles of Pellegrino and walked into the living room. Ryan was slumped back into the couch, arms crossed, chin resting on his breastbone. His gaze tracked her around the furniture until she stood in front of him.

She handed him the water. "*Áukî-ni?*"

"Friends." Ryan's hand slid over hers. "Always." He squeezed her fingers before he took the bottle.

Nicky sat across from him. She opened her water and took a sip.

"What else?" he asked quietly, sitting up straighter, his expression centered, calm.

"A couple other things that came up in the Sandra Deering case." She paused. "Look. If you don't want to talk about it—"

"It's okay, Nicky. If I can help, I'd like to."

"Her final UNM class presentation was on missing Fire-Sky tribal members. But she didn't use that term. Instead she used *perdido*. Lost. Juanita Benami said the same thing to me. She said I had to find Sandra, or she would be lost." She leaned forward, twisting the bottle in her hand. "And when I was researching Sandra in the tribal registry, I looked at Savannah's ancestry, too, and saw *lost*, and another word next to some of her ancestors—*gone*. No cause or date of death. Just lost or gone. What's the difference?"

"*Gone* is easy to explain. It means that individual left their People on purpose and never returned." His voice turned grave. "Maybe they committed a crime so unforgivable, they were banished by the elders. Banishment is rare now. They are generally allowed back after a period of time. I know of a few banished who have returned. You might say I was one of them."

Ryan took a drink before he continued. "They went to another People, to marry or for another reason."

"Another people?"

"Another tribe. Moved away from the reservation, divorced their culture, adopted another." He gave her a candid look. "The rez isn't an easy place to live sometimes. Those who have gone usually don't return. Mostly, their family or clan knows their fate. In many ways, *gone* is not a happy word. But it is better than *lost*."

He paused, his gaze distant. Nicky wiped the condensation on the glass bottle and waited.

"*Lost* means they did not leave—or die—of their own free will. Maybe they went on a hunt and disappeared. Or maybe their body was found, but something of them was missing. Taken. Fire-Sky People and their enemies did that to each other during times of war. Killed and took part of the victim as a trophy so the spirit wanders lost, unable to return and defend their lands and their People. Tsiba'ashi D'yini caciques and elemental war chiefs perform very sacred chants and dances to heal a lost one, to calm their spirit. But it's dangerous. Done improperly, the dead can come back to haunt the living."

"So, taking an organ from the body . . . That explains the law the state passed—disposition of Native American remains."

"Pueblo religious practices and culture call for a person's body to be intact at burial, so the whole person can find spiritual peace. It's a major reason traditional pueblo Indians don't become organ donors. Sad there needed to be a law, huh?"

"Yeah." It was also why she liaised so closely with OMI when they autopsied a member of Fire-Sky. Two highly publicized cases—both from Laguna Pueblo—had led to this law. Evan Martin had been struck by a van and killed. OMI kept the man's brain, ultimately cremating it. The family didn't learn until eighteen months after the burial that the body wasn't intact. A year later, Alicia Waseta was killed by a BIA vehicle. A doctor at OMI took her heart as part of a UNM study on a rare heart condition. The family eventually received the heart and was able to bury it next to her body.

"You said the men in Santiago Analla's family had 'faraway eyes.' I thought that was the Rolling Stones' only country music song," she said with a half smile. "I've heard the term a couple times in the last few days. Could you explain it?"

"'Faraway Eyes,' huh?" Ryan grinned. "*Tee'e huwana'ani*. Psychic. Clairvoyant. Sixth sense. There are lots of terms to describe it in your world." His face became serious. "You have it, I think, but you fight it. Then again, Savannah would say it's nothing more than the fact that you do good police work."

He leaned back and crossed his arms again, but this time he was relaxed.

Nicky chewed her lip. She'd never seen or sensed things until she came to the reservation. But Juanita Benami said she would need both 'faraway eyes' and good police work to solve her granddaughter's disappearance.

"Does it mean I've been witched?" Her cheeks heated as she asked the question.

Ryan laughed.

"You've probably been witched dozens of times over the last five years by people you arrested, or their families. Some of the traditional Indians on the force really let it get to them."

"No kidding. A couple of them won't even patrol parts of the pueblo alone, or take calls from certain tribal members. There's always complaints about the lack of police presence in some of the villages." She hesitated. "But don't pueblo witches have to break the skin? I thought they used sharp objects, and I don't think I've ever—"

Ryan's face suddenly shuttered, his expression blank. There was a change in the atmosphere of the house. A door snicked closed.

Someone was in the kitchen. She met his eyes and shifted back in her chair.

"Some do break the skin," he finally replied. "But that's very powerful and awful magic."

"Ryan, Juanita Benami said a witch holds Sandra. She said the witch will inject her with evil if she's not found. Take her heart and spirit."

Nicky rubbed her knuckles over her mouth, staring into the darkened kitchen.

"Under Santiago's name in the tribal registry, someone had written 'Witched' next to the cause of death," she said.

Ryan looked at her, a white pinched line around his lips. Seconds ticked by.

Soft footsteps sounded on the floor. A slim, dark shape appeared in the archway between the kitchen and living area.

"I wrote it," Savannah said into the silence. "After Ryan came back and told me how Santiago really died. That he'd injected himself with drugs. He'd pierced his skin with a needle, and allowed evil to flow into his body."

She stepped out of the dark. The light from the lamp caught and reflected off the lenses of her glasses and the wetness of tears on her cheeks.

Nicky's chest constricted. Ryan dropped his head into his hands.

"They found it, you know? During the autopsy. The needle mark on my brother's arm. But until Ryan told me"—she came up behind him and placed her hand on his head, her face softening with such love Nicky blinked—"no one knew what it meant. Or even cared. The FBI and BIA marked him as another stupid Indian teenage suicide. He was a statistic to them."

"I'm sorry, I'm so sorry," Ryan whispered.

Savannah wrapped her arms around his shoulders and buried her face in the back of his neck.

"You have to stop blaming yourself, Ryan," she murmured, her voice thick with tears. "*You* listened. *You* changed. *You* are a different man, and I bless the day you truly came into my life, and back home."

Savannah caught Ryan's chin in her hand. She tilted his head and used her shirttail to wipe the tears from his face before she leaned down and kissed him tenderly on the cheek. He closed his eyes and swallowed. When she let him go, Ryan reached back his hand and clutched the one Savannah had placed on his shoulder. She straightened and wiped her eyes.

"Don't you see, Nicky? Sandra's grandmother was talking about drugs. She either knows or is afraid Sandra's using again," she stated calmly. "Drugs are the 'witch' that gets under the skin. They're evil and make people do unspeakable things. There's no magic here." Savannah's voice was filled with quiet conviction.

It all made sense. Based on Fire-Sky tradition and culture, it was a very short leap to link needle marks and witching.

But there was still something she was missing, and it made her uneasy. Sandra's disappearance didn't fit the mold of the addicted or transient tribal members who showed up on the reservation once their drugs or alcohol or money ran out. Nor did the woman appear to be a suicide risk, even though all the signs pointed in that direction. It was all too pat, too obvious.

Nicky stood, interrupting Savannah and Ryan's murmured conversation.

"It's late. I think I'll head home, start fresh tomorrow. I haven't had a chance to stop by Juanita Benami's house or search Sandra's car—"

Her phone rang. She recognized the Dispatch number, and was about to answer it when Ryan's phone buzzed.

He looked at her, and Nicky stared back at him with deep foreboding. She wasn't on call tonight. Neither was he. There were only a few reasons they both would be contacted to come back in, none of them good.

She walked away from Ryan and Savannah, and pressed the icon to answer.

"Matthews."

"Sergeant, we have a report called in from Western Rail. One of their conductors said they've been involved in a train-pedestrian collision near Peetra Road. Officers dispatched to the scene have confirmation of what looks like a single fatality. Fire and Rescue has been called, and OMI is on standby."

Nicky's stomach sank.

"Ten-four, Dispatch. I'm on my way."

CHAPTER NINE

Sandra Deering was dead.

Nicky kept her expression flat, her hands clasped behind her back as she stood at ease in the captain's office. Outside the large picture window, the parking lot was almost empty. It was past six P.M., and most of the day staff had left.

Captain Richards handed the Sandra Deering folder to Lieutenant Pinkett and leaned back in his chair. It creaked loudly in the silence and her gaze slid back to the men. Pinkett shifted to stand behind the captain. A united front.

Captain rocked forward and placed his elbows on the desk, hands steepled. He stared at her, his icy green eyes hard and cold.

"You went to the funeral." His gaze swept her class A's.

"Yes, sir."

"I saw in the report Deering's head was crushed. OMI had to do identification by fingerprints from a severed hand. So, no open coffin?" He smirked and watched her closely.

Insensitive prick. She didn't rise to the bait.

"Yes, sir."

Recovery of Sandra's body had taken hours and been absolutely brutal. The team she'd assembled walked over a mile and a half in the dark to find all the parts. They'd even had to call in Animal Control to chase off a pack of stray rez dogs attracted to the scene by the smell of blood.

"Did you get a chance to reinterview . . ." He flipped the pages of a stapled sheath of papers. "Juanita Benami. Deering's grandmother, correct? Or the boy about the toxicology results?" He snapped his fingers and Pinkett handed him the folder.

"Squire Concho," Nicky said.

"What?" His gaze shot to hers.

"The boy. Sandra's cousin. Squire Concho. He's devastated—they're both devastated—by her death."

Nicky and Jeff Gabriel, a Keres-speaking officer, visited Juanita Benami's home to give her the news of Sandra's suicide. It had been gut-wrenching. Squire tried to remain stoic, but within a few minutes his face had crumpled and he'd run out the back door, sobbing. The grandmother sat white and still as Jeff haltingly told her the news, tears slipping into the deep wrinkles of her face.

Captain stared at her unblinkingly, lips pursed under his thin graying mustache, before he dropped his gaze to the desk. His finger moved across the paper as he read.

"Let's see. Marijuana, alcohol, and heroin. Injected heroin. Fresh needle marks evident on her arm. This girl got around."

A lump lodged in Nicky's throat. Evil had seeped into Sandra from the breaking of skin. She'd been witched, just like Santiago Analla. Same trajectory. Same ending.

Nicky pressed her lips together, wrestling with her unwillingness to believe any of it. Why had Sandra polluted her body with poisons and killed herself in such a brutal manner when, according to family, friends, and her professor, she'd been actively and enthusiastically planning for her future?

"About the reinterview, sir." She cleared her throat. "I thought I'd schedule it next week," she said. "Her family is still grieving and I wanted to give them some time—"

Captain cut her off. "No. Get it done by Friday. I want a final report submitted on Monday. And press her relatives about the plethora of drugs found in her system. She may have had a source on the reservation. You know how well my zero-tolerance campaign has worked in the last year. Wouldn't that be a feather in our caps if we rid the pueblo of another drug dealer?" he said over his shoulder to Pinkett, his mustache twitching with a smile.

Nicky wet her lips. She wasn't ready to let this case go. There were still too many missing pieces.

"But sir . . ."

Both Captain and Lieutenant Pinkett swiveled to stare at her, Pinkett's eyes wide. Captain's face took on a tinge of red and his lips turned down. Nicky set her teeth. One wrong step and there'd be another reprimand for insubordination in her personnel file.

"Don't you find it odd Sandra's toxicology report came back so quickly?" She swallowed, sick about what she had to say next. "I mean, the state crime lab is backed up for months. They expedite samples on a high-profile case, but this? A suicided Native American nobody?" She tried not to choke on her words, to keep them light, casual. "We haven't even received tox reports from the train-bicyclist fatals, and that happened before Deering's death."

The high color left the captain's face and his shoulders relaxed. He tipped his head to one side and stared at her, brows furrowed.

"And, sir," she said, "I have questions about the autopsy report—"

Pinkett cut Nicky off. "Why? The final document is pristine."

"That's very atypical for the particular pathologist, Lieutenant. David Saunders?"

"Oh. Saunders." Pinkett snorted. "He still has a huge chip on his shoulder when it comes to dealing with Indians."

"What's this about?" Captain swiveled halfway to Pinkett, the creaking of the chair harsh.

"It was before your time here at Fire-Sky, sir. Saunders is one of the OMI docs who took hearts and other internal organs from autopsied Indians without permission back, oh, ten or fifteen years ago. He's kind of a pill to work with, always sloppy in his autopsy reports for pueblo tribal members," Pinkett said.

Captain gestured to the folder. "But there's nothing wrong with Saunders's autopsy report this time."

Nicky hesitated. "No, sir, but my instincts—"

She clamped her jaw. How do you tell your bosses about hallucinogenic visions of an old woman's face in the glass, most likely brought on by sleep deprivation? Or chasing after a hopping white bunny that represents an underworld spirit, and not get fired?

"You're not paid to follow your instincts, Sergeant," Captain said in a patronizing tone. "You're paid to close cases like this: simple suicides perpetuated by drug addicts. I want the final report in my office, on my desk, Monday morning."

"Sir—"

"Matthews. Am I not making myself clear?" His cold gaze bored into her.

"Yes, sir," she said, her voice tight.

She'd had enough, and pivoted to leave.

"Matthews. You are not dismissed." Captain drew out each word. Heat rose in her face and she gritted her teeth. He pulled his chair forward and moved the mouse on his desk. The bright light of the screen made his visage glow blue. His fingers clicked the mouse.

"What's going on with the threatening emails you've been receiving? From, er, Acid Rain."

"Yes, sir. The emails link Acid Rain to Howard Kie in one of the message lines. He appears to be a friend of Sandra Deering."

Captain's brows beetled as he looked back and forth across the monitor. "Rabbits, knives, and hearts." He looked up at her, one eyebrow cocked. "You considered these threatening?" His tone was mocking.

Pinkett shuffled around the chair and pointed to the screen, his shaved head shining under the fluorescent lights.

"This is the one, sir, that caused us to send them emails to the FBI Cyber Division." His gaze flickered up to Nicky as Captain opened the file and sat back.

Red and yellow flashes colored his face from Howard Kie's last email message, the one that triggered her to report it to Pinkett. It started out with dozens of white rabbits hopping around the page, their movements becoming more and more frantic, until one by one they were impaled by a flying knife and exploded into fiery balls of light.

Under any other circumstances she would've dismissed the emails and Howard Kie as a nuisance, doing nothing more than sending uniformed officers to threaten him with arrest—or maybe offer him help. It was more than obvious the guy had mental health issues. But taken together, the messages were deemed threatening.

The emails had stopped immediately after she'd reported them to the FBI. She hadn't heard from Howard since.

Captain made a noncommittal sound.

"What's the status?" he asked.

"Still pending, sir," Nicky answered.

She didn't tell him Mike Kapur, her contact at the FBI Cyber Division, was scheduled to call her personal cell later that evening. He'd texted a couple hours earlier, saying he'd found something interesting about her threatening email case. No matter what Captain said, her *instincts* told her his information might open a whole new perspective on Sandra's death.

"Well, in my opinion, the emails don't appear to be related to the Deering suicide. Just some stupid drunk Indian with too much time on his hands," Captain said. He sent her a challenging look.

Nicky's hands curled into tight fists at her side, hot words on her tongue, ready to tell her captain where he could—

Pinkett's eyes widened and he gave her a tiny shake of his head. She swallowed. Captain leaned back in his chair, arms crossed, his lips twisted into a satisfied sneer.

She'd risen to his bait this time, damn him. Nicky slowly relaxed her hands. She wouldn't bite.

But one day . . .

The expression in Captain Richards's eyes promised her that one day couldn't come soon enough.

CHAPTER TEN

Nicky pulled her truck onto the Kuwami K'uuti unpaved overlook and stepped out onto the hard-packed dirt. Her face relaxed into a faint smile as she leaned against her unit and soaked in the warmth of the setting sun. The panoramic view of distant mesas and the sloping plateau below, dotted to the horizon with scrubby piñon and juniper, made her heart swell. This evening the sun had painted the brush and trees orange and stretched their gray-brown shadows eastward behind them. A small village—Chirio'ce (the rez kids called it Cheerios)—stood on the flattened top of a broad hill, just visible to the south. The colored rays of the sunset made the weedy trailers and junked cars stark and picturesque instead of tired and sad.

Behind her, the landscape started its rugged upward climb to the summit of Scalding Peak. Piñons quickly gave way to taller pines, jagged tumbles of rocks, and miles of dirt road that led up to the sacred shrines of the mountain, off-limits to anyone except the elemental war chiefs.

The breeze hummed through the trees. It snagged her ponytail and fluttered the ends against her cheek. She breathed in the dusty pine-scented air. The bluff was quiet and private, a perfect place to wait—and think.

Nicky tightened the band on her ponytail and absentmindedly combed her fingers through the ends of her hair. The perfect autopsy and the expedited toxicology report were unusual. She didn't like unusual in her investigations.

Which actually brought her full circle to Howard Kie, the guy from the mini-mart canvass, and the reason for Mike's off-the-record call.

The sun disappeared below the horizon and the breeze turned chilly. Nicky reached in through the open driver's-side window and grabbed her jacket. She shrugged it on and checked the time on her cell phone.

Howard Kie hadn't even been on her radar as connected to Sandra until days after her suicide when Nicky's inbox filled with a flurry of bizarre emails. They had all been written by "Acid_Rain," but only one could be definitively linked to Sandra because of the subject line. He'd written: *Sandra is My FRIEND*. The body of the email had been cryptic and paranoid, saying he was being watched, and that Sandra's death was a warning to them all. The following emails contained the rabbits, knives, and hearts Captain had used to mock her.

Her cell phone rang, right on schedule. Technically, she wasn't supposed to get involved in the email investigation because she was still the potential victim of a possible crime. But when Howard's name came up in Sandra's case, her focus shifted.

She needed information. And sometimes you had to bend a few rules.

"Hey, Nicky."

"Mike. Thanks for this."

"Yeah, this Howard Kie guy," he launched in, rapid-fire, "must have installed some pretty sophisticated software since the last time he popped up for a trace. Honest to God, the only reason we knew where to start this time was your tip, and even then it still took us a friggin' *week*. I would love to recruit his ass if he wasn't mad as a hatter."

"What?" Nicky said sharply.

"You know. A few sandwiches short of a picnic. Not the sharpest tool in the shed?" When Nicky didn't respond, he muttered, "Tough crowd. Anyway, the setup to cloak his location and identity was brilliant, like nothing I've ever seen. But I doubt he could pass the mental eval."

"No. What do you mean, *since the last time*?"

"I mean a couple of years ago he sent a bunch of emails to the FBI bureau chiefs in New Mexico and Arizona about some kidnapped and murdered Fire-Sky tribal members. You remember. The ones found in the Chiricahua Wilderness. I have their names here. Um . . . Maryellen Kay-sh—"

"Maryellen K'aishuni and Vernon Cheromiah." Nicky pressed her hand against her throat. "Maryellen had Down syndrome. They thought at first she'd wandered off. Vernon was the tracker her family hired to find her."

"Yeah. Sad. Anyway, the emails had the same shit about rabbits, hearts, and knives. I don't have clearance, so I couldn't get access to the whole file, but I was able to sneak a cyber peek at a couple of pages. It seems the FBI sent a team in to talk to Howard because of the rabbit reference. Weird, huh?"

Rabbits. Ryan said they were an omen of death, of restless underworld spirits. His statement came back hauntingly. *Whoever Wind Mother wants you to rescue is either already dead or will be soon.* She shivered.

Was that why Howard was using those images in the emails? Had he linked the rabbit Nicky followed after the mini-mart break-in to Sandra's death?

But how was any of this related to the Chiricahua murders?

The uneasy feeling crept into her head again.

"Can you send me that info, Mike? I'd like to interview Mr. Kie but need these emails cleared up before I can get involved. Protocol." Still, she could drive by Howard's trailer tonight, just to check on him.

"Sure. I'll attach them to my final report, make it official. You should have it in the next couple of days." He paused. "You do realize none of what I've told you merits an off-the-record phone call."

"Yes, Mike, I do."

His voice dropped, but there was an edge of smug satisfaction. Mike loved to impart bureau gossip. She could picture his Cheshire Cat grin on the other end of the line.

"Two things. First, Howard set up a bunch of cyber traps to alert him to anyone who came sniffing around his Net presence. Once I found him, I hung out and watched his online activity. The thing is, I, apparently, was not the only one with an interest in your Mr. Kie. Someone else had a hard-on for him, too, and got caught. Howard was alerted and just up and digitally disappeared."

Was that why Howard's emails had stopped so abruptly?

"Who? Another agency?" she asked.

"No idea. I tried to trace the source, but came up empty. But that's not even the most interesting thing about your guy."

"Spit it out, Mike." Tension coiled in Nicky's chest.

"Nicky, Nicky. Can't a guy indulge in a little foreplay? A little cyber phone sex?" He chuckled at her impatient huff. "Turns out Howard Kie's FBI file has some tags on it. I checked them out. A couple were placed two years ago, right after the Chiricahua murders and the FBI personal visitation to his abode, but . . ." He stopped again, obviously enjoying himself.

"Come on, Mike," Nicky coaxed. "How about I send you some nice Hatch green chile if you cut the crap?"

"*Aaannnd* she comes through in the clutch. Do you know what passes for spicy on the East Coast? Del Taco. I want the hottest stuff you can find this time," he said. "Okay. The tags function to automatically send anything new in Howard Kie's file to a series of IP addresses."

"Can you—?"

"No, I'm not going to trace them," he said. She snapped her mouth closed. "I like my job and want to keep it. But I do kinda recognize one of the addresses because . . ."

He paused dramatically, but Nicky already knew what he was going to say. The skin prickled on the back of her neck and she clutched her phone tighter.

"It's a server in your system. Turns out someone on the Fire-Sky Reservation is cyber-stalking Howard Kie. So, by extension, he or she knows about you. Oh, and, by the way, the last tag was only placed a couple of weeks ago."

He let out a snigger.

"Looks like you got an FBI mole in your midst. Or maybe I should say, rabbit."

CHAPTER ELEVEN

Nicky sat in her unit and stared into the night. She'd started her Tahoe, ready to head home, but she normally used the drive to her small house in Bernalillo to unwind from her day. Her mind was running way too fast for that. She would stay, parked and quiet, until she could organize her thoughts.

The breeze had dropped to nothing. The trees and chamisa skirting the lookout were still. The hum from the truck's engine was a low, soothing background sound and the heater blew warm air into the cab. Nicky tipped her head back and fixed her eyes on the ceiling. The complications of this case—the layers of information—left her edgy and tight. She breathed deeply in and out, relaxed her body, forced tension away. Her eyelids fluttered closed.

Something else was going on at Fire-Sky. FBI thought Howard was the key, but she wasn't so sure. Still, Howard seemed to be a link between two pueblo tribal members murdered in the Chiricahua and Sandra Deering's suicide.

Why, why, *why*? How were they linked?

She didn't know much about the murders, and made a mental note to read the files. What she did know was the victims found in the Chiricahua cave—Maryellen and Vernon—had gone missing.

Her eyes moved rapidly beneath closed lids. A hand twitched on her lap.

Missing. Maryellen and Vernon had gone *missing*. Sandra had gone *missing*. Sandra's presentation was on the *missing*.

No. The UNM professor had changed the title of Sandra's presentation to "The Hearts of the *Missing* Still Beat." But the word Sandra had used was *perdido*. Not missing. *Lost.*

Was this the link? Were all these people lost? According to Ryan, that would mean something vital was taken from their bodies. Their spirits could not rest.

Nicky's thoughts meandered in the blackness, clues, evidence, and faces swirling in a slow tornado above her, assembling, disassembling, trying to fit together and build the answer. But black holes of missing information made the structure weak. It would collapse, only to come together again.

As she drifted, the purring of the truck's motor changed. Once soothing, it took on an edge, a buzzing, like thousands of distant bees. The air vibrated with it. It penetrated her skin and seeped into her body, until everything around her was humming.

Nicky's scalp prickled. Her breath stuttered and her flesh crawled with a bone-chilling cold. Fingers curled into fists. She was being watched. Could feel the icy burn of it on her face.

Her eyes popped open. Slowly, slowly, she rolled her head to look out the driver's-side window. She choked back a scream.

Juanita Benami stood next to her truck. She stared unseeingly through the glass, eyes glazed white, her expression frozen in a rictus of grief. A dozen glinting chains and pendants hung around her neck, stark against her black dress.

Nicky sat up, never breaking eye contact, and placed a shaking hand on her weapon. But as she slipped her fingers over the butt of her sidearm, the old woman—her body like a rag doll—was yanked away, back into the dark shadows of the trees not twenty steps from the truck.

And there, she changed. The black of her shoes crawled up her legs to become tall moccasins. Dark, rusty clothes transformed around her hunched body into a deerskin dress and cloak. Her silver jewelry slithered and snaked from her neck to weave into a gleaming breastplate of shell, turquoise, onyx, and coral. Long white hair swirled out of the bun at the back of her head, ruffled in an unearthly breeze, and her eyes now glowed a deep golden brown in the light of the rising moon.

This ancient woman had visited Nicky before. She was the face reflected in the glass.

Ánâ-ya Cáci. Wind Mother.

As if she heard Nicky's thoughts, she bowed. Then she lifted her face and arm toward the black slopes of Scalding Peak. The chamisa behind her shivered and swayed, and a dozen white rabbits poured out to hop around her feet, only to burst into bouncing spots of light.

Like Howard Kie's email.

The apparition turned back to the truck, and Nicky's breath strangled in her throat. The flesh was gouged away from her skull, her eyes and mouth gaping black pits. She raised her hands and the globes of lights surrounding her streamed into the dark openings of her face. Her chest swelled as she tipped her head to the sky and blew the light at the mountain.

Nicky kicked open her door, and planted her feet on the hard-packed earth. Her gaze followed the balls of light as they swirled upward. Their unearthly glow faded, then disappeared into the blackness of the rocks, like they'd entered holes in the mountain.

Not holes. Caves. This side of Scalding Peak, the side exposed to the southern plateau of the reservation, was riddled with caves.

The humming that filled the air stopped and Nicky jolted awake. Disoriented, she sat in her truck. Memory flooded her as she swiveled her head to stare out the window. The old woman and the rabbits were gone.

She opened the door, breath harsh, and climbed out. Fumbling at her waist, she switched on her flashlight and pointed it at the heavy shadows that lurked between the branches and leaves. Her breath came easier as she crept forward and angled the beam at the ground. There were no footprints, no paw prints. She knew there wouldn't be. But . . . brows knit, she knelt and touched the powdery dirt.

The ground seemed to have been swept clean.

Nicky stood and gave the slopes of Scalding Peak one last lingering glance, before she slid back into the driver's seat of her unit. She started her truck and stared for a long time at the trees and bushes.

She'd swing by Howard Kie's trailer tonight.

Might as well. The drive home would offer no chance for her to unwind now.

CHAPTER TWELVE

Howard sneaked another peek out of the dirty blinds, disturbing the thick layer of dust, and sneezed loudly. He'd tried to muffle his sneezes, but they made his head hurt too much. Like his eyes were stretching out of their sockets.

He popped a beer and guzzled half of it as he sat in the chair he'd placed by the window, tense with anticipation. They would come. They had. Almost every night. He wouldn't have even noticed except he'd been up late, on his computer.

His hand went unconsciously to his mouth and he chewed on his thumbnail, nibbled off little bits, and spit them onto the floor. He'd have to sweep them up later, or witches might find them. They'd left him alone since he'd started sweeping his paths.

A car growled by on the road and he wanted to see. But no more sneezing. Someone might hear. He pulled his T-shirt over his mouth and nose, parted the blinds again, and froze. Eyes bulged behind the lenses of his glasses and his heart thundered almost out of his chest. They had come. Again.

His gut roiled anxiously and he brought the can up to his cloth-covered mouth for a drink before he remembered. He moved the shirt down just enough and quickly gulped the rest of his beer, then pulled the shirt back up.

It was a police car, unmarked. Well, not a car. A police SUV. But it was different than the other tribal truck that came by, the one with the medallion on the doors, or the big black pickup. It turned onto the dirt road that went right past his trailer, crawling along. He knew what would happen next. Like all the others, it would slow as it passed by his house. Or stop. And whoever was in the vehicle would stare hard at the dark windows.

Only this time he wasn't there. Just pretended he was.

His fingers twitched on the mini-blinds.

What did they want from him? The drive-bys had started a few weeks ago. Always at night. Sometimes very late. No one ever got out, but he couldn't see in the car windows, either. Dark tint. It saved the upholstery and dashboard from the harsh New Mexico sun. He didn't have dark tint, and his car was trashed inside.

The truck slowed near his driveway, just like all the others.

Howard stiffened. It pulled up to his trailer. Headlights swung in a sharp arc that cut over scraggly brush and weeds before they spotlighted the white aluminum siding and dirty, curtain-covered windows. He held his breath as it stopped a few feet from the front and sat there, the engine thrumming. Felt the vibrations through the air across from the road. But he was safe, hidden.

And he waited, hardly daring to breathe. The driver's-side door opened. It was the lady cop who'd asked him about the mini-mart break-in. The one he'd sent his emails to, the one Sandra said wouldn't help.

His lips trembled and he pressed them into the T-shirt.

The one who hadn't helped.

Sandra had been right, and now she was dead.

He tried to suppress the sob, but it escaped. Sandra was dead, and it was his fault. He never should have contacted the cop about the war chiefs. He never should have told Sandra about the conspiracy of the lost on the reservation. The war chiefs had taken their revenge. Sandra had been murdered for their rituals. His friend. How many was that now? Sandra knew. She'd found out, and then he'd gone and painted a target on her chest.

This bunch of war chiefs were evil people—*dzaadzi dawaa han'u*—craving only power, not honor. They rejected him from their ranks so they could hide their treachery, and he was qualified by blood. He would make a great war chief.

The cop, Sergeant Matthews, stood for a long while next to her car door, the dim light from the interior casting shadows across her face, before she walked to the front of his trailer, her right hand tight to her leg. She didn't climb the cinder-block steps, but leaned over to knock, a hollow pounding he wouldn't answer. Not tonight. Not ever, he thought with a sneer. His vision blurred and he blinked. Wetness dripped down his face.

She'd broken trust, this stupid white cop. Told someone and they invaded his computer, had fallen into one of his traps. He stopped the emails. Stopped trying to help her. Acid Rain was gone. It had been a good name, too. So had Sandstorm.

Another sob broke and he cried in earnest and watched the cop from the small adobe house across the road. It had been empty for over a year. Who would want to rent it when the tribe built new homes and apartments near stuff? All that was out by his trailer was that stupid mini-mart. He swiped his eyes.

After the online attack, he'd asked the owner, Mr. Saenz, if he could stay there awhile. Said the septic tank in his trailer needed to be pumped. That he'd pay him a hundred bucks after he got his check, but he didn't have the money until Distribution Day. It was coming up soon. Everyone on the rez was excited because they'd heard it was going to be thousands of dollars each.

And since he was full-blood, he got more than others. That's the way it worked since the casinos opened. But he wouldn't get the bonus. No way was he showing up to sign the register. Too dangerous. The war chiefs would find him.

The cop went back to her truck and climbed in. His breath shuddered in and out as he waited for her to leave.

She sat there, in her cop car, for a long time. Then she backed out and drove away.

Howard slumped in his chair. He tipped his head back and closed his eyes. They burned and his muscles were heavy because he hadn't slept enough in the past few weeks.

And because of the beer. Another sob escaped.

He could have stopped all of this. All of it. He could have taken his place with the war chiefs and stopped their wickedness, their evil. If they had let him in to his rightful place in the tribe, beer would never have been an issue. Sandra would still be alive. So would a dozen others. Maryellen and Vernon and Kim and Berna and Harley and . . .

He succumbed to a huge yawn.

No one had listened to him. Not the FBI, not the rez police, not the tribal elders. No one.

He'd show them. He would find out when the war chiefs next traveled up Scalding Peak for another sacred ritual. Track them and take pictures. Then he would have evidence—not dreams—to give them. And the elders would let him be a war chief because he'd expose them.

And they would stop cutting out the hearts of his People.

CHAPTER THIRTEEN

"What do either of you know about Maryellen K'aishuni and Vernon Cheromiah?" Nicky asked.

Savannah jumped at her sudden question. Both she and Ryan laid their forks down.

Nicky's gaze swung from Ryan's placid frown to Savannah's wide eyes behind her lenses.

Savannah grabbed the half-full bottle of wine and poured herself another measure before jutting her chin at Nicky's glass.

Nicky shook her head. "I've got to drive home."

"You can always stay here," Savannah murmured.

Nicky stared at her. Savannah's hand was trembling.

"I didn't really know Maryellen at all," Ryan said. "But Vernon was a conservation officer for years. After I came back to the rez, we overlapped for a few months before he retired and started guiding hunts."

FER—Fire, EMS, and Rescue—shared a building with the Conservation Department. The two groups hung out all the time, playing pickup basketball day and night on a half-court tucked into one side of the fenced recreation yard. They had rival coed softball teams that competed against the police department in a summer league. She was recruited when they were short of girls, but she wasn't very good. Ryan laughingly called her a warm body. Savannah was much better, but the guys still only put her in as short outfielder. At least she got on base most of the time.

"Maryellen was kind of a fixture at Feast Days and around the rez in general. She was very sweet. Her parents took her everywhere. They were devastated by her disappearance and murder. She was their only child," Savannah said, staring down at her plate, hands in her lap.

Nicky's eyes narrowed. Savannah knew something upsetting about Maryellen. She tamped down her need to press her friend for whatever was bothering her. She would let Savannah recover and circle back to it.

"What do you remember about the murders?" Nicky asked Ryan.

Ryan watched Savannah, too. "Probably not much more than you. The search went on for a couple of weeks, but they found nothing. Best theory? She wandered away, fell into a ravine or mine. The area's riddled with them. This was probably something I read in the papers, but . . ." He scratched his head. "I think the K'aishunis said there was an old pickup parked at the campground. It was gone the next day. They thought someone might have snatched her, but nothing came of it.

"And Vernon. The K'aishunis hired him when the organized searches found nothing. He was legend here on the rez for his tracking," he continued. "Biggest elk and deer guaranteed. Used to call himself the Prince after Prince Humperdinck in *The Princess Bride*. You know. He could *track a falcon on a cloudy day*." All three of them said that last part in unison, grinning.

Nicky flashed a glance at Savannah. She'd recovered a little. Good. Hopefully she wouldn't retreat now.

"We were all shocked when he was found murdered. Vernon could live off the land and hide in plain sight. You could walk right by him and never know he was there. How he was caught and killed is a mystery no one could explain. He was too wily. Too smart." Ryan gave her a narrow-eyed look. "What's this all about, Nicky?"

Something clicked in Nicky's brain.

"This trip the K'aishunis took to the Chiricahua. They did it every year, right—like a pilgrimage?" she asked.

"Yes," Savannah said. "Maryellen's father, Jim, is very traditional. Very, *very* traditional. He was convinced there was an underworld link between the Chiricahua and Scalding Peak." She wrinkled her nose.

"And I mean a *physical* link—like a tunnel or caves—so you could journey from one place to the other. He said petroglyphs and pictographs deep in some of the caverns down there are exactly like those found on Scalding Peak. He'd take his family to Arizona every year around summer solstice to chant and pray, hoping the way would be opened to him."

Nicky stared at her, eyebrows raised. Savannah squished up her face and shrugged. "Our families are of the same clan, and he and my dad were in the same class in school. They were good friends and whatnot. My dad would invite them over for dinner and they'd talk. That's how I got to know Maryellen." Her face closed off again.

"So . . ." Nicky drew out the word as pieces of the puzzle assembled in her head. "If the K'aishunis had been traveling annually to the Chiricahua for . . . how long?" She gave Savannah a questioning look.

"Since before Maryellen was born. Over thirty years."

"Why did Maryellen wander away *this* time? Had she ever done it before?" Nicky asked.

"I don't think so. They were very protective of her because of her Down syndrome. And other reasons . . ." Savannah's voice trailed off. She took another bite of pasta.

"She disappeared in the morning, right?" Nicky leaned forward and propped her elbows on the table. "As she was going to the showers. By herself. Alone. The file said her mom didn't follow right away because animals had gotten into their food. Maryellen had gone by herself the day before, so she wasn't too worried."

"That's what her mother, Dinah, told us later. She felt so guilty about it. Said she'd failed her daughter too many times," Savannah replied.

"Her parents believe she was snatched—kidnapped—although there is no evidence for that except the truck. And Ryan, you said Vernon was too savvy to be caught if he didn't want to be."

Ryan nodded.

Nicky tapped her lip. "Everyone on the reservation knew about the K'aishunis' annual pilgrimage. What if Maryellen's abduction and murder was planned? What if someone tampered with the food, hoping her mother would be delayed so he or she could get Maryellen alone?" Pieces of the puzzle were coming together. "What if Maryellen *knew* her kidnapper? Would she have willingly gone with someone she knew? What if Vernon also trusted his murderer? Could he have been tricked into helping someone who was also ostensibly searching for Maryellen?"

Ryan folded his arms across his chest, a frown on his face. "I'm sure the authorities thought of all that. Eliminated every possibility."

"There were a lot of tribe members who continued the search after the police and rangers called off their efforts," Savannah said. "I wanted to go, but Dad had his heart attack around that time. He really wanted to help out, too. We just couldn't."

"I was away, in Dulce, at Jicarilla. My cousin was getting married," Ryan said.

"And I was at a conference and training in Seattle," Nicky said, but she'd covered shifts later because some of the Native cops volunteered for the search. "This guy would have blended in. He might even be on a list of people who volunteered." Her voice held underlying excitement, but Savannah was adamantly shaking her head. "What?"

"I don't believe Maryellen would have gone with anyone, even someone she knew. She was mentally disabled, but not dumb. It had been drilled into her she was never to go with strangers or friends without her parents' permission. I know this," Savannah said.

"Anyone can be tricked, Savannah," Nicky countered. "Maryellen was probably more susceptible because of her disability."

"No. Maryellen practiced with her mom. Role-played. They made sure she was never taken advantage of again."

"Again. What do you mean, *again*? Come on, Savannah. I need info," Nicky pressed. "It might be important."

Savannah dropped her eyes, her hands knotted on the table. Finally, haltingly, she said, "Dinah K'aishuni practiced with Maryellen because, back when I was still in high school, around the time Santiago died . . ." She looked at Nicky, her mouth turned down, eyes moist with tears. "Maryellen was raped and got pregnant."

Shock reverberated through Nicky's system. Ryan's face paled, and his knuckles whitened as he clutched his fork.

"Dinah never told the FBI because . . . because she couldn't. She couldn't bring shame on her daughter like that. Then everyone would know on the reservation, and she had kept it so secret. Hidden." Her expression begged for understanding.

Nicky ground her teeth. *Hidden*. Dammit. That meant a Family Meeting and negotiations with the perpetrator. Which meant the guy might still be loose on the rez to commit other crimes. Family Meeting was one tradition Nicky could do without.

"I need to speak to Maryellen's parents. There are K'aishunis living in Chirio'ce."

Savannah shook her head.

"That's an uncle and cousins. Maryellen's parents aren't here anymore. Aren't on the pueblo. After they came back two years ago, after her murder, they left. Something happened here at Fire-Sky. I—I'm not sure what it was. Something bad. Personally, I don't think Dinah could have stayed, with all the memories. They live in Nebraska now."

She paused, her face tight, and said, "Nicky, they are *se fue*. Gone."

CHAPTER FOURTEEN

"Sergeant Matthews? Sorry to interrupt. Mrs. Benami and her grandson would like to speak to you."

A flare of anticipation sped Nicky's heartbeat. This was the third time they'd come to the station in the last few days. The first two times she'd been in the field and missed them, too busy with a rash of residential break-ins in Salida.

She swallowed on a dry throat. She had been too unnerved by her dream at the lookout and needed time to process it, to think about what it meant and how it fit into Sandra Deering's case. She'd come up empty so far. But now . . . they must have more information. Why else did they persist? She exhaled a calming breath and something inside her settled.

Nicky flashed a smile at the young officer by her desk. Cyrus Aguilar was a graduate of the U.S. Indian Police Academy in Artesia and had been working at the department for a couple of months. He was a home-grown Tsiba'ashi D'yini kid, halfway through his sixteen-week field training. Brass had him working swing shift, but he wasn't allowed to patrol alone. That wouldn't happen until he could prove himself.

"Can you escort them into room three for me, Aguilar?" she requested. "Take them a couple of bottles of water. I'll be there in a minute."

"Sure, Sergeant."

"And Aguilar?"

"Yes, Sergeant?"

"Ms. Benami only speaks Keresan. You speak Keres too, right?

"Yes, ma'am. Not as fluently as I would like." He shrugged and his lips quirked up in a half smile. "But I'm taking classes at the Hummingbird Community Center."

Aguilar was a lean, nice-looking young man, his straight black hair pulled into a long braid. His eyes were always shining with a sense of purpose. A good role model.

"Her grandson, Squire," she said simply. "He's a little lost now."

"But you think he's a good kid." He hesitated. "I've seen him at the center. We've never spoken."

"I want you to sit in. Squire translates for his grandmother, but I'd like a second set of ears."

Cyrus stood taller. "Thank you, ma'am. I'd be proud to help."

Nicky quickly completed her report and sent it to her lieutenant. She pulled on her blazer before heading to the small conference room.

Aguilar stood just inside the door. Squire sent her a sideways glance as she stepped across the threshold. He fiddled with the lid of his water, twisting it on and off. Juanita held two plastic bottles upright on the table, a third tucked into her purse. It was human nature to take something free, but in Indian Country it could also be construed as a "gift," an offering.

"Mrs. Benami, Squire, I'm sorry I've missed your visits."

Squire stared at her, his expression surly, but she thought she saw a flash of uneasiness in his eyes. He was dressed completely in black, his stringy hair hanging in his face.

"If you don't mind, I'd like Officer Aguilar to stay," she said pleasantly.

Squire leaned close to his grandmother and thrust his chin at Aguilar as he spoke.

The old woman's brows knit. She stared at Aguilar. As was tradition and out of respect, he did not meet her eyes. When Squire finished speaking, Juanita nodded, and Nicky slipped into the chair across from her. Aguilar sat next to her.

"How can I help?" she asked.

The woman cocked her head, listening to Squire's translation. She murmured to him and knocked on the table with her rings before she stretched her arm across the top.

"Please take Grandmother's hand," Squire said.

His voice shook and Nicky's pulse fluttered in her temple. She tamped back her disquiet and took Juanita's hand. The old woman's fist opened at the last second and locked across Nicky's fingers. Her hand was cold and damp from the water bottle's condensation, and something flat and rough-edged pressed uncomfortably into Nicky's palm. She stiffened and her gaze darted to Juanita's face. The woman narrowed her eyes before her expression blanked. Nicky almost yanked her hand away, but Juanita tightened her grip, making the object between their palms bite into her skin.

"*Dza*. Nah." She pressed her other hand over the top of their entwined ones and gave Nicky a smile. "Is o-kay."

She turned her head to Squire and spoke in Keres, dentures flashing between thin, colorless lips, voice rusty and with little inflection. He translated as she spoke.

"Grandmother says you know why she is here," Squire said. Officer Aguilar cocked his head and leaned in a little.

"Sandra was witched. She did not kill herself. Grandmother says you and the police think Sandra was high on drugs, but she wouldn't do that." His expression was fierce. "You searched her car and her room. There was nothing. No drugs. Did you talk to her friends?"

"They said she didn't even drink. That she attended AA meetings in Albuquerque. But Squire"—Nicky gentled her voice—"that doesn't mean she didn't—"

"No! Somebody did this to her. That's why we're here. We have proof."

Nicky exchanged a look with Officer Aguilar. "Go on."

"We're here to tell you what is happening now and why you must continue the search, no matter what your chiefs command. Sandra's not at peace. Her spirit wanders and comes to our home. Something was . . ."—forehead puckered, he licked his lips—"empty when you found her body. *Empty*." He gave his grandmother a glance.

Juanita nodded and squeezed Nicky's hand.

"I don't understand," Nicky said. "We retrieved Sandra—*all* of her—from the field. The autopsy report showed she was complete. She was buried *complete*. What do you mean, *empty*?" Nicky addressed Juanita, her confusion very real.

The object between their palms felt hot now, burning her skin.

Squire spoke, his voice hushed. "Our house is surrounded by an old metal fence. To come into the yard, visitors must pass through the gate. It's always latched." He looked at his grandmother. "The latch is rusted, and must be pushed up hard for the gate to open. It isn't easy," he insisted.

A breath rushed out of Aguilar, and Nicky shot him a glance. He was rigid in his chair, his face gray.

"What?" she whispered, her scalp prickling. The burning against her palm intensified. She cleared her throat and tried to regain her authority. "What does it mean?"

"It means either you lied to us or someone has lied to you, Sergeant Matthews. You told us Sandra was complete, but she wasn't." Squire's voice broke.

Nicky frowned at the accusation. "I did not lie to you," she rapped out. There had been no reason to question OMI because everything had been perfect on the autopsy report.

Too perfect.

No. Her eyes widened. Juanita caught her gaze and nodded slowly.

"How do you know I was lied to about Sandra's body?" Nicky said, her throat tight.

The answer came from Cyrus Aguilar. "Because the gate to the house won't stay closed." His voice was hushed.

Squire's lip trembled and he wiped away a single tear, wetness smeared across his cheek.

Aguilar continued. "The body in the ground is not whole, so she cannot rest. She is wandering, afraid. Confused. She's trying to come home. To a safe place. To her family. She doesn't know she's dead." His voice choked on the final word.

He repeated what he said in Keres, and Juanita Benami's face crumpled in grief. She sucked in a small, heart-wrenching sob, and turned their linked hands over, releasing the object between them into Nicky's palm.

It was a silver pendant with radiating arms—like a sun. Most of the arms were filled with slim sticks of red coral. One held a bright piece of turquoise tucked into the thin silver slot and another was empty. Nicky caught her breath.

Empty.

Tears trickled down Juanita's face as she smoothed her fingers over the pendant. Nicky clutched the woman's hand, wanting desperately to take away some of her pain, but she shook her head and pulled away.

Aguilar touched Nicky's arm.

"Someone deliberately . . . *took* a part of her body, so Sandra Deering's soul is broken and alone. *Esta perdida.* She is lost."

CHAPTER FIFTEEN

"It's very old," Ryan murmured, holding Juanita Benami's pendant on the tips of his fingers.

"How can you tell?" Nicky asked.

"The tooling. Patina. No maker's mark. And the design. I would guess it was made a generation or so after the Spanish friars arrived and converted the tribe to Catholicism." He smiled faintly. "This fellow was probably a rebel, resisting conversion in his own way."

"I don't understand," Nicky said.

"There are twelve spokes or points in this pendant. It's not a sacred number in Fire-Sky culture, but very significant to Christianity. Normally, the spokes on this type of jewelry represent a series of Earth or Sky or Fire gods. Because of the design and color of the stone—red, or coral—the maker was from a Fire Clan. There are more than twelve gods in the Fire Clan host. Fourteen, I think. Sixteen for—"

"Sky and eleven for Earth," Savannah finished. "Water Clan doesn't have pendants like this."

"So twelve spokes are unusual?"

"Not anymore. Most Indian silversmiths do as many points as their design calls for. The bigger the piece—the more points—the more money. But the real difference in this piece is the middle section, here." He pointed to the center of the pendant. "This silver oval is divided into four chambers with a cross. More Christian symbolism, so it served its purpose—fooling the priests. But it's actually a depiction of a heart. See? Two smaller chambers above the horizontal bar, two larger, below—atria and ventricles. The heart is considered the residence of the soul."

Savannah touched one of the tiny drops of silver at the end of a spike. "This pendant is a Fire Clan symbol. It's called a Spirit's Heart. At the time of conquest, it and other Native religious objects were banned. If a member of the tribe was found making anything like this, they could lose a hand, or worse. Thus, the Christian elements."

"There's an empty slot, a piece missing," Nicky pointed out. "More symbolism?"

"Yes, just like the turquoise stone that replaced a coral one. The original story of the Spirit's Heart involves a Fire deity and his four-teen children, so fourteen stones in fourteen spokes. As the years passed, some of the children left to join other clans in marriage, or were killed in hunts or wars, or disappeared, never to be found. What happened to them determined whether their stone would be replaced and with what.

"Marriage would mean a replacement that symbolized the joining clan. Turquoise for Sky." Ryan laid the pendant on the black velvet he'd brought to Savannah's. "Onyx for Earth, mother-of-pearl for Water. But if the child was lost or died tragically, its spirit would wander, restless and empty." He hesitated. "So, nothing."

"Juanita Benami probably gave this to you because of the lost stone. She believes it represents Sandra, and now it's your problem, not hers," Savannah said dryly.

"Juanita and Squire believe Sandra's soul is lost. That explains why you continue to be visited by the spirit of the ancient one, Nicky. Maybe there is still a wrong that needs to be made right," Ryan said. "And you've been chosen."

Savannah rolled her eyes. "Oh, for God's sake," she muttered. The timer buzzed. "Enchiladas are done, so no more talk about visions and wandering spirits. Do you want to eat at the counter?" She pulled a dish of mouthwatering green chile enchiladas from the oven and set it on a trivet.

As Nicky shifted to a barstool, she eyed Savannah, who caught her gaze and stilled.

"What did you do, Nicky?"

Nicky scrunched up her face and confessed, "After Juanita and Squire left, I called and left a message for Julie Knuteson at OMI, about a follow-up on Sandra Deering's autopsy."

"*Really?*" Savannah threw up hands still encased in oven mitts. "There was nothing suspicious about her suicide, your words. And Captain Richards ordered you to close the case. You did turn in your report, didn't you?"

"Pending Sandra's UNM email and dorm information. I still haven't heard from them," Nicky said defensively.

"Fine. But if they'd found something, don't you think they'd have contacted you by now? If the captain finds out you're still working on this, he's gonna be *ecstatic* you disobeyed direct orders. He's looking for an excuse—"

Nicky cut her off. "There was nothing suspicious about your brother's suicide, either." Savannah's shoulders stiffened. Nicky hated bringing up Santiago's death, but it made her point. "I've been thinking about this and have come up with a possible link. You both know the guy who did Sandra's autopsy—David Saunders—has taken body parts before." Nicky looked back and forth between Ryan and Savannah. "What if he's done it again? What if he's been doing this all along and lying about it on the final reports?"

"And how will you explain your reasoning to Julie? To anyone?" Savannah asked. "Sandra's grandmother told me her gate doesn't close so that means Sandra's spirit is walking the earth, and OMI must have lied? Or how about, the final report OMI sent me was *so* well done, *so* complete and flawless, it made me suspicious?"

Ryan grinned and Nicky smiled a little sheepishly. "I'll probably say I had a hunch or something. It's a cop's go-to for lots of things."

Savannah humphed and pulled off her mitts. She passed Nicky and Ryan plates. "Eat. And no more surprises. Agreed?"

"Agreed," Ryan said and held out his plate.

Nicky pressed her lips together and scooped enchiladas. Savannah handed Ryan a cold Pellegrino, then reached back inside the refrigerator for an open bottle of white wine.

"Nicky?"

She took a bite of enchiladas, shook her head, and avoided Savannah's gaze. Her next bit of information would make her friend go ballistic.

Savannah stopped and stared. Her eyes narrowed.

"Jeez, Nicky, there's *more*? Spill, before I hit you with something."

"I'm heading up to Santa Fe to meet someone after dinner. So, no. No wine. I'll have a water, too. A bottle of Pellegrino would be great." She was babbling.

Savannah and Ryan's words tumbled over each other. "Santa Fe? Dammit, Nicky. Who?" "So that's why you have your mom's car."

"It's not a date," Nicky said defensively, stalling. "I got a text yesterday."

Both Ryan and Savannah said nothing, but Savannah's anger was almost palpable.

"From Dax," Nicky finally admitted.

Ryan's eyebrows flew into his hairline and Savannah actually growled before she snapped, "I knew it! And you're actually going?"

"He says he has important information about something going on at the pueblo, and he couldn't tell me over the phone or by text. Too many eyes and ears."

"Yeah, like his wife's!"

Nicky winced. She wiped at imaginary crumbs by her plate.

Savannah was silent for a beat. "I shouldn't have said that. I'm sorry. But after all that happened? After all he put you through?"

Nicky gave her a steady look and Savannah's speech faltered.

"It's just that he hurt you so much. . . ."

"It's been years. I was over him—*all* of it—a long time ago. I'm happy with the way things turned out." She gave Savannah's arm a squeeze and smiled brightly at her and Ryan. "And just because I'm going to meet him doesn't mean I trust him. But he's so well connected, he might really know something. And he's provided good information in the past."

"You don't know what this is about?" Ryan forked a bite of enchilada into his mouth.

Nicky shook her head.

He swallowed. "Then go. But be sure to take some antivenin. That guy is a snake."

CHAPTER SIXTEEN

Esta perdida. She is lost.

Nicky scanned the darkened streets of downtown Santa Fe looking for a parking spot on a crowded Friday night. The area was filled with trendy restaurants and bars. And, if the license plates were any indication, lots of out-of-state tourists.

Cyrus Aguilar's words kept running through her head. They were all she'd thought about on the drive up. And because the consequences of her actions were probably not going to go unnoticed by her captain and lieutenant, they'd caused her to lose quite a bit of sleep the night before.

Savannah was right. Her superiors expressly ordered her to close the case. No matter what she found, Captain would use it against her. She could be looking at reprimand, suspension, or worse.

Nicky touched the Spirit's Heart pendant, running her fingertip over the small oval center. It sat flat on her skin above the deep V of her tunic top. Ryan had run a long silver chain through it and hung it around her neck, murmuring, "Keep this close to your heart, okay?"

She straightened her shoulders. She'd have to risk her captain's ire. There were too many questions about Sandra's death that still needed answering. It was a puzzle she was compelled to solve.

Taillights flashed red as a car pulled away from the curb. She tucked her mother's sporty two-door Mazda into the parking spot.

On the crowded sidewalks her boots clipped with each step, but she was glad for the walk. The meeting place with Dax was only a couple of streets away. If anyone saw them together and reported back to his wife, it could get real ugly real fast, and she had enough on her plate. But he'd been adamant his information was important. She huffed out a breath. And this was the only way he would tell her.

Dax Stone. Chief of the New Mexico State Police. Only child of a politically well-connected family. He had cousins from Texas and Colorado in Congress, the ear of the governor, and made it clear he was angling for political office at the national level. Dax was movie-star handsome and charismatic, and she'd been dazzled when he'd focused his attention on her the summer before her final year of law school. She'd been awarded a prestigious internship at the DA's office in Albuquerque where she'd caught his eye. They'd indulged in a torrid secret affair that ultimately blew up in her face and left her career in ruins.

Nicky turned into a narrow street. *He'd* indulged. She'd fallen in love, and he'd whispered he felt the same way, but his life was too complicated, his family had expectations. If she could only wait for him to sort out his obligations before they went public . . .

She'd believed every word, every lie, and fervently agreed to do whatever he wanted.

Had anyone else in the history of the world been so stupid and naive?

Nicky read the unobtrusive gold lettering above the door of the restaurant. This was it. She wavered, sick anticipation sliding through her, before she clutched the Spirit's Heart pendant in her palm. The silver prongs bit into her skin. She hoped it would give her the strength she needed to walk in and act like she was doing him a favor.

And that the scars of their affair were completely healed and had faded into nothingness.

She released the pendant and stepped inside, catching the eye of the black-clad maître d'. Before she could open her mouth, he beckoned her to follow him, a knowing smile on his lips.

He led her through a darkened maze of black-draped tables and booths lit by flickering candles. Smoky jazz was playing loud enough that the murmured conversations of couples were private, yet soft enough that it didn't interfere with their exchanges. The whole place was intimate and oozed with an illicit atmosphere.

A place where men and women brought their lovers, not their spouses.

Her lips twitched. Dax should feel right at home.

They stopped before a curtained alcove and her guide rapped against the wall. The ridiculousness of the situation almost made her laugh out loud.

Suddenly her nervousness melted away. This was the Dax she'd known in the past. All drama, no substance. He hadn't changed.

But she had.

"Come." His voice was deep and strong. It once sent shivers over her skin.

The maître d' opened the black velvet drapes with a subdued flourish.

"Chief Stone. Your guest has arrived."

Dax stood slowly, his dark blue eyes never leaving her face. Age had only made him more outwardly attractive. His build was athletic, his shoulders and chest wide and slabbed with lean muscle. He was tall, dwarfing her by more than half a foot. Wavy black hair with a sprinkling of silver threads swept back from a smooth, wide brow. Stark cheekbones squared into a strong jaw and chin, and masculine lips quirked into a charming smile below a straight, bold nose. One eyebrow struggled to lift upward.

Oh, dear God, he'd gotten Botox. She couldn't stop her grin.

He took hold of her upper arms, obviously mistaking her reaction as welcoming, and leaned in to kiss her, his eyelids drooping seductively.

Nicky turned her head at the last second and his lips landed on her cheek. She slipped out of his grasp, sat down, and clutched her hands together so she wouldn't rub off the feel of his mouth on her skin.

Dax murmured something to the waiting maître d', and slid onto the buttery black leather of the seat. As the man left, he drew the curtain back in place.

"Dax." She kept her expression relaxed and pleasant.

"Nicky. You've only become more beautiful since I last saw you. It's been, what, two years?" His smile was wistful, but his gaze roved possessively over her neck and breasts.

"Since I graduated from BIA training and was promoted to agent."

"I'm glad I could help you with that," he said.

A small flame of anger ignited. She placed her hands flat on the table and leaned forward.

"First of all, it was part of the settlement. Second, I didn't need your help. I earned my place there two years earlier than we'd agreed upon." She sucked in a deep, settling breath.

"Of course," he said soothingly, but she could see a mocking glint in his eyes.

"Why am I here, Dax? What's so important and so secret that you couldn't tell me over the phone?"

"Nicky!" he chided, reaching across the table to cover her hand with his. "Can't two old love . . . *friends* meet for dinner and talk about good times past?"

The curtains swished open and a waiter rolled in a cart with an iced bottle of champagne and the mouthwatering smell of steaks.

Nicky tried to pull away, but Dax clamped his fingers around her wrist.

"I remembered what you like . . . to eat," he murmured provocatively, and grinned as she irritably snatched her hand back.

The waiter placed their plates before them and disappeared through the curtains.

A reluctant smile tugged her lips.

"Ass. You always did know how to get to me."

"Eat your steak. I told them rare." He gave her a genuine smile, and cut into his.

"I ate before I came."

His smile froze. "Too bad. They do a mean steak here."

Nicky looked around the alcove. "What is this place?"

"A place that caters to celebrities and politicians," he said between bites. "Discreet. I've used it a few times before in the past when something . . . delicate came up."

She could imagine.

Carefully, he put down his silverware.

"Why do you avoid me? What we had was great. What we could still have."

Nicky gave a snort, and he frowned.

"Seriously, Dax? Have you *seriously* forgotten what happened?"

"It was a long time ago."

She interrupted him, her voice sharp. "Your wife came to my house—"

"Fiancée," he corrected.

"Oh. Excuse me. Your *fiancée* came to my house, poisoned my dog, and tried to *kill* me."

"That's why I couldn't leave her for you. Her mental state was too delicate. She's better now. She's gotten help since then." But as he said it, his gaze slid away.

"Because it was *mandated* in the settlement," Nicky snapped. "So she wouldn't go to jail for attempted murder."

Not that it would've ever happened. Nicky had gotten a stomachful of the justice system back then. Her idealistic image of equal justice for all shattered into a million pieces when it fell on her head like a ton of bricks. Rich and politically connected families like the Randals *did not* have daughters who went to prison, even if it meant ruining the life of a lowly middle-class law student.

Nicky didn't know how they'd managed to hush up the scandal, while at the same time causing all of the blame to fall on her. By the end, she had to drop out of law school and mortgage her house to pay for lawyers. It took Dax pulling her aside at a deposition, offering her money to cover her debts—and begging her to let it go—for Nicky to concede defeat. Hush money, she thought bitterly. He'd married Janet Randal weeks earlier, in a lavish ceremony attended by celebrities and national politicians. For Nicky, his offer had been the nadir of the whole affair.

She'd agreed to a settlement, but with stipulations, one of which was admission to the Police Academy. The injustice of the courts made her sick. She decided instead to become a cop. Direct, frontline action, instead of talk, backstabbing, and delay.

But Dax had one final twist, one last lie to perpetuate. Instead of the Santa Fe Department of Public Safety Law Enforcement Academy, he'd gotten her admission to the U.S. Indian Police Academy in Artesia. The Randals lived in Santa Fe. They didn't want her near them.

She would never admit it to him, but it was the best thing to happen out of the whole sordid situation. She loved where she was and what she did.

Nicky swallowed her anger. "Why did you want to meet with me?"

"I miss you, Nicky. I miss us. I made a mistake when I let you go. I wanted you to know that." He gave a self-mocking laugh.

Five years ago, she would have given anything to hear him say that.

"So the information was a ploy?"

"I do have something to tell you, but . . . I wanted to see if we could come to an understanding. I can't leave Janet. And I still want to run for Congress. That means there's no future for us."

She raised her eyebrows.

"Look, I'm trying to be honest. You're the best I've ever had." His voice became intense. "I want that again. Nicky, Janet is in New York with her mother for a few weeks. Stay with me tonight."

Funny, but she believed him. And she was tempted. Her sex life had been nonexistent since Dax. She'd wanted only him at first, then vowed off anyone connected to law. Since those were the only men she'd met in the past five years . . .

"No." She was proud how firm her voice sounded.

His eyes narrowed. Chin lifted, she stared at him defiantly. Finally, he gave her a rueful smile. "Can't fault a guy for trying."

Time to end this before she changed her mind.

"It's getting late, Dax. What's this information you have for me?"

He crumpled up his napkin and tossed it beside his plate, suddenly all business.

"I've heard from an inside channel you have a couple of FBI agents working undercover on your Tsiba'ashi D'yini Reservation." His pronunciation was perfect. "Not even your chief of police knows."

Two agents. She'd thought there was only one.

"How about Richards?" she asked quietly.

"No. Your jackass of a captain is in the dark, too."

There was no love lost between the two men. It went back even further than her and Dax's association.

"I know about the agents." Well, she knew about *one* of the agents. It was a little white lie, but she relished his look of surprise. "You aren't the only one with 'inside channels.'"

This time his chuckle was real. "Why doesn't that surprise me?" he said softly before his expression became serious again. "But do you know why they're in place?" He answered his own question. "No. Because if you did, you wouldn't be so complacent."

Nicky's instincts rattled off an alarm in her head.

"The FBI hasn't told anyone—not even the BIA—because they don't want to scare him away, have him go underground. They don't want leaks," he continued.

"Scare *who* away?"

"Nicky, the FBI think they've tracked a serial killer to the Fire-Sky Reservation. And they believe he's targeting Tsiba'ashi D'yini Indians."

CHAPTER SEVENTEEN

Nicky pressed her foot down on the accelerator until she was flying over the dips and hills in the road. Normally the roller-coaster feeling relaxed her, as did the stark beauty of the late spring landscape. But she had too much going on in her head to enjoy it.

Dax's information was making her crazy. A serial killer preying on Fire-Sky Natives.

At the restaurant, she'd stared at him openmouthed, knowing—*knowing*—that *this* was the reason for the ancient one's visitation. Somehow *this* was tied to Sandra Deering's pursuit of the lost tribal members. Despite her rapid-fire interrogation, Dax knew nothing more than what he'd told her. Couldn't even answer the simplest questions.

Like how many people had been murdered.

At a bend in the road, she slowed her unit and scanned the countryside, looking for anything out of place—for anything that might need intervention. Because that was her job. To help the people of the pueblo. Keep them safe. Sometimes it was thankless. Sometimes heartrending, and sometimes uplifting. But it was never boring. It had taken a long time to realize she'd done the right thing by becoming a cop—that she was in the right place, doing work she absolutely loved.

So why was she wavering *right now*? Her fingers flexed on the steering wheel. In her possession was potentially lifesaving information: a serial killer in the midst of the people she was sworn to protect.

And she didn't know what to do with it.

The road straightened, a flat line pointing true to the small community of Ruby Crest and the Feast Day coordination meeting held in the bingo hall off the adobe church. It was the first joint meeting of everyone involved. As many as two hundred people usually showed up, including parade participants, dance and float managers, food and craft vendors, security for the weekend's festivities, and casino coordinators.

Traffic thickened, as much as it could on the two-lane road, with cars and trucks filled with residents streaming to the gathering. She drove up behind a battered blue pickup truck, the bed filled with chattering men and women, some with small children on their laps. An older man, shadowed face under a sweat-stained Stetson, stared at her. He dropped his chin in recognition before he looked away.

Her phone rang, and Bluetooth picked up the call. She glanced at the radio display. Julie Knuteson's name scrolled across the screen. Nicky's stomach tightened. Finally.

"Hey, Nicky. I got your message. Sorry I didn't get back to you right away. We're down a man here and swamped. Multiple traffic fatalities, two unattended deaths, one murder-suicide, and a partridge in a pear tree. Just since yesterday. I haven't had a second to breathe."

Nicky made a sympathetic noise.

Julie worked at OMI in Albuquerque. They'd become friends when Nicky was assigned as the tribe's liaison to the agency two years ago.

"Why didn't you call my personal cell phone?" Julie asked. "I'd have gotten back to you sooner."

"And interrupt the first vacation you've had in a year? Not a chance. How was the wedding?" She slowed her unit to let a car pull in front of her.

"Fine." But her voice was less than enthusiastic. "I don't know what my sister sees in that woman. Her new wife is a total ass, and I'm not saying that in a homophobic way. She'd be an ass if she were a man, too. I give them a year, tops."

Nicky chuckled. "You can't choose your family," she said, thinking of her mom. "And how are you doing?"

Julie had broken up with her live-in partner earlier that year after naked pictures of him with another woman were sent anonymously to her phone.

"Oh, I'm fine. Nothing like showing up 'stag'—or do I mean 'doe'?—to a lesbian marriage ceremony. I was hit on so many times, I started to feel a whole lot better." She drew in a deep breath. "And I'm kind of seeing someone now. A guy I work with periodically. I know it's fast after . . . you know."

Nicky could almost hear Julie's grimace through the phone.

"Hey. No judgment. I'm the *last* person to give dating advice."

They both laughed, before Nicky continued. "Look, I know you're busy, but . . . I have a kinda-sorta ticklish situation that needs discretion." The car in front of her stopped at a crosswalk to let a group of young men in cowboy hats swagger across the street.

"Did you kill someone? No problem. I'll do the autopsy and totally say it was natural causes."

"Funny. I'll keep that promise in my pocket for another time."

"Seriously. Anything you need."

"Wait till you hear, then make your decision." She licked her lips. "David Saunders did an autopsy on a Fire-Sky Tribe member a little over a month ago—"

"Saunders," Julie spat. "That son of a bitch is why I was called in to work last night. He's AWOL. Up and decided to take a leave of absence early last week. No one's seen him since. Sent an email to the ME saying he'd been asked to speak at some forensics conference in Italy. Didn't get anyone to cover his shifts or call, and left a bunch of open cases."

Nicky's every nerve went on high alert. This was a completely off-the-wall coincidence, and she didn't believe in coincidences.

Traffic slowed to a crawl as she entered the town. The church was ahead on the right. Dozens of trucks and cars were parked in dirt lots on either side of the road. Nicky turned her unit into the lot on the far side of the building, found an open spot, and parked.

"The Native woman he autopsied—Sandra Deering—I need you to review her files. His notes, the CT, photos. All of it. Search for anything he might have overlooked, or . . ."

"Or what? Falsified?" Julie's voice was serious. "Nicky, what's going on?"

"I don't have anything concrete yet. Just a hunch. And Julie, I need you to keep anything you find quiet. For now."

The silence on the other end of the line stretched. Nicky stared out of her unit over the edge of the high bluff and into a sweeping grass-and-scrub-filled valley. Cattle dotted the landscape, and Scalding Peak loomed against the sky. The sun sat low on the horizon. Feast Day meeting would start in five minutes.

"What's the name again? Sandra . . . ?" Julie asked.

"Deering." Nicky's shoulders relaxed. "Train-pedestrian. Ruled a suicide." She gave the date.

"Let me pull it up. I'm putting you on speaker."

Nicky heard the tapping of a keyboard.

"Here it is. Yeah. David signed off on the report, along with Jim Harrison, his supervisor." There was a pause. "That's weird."

"What? What's weird?"

"The report. David didn't have to resubmit because of modifications or changes. He always makes changes. We all do. That's why we have a tracking system that layers revision, for legal purposes. This report is perfect." Her voice held a note of misgiving. "Too perfect. Hold on." More tapping. "Damn it. Why didn't anyone notice this?" Julie said.

"What?" Nicky licked her lips.

"All of the OMI pathologists are assigned a sequentially numbered series on their autopsies for tracking purposes. Mine begin with my initials followed by a number. You know, JK1, JK2, and so on, but more complex. No skips in sequence because of legality issues. Each body received is logged in by a technician and CT-scanned before it's turned over for autopsy. David usually takes the train-pedestrians, so the tech would have used his next sequential file number for Sandra Deering. But I just pulled up all of David's cases for the last couple of months, and . . ."

"What?"

Julie gave an odd little laugh. "So, Nicky, do you ever get hunches about the lottery? Because if you do, please tell me. I am ready to be rich. David's cases. They're not sequential. There's a file number missing."

"Which file?"

"The one right before Sandra Deering's officially submitted autopsy report. He's somehow deleted a file that should *never* have been deleted," Julie muttered. "What the hell?"

The cool evening air wafted through the wide double doors of the church hall and into the stuffy, crowded interior. Tables normally used to serve punch and cookies after services sat on a dais at one end of the long room. Excited conversation and laughter filled the air: English, Spanish, and Keres, but the sounds weren't distinct. Too many people speaking at once. Careful rows of chairs had already been moved into more intimate circles. As they crept toward the stage, the Fathers shook hands and chatted with parishioners.

The lingering smell of tobacco from those smoking outside mixed pleasantly with the scent of strong coffee. Nicky filled a Styrofoam cup from a large silver urn and added a packet of artificial sweetener. She grabbed a couple of store-bought cookies—the homemade ones were gone already—and stood back, searching the crowd for black shirts with SECURITY emblazoned in large white letters across the back. Underneath, in smaller print, was POLICE, MEDICAL, FIRE, or CONSERVATION. It was the uniform of the emergency personnel for the fiesta, worn with their duty belts and cargo pants. Her gaze snagged on a mixed group of black shirts in the middle of the room. Nicky munched an iced oatmeal cookie as she detoured past them toward Savannah. Her friend waited at the edge of the stage, a yellow legal pad clutched against her chest.

"How'd it go with Dax Friday night? I was *extremely* good and didn't text or call the whole weekend, so you'd better give me a straight answer, or else," Savannah threatened.

"It was fine." Nicky's gaze ran over the people already sitting onstage.

"Fine? That's all I get?" Savannah asked, her eyebrows raised so high they disappeared under her bangs. Nicky sipped her coffee to hide a smile.

Savannah tugged her into an unoccupied corner of the room.

"Ryan and I have been *sick* with worry—" Nicky rolled her eyes and Savannah corrected. "Okay, *I* have been sick with worry you did something idiotic, like sleep with him. Ryan said you were a big girl and could make your own stupid mistakes."

Nicky gave a crack of laughter. That sounded more like Ryan.

She leaned in close to Savannah. "He offered. Wanted to restart our relationship, if you can believe it. Said I was the best he'd ever had, like I was some kind of gourmet treat," she finished dryly.

Savannah snorted, but her expression relaxed. "Where did you meet?"

"Some restaurant in Santa Fe. Very clandestine. I had the feeling he'd used it before." She felt a stupid pang in her chest, but she ignored it, and searched the room for Ryan. He stood with a group of security people, talking to a couple of conservation officers, one she didn't recognize.

"So, what was the information Dax had? Or can you tell me?" Savannah asked.

"It was about the FBI undercover operation on the pueblo. Seems there are two agents, not one."

"Two, huh? Wow. There must be something pretty big going on. He didn't say anything about who they are or why they were here?"

Nicky shook her head, careful to keep her face neutral. She couldn't meet her friend's eyes, so she focused on the new conservation officer talking to Ryan.

The man's dark brown hair was cropped short, with threads of gray. White or Hispanic. Maybe mid- to late thirties in age. While Ryan was lean, this guy was bulky, with muscular shoulders and arms. His stance was erect, shoulders back, head up. Definitely ex-military. It wasn't unusual for the different tribes to hire ex- or retired military, because it didn't take much training to get them up to speed for police or Conservation. They were the only two organizations on the pueblo who made arrests and carried sidearms.

It also didn't take much training to get ex-military up to speed in the federal agencies. DEA, Homeland. FBI.

Maybe he sensed her stare, because he stiffened, before his shoulders relaxed. Coffee cup in one hand, he hooked the other thumb in his belt and stared around the room, even as he responded with a smile to something Ryan said.

Ryan sent her a swift glance and half grin, and gestured for her to come over.

"Come on." Nicky nodded back at Ryan. "Let's go meet the new guy."

"Ryan can't stop talking about him. They really hit it off. It's 'Martin this' and 'Martin that.' Major bromance." Savannah grimaced. "Skeezy PJ is with them. I'll stay and get a seat."

"Okay. Catch you after the meeting." Nicky dropped her empty cup in a wastebasket and edged toward Ryan and the new hire. She met his gaze, glad she was still some distance away so he couldn't see her jolt of surprise.

Light eyes. Sky-blue in a tanned face. For some reason, she'd expected brown. His smile gone, he studied her from head to toe, his expression flat and assessing. She bristled inside, picking up hostility before she casually broke off eye contact.

Her gaze flicked over the rest of the group. Most of them watched her, some called out greetings. PJ, the little scumbag, undressed her with his eyes, and Valentine, who stood behind Ryan, completely ignored her.

Coffee in hand, Ryan gave her a one-armed hug. "Hey, Nicky. Savannah didn't want to come?"

She shook her head and squared off for her own cool appraisal of the new conservation officer. She'd guessed right. Hispanic. About thirty-five, and good-looking, although his nose was slightly too large and his lips a little thin.

The Feds were so obvious.

"I don't think you two have been introduced," Ryan said, a note of underlying humor in his voice.

So, he suspected, too.

She held out her hand. Martin's grasp was warm and strong. Her muscles tightened and her whole body took notice of the man in front of her. The air suddenly felt charged.

"Sergeant Matthews is on the police force, but she's also a special agent with the BIA. She's coordinating security for the festival weekend, and will be our supervisor for Friday night," Ryan said.

Thank God Ryan filled in the conversation gap, because she wasn't sure she could speak just yet. She forced a smile and released his hand, before flexing her tingling fingers. He smiled back, but his eyes were narrowed, his face stiff.

"Sergeant Matthews. I've heard a lot about you," he began. Her lips twisted and he continued hurriedly, "Nothing bad. Really. Only admiration."

She ignored Valentine's snort.

How much did he really know about her? How deep was her file at the FBI? If he really was an agent.

Nicky finally unstuck her tongue from the roof of her mouth. "I'm sorry, I didn't catch your name . . . ?" Her voice sounded husky to her ears.

He blinked rapidly and fidgeted with his coffee cup, like he was having trouble processing what she'd said. *Well, son of a gun.* She suppressed a smile. He was as shaken by their introduction as she was. Some of the tension drained out of her.

"Yeah. Sorry. I'm the newest hire for the Conservation Department. Been here only a couple of weeks. Out of Arizona. Yup."

Nicky bit her lip to stop a smile. He was rambling.

"Sorry." He took a deep breath. "Name's Martin. Frank Martin. I look forward to working with you, Sergeant Matthews."

CHAPTER EIGHTEEN

Nicky groaned softly and relaxed into a cushioned chair in Savannah's den. She twisted the top off a bottle of cold water, took a drink, and cradled it against her shirt. Feast Day meeting had run long—like it did every year. A plate sat on a tray table next to her, crumbs the only remains of the sandwiches and chips she and Savannah had eaten a few minutes earlier. It was dark outside, and the patio door hung open. Crickets chirped and cars drove by. A dog barked in the distance. Pueblo night music.

Savannah sat and typed her meeting notes into an email for her boss. She'd periodically fired questions at Nicky. "How many people would you say showed up? Was anyone prominent missing tonight?"

But Savannah had been silent for the last ten minutes.

The warm air wafting through the screen door made her sleepy, and Nicky let her eyelids drop. She drifted, sifting through her conversation with Julie Knuteson at OMI, with Dax in Santa Fe, and her introduction to Frank Martin.

Words and impressions became like smoke, ephemeral, swirling around and around together. They twisted into a tightly woven rope that snaked around her neck. It changed to metal, cold against her skin. Something heavy tugged at the chain. A presence stood before her, its hand pressed into the skin of her chest, icy as death. It steadily warmed until it burned with the intensity of a thousand red-hot knives. The pain was intense, but she had to bear it, had to wait until the dream gave her an answer. Suddenly heat flashed like the sharp steel of a blade, and plunged into her chest toward her beating heart.

Nicky gasped and her eyes popped open.

"I'm glad you're still wearing the Spirit's Heart," Ryan said. He sat on the sofa, his empty plate stacked on top of hers.

The pendant was clenched in her hand. She opened her fingers and studied the rays of coral and the single turquoise stone. The empty spoke was black and hollow.

"You were dreaming."

"Hmm." She tucked the pendant inside the V of her shirt and set her bottle of water on the side table. He'd turned off the lamp, so the only light was from the kitchen. Nicky glanced at Savannah. She still sat at the bar, her back to them, scrolling the screen of her computer, only to stop periodically and make a notation on her yellow pad.

Nicky yawned and ran her hand over her hair, caught her ponytail and gave it a flip.

"So, is Frank Martin FBI?"

"Probably. Ted said they were in the army together. Afghanistan. When the job came up, he gave him a call." Ted being Ted Brighton, the Conservation Department's captain.

"Convenient."

"He's actually qualified. Went through Land Management Police Training at Glynco, and was working at the Tohono O'odham Reservation in Arizona before he transferred. I don't know dates, though."

"I can pull up his file," Savannah called back to them.

"If he's FBI, I wouldn't trust the information in it." Nicky grabbed her water and took a drink.

"What's going on that they need an undercover operation on the rez?" Ryan asked. "I mean, I know they have federal jurisdiction on a lot of things."

"Yes," Nicky agreed. "The Major Crimes Act includes murder, manslaughter, kidnapping, every assault imaginable, arson, burglary, robbery, child abuse."

"Fire-Sky police do all of that," Ryan said.

"But the Feds have resources we don't," Nicky pointed out.

"We would've heard about any of those crimes. You know how gossip and rumor spreads on the pueblo," Savannah added, hunched over the computer.

"Since everyone in the FBI does a rotation through Indian Country, I'm sure they've all been briefed about how fast information travels here. That's probably a big reason they're so paranoid and secretive about everything. And a pain in the ass to work with." Nicky sighed. "It's just that they don't know the territory, don't know the culture. They come to the rez, order people around—"

"Then have to ask directions to get back onto the freeway when they leave." Savannah scoffed.

"I'm cross-commissioned for Indian Country and federal. So are a lot of other cops on the pueblo. They should do us the courtesy—"

"Surely your captain or chief have been briefed," Ryan interrupted.

Nicky shrugged. She wanted to tell them Dax's information, but if what he said was true, it could mess up the entire operation, potentially put more people in danger. Until she had more intel, she'd keep quiet.

Time to change the subject.

"Julie Knuteson from OMI called me back."

Savannah swiveled around. "And?"

"She's going to look into the Sandra Deering file."

"And?" Ryan asked softly.

Nicky pressed her lips together. "The doctor who did Sandra's autopsy has taken an unauthorized leave of absence. He left a message saying he was going to some meeting in Europe, but no one knows where he is."

"That doesn't mean anything, Nicky," Savannah said. "Are you sure you want to do this? If Captain Richards finds out, the consequences—"

"I need to know."

Savannah turned away. "You and your stupid puzzles." She scrolled through her emails. "Fine. If you get fired, you can always get a job at McDonald's or Blake's. I hear managers make pretty good money. Oh, *shit*." She clamped a hand over her mouth.

"What?" Nicky and Ryan said at the same time.

"I just got an updated email of the notables attending the fiesta. Dax Stone, chief of the New Mexico State Police, is now on the list. *And* he's going to be onstage during distribution. Along with the tribal governor and the governor of the state!"

Nicky hurried over and scanned the list. "At least Janet's not coming. He said she was with her mother back East."

"That's probably why he'll be at Feast Day. Because *she's* not here and *you* are."

Nicky exhaled a shaky breath. She didn't want to be seen with Dax, much less speak to him.

Ryan joined them. "What's going on?"

Before Nicky could explain, Savannah said, "Dax hit on her the other night. Wants her back on the sleazy side. Said the sex was the best he'd ever had."

Ryan grinned as Nicky's neck and face heated.

"Wow. Hidden talents." He laughed.

"Shut up, both of you."

"What'll you do if he tries to talk to you?" Savannah asked. "It will definitely stir up old rumors and gossip."

"That's gonna happen even if he doesn't speak to you," Ryan observed. "Just his presence is going to be a problem."

"Yeah. Captain Richards and his crew already think you slept your way to the top. Those misogynistic idiots won't ever believe a woman can climb to your rank and position so quickly without help, especially since you left so many of them in your dust." Savannah tucked her arm around Nicky's waist and gave her a hug. "But it really is best if you avoid Dax Stone."

Nicky swallowed. "I know."

Ryan tipped his head to one side. "Who are you partnered with on Friday?"

"Since I'm supervising, I was going to float. Are you volunteering as guard dog?" It wouldn't be too difficult to shift the personnel roster around.

"Sure. He'll be less likely to approach you if you're paired with a big scary guy." His eyes twinkled.

"Big scary guy, huh? To protect little ol' me from another big scary guy? I don't know whether to shoot you or kiss you."

"I think it's a good idea, Nicky," Savannah interjected. "Another man between the two of you—as sexist as it sounds—may make Dax think twice about propositioning you again."

"Wait!" Nicky raised her eyebrows. "How about I kill two birds with one—heh, heh—*Stone.*"

Savannah groaned. "That pun makes no sense, you know."

"Yes, it does. It was brilliant," Nicky stated firmly. "I can keep Dax at arm's length, and I can get to know a new employee on the reservation. Evaluate him, interrogate him, look for cracks in his probable FBI armor." She smiled, more excited than she should be.

Ryan and Savannah exchanged a glance.

"I'll assign our new Conservation agent Frank Martin as my partner for Feast Day. That will definitely make for an interesting weekend."

CHAPTER NINETEEN

Because the Catholic Church officially decreed three saints were martyred on a single day, the Feast of Saint Denise, Andrew, and Paul—DAP Day—was celebrated May 15 for over two hundred years on the Fire-Sky Reservation. But about twenty years ago, the pueblo changed the fiesta to the last weekend of the month for their Feast Day, or *bá-sku*. Since the school year for most districts in the state ended the week before, and it coincided with a federal holiday, the pueblo wanted to maximize the attendance of New Mexico families before they scattered for summer vacations. The change caused a major rift between the more religious, traditional members of the tribe, and those who saw the decision as both logical and economically more feasible.

"In the end," Nicky said, "money won out."

"Well. I hate to say this . . . but doesn't money always win out?" Frank Martin asked her as they patrolled through the crowded streets surrounding Salida's plaza.

People lined up at booths to grab dinner as the sun sank in the west. Nicky smelled fry bread and lamb, mixed with the sweet savory scent of kettle corn and funnel cakes. Drums and chants sounded from the distant plaza, part of a series of entertainment for the tourists and Natives.

Nicky glanced at him out of the corner of her eye. His black polo stretched tightly over muscular arms, body armor making his chest even broader. A woven leather Sam Browne without the suicide strap wrapped across a flat stomach, his sidearm slotted in a holster on his right. He'd clipped his radio and flashlight within easy reach, as well as a pouch for extra magazines. An ornate silver and gold badge, its colorful Conservation Department medallion fixed in the middle, sat prominently on his belt. His boots were brown leather, laced up over his ankles. Very military, very masculine. He'd hung his sunglasses in the neck of his shirt.

Frank leaned down to pick up an empty plastic soda bottle and dropped it into a recycle container.

"Does the money always win out?" Nicky repeated slowly. "Very cynical, Agent Martin." She resumed her scan of the crowds. The embroidered Fire-Sky logo over her left breast and the POLICE in large white letters across her back were the only relief from the head-to-toe black she wore except for her gold shield clipped to her duty belt. "Considering the crowds will only get bigger this weekend because of the fiesta's date change, I would have to say yes in this situation. But I like to think other things are more important than money." She wrinkled her nose. "Oh, dear. I may have to eat my words. Today is per capita distribution."

He laughed, and a smile tugged at her lips. She was enjoying herself.

"This is a nice break from work. It seems all PJ and I do is remove rattlesnakes from every conceivable nook and cranny in the pueblo. We've been getting two or three calls a day at the department since it's warmed up."

Nicky pulled her face into a grimace and shuddered. "Better you than me. I thought Animal Control did that."

"They kill them. We catch-and-release them alive, far, far away from people."

They walked around a group of laughing teens sharing a funnel cake.

"So, is this your first fiesta? Or did you attend Feast Days at O'odham?"

A veil dropped over his eyes. Although he was still smiling, it seemed forced. She wondered if she'd struck some kind of nerve. Or if he'd ever actually worked at Tohono O'odham at all. Just part of his cover.

"Feast Days were different there. I was never assigned to patrol."

Hmm. End of subject.

They walked in silence until they neared a large white tent. A long line of people and families, chattering excitedly, snaked inside. The enticing smell of grilling burgers wafted on the breeze.

She unclipped her phone from her belt. It was almost six P.M.

"Speaking of eating my words, are you hungry?" DAP Day officially opened at one P.M. on Friday, so they'd started patrol after lunch.

"I guess."

She sighed dramatically. "Well, if you only guess, you aren't hungry enough for a secret recipe, Fire-Sky double-green-chile cheeseburger with special sauce and seasoned, fresh-cut steak fries." Nicky leaned in to him and caught a whiff of woodsy aftershave. She took another subtle sniff. He smelled good. "I've heard the secret is ten percent buffalo meat mixed into the beef," she stage-whispered. "And I've also heard the Laguna Burger is better, but that's strictly between you and me. Saying it out loud would be a firing offense."

He smiled slowly. This time it reached his eyes.

"Is that what the line is for?" He indicated the growing throng of people.

"It is. But there's a special VIP entrance around back that will take us straight to the source." Nicky wiggled her eyebrows. "Are you game? 'Cause I'm buying."

"All right. I have to confess my stomach's been growling for over an hour. A few minutes ago, I had to restrain myself from grabbing some little kid's Frito pie," he admitted.

Nicky chuckled and pulled her radio from her belt to report they'd be at dinner for the next thirty minutes.

"Confession's good for the soul, Frank," she said lightly, but her steady gaze caught and held his.

Not breaking eye contact, he said, "I'll remember that if I ever need absolution, Sergeant Matthews."

"Nicky. Call me Nicky."

"All right." He smiled. "Nicky."

She led him around to the back of the tent. Within minutes they clutched bowed paper plates heaped with burgers and fries. They shouldered their way through the crowded tent to seats. Frank took a bite of his burger and moaned.

"See? What did I tell you?" Nicky dug into hers. They ate in companionable silence.

The noisy chatter in the tent dropped when a cluster of newcomers entered, but picked back up quickly when the crowd recognized them. Lights flashed as people held up cell phones and cameras.

"Is that the governor?" Frank asked.

Nicky twisted around on the folding chair and studied the group by the grill.

"Yes. Both of them."

"Both of them?" Frank stared at the knot of well-dressed individuals behind them.

"Both of them." She picked up the last piece of her burger, popped it into her mouth, and sighed at the flavorful burn of green chile.

"The governor of the state of New Mexico and Fire-Sky's governor, along with most of the tribal council, a couple state senators and reps, and casino people."

Frank raised his eyebrows. He sat with his elbows on the table, empty plate in front of him.

"The New Mexico governor has shown up for Distribution Day ever since she was elected. The tribe's done amazing things with jobs and employment, even during the last recession."

Frank dropped his light blue gaze to her face. Nicky jolted every time she saw his eyes.

"So, let me get this straight. Fire-Sky Pueblo hands out a certain amount of money every year to each member of the tribe because . . . ?"

"Because of blood."

Frank raised his eyebrows. "Blood."

"Ancestry." Nicky took a drink of water before she explained. "To be a registered member of the pueblo, you must prove you possess one-half degree Tsiba'ashi D'yini blood. A naturalized member must prove they are one-quarter degree Fire-Sky blood, but contain a total of one-half degree Indian blood from federally recognized tribes."

"Degree?"

"Percent. So, fifty percent means one-half degree. The more Fire-Sky blood you possess, the larger your distribution check."

Frank frowned. "And how large are these checks?"

"It changes every year, depending on the profits from tribal industries," Nicky said. She lowered her voice. "This year, full-bloods will receive over ten thousand dollars each."

"Jeez. And they hand the checks out tonight?" His voice held an incredulous note. "Isn't that asking for trouble?"

"Not real checks. The actual money gets deposited into special accounts at the end of the month once all the signatures and other information is confirmed. But, if you show up tonight to sign the register, you get a bonus." She tilted her head to indicate the group of VIPs behind her. "Peter Santibanez—PJ's father—came up with the idea after the casino opened. He sold it as a way to show unity on the pueblo. A we-are-one-people-and-can-be-successful kind of thing." That statement was straight out of Savannah's mouth, only she said it in a way more cynical tone of voice. "The press and politicians love it. Tribal members and families are invited onstage to shake hands and receive their money as part of the show tonight."

A cool breeze blew into the tent from an open flap. Nicky shivered and rubbed her arms.

"You're cold," Frank stated. "Why don't you stay here and clean up? I'll go over to the command center and grab our jackets."

"Thanks." Nicky smiled at him.

Time seemed to stop.

His mouth quirked up on one side. "Well." His voice was rough. He cleared his throat. "The burger was great. I owe you," he said and walked out of the tent.

Was it Frank's voice that caused goose bumps to break out on her skin? Or was it the dropping temperature?

Nicky stood and gathered the remnants of their meal. She dropped the trash in the large plastic barrel tucked in a small alcove, before arching her back in a long stretch. The rear of the tent was open. She'd wait there for Frank. Turning, she ran into a hard body standing directly behind her.

Nicky stepped back to apologize, looked up into Dax Stone's dark blue eyes, and froze.

CHAPTER TWENTY

Nicky cursed under her breath as she stumbled back. Dax's hands steadied her, his gold wedding band winking in the flashing lights of the cameras. Shouts of, "Governor! Over here," rang out. The VIPs, their backs to her and Dax, laughed and held up plates filled with Fire-Sky burgers as the press and tourists snapped photo after photo.

"Dammit," Dax muttered. "Quick, outside."

He tugged her through the back opening of the food tent. It was pitched at the edge of a large dirt lot that held a few dozen cars and trucks. The fiesta-goers must all be at dinner, because it was otherwise deserted.

Great. Her arm gripped in his hand, Nicky trailed a half step behind him.

The sun had dropped low on the horizon and glowed golden through thin, streaky clouds, but there was still enough light that the two of them threw shadows on the hard-packed ground. Applause from a distant audience watching the traditional dances carried on the breeze.

Dax guided her to the side of a panel truck and Nicky mentally kicked herself for the situation she was in. It was her own fault. Given his political aspirations, she should've known he'd be nosing around the governors.

He must have been watching her, because the one time her partner was out of her sight and useless as a guard dog, Dax had pounced. And if she couldn't get away from him, she'd have to deal with stupid introductions and awkward explanations when Frank came back with their jackets.

"So who was that guy you were sitting with? You looked pretty cozy. Is he why you turned me down in Santa Fe?" The hand on her arm tightened.

Nicky's anger flared. She shrugged off his grip.

"That would make it easier for you, wouldn't it, Dax? If I were involved with someone, there'd be a justifiable reason for me to say no."

Instead of becoming angry at her declaration, his body relaxed, and a dark, sexy smile quirked his lips.

"So, you're telling me there's a chance." He quoted one of his favorite movies. "Come on, Nicky. Remember how great we were together? We could have that again."

She was in no mood to be charmed.

"I don't get it," she said. "We've barely seen or spoken to each other for the last five years. Why are you bothering me? Why now? Why here?"

But he didn't answer her questions. Instead he stiffened, his cool charm dissipating like smoke. His brows snapped into a hard line. He took a step toward her, crowded her back against the truck.

"I'm *bothering* you?"

She blinked up at him, her face going slack. His gaze dropped to her mouth and he leaned in, lips quirked into a half-smile. Warm breath bathed her cheeks. Nicky took a deliberate half step forward and raised her face to his.

"Do you think this little display of masculine intimidation is going to work on me, Dax?" She kept her voice musing, curious.

His eyes widened. He slowly arched his head and shoulders away from her.

"Do you think after a whole year where your wife's family and their lawyers threw everything they had at me—and *ruined my life*—that I would fall into your arms?"

He shuffled a cautious step back from her. "Uh, look, Nicky, all I wanted to do was talk—"

"You need to stand down, Dax. I'm a completely different woman now. And this woman doesn't want anything to do with you."

"But what about all the help I've given you over the years? The tips? The back-channel information? I've tried to make up for what I did. Dammit, Nicky, you owe me."

Nicky's chest swelled as she drew in a long breath. Her hands closed into fists. Dax took another step back.

"I *owe* you?" she snarled. "Why, you son of a—"

"Sergeant Matthews?"

Both of them snapped their heads around. Frank Martin walked toward them but held Dax's gaze. He handed Nicky her jacket, settled in beside her, and crossed his arms over his chest.

Nicky eyed both men. Frank wasn't as tall but he probably outweighed Dax by twenty-five pounds. She smirked. Not that she'd needed him.

Dax recovered quickly. He flicked a hard glance at Nicky. "Aren't you going to introduce us, *Sergeant Matthews*?"

Nicky pinched her lips tight at Dax's tone.

"Agent Martin, Dax Stone, chief of the New Mexico State Police," she said in a clipped voice. "Chief Stone, Conservation Agent Frank Martin, Fire-Sky Pueblo."

Dax Stone held Frank's stare for drawn-out seconds, then gave him a politician's smile and extended his hand. "Agent Martin."

Frank widened his stance and dropped his arms to tuck his thumbs in his belt.

Dax withdrew his hand and the smile melted off his face.

"Well, it looks like you have yourself a champion, Nicky. But there was no need to step in, Agent Martin. Nicky and I are old . . . friends." His lips curled. "She's perfectly safe with me."

"That's where you're wrong, Chief. I didn't step in to help *her*," Frank replied.

Nicky snapped her head toward Frank. A slow smile stretched her mouth.

"Sergeant? We're wanted by the stage," Frank said. "If you'll excuse us, Chief."

They pivoted and strode away, leaving Dax Stone alone in the growing shadows.

As they walked around the tent toward the street, he muttered, "Dax. What the hell kind of name is Dax?"

Nicky gave a crack of laughter. He cocked an eyebrow at her, but she shook her head. Frank matched her step for step.

CHAPTER TWENTY-ONE

Nicky crossed her arms and smiled. Another Tsiba'ashi D'yini family ascended the steps of the outdoor stage. The mother helped a little boy of about three up each rung—step-stop, step-stop—and the crowd was eating it up. The child jumped the last step and ran to his dad, already onstage. An older girl dressed in traditional costume followed Mom. White shells sewn into her shirt declared her elemental clan as Water.

"Darlington Xavier Stone." She glanced at Frank.

"You're kidding." A smile tugged his lips, but whether it was because of Dax's real name or the antics onstage, she didn't know.

The little boy took the ink-dipped eagle feather and made his mark in the registry, but he didn't want to let the pen go. The crowd laughed as his father chased him a few steps before he scooped him up and snagged the feather.

"Nope. That's his real name," Nicky replied.

Dax was onstage now, part of a long line of VIPs glad-handing the invited families. He stood taller than all of them, his black peaked cap with its chief's insignia pulled over his brow.

"Well, he seems like a real jack-hole to me. So, what's on the scroll?" Frank asked as the tribal governor handed one to the father.

Some of Nicky's tension drained with the change in subject.

"It's a signed commemorative certificate, suitable for framing. Personalized with the family's name, the date, and the amount of the per capita distribution check. But only people invited to the stage actually get a certificate. They have to apply for that privilege, too. Peter Santibanez chooses those he considers worthy."

"Worthy?"

"People who won't embarrass the tribe if the press researches them. Individuals without criminal records, full-bloods." She gestured to the stage. "Intact families like the Bahes. Joshua, the dad, works as a sous chef at the Fire-Sky Resort. His wife, Celia, is a cashier at the casino. They have the requisite two cute kids." She smiled as the little boy gave Santibanez a hearty handshake and the crowd laughed in coordinated response. "Good people. It's all very political."

"Peter Santibanez is PJ's father, my partner at the Conservation Department."

"Yeah. Peter Senior is the head of F-S Tribal Enterprises. He's the man at the mic. A lot of people on the rez think he's where the real power lies because he controls the purse strings of the tribe."

Santibanez's teeth flashed white against his skin as he grinned and shook the hand of the next person on the stage. His long hair was wound into a traditional wrapped bun, but he was dressed in a stylish black suit and a stark white shirt. He wore a silver and turquoise bolo tie and a chunky turquoise ring and watchband on his hand and wrist, his declaration he was elemental Sky Clan.

Frank nodded to a line of tables underneath canopies that bracketed one side of the audience. "What's going on over there?"

"Tribal members signing in to get the bonus."

Savannah sat at the nearest table. Nicky caught her eye and waved. Her friend said something to another volunteer, got up, and hurried toward Nicky and Frank. She, too, was dressed in traditional clothing.

She hugged Nicky. "Don't say a word. Peter Santibanez insists that anyone who works the registration tables has to come 'Full-Indian.'" She mimed air quotes and rolled her eyes. "I wanted to back out, but my mom wouldn't let me. Since I didn't have anything appropriate, she dug this up from her grandmother's stuff."

Even with her owlish glasses and modern haircut, Savannah looked beautiful and exotic in her Native dress. The soft deerskin had been brain-tanned white, contrasting gorgeously against her golden skin. Her shirtfront and the ridges that ran along her shoulders and down the sleeves were beaded with iridescent mother-of-pearl. A colorfully woven wool belt wrapped around her slim waist, and her straight white skirt dropped over cream-colored moccasins. Ryan's comment about Savannah jumped into her mind:

To Savannah—to many Indians—their ancestry, their DNA defines them. It colors actions and decisions. Has nothing to do with traditional or nontraditional practices. It's much more elemental than that.

"So, aren't you going to introduce me to your partner?" Savannah winked at Nicky.

"Frank Martin, Savannah Analla. Savannah works with Public Safety at the police department. Frank was just hired at Conservation."

Savannah held out her hand to Frank. "Ryan Bernal has told me a lot about you." She grinned. "So are you enjoying DAP Day? Has Nicky been filling you in on the history? Do you have any questions? Can you tell I've had too much coffee?"

Frank, who initially looked a little taken aback by Savannah's chatter, chuckled.

"I was about to ask Nicky—Sergeant Matthews—about how the registration works. Does everyone have to sign in tonight to get their check?"

"Nicky, huh?" Savannah's grin widened. "The sign-in during the fiesta is to get a bonus payment, but the actual registration starts on the first of January. It goes until June first. If a tribal member—regular or naturalized—wants to receive their check, they have to"—she held out a hand and ticked off her fingers—"one, bring their written ancestry and Certificate of Indian Blood to the enrollment offices, and two, update their registration in a database set up specifically for per capita distribution."

"Certificate of Indian Blood? There's a DNA test that proves a person is specifically from the tribe?" Frank asked. "I imagine with a large payout you get people coming out of the woodwork saying they have Fire-Sky ancestry."

"No DNA test or blood test or anything like that is officially recognized," Savannah replied. "The CIB is a federal requirement that calculates the degree of Indian blood from our lineal ancestry. A lot of tribes use it as part of their documentation."

An infant wailed in the background.

"Even babies born this past year get a check with the right paperwork," Nicky added.

"Yep. And the casino hotel is filled with tribal members who don't live on the reservation but come in specifically for DAP Day and the bonus." Savannah's gaze swept the crowd. "The number of people on the pueblo swells for a few days because a lot of our transient population return."

Nicky gave Savannah a sudden, sharp look. A light switched on at the edge of her mind. Transient population returning to register . . . But before she could grasp its meaning, new names were announced over the PA system.

"Juanita Benami and Squire Concho. We welcome you today. Grandmother Benami has endured the tragic loss of her granddaughter this year," Peter Santibanez said in sorrowful tones.

The crowd quieted and stood. Squire, his hair in a tidy braid, was dressed in cheap black slacks and a wrinkled white dress shirt buttoned all the way to his chin. He helped Juanita up each step. The old woman paused to catch her breath at the top before she hobbled toward Peter Santibanez. He bowed and took both of her hands in his, murmured his condolences, then passed her to the governors, who, with sad smiles, gave her the rolled certificate.

But instead of continuing down the VIP line for more handshakes, Juanita shuffled to the front of the stage, Squire by her side, and searched the crowd. She tugged his sleeve and Squire bent down, nodded, then he, too, searched the audience. He caught Nicky's gaze and said something to his grandmother. Juanita turned her face toward Nicky. Slowly she held out and shook her certificate.

Nicky's focus blurred and, for a flickering instance, the tiny woman dressed in black became the ancient one. She sucked in a faint gasp and stilled.

"That son of a bitch. Peter Santibanez just exploited Sandra Deering's family," Savannah said.

Her vision cleared. Nicky shook her head and stared at the stage.

"Sandra Deering?" Frank asked, his tone sharp.

"Dear God, how could I have missed this?" Nicky whispered. Pieces of Sandra's puzzle that had been haunting her started to fall into place. With a quick, "Excuse me, Frank, I need to speak to Savannah," she caught Savannah by the arm and dragged her out of his earshot.

"Savannah, what happens to Sandra's per capita distribution? Does the family get it?" She flicked a glance at Frank. He stood where she'd left him, but his body was stiff and his arms were crossed.

"No. It gets added to the money used for tribal improvements and new business ventures. Why?"

"Does the PCD database list include the individuals who *didn't* register for their annual checks?" Nicky asked. "And the reason why they didn't register?"

"Yes, if there is one. The tribal council would need that information to justify taking the money."

"Do they check the list of the missing people—the ones who miss the deadline—against any other databases?" Nicky pressed.

"They check it against deaths and births, and cross-check it against last year's PCD—" Savannah stopped and her eyes widened. "Oh, my gosh. Sandra's list of the missing! She got it from the Distribution Day database."

"That's why the *official* missing persons reports didn't help. Most of those people are addiction transients. They disappear for months on end, only to come home for Per Capita Distribution Day. They aren't truly missing. But Fire-Sky members who *don't* show up from one year to the next . . ." She let her voice trail off suggestively.

"We Indians have an unofficial name for distribution money," Savannah said. "*M'aat'i sá-wáka*. Do you know what that means?"

Nicky's heartbeat accelerated. She turned her head back to the stage. Juanita Benami and Squire were gone.

"Yes. It means 'blood money.'"

CHAPTER TWENTY-TWO

Fiesta security personnel gathered in the morning at the church's Bingo Hall for breakfast and to go over assignments for the day. Nicky chatted with Ryan and Frank, a half-empty cup of coffee in her hand, when Savannah stalked inside and dropped the *Albuquerque Journal* on the table.

"Have you seen this? I thought you were going to stay away from Dax Stone."

Nicky dragged the paper in front of her. Above the fold, there was a color picture of the governors, smiling and holding up their Fire-Sky burgers.

"Isn't that one of the reasons you wanted Frank to be your partner? Your scary guard dog?" Savannah kept her voice low, but she was obviously upset.

From across the table, Ryan stood and craned his neck. Frank, who'd been sitting next to her, pulled his chair closer.

"Scary guard dog, huh?" he said warmly in her ear.

Nicky bumped his shoulder with hers and gave him a half smile. "Yeah. Sorry."

"Would you two stop flirting," Savannah snapped, "and look at the photo? There." She stabbed a finger at a spot between the governors' heads.

Nicky studied the picture more carefully and it made her feel a little sick. She and Dax were standing behind the VIPs, his hands clasping her arms, his wedding ring prominent. Their pose was close, intimate.

"Wow. Isn't it amazing how in focus everything is in the picture? Digital camera technology—"

"Shut up, Ryan." Savannah handed Nicky her cell phone. "That's not all. Did you know there's an online gossip site, based out of Santa Fe? Mostly it tracks celebrities and actors, but not always. Look what showed up on it last night."

A picture of Nicky and Dax silhouetted next to the white panel truck was displayed on the screen. Below, the caption read:

Divorce rumors have been swirling around New Mexico power couple Janet Randal Stone and Dax Stone, NM state police chief. Could this old flame be the reason?

She tried to hand the phone back to Savannah.

"No. There's more. Keep scrolling."

Nicky swiped through half a dozen photos of her conversation with Dax the evening before. She stopped on one where she was only inches from him, her face tilted up. Her stomach fell. The caption read, *Prelude to a kiss?*

"That's where I stepped in. I thought you were going to deck the guy," Frank said over her shoulder, loud enough that a couple of people nearby turned their heads toward them.

Nicky handed the phone back to Savannah. "I didn't see a photographer. I thought we were alone." Her face felt stiff.

"There was a guy with a camera, smoking under a tree," Frank said.

"Do you think Janet is having Dax followed? Jeez, Nicky. That's all you need is to be called as a witness in Dax's divorce. All the old stories will be stirred up again." Savannah's brows crinkled and her lips pinched thin.

"Nothing happened last night. The best thing to do is ignore it," Nicky said firmly. She glanced at her phone for the time. "Our shift starts at ten, Frank. Let's go."

Nicky caught a few surreptitious glances from some of the people in the room. Manny Valentine gave her an insolent stare, and the sick feeling returned. He would go straight to Captain with this information.

She tugged the Spirit's Heart pendant from under her shirt and squeezed it. They'd had such a breakthrough yesterday when they'd figured out where Sandra had found her "lost" tribe members, but a lot of investigative work still had to be done.

With all that was happening on the Sandra Deering case, she did not need a Dax Stone distraction right now.

CHAPTER
TWENTY-THREE

The Bernalillo Starbucks was crowded for a Sunday morning. Nicky swirled her latte, waiting until Frank sat down with his coffee before she took a sip.

Ready for another day of patrol—the final day of the fiesta—he was dressed in his black polo and camo cargo pants, sunglasses perched in his hair. He rested his muscled forearms on the table, fingers laced around his coffee cup. His hands were large, nails blunt and clean. No ring.

"Sure you don't want anything else? Since you got up early, I'm buying." His light blue eyes smiled.

"I'm good." She pressed her lips together, but couldn't completely stop them from quirking up on one side. The heat from her coffee tingled against her tongue as she took a sip, and she fleetingly wondered if the warmth in her chest was from her drink or from Frank's presence across the table. They'd spent Saturday at the fiesta, partnered again, and he hadn't pressed her about Dax or the mess Friday night. In fact, despite all the hours they'd spent together in the last couple of days, their topics of conversation had been impersonal. Safe.

Maybe it was time to change that.

They both had agendas. She, to figure out why he was at Fire-Sky, and he—she gave an internal shrug—probably to find out what she knew about the Sandra Deering case and how it related to the Chiricahua murders.

But there was something else going on she wanted to explore. Her attraction to this man ran fast and deep. Either he was a great actor and she was reading him wrong, or the feeling was mutual. If it was mutual, she would use it against him and hope it wouldn't come back to bite her. She had a strict no-fraternization rule. Still . . .

She swirled her coffee again, her smile coy.

"So. Do you really want to talk about your assignment today, or . . . ?" Nicky let her voice trail away.

"Or?" he answered, his tone light.

"Or do we get to know each other better? Like, who is Frank Martin?"

He chuckled. "Can you narrow it down a little?"

"Wow. That much to tell," she teased playfully.

"No. Not really." His smile deepened.

"Okay. Let's start with an easy one. Where are you from?"

"Tucson. I grew up there. How about you?"

"Albuquerque, born and raised. Family?"

"Dad and Mom live halfway between Benson and Tombstone. Three older sisters." He waggled his eyebrows. "Hand-me-downs were the worst." Nicky burst out laughing. "How about you?"

"My mom and dad divorced when I was about ten. Dad passed when I started high school." Frank murmured condolences. "My mom traveled, so I spent a lot of time with my grandmother. Siblings . . ." Nicky toasted him with her cup. "Too complex for coffee, so let's move on. How'd you come to be a conservation officer on an Indian reservation? It's not a career many people know about."

"It wasn't a straight path by any means. I played baseball in college. Had a scholarship. Catcher. Thought I was going to be the next Pudge Rodriguez." At her blank look, he said, "Gary Carter?" She shook her head with an apologetic smile. "Johnny Bench?"

"I've heard of him!"

"You're not a baseball fan?" Frank's voice held an incredulous note.

"Not really. Is that a deal-breaker?" She raised an eyebrow.

"Maybe. Are we making some kind of a deal here?"

"Maybe," she repeated softly. "But you haven't made the connection,

Agent Martin. How do baseball and conservation go together? Please continue," she directed, using her best interrogation tone.

"Uh-oh. That law-school background is coming out."

Nicky couldn't stop the tightening of her expression. She turned away from him and scanned the early morning crowd, sipping her coffee to cover.

Frank stretched a hand across the table.

"I'm sorry," he said. "It's just that the guys talk."

"And with Dax Stone showing up at the fiesta, the photos in the paper . . . I'm sure the gossips are working overtime." Nicky set her cup down and checked her phone. Taking a deep breath, she managed a bright smile. "Ancient history is not the topic of study this morning. Baseball is." She put her phone down, screen up, and tapped it. "Ten more minutes and we need to get to work." Deliberately softening her expression, she said, "I'm still interested."

His eyes flared as he picked up her underlying message. Good. For a moment she'd lost sight of her goal. It wouldn't happen again.

"Baseball, right. So, the athletic department encouraged certain degrees and classes that—let's just say—wouldn't interfere with practices or the season and would make it easy to keep up our grade-point average. Math appreciation, communications . . . I took one called Forests and Society. Really liked it. That led me to the conservation biology degree at the University of Arizona."

"So you got your degree and went into the military." At his quick look, she smirked. "You're not the one only who hears gossip."

"No. I dropped out of college and went into the military."

"Why?"

"Convergence of bad luck?" He shrugged and took a sip of his coffee. "Honestly? Immaturity. The coach brought in a new kid. He was a better catcher than me and took my first-string position. I didn't get to play much anymore, so I quit." He hitched a half smile. "And there was this girl."

"Let me guess. Your one and only true love. Life wouldn't be worth living if she wasn't in it. And she broke your heart."

He chuckled. "Right in one. She dumped me after I left the team. Next thing I know, she's dating my replacement. That was pretty devastating. I dropped out of school and joined the army as a grunt."

"You were in Afghanistan."

"Three tours. Demolition. With the scouts. We were dropped in the backcountry to find Taliban hideouts. I blew up caves."

"Was it rough?"

"Surprisingly—most of the time—it was amazing. The places I was stationed were very much like the mountains in southern Arizona. Still, it was no walk in the park."

His smile was gone. Had he lost buddies out there? She didn't know him well enough to ask.

Nicky tried to lighten the mood. "Well, you came to the right place if you want caves. Scalding Peak is riddled with them."

"Except they're off limits to non-Natives, right? Because they're sacred and the war chiefs do rituals up there. That's why I'm paired with PJ for the duration of my training. He was a war chief, so he still has partial access in case we need to go in."

Nicky shook her head. How could she explain PJ Santibanez to Frank?

"No. PJ has never been a war chief. He might have trained to be one—" She glanced down at her phone. "Ten minutes is up. We've got to get going. Looks like we'll have to finish this fascinating conversation later."

"How about over dinner?" he said. "I owe you for the Fire-Sky burger."

Her heart rate sped up. "Not tonight. The fiesta goes till ten."

"Later this week, then. Give me a call when you have a free evening. Let's exchange numbers."

"Okay." Nicky told herself she was accepting his invitation because she needed to gather information.

If she could only keep the stupid smile off her face. She took a sip of her latte and wrinkled her nose.

"Do you mind watching my stuff? I need to get a warm-up for my coffee and hit the ladies' room."

At his "No problem," she walked to the back of the shop, her step light. She stopped to hand her drink to a girl behind the counter to microwave, before she ducked into a narrow corridor.

"Here's your coffee, Officer." Nicky smiled her thanks to the barista and took a sip. Too hot. She swirled her drink and looked for an opening in the line of customers, neck craned to find Frank.

A phone rang, and she automatically slid her hand to her belt. Her skin prickled. The clip was empty. She checked her pockets. Not there. Had she dropped it?

No. Relief swept over her. She'd left it on the table, her purse and jacket hung on the back of the chair. Jeez, her little chat with Frank had really messed with her head this morning.

Nicky sidestepped between two large men with the Santa Ana Star Casino logo embroidered on their shirts. Frank stood by their table. Her phone was in his hand.

"I'll take that," she rapped out, palm up.

"Oh. Sorry. It started ringing, so I just . . ." He handed her the phone and flashed a sheepish grin.

Nicky checked the screen.

Julie Knuteson, MD, OMI
505-555-8891

"Excuse me." She walked a few steps away from him and answered. "Julie?"

"I've got something." There was barely suppressed agitation in Julie's voice. "Can you come by the lab today?"

Nicky glanced at Frank. His head was down but tipped in her direction. The barista called out an order, and a guy picking up his coffee blocked her view of Frank for a moment. "I can't talk now. And I can't come today. How about tomorrow?"

"Tomorrow after work," Julie said. "Text me."

"Okay. Gotta go." Nicky hung up. She took a deep breath and deliberately relaxed her body. "Ready, Frank?"

His gaze swept her face. "Everything all right?"

She clipped her cell to her utility belt, grabbed her jacket and bag, and started for the door.

"Yeah. My contact at OMI. A dead body brought in last night could be a Fire-Sky overdose. I'm the tribe's liaison, so she gave me a heads-up call." Nicky tried to inject enough ruefulness in her voice to make her story appear true.

He made a noncommittal sound and held the door for her.

Nicky glanced at Frank as she stepped outside. Even though he'd had her phone, he hadn't learned anything important. And he'd backed her up with Dax on Friday night. Still, she vowed to be more careful around him going forward.

CHAPTER TWENTY-FOUR

Nicky and Frank headed into the village of Salida for patrol. The crowd had thickened after the conclusion of Sunday Mass, and tourists and residents mingled on roads blocked off from vehicle traffic. The tent canopies and booths that lined the narrow streets displayed Native crafts and painted pots, homemade clothes, jewelry, and leather goods. People gathered at stalls selling breakfast burritos and bags of deep-fried sugar donuts, their sweet-savory scent like a siren's call in the crisp morning air.

"*Bitch!*" A woman stepped into the street and jerked her hand in an arc.

A shower of dark liquid seared the skin of Nicky's left hand and splashed in the V of her shirt. The arm and shoulder of her jacket steamed where it caught the bulk of the fluid. She hissed and twisted away.

Training kicked in immediately. With a burst of adrenaline, she lunged at her attacker and slammed her to the street. The woman screeched and scored the side of Nicky's face with long red nails. Nicky quickly flipped her over, knee in her back, and pulled out a pair of handcuffs. The woman kicked mightily, and Frank fell on her legs.

"You got this?" Frank asked.

"Yeah." She jerked one wrist behind the woman's back and clicked on a cuff, before she grabbed and twisted the other arm. Her fingers bit into skin.

Frank reared up behind her and knelt across the woman's calves, radio in hand. "Ten eighty-two, repeat, ten eighty-two on the north side of the plaza."

"Copy that. On our way."

"Get off! You're hurting me! Police brutality! Bitch, get off me! It was an accident! I swear it was an accident. Dax! *DAX!*"

Her screams drew a crowd. Some of them held up cell phones to record the spectacle.

Nicky heard running footsteps. Breathing hard, she clicked on the second cuff, stood, and hauled the woman to her feet. Three men raced toward them, Officers Manny Valentine and Cyrus Aguilar close behind.

"Get off her! Let her go!" Dax yelled, his face ashen. "Janet, honey, are you all right?"

Frank stepped in front of Nicky and the woman, one hand out, the other on his ASP baton.

"All of you, stop right there. If you take another step, I'll arrest you for interference with the lawful duty of a police officer."

They slid to a stop. "You and what army?" growled one of the guys with Dax.

From his aggressive demeanor, Nicky guessed he was one of Dax's state cops, maybe even a bodyguard. Except Dax and his men were dressed in jeans, so they weren't here in any official capacity. Her brows knit. Then why—?

She stiffened, muscles rigid. *No. It couldn't be.*

"She attacked me. It was an accident, and she attacked me." Sobbing, the handcuffed woman struggled to reach Dax.

Nicky spun her around, and stared at the lovely, gamine face. Her cap of white-blond hair was mussed, and dirt streaked her skin and clothes. But the hatred blazing from the blue-green eyes jolted Nicky. Coldness slid to her core. "Janet. You changed your hair. I didn't recognize you."

"Bitch!" she screeched again, before she lifted her head up and wailed plaintively. "Dax. Please help me. Save me."

Dax and his men stepped forward again, but Valentine and Aguilar had circled around and created a shield with Frank at its center. Nicky glanced to either side. Two more Fire-Sky officers—Gallegos and Montoya—flanked her and Janet Stone on the left and right.

"What the hell is going on? Nicky? What have you done to my wife?" Dax inched closer, his tone harsh now.

"Chief Stone, I don't care who you are. If you take one more step, I will not hesitate to bring you to the ground and cuff you, sir." At the intensity of Frank's voice, Dax blinked.

Janet twisted back to Nicky. "This is all your fault," she shrieked. "If you hadn't contacted him, hadn't wanted him back, this never would've happened. Why can't you just leave my husband alone?"

The adrenaline pumping through Nicky exploded into anger. Her hand tightened on Janet's arm, two seconds from shaking her teeth out. She took a long steady breath.

"Dammit, Janet. I want *nothing* to do with him."

"You lie! I saw the pictures. I saw them." Janet disintegrated into sobs, her slight body shuddering with them. "I saw them."

"Nicky, please. Let her go. I'll take her home, okay? Just let her go," Dax begged. "Janet, sweetheart, it'll be okay."

"Montoya, Gallegos," Frank barked, "take the detainee to Command Post One. Make sure you read her her rights. She's being charged with assault on an officer." He looked at Aguilar and Valentine. "Go with them. I'm taking Sergeant Matthews to first aid."

Manny Valentine swiveled sharply. Nicky met his gaze and his face paled as he stared. He and the other officers escorted Janet down the street. She resisted at first, but soon fell into step.

Dax motioned for his two bodyguards to follow. The crowd of tourists and Indians started to disperse.

"Frank, I need to go with them," Nicky said urgently. "None of those officers have jurisdiction for non-Indian on non-Indian crime because they're tribal. I'm federal. I'm the only one who can make the arrest."

"You will, but after we have you checked out." The fingers of Frank's hands were warm on her cheek as he tilted her head to one side. He grimaced. "She clawed you good." His gaze dropped. "How's your hand?"

She flexed her stinging fingers. Fluid-filled blisters had already formed. It would hurt like the devil once her adrenaline rush subsided.

"Nicky. Please. Let her go." Dax touched her arm and she shrugged him off. "She didn't mean it. She's still . . . sick. She still needs help."

Frank threw him a glance, his lips turned down in a scowl.

"And you're the only one who can help her. Rescue her from herself." Nicky glared into his eyes. "Why did you have those two goons with you today, Dax? Were you expecting trouble? And why was that photographer following you Friday night? Did Janet hire him?" Realization hit her like a fist. "Or did you?"

Dax stood as if cast in stone. He dropped his gaze. She pivoted away, disgusted by the whole situation, and headed toward the first-aid station. Frank fell in beside her.

Nicky called over her shoulder, "Must be nice to be Janet's champion. How grateful will she be if you save her from the evil other woman? Grateful enough to stop talking about divorce?" Her voice wobbled at the end and she clamped her lips closed.

They walked in silence through the crowd, Nicky cradling her hand.

"It's my own fault," she finally admitted.

Frank raised his brows, but didn't say anything.

"I knew Dax was a snake, and I just made the mistake of getting bitten. Again."

A man dressed in the same black polo and khaki cargo pants as the EMTs met them at the door of the first-aid trailer.

"Hello, Sergeant. I'm Dr. Laughton. I heard you had an encounter with a cup of hot coffee out there on the mean streets of Salida. Let's get you out of this jacket."

Nicky shrugged out of her dirty, coffee-stained jacket and handed it to Frank.

The man gently grasped the unburned skin of her arm and stared at the blisters on her hand. "Tip your chin up. Thank you. Okay. Burns on your chest and neck, and some nasty scratches on your face. Let's head inside so we can get them cleaned up."

Laughton shot her a smile and stepped between her and Frank, who hovered behind her. Frank rocked back on his heels and scowled.

Nicky gritted her teeth and nodded in assent. She barely registered the doctor other than to note he was tall and blond. Her numbing spike of adrenaline had worn off and her burns felt like they were on fire. Though she tried to suppress it, her whole body shook with reaction. The doctor helped her up the retractable metal step of the mobile medical unit.

To divert herself from the pain, she studied the little room. Brightly lit, cool, and smelling of antiseptic, it had been modeled into a small clinic with an examination table and instrumentation, including a scale, a blood-pressure cuff hooked to the wall, and a sitting area under a large, curtained window. There was even a sterilizer next to the sink. All of the cupboards were labeled with their contents, and a compact refrigerator tagged with a NO FOOD OR DRINK sign was tucked along one side of the room. A short Native American woman, her black hair rolled into a bun, stood quietly. Scissors, gauze, a tube of salve, and a plastic cup of ice were on the counter next to her. Nicky recognized her as a CMA from the Fire-Sky Clinic, and gave her a quick hello.

"So, there was a wrestling match, too?" Dr. Laughton smiled, straight white teeth flashing briefly. "Wish I could have seen that. Mary, rinse off her hand with half-and-half Betadine and sterile saline. Officer, you can have a seat over there." He directed a flat, hard look at Frank, and gestured to the chairs. Frank crossed his arms and didn't move, his face a mask.

Laughton gave him a faint sneer, and turned his back to him. "As far as you know, this was only coffee, right? There was nothing else added?"

Nicky sucked in a breath as Mary cleaned the grit embedded in the blisters of her hand. "I don't know. Cream and sugar?"

"I had one of the officers on scene collect the cup for testing," Frank said. Laughton glanced at him.

Nicky blinked and caught Frank's gaze. "What? I didn't see—it was just coffee, right?"

"You were busy with Chief Stone at the time. And people throw a lot of bad things at cops. It was just a precaution," he said.

"Yes. He wouldn't be doing his duty if he didn't protect you *after* the fact, would you, Agent Martin?" Laughton said.

Eyes narrowed, Nicky looked back and forth between the men. "What's going on? Do you two know each other?" she asked, an edge to her voice.

"Nope," Frank said.

"Not at all." The doctor turned his back to Frank again. "I need to examine the rest of these burns. To do that, I'm going to have to remove your shirt." He grabbed the scissors.

"Wait, Doc. I can pull the shirt over my head—"

The trailer door burst open. Ryan and Savannah practically tumbled inside.

"We heard what happened," Ryan said.

"Are you okay?" Eyes wide, Savannah clutched a folded black polo against her chest. "I brought this for you to wear. Oh, Nicky. Your hand," she whispered.

"I'm fine, right, Doctor? He's going to bandage me up, and then I'm back out on patrol," Nicky reassured her.

"Well . . ." Laughton frowned. "I think it would be best if you went home, Sergeant. Your left hand will be almost worthless for a day or two. I'll write you a medical leave excuse."

"No. I still have an arrest to make, and . . ." She scrambled for a reason to stay. "And I can't leave my partner. He's new and this is part of his training. Right, Agent Martin?"

"Nicky, please do what the doctor says. Frank won't care." Savannah turned and placed a hand on his arm. "Right, Frank?"

Frank frowned and nodded slowly.

Nicky blew out a long breath. She was meeting with Julie Knuteson at OMI tomorrow night about the Sandra Deering autopsy. A day at home would allow her to review the files one more time, see what she had and what was still missing.

"All right. Wrap me up good, Doc. After I'm done today, I'll head home, and take tomorrow, too. But I want to work Tuesday. The war chiefs are doing their Blessing Ceremony, and I have a feeling I'm going to need all the help I can get moving forward."

She smiled around the room, trying to lighten the tension. Savannah visibly relaxed, Ryan nodded his head, and Frank's mouth curved in a half smile.

"Okay. And since you have a clean shirt to wear, I'm gonna cut you out of this one and get you patched up. But without an audience. Everyone out," Dr. Laughton ordered.

Nicky promised to text Savannah and Ryan, and they filed out of the trailer.

Frank didn't budge. "I'm staying with my partner."

Nicky's gaze flew up to his.

Laughton was cutting through the sleeve of her shirt but paused to say coldly, "I gave you an order, Officer. You are dismissed."

Frank widened his stance and looped his thumbs in his belt. The room bristled with tension.

"It's okay, Doctor. He has to view my injuries for the arrest report," she said. "And he can hold my necklace." She reached her hands up to unlatch it, but Frank stepped behind her.

"Let me do that," he murmured. His fingers were gentle as he removed the Spirit's Heart pendant from around her neck. Mary handed him a cup of water from the tap. He dropped it in to rinse off the coffee.

Laughton finished with her shirt, then quickly detached the Velcro straps holding her light body armor in place. He snipped off her thin tank top, leaving her black crossover sports bra in place.

The cool air of the room hit her coffee-damp skin and magnified the pain of her burns. Mary stepped forward and cleaned them with ice-and-saline solution. Dr. Laughton coated the top of her hand in Silvadene and applied gauze and tape.

Tears welled in Nicky's eyes, in part because of the pain, but also because of the whole stupid situation with Dax and Janet. Ugly gossip would fly around the police department because of this incident. Maybe she should ask for the whole week off and let it die down.

She raised her uninjured hand to dash away the wetness around her eyes, when Frank pressed a tissue into her fingers.

"Thanks." Her voice was husky, strained.

He shrugged, his expression unreadable. But when she grunted as

Laughton dabbed salve onto her neck and face, Frank picked up her un-injured hand and held it. He let her squeeze as hard as she needed.

Mary and Laughton were maneuvering the clean black shirt over her head when there was a sharp knock on the door.

Laughton nodded to Mary to open the door when the shirt was in place.

Cyrus Aguilar climbed up the steps. He wouldn't meet Nicky's eyes.

She slid off the table to her feet. Her burns throbbed with each beat of her heart. "Officer Aguilar. Please report."

"Sergeant Matthews." His voice broke and he cleared his throat and started again. "Sergeant Matthews. Lieutenant Pinkett said to inform you the captain has released Mrs. Stone from custody, and—and that he has determined the incident was no more than an unfortunate accident. There will be no arrest. The injury report will reflect the coffee spill and your resulting burns were unintentional. You are also ordered off duty tomorrow and are to leave the feast immediately." His glance flickered to her face, then away. "I'm—I'm sorry."

Nicky didn't say a word. She wasn't sure she could. Mary held a plastic bag containing her shredded clothing, vest, and jacket. Instructions and salve were on top. She reached for her gear, but Frank put a hand out to stop her.

"Are you okay to drive? I can take you home."

"I'm fine. And I need my unit," she said in a low voice.

Nicky took the bag of clothes and, with as much dignity as she could muster, walked out of the trailer and headed to her vehicle. Frank and Officer Aguilar flanked her.

When she slid into her truck, Frank handed her the Spirit's Heart necklace. She'd forgotten it. Nodding her thanks, she wrapped the delicate chain around her uninjured hand, and lifted the pendant up to stare at it as it twirled and dangled. The black, empty slot caught and held her attention. This was her talisman, she thought fiercely. An Indian rosary, to remind her of her purpose on the pueblo. All else was distraction.

She shifted the truck into gear and pulled out onto the narrow street. In the bright sunshine behind her, people streamed from booth to booth, or headed to the plaza by the church to see the chanted prayers and dances.

Before she turned onto the main road, Nicky glanced in the rearview to see Frank and Cyrus. They stood side by side as if in vigil, and watched her leave.

CHAPTER TWENTY-FIVE

Nicky pushed open the doors of the New Mexico Scientific Laboratories in Albuquerque and walked into the soaring lobby. The curved glass wall in front of her extended up multiple stories. Huge abstract landscapes decorated the large open space. In contrast to the cold, clean lines of the modern architecture, the temperature was surprisingly warm. The position of the blue-tinted glass, which faced southwest and captured the heat of the afternoon sun, probably had something to do with that.

She produced her Fire-Sky police ID and signed in to the visitors' log at the security desk. Julie had asked her to come late, after much of the day staff had left work. The guard gave her a visitor's pass and buzzed her into the OMI reception area.

Dr. Julie Knuteson was waiting for her. Nicky gave her a quick hug in greeting.

"What happened to you?" Julie asked.

Nicky made a face and held out a lightly bandaged hand. "A run-in with a cup of hot coffee. I lost," she quipped. "But it's a lot better today. How are you doing?"

Julie shook her head, her smile tight. The smattering of freckles across her nose and cheeks stood out against a pale, pinched face. She was a couple of inches taller than Nicky, and larger. She'd been an athlete in high school and college, but her muscles had melted into softer padding from long hours in a demanding, sedentary career. She wore blue slacks, a slim belt resting on curved hips, and a cream blouse.

Nicky touched her arm and searched Julie's gray-blue eyes. The skin between her brows was pulled into furrows. "That bad?" she asked.

"You have no idea," Julie replied with a sigh. She brushed light brown hair from her forehead, but her fingers stayed to massage her temple. "Let's get out of here," Julie muttered. "I don't want to say anything until we're in a secure area."

A lump formed in Nicky's gut.

Julie led her to the OMI portal, holding her ID card to the metal lock until it clicked. She pushed it open and headed down a labyrinthine series of apricot-painted corridors. A few people, laden with briefcases, bags, and purses, called good night as they passed. But other than polite replies, Julie was quiet, the soft tap of their shoes on tile the only sound other than the low hum of fluorescent lights overhead.

They pushed through doors into the stairwell and descended into another, narrow corridor. As they approached the region of the building that housed the morgue, the smell of the air changed subtly. Julie once told her a state-of-the-art exhaust system had been installed when the labs were built, but it didn't matter. The dead always marked those around them.

Julie stopped abruptly. She rubbed her palms together and sucked in a breath.

"Before we go any farther, you have to know . . ." She exhaled. "I know you told me to keep anything I found to myself, but . . . but I brought someone else in. Don't worry. I've sworn him to secrecy."

Nicky curled her fingers. "Who?"

"He won't say anything, I promise, and he has the expertise to evaluate—"

A door closed and keys jangled as another person stepped into the hall. "G'night, ladies."

Julie's lips pressed in a tight smile and she waited until the man was gone.

"He has the expertise needed for what I found. And I trust him. Remember I told you I was seeing someone new? This is the guy." Her tone brightened. "I've worked with him for a couple of years now, ever since he moved to New Mexico, but it wasn't until after my breakup with Brian-the-rat that he asked me out. Said he'd admired me for a long time and thought he'd never get his chance." Julie's eyes glowed, her speech animated and fast. "He's part of the state's transplant recovery team, so he's always at OMI, harvesting tissue. And he's on this *amazing* research fellowship studying modifications in UW—"

"Wait." Nicky tried to slow her down. "What's UW?"

"UW solution. It's an organ preservation compound developed by the University of Wisconsin—UW—that limits ischemic damage from prolonged storage of harvested organs before transplant. It also improves myocardial function in early post-transplant, but Lio believes the modifications he's made with a specific type of adenosine to maintain high ATP levels, and the radical oxygen scavenging components he's added, plus hydrogen—"

"Wait. Leo?" Nicky felt like Alice down the rabbit hole.

"Sorry. It's just so exciting. He's working on prolonging the number of hours an organ can be stored before transplant. It will save countless lives because timing is so critical for successful outcomes—"

"Julie. You lost me again. Organ storage?"

Julie laughed. "Okay, I'll stop. And it's Emilio. He's a great guy, but he has a few, um, idiosyncrasies. Still, he's been a huge help with your case. He's waiting in his lab." Julie paused and leaned in close. "Did you know physicians are sometimes referred to as little-*g* gods because they can hold the lives of their patients in their hands? Well, transplant surgeons are known as big-*G* Gods, because they hold your soul in theirs."

She bustled the rest of the way down the corridor and stopped at a door near the end. Nicky pressed her lips together and followed more slowly. What was so bad that Julie needed to bring an expert in for Sandra Deering's case?

Julie led her to a small, cramped laboratory. "Stay here. I'll be right back." She disappeared down the hall.

Nicky looked around. Long metal counters topped with tall shelves ran the perimeter of the room. On the shelves sat dozens of mismatched glass and amber bottles, all jumbled together, their contents identified with handwritten labels. Although lights gleamed white and blue from under the shelves, the windowless walls and darkened ceiling created a cavelike atmosphere.

But it was the series of glowing glass vessels dotting the top of the lab benches that drew Nicky's attention. Each was the size of a fish tank with a tightly sealed lid. Clear plastic tubing snaked inside, bubbling gases through liquid. Outside the tanks, the tubing ran along the underside of the shelves and connected to metal canisters chained to the wall.

Posted yellow and black triangular signs with stylized exploding containers hung at the end of the benches, and large red, black, and white stickers plastered on the smooth cylinders read:

DANGER: COMPRESSED HYDROGEN. FLAMMABLE GAS. NO SMOKING. NO OPEN FLAMES.

WARNING: COMPRESSED OXYGEN. NO SMOKING OR OPEN FLAMES.

Condensation on the sides of the bench-top chambers obscured the view of what they contained. Nicky stepped forward, wiped her hand against the chilly glass.

And reeled back with a sharp indrawn breath.

Fist-sized and purple-pink, a heart pulsated inside, suspended with clamps and wires in the clear, cold liquid.

Eyes wide, her gaze darted around the room.

A tank labeled LIVER/BOVINE stood next to one that read KIDNEY/OVINE. Another, LUNGS/HUMAN—SMOKER.

Her attention flew back to the container in front of her. "Heart, human. Traffic fatality," she whispered and rubbed her hands over her arms.

"Nicky—"

Flinching, she spun around with an intake of breath.

"This is Dr. Emilio Meloni, transplant surgeon extraordinaire. Lio, this is Sergeant Nicky Matthews. She works at the Indian reservation I told you about."

Julie's body obscured the man as she gave him a light kiss. She held his hand when she shuffled to stand beside him, her smile wide. His other hand jingled coins or keys in the pocket of dark gray trousers.

Lio Meloni was whipcord-lean, a few inches shorter than Julie. He was probably in his late thirties or early forties, but it was hard to tell because he had one of those smooth boyish faces that defied aging. Both deep and fine lines crisscrossed the skin around dark brown eyes, and there were faint, crepey circles beneath, as if he were perpetually sleep deprived. Brown whiskers stubbled his face, but the top of his head was shiny in the fluorescent under-shelf lights. Premature baldness, and he had the overt confidence to carry it off.

A slim leather belt wrapped his waist and the sleeves of his light blue dress shirt were rolled to his elbows. He stepped too close and grasped her hand firmly with faintly sticky fingers. Nicky pulled back a little at his exuberance.

"Hello, Sergeant," he said in greeting, his smile a little lopsided. "Welcome to my lair. I mean, not really, of course. Just feels like one. No windows." He bounced on his toes.

Nicky relaxed a little. He was charming.

"I thought only mad scientists or evil geniuses had lairs," she countered. "Which one are you?"

Lio grinned and his eyes crinkled until they almost disappeared. "Definitely a mad scientist. The bubbling organs and creepy lighting add to that Dr. Frankenstein ambience I'm going for."

She laughed. He seemed all right. And she was glad, for Julie's sake.

"Don't worry, Nicky. He received written permission from the next of kin for all of the human tissue in here," Julie said. She bestowed a beaming smile on Lio.

He bobbed his head. "Damn straight. I am well versed in New Mexico state laws, especially the ones that pertain to Native Americans. What happened here?" Without warning, he scooped up Nicky's bandaged hand. "And your face." His lip curled a tiny bit.

Nicky tugged her hand away. Was one of his idiosyncrasies the casual invasion of personal space? "Clumsiness and hot coffee."

A single eyebrow flicked up. "You okay?" At her nod, he leaned back to pull a disinfectant wipe and clean his hands.

Nicky, a little insulted, raised her eyebrows at Julie, who shrugged and mouthed, *Quirks.*

Lio, apparently oblivious, asked, "Shall we get started?" He ushered her to a counter arrayed with three flat computer screens. The bubbling tank filled with the sheep's kidney rested a couple of feet away. Nicky swallowed and took the middle chair, Julie the one on her right. A faint astringent odor teased her nose as Lio sat beside her.

Julie rested her hand on the mouse. "So, like I told you when you called, David Saunders was able to—I thought—delete an autopsy report, which, because of legal issues, is strictly prohibited. The first thing I did was to pull the replacement file up and go over his notes, CT scans, and photos." She launched a computer file on the middle screen. It filled with a color photo of a mangled torso.

"This is the file designator." She pointed to a series of letters and numbers at the top of the picture that detailed the specifics of OMI's intake system.

Nicky's gaze remained glued to the remnants of Sandra Deering. Never having encountered the young woman on the pueblo, she only knew her because of her tragic death, what other people told her, and the sorrow and pain her family experienced. The picture was both sad and sobering. She swallowed unexpected emotion.

". . . technician checks the body into the system and assigns the file number, does the CT scan, and assembles the initial report," Julie finished.

Nicky had escorted the OMI van with Sandra's body back to Albuquerque the morning of the suicide. "I received a receipt for the body, but I don't remember a number like that on my paperwork." She tapped the screen. "Or in the email OMI sends out."

"No. What you get is a placeholder that keeps us honest. That way, you can call us to account if we lose the body," Julie explained. "When I studied the file David submitted, I couldn't find anything wrong. The body was damaged, but the police and search teams did a very thorough job in collecting it at the scene. It was pretty much all accounted for and I know that's not always the case with train-pedestrians. I accessed David's computer to see if I could dig up the original file, but couldn't find anything." She flashed Nicky a conspiratorial glance. "At first."

A few keystrokes, and a blue screen with scattered folders popped up in front of her.

"David partitioned off part of his hard drive. All I needed was his password," Julie said.

"How did you figure that out?" Nicky asked, impressed.

"Not so hard." Julie grinned. "He had it taped to the inside of his office desk drawer. Once I had access, I found the *original* autopsy file, along with some other very interesting things."

"Amazing. Passwords taped in his drawer," Lio muttered, arms crossed, knee bouncing. "Pull up the relevant CT images, babe. Show her what you found."

Julie clicked the mouse. Three images came up, one on each of the screens. All were vertical CT slices of Sandra Deering's torso. The first two were similar, but the third . . . Nicky leaned forward to study it.

"This first image was done by the technician." Julie pointed to a screen. "It's annotated with the *correct* file number—the missing file. The second image was one David did himself a few hours later, after he was assigned the autopsy. See? It's annotated under the same original file number. I think he must have seen a problem and thought a mistake had been made." She paused. "The third image was the one he submitted in his final report."

So these scans were the key. Nicky asked the obvious question. "What makes them different?"

Julie pressed enter on the keyboard. Each of the three scans shuffled through a series of thin sections of the chest cavity—like a movie—then repeated in a loop, over and over again. Nicky watched them carefully, mentally comparing what she saw on all three screens.

She pointed to the first two revolving images. "Something's missing in these that's present here." Her finger shifted to the third series of pictures as they flashed around. Even to her own ears, her voice sounded constricted.

Needlelike prickles washed over her skin and she suddenly knew what was missing. Knew with certainty why Juanita Benami told her Sandra's spirit was lost because the gate wouldn't close. Knew why Squire insisted Sandra hadn't killed herself. Why she'd had visions of the ancient face of Ánâ-ya Cáci and the white rabbit, and why Howard Kie sent the odd images in his emails.

And why two undercover FBI agents were on the Fire-Sky Pueblo, hunting for a killer.

She disentangled the chain from around her bandaged neck and held the Spirit's Heart spray of silver and stone in her fist. This explained the missing piece of the pendant. The missing piece of the puzzle that was Sandra Deering.

"It's her heart, isn't it? It was gone when she was brought to OMI. Either it wasn't retrieved at the scene, or . . ." Nicky's throat tightened.

Julie finished her thoughts. "Or she didn't have it when she was hit by the train because someone had already taken it from her."

CHAPTER TWENTY-SIX

Nicky stared at the computer screens. "You don't think David Saunders took the heart? He has a history." She felt numb.

"No. Her heart was removed before she was placed on the train tracks. Probably within a few hours, so time of death wouldn't be suspicious," Julie said. "But without the body, it's going to be hard to prove." She stopped the revolving scans and clicked through more keystrokes. A single color photo now dominated the panel in front of Nicky.

"Whoever did this thought the train would hide his—or her—dirty work. It did for the most part because the technician didn't suspect anything was wrong. But once the body was cleaned up and processed for evidence—which is David's job as pathologist—he found this." Julie picked up a stylus, touched the screen, and drew the tip down a long seam in the middle of the damaged chest. "A median sternotomy. It's how they took her heart. He should have stopped and called the police when he found it. But he didn't. Instead, he cut further. Basically, he destroyed evidence."

She opened another autopsy photo marked with black triangles. "David placed arrows at the arterial and venous dissection lines, and included measurements." Julie paused. "This is why I called Lio, Nicky. Since our autopsy technique differs from what I saw here, I suspected—"

"Let me take over now, babe." Lio scooted his chair forward. "This was no butcher. Whoever did this is trained. Meticulous. The dissection of the great vessels was such that this heart could have been used in a transplant. See here." He pointed to two small, rounded openings. "The superior pulmonary artery and aorta were cut to the correct length for retrieval." He grinned at Nicky. "Couldn't have done a better job myself."

Nicky stared at him, hand pressed against her lips.

Lio sobered. "Sorry. That was callous. Anyway, I think this woman either died or someone murdered her and removed her heart. Afterward, it was the work of a butcher to then throw her body on the tracks. Horrible." He shuddered.

"Don't the trains have cameras? Couldn't you tell she was already dead before . . . you know." Julie grimaced.

"The video showed Sandra lying between the rails. She wasn't moving, so we assumed she'd passed out. Her toxicology report found enough drugs in her system." Nicky tore her gaze from the picture and focused on Julie. "Why do you think Saunders kept this quiet?"

"Pretty obvious. A heart was missing from a young Native American woman and David was her pathologist. If this came out, the press and OMI admin would have skewered him. He's still pretty bitter about the last time, and that was, what? Over fifteen years ago."

"Yes." That answer matched her supposition, too. "Makes sense."

"But it looks like he did tell someone." Julie clicked on an icon and an email page popped up. "And he sent whoever it was the original autopsy report and files."

The recipient email address gave her no information, just a series of numbers and letters.

"Can I get a copy of this?" Nicky could guess the final recipient. Or, at least, which bureau.

"I brought a spare flash drive. I'll copy whatever you need," Julie said.

"He put a different heart in her chest for the third CT scan. Do you think he left it there?" Nicky asked.

"I don't know."

"That should be easy enough to check," Lio said. "Dig her up."

"Traditional Fire-Sky burial practices don't include preservatives," Nicky said. "Bodies are buried in a blanket, not in a casket. By the time I got legal permission, there would be nothing left to check."

Even if the substitute heart was still buried with Sandra, it wouldn't matter. It wasn't hers. Nicky would have to find the actual heart, or Sandra's spirit would wander lost.

This was why she'd been visited. This was the ancient one's task for her.

Julie's quiet voice interrupted her thoughts. "Hey, Nicky? There's more. David has a DNA database on the partitioned side of his hard drive with hundreds of entries, probably from autopsies he's done. I opened a couple and recognized the CODIS series of genetic identifiers because we use them as part of our analysis. I'll cross-check them with OMI's files, but it could take a couple of days. It's just . . . well . . . some of the other genes he's got in his database aren't normally used in forensic identification of remains." Her brow furrowed. "And I don't know what to make of it."

Nicky banged on the trailer door, oxidized white paint so old it powdered the side of her fist.

"Howard? Howard, come out. Now! I need to talk to you!"

The engine of her unit hummed quietly in the warm night, its headlights eerily lengthening her shadow across the rusted side panels of the mobile home. Thick clouds scuttled across the dark sky, the metallic taste of rain in the air.

"It's Sergeant Matthews." She drew in a deep breath and released it slowly before she spoke again. "Come on, Howard. I need to talk to you. Please." He had to know something. And if he did, he might be in danger.

The hair on the back of her neck stood up. Or he might be the killer.

Because she was officially off-duty—medical leave due to her burns— she hadn't called for backup. Still, she'd tucked her sidearm into a concealed holster at her waist.

"Howard!" Again she hammered the dusty, dented aluminum.

Sandra Deering, Maryellen K'aishuni, and Vernon Cheromiah were linked now. Victims of the same murderer, she was sure of it. They were also linked by Howard Kie's emails. Rabbits and hearts and knives, images he'd used for *both* cases.

Nicky found no answers in the K'aishuni and Cheromiah files. Their cause of death was listed as homicide. The autopsies, handled by the FBI, were probably as fake as Sandra Deering's.

What was the FBI hiding? Had they covered up at OMI in Albuquerque, too?

It was full dark. A single fat drop of rain fell on Nicky's cheek as she stared at the trailer door. She needed to speak to Frank Martin, tell him she'd figured out who he was and why he was here. If the FBI had Sandra Deering's original autopsy file, it was time for them to cooperate, or she'd spill everything she had to the press.

She also had to question Maryellen's parents, ask them why they'd left the reservation. What had happened in the weeks after Maryellen's murder that made them turn their backs on their culture and people?

A rumble of thunder sounded in the distance, the smell of rain stronger.

Backing down the steps, Nicky stared at the trailer, searched for any sign of Howard's presence. His *ranfla* was under the listing carport, but no light flickered through the curtains in the front window.

Fist tight, she thumped the aluminum frame. "Dammit, Howard, open up!" She needed some answers from Howard Kie.

A second shadow loomed from behind her. Nicky spun on her heels, hand on her weapon. In the harsh glare of the headlights stood a small silhouette, features obscured.

"Hey. You lookin' for Howard? He's not there," came a friendly voice.

Nicky stepped out of the light and the figure resolved into a young girl carrying a plastic mini-mart sack, staring at the side of the trailer.

The girl nodded at her looming shadow. "That's cool. Kinda scary, huh? You're a cop, right? Howard lives over there now"—she tilted her chin to the side—"in Mr. Saenz's old house. Moved there when all the other cars started driving by his trailer. Said people are watchin' him. I saw your truck another time."

A screen door banged in the distance.

"Gotta go. They're waiting on dinner." She held out her bag. "Check over there. But be careful. He doesn't like you stepping on his clean dirt. He sweeps it all nice. Sometimes even vacuums. He's kinda weird." She left, feet crunching in the gravel, her body blending into the darkness.

Howard was being watched? By whom? More questions that needed answers.

Nicky turned off her truck and grabbed a flashlight. She headed toward the decrepit old house the kid had pointed out, keeping the strong beam of her light pointed at the ground. Ten feet from the door, she halted and looked behind her. The front windows had a perfect visual line to Howard's trailer. If he was in there, he'd have already seen her. A door had slammed a few minutes ago. He was probably gone now, out the back and into the brush.

Edging closer, she swept the light across the dirty windows, covered on the inside by bent mini-blinds. She could imagine Howard sitting next to them, peering out. Heat spiked up her neck as she stepped into the cleared area around the front of the house and pounded on the door.

"Howard? It's Sergeant Matthews from the Tsiba'ashi D'yini Pueblo police. I need to talk to you."

She tried the doorknob. It was locked. A few more drops of rain fell, pinging on the metal roof, and a cool breeze kicked up. It swirled around her and tugged at her hair and clothes—the tickling start of a downdraft from a cloudburst coming closer.

Nicky took a deep breath to tamp down her seething emotions. With her hand splayed against the rough stucco, she tipped her face up to the dark sky. The clouds were so low they were like the soft gray ceiling of a vast room.

Why was he avoiding her? Avoiding everyone?

If Howard was hiding in the sage and chamisa, he was going to get wet. But he could be tucked into a shed, or under a car or truck. Anywhere in the neighborhood he knew and she didn't.

She dropped the shaft of light to the dirt to check for footprints. Her eyes narrowed. The ground had been swept clean. The only tracks she saw were hers.

Nicky hurried to the back of the house. There was another large pad of dirt. She squatted in the bunchgrass to the side and let her light rake over the ground.

No tracks, no nothing. The same swept dirt.

The rain started in earnest and the drops landed darkly in the clean field around the back door, little round balls of water that sat on top of the dirt, only to shrink away as the earth sucked them down.

The sound of rain crescendoed. Whether she liked it or not, she was done here.

By the time she slid into the seat of her unit, her shoulders were soaked. From the console, she grabbed a handful of napkins and wiped her face as the downpour drummed on the windshield and roof. Lightning split the sky, illuminating the scrubby neighborhood in brilliant blue light. She sat for a moment, rubbing her finger across her lips. Maybe the little girl—or her family—had more information about Howard Kie.

She backed her truck down the driveway and drove in the direction the girl had walked. When she arrived at the home, its front door was open and the girl, a baby on her hip, rocked back and forth over the threshold. Nicky darted through the pouring rain to the covered porch and shook the water from her hair. The scent coming from inside the house was warm and stale.

Light above the entryway spilled over the girl's round face. Straight black hair fell to her shoulders, above a ratty T-shirt, jeans, and cheap pink shoes. She was thin, about twelve, Nicky guessed. The baby stared at Nicky, eyes unblinking, chubby cheeks and a button nose over lips smeared with a ring of food. A half-chewed Vienna sausage was clutched in one fat fist. The fingers of the other hand held the nipple of a bottle filled with a purple liquid.

"I was watching. He wasn't there, huh?" the girl said. "My stepdad says he's crazy." She glanced at the bandages on Nicky's hand and neck.

Nicky gave the girl a rueful smile, taking in the noise of the TV and the cluttered hallway behind. Movement caught her eye as another little girl, this one about six or seven, peeked out from a back room.

"No, he wasn't," Nicky answered. "And I was really hoping to talk to him. Do you see Howard a lot? When is he home?"

The girl shrugged, jostling the baby, who stuck the bottle in his mouth.

"All the time, I guess. But me and Valeriena"—she gestured with her chin—"are at summer camp during most days now."

"Is your mom home? Maybe I could talk to her, see what she might know. I'm Sergeant Matthews. What's your name? And who's this little sweetie?"

"I'm Venetia and this is Victor." The baby wore a dirty, unsnapped onesie and a full plastic diaper, his legs and feet bare. "Nah. My mom and Bobby are at the casino. They should be back pretty soon." Her smile had disappeared and the expression in her eyes was wary now.

"Bobby?" Nicky winked at the baby and tugged a tiny toe. He clamped four little teeth on the nipple and ducked his head into his sister's shoulder. She couldn't coax a smile from him.

"My stepdad. He's Victor's pop."

"They been gone long?" Nicky asked with a smile. "You had to get dinner? What did you eat?"

"I'm old enough." Venetia scowled. "I'm twelve, so I can stay at home alone. That's what the judge says. Maybe you should go." Her bottom lip pushed out and she notched her chin up.

The younger girl crept up behind Venetia and spoke. "Vienna sausages and applesauce! And grape Fanta." That explained the purple liquid in the bottle. "I'm seven. Victor isn't even one year old. He can't walk good yet." Venetia tried to shush Valeriena, but she was obviously a chatterbox.

"Hey, you got bandages," Valeriena said. "You really lookin' for that guy from over there? He's kinda scary. He sweeps the ground all the time and I asked him why and he said to keep away very bad witches and spirits, like on Halloween."

Victor dropped his bottle. Valeriena bent to pick it up, wiped the nipple on her shirt, and gave it back to him.

"Veni stol twenty dollars from Mommy and Bobby 'fore they left to get drunk. She used that to buy a good dinner. I'm not hungry anymore, but we had to hide the rest, otherwise Bobby gets real mad, 'cause it's a waste of distribution. But he's super-happy now, 'cause of distribution Victor's gonna get he didn't have before."

Venetia frowned at her sister. "Take Victor and go watch TV, 'kay?" She passed the baby to Valeriena, who settled the little boy on her hip, her arms barely able to encircle him. She leaned to the side for balance. The two of them looked like a large Y.

"'Bye, lady police officer. Hope your hurts get better soon. Victor smells like pee, Veni. We got more diapers?"

Venetia dropped her gaze as she shook her head. "Didn't have enough money."

Once Valeriena and the baby disappeared in the back, Nicky said, "Who can you call to come stay with you until your mom gets back?" When Venetia made to argue, Nicky cut her off. "Call someone, or I'll take you to CPS. Child Protective Services—"

"I know what they are. And then what? We stay for a couple of days and they give us right back here," the girl replied, her upper lip curled.

The rain had slowed to a gentle hiss on the roof and earth. Nicky crossed her arms and waited silently, knowing what Venetia said was true, but refusing to budge. The children weren't safe alone at night by themselves. She couldn't change much in their lives, but she could help them right now.

Venetia shifted on her feet, mouth turned down. "My aunt. I can call her."

"Okay. Do it. I'll wait until she comes. And if she doesn't . . ." She let the statement rest on the air. "Lock the door and only open it to me or your aunt. I'll be back in a few minutes."

Nicky waited until the lock engaged and jogged back to her unit. She drove to the mini-mart, empty of customers because of the rain and the time. The clerk was a sleepy-eyed young man with a precision faux-'hawk. She asked him questions about Howard Kie and the little girls, modifying her purchases because of his answers.

The front window of the store was slick with rain, the broken plate glass from the burglary replaced. She'd purposefully avoided looking at it, building up her courage. Finally, while the clerk ran her card, she walked to it and stared at her pale reflection, warped by the streaming water, and searched the other images reflected from the inside of the store. Mirrored in one corner was a magazine rack behind her and she laughed out loud, getting a curious smile from the clerk.

Kim Kardashian *was* in the window.

Nicky shook her head, gathered her bags, and headed to the door when she saw a bulletin board covered with ads.

"Hey. Can I have a couple of these pushpins?" she asked.

"Take what you need, Officer."

With the pins in her sack, she hurried out to her truck. The rain was a drizzle now and the air smelled clean and fresh. Thunder sounded, but distant. There would be more rain, probably on and off all night. Hopefully it would clear up for the Blessing Ceremony tomorrow.

Nicky drove to Venetia's house and dropped off more food, diapers, and wipes with the girl, who assured her the aunt would be there in the next few minutes. Eyes wide, she stammered her thanks.

"I'll wait until she comes," Nicky said. "Lock the door."

Back at her truck, Nicky grabbed the last grocery sack and headed to the old adobe shack. The downpour had erased her footprints. Instead of leaving more, she stepped around the open area, balancing along the rocks lining the yard. When she reached the front, she pinned the bag on the door and left the way she came.

Nicky waited for the children's aunt, who was very apologetic. They chatted about the situation, and once she was confident the kids were safe, she left, dissecting the last couple of days as she drove. There was so much to process, so much information running around in her head, she hoped she'd get some sleep that night.

But when she finally got home, that faint hope shattered into a thousand pieces.

Someone had smashed out the front windows of her house.

Howard crouched behind an old lawn mower in the leaky, spider-filled shed by his trailer, muscles taut, until the purr of Agent Matthews's engine faded into the patter of rain. Shivering, he swiped his hand over his head and neck, chasing tickling legs as they scurried across his skin. His brain ached, like drums beating behind his eyes. He was cold, wet, and his glasses kept fogging up. But he had discipline. The same discipline you needed as a war chief, and he stayed patient and still until she really, really left, instead of just driving to the mini-mart and back. He almost fell for it the first time. Almost got up and went home.

Slowly and stiffly, he stood and left the shed, heading to the adobe shack. His shoes squelched in sandy puddles. When he could, he stepped on rocks or bunchgrass, so the witches and evil spirits would lose his trail.

The war chiefs were still after him and he was tired from the fear he felt all the time. Sick from the lack of beer. But he could think better, and he had to be vigilant. Howard shuddered. They took the hearts of their enemies so they would wander lost. And he was their enemy because he would expose them.

They would be at the Blessing Ceremony tomorrow night in Salida and he would spy on them, disguised. His clan mask—a family mask— was good. The guy at the mini-mart said he'd give him a ride. He would figure out their game and gather evidence, prove they killed Sandra to cover up their crimes and killed others to increase their power.

Howard glanced at the house and froze.

There was something stuck to the door, but its outline was fuzzy through his fogged-up glasses. He crept closer, each step placed carefully so he wouldn't leave tracks. A large bag of Flamin' Hot Fritos was pinned to the wood. The cop had left a peace offering, an apology.

Suddenly delighted, he smiled. It was a good sign. And he had something to offer in return.

CHAPTER TWENTY-SEVEN

Howard let the tips of his blue-powdered fingers brush the cop's jacket before he darted into the Blessing Ceremony crowd. It was like he glided through the *tsa'atsi*, so fast no one could see him. He pivoted to see if the lady cop had noticed, and bumped into a *bishbiina*, a Sky-Bird person, which knocked his own mask askew. All he could see now was down. The forked branch he'd stuck into the hole near his left ear sagged and he stopped unsteadily to twist it back in place, then righted the mask.

His chest swelled with euphoria. Free. Out of hiding, but still hiding. The chill air deep in his lungs made him part of the night, the tiny stones that poked through the soles of his moccasins made him an extension of the earth. He wanted to yell and chant and dance because whoever had been tracking him—including Sergeant Matthews—would not know him. He was not Howard now, but the sum of his ancestors. Part of those who lived in his family's *kəətsi* mask.

People streamed around him as he swayed on the road, invisible. But they weren't people, they were *hanutra*. Sucking in a great, happy sigh, he smelled the mud and wood and stink of antelope hide that made up his mask. Breathed in the essence of his father and grandfather and all his fathers from the Beginning. From *naha'aya*. From the Day before Yesterday. He did it again. His chest inflated, absorbed the power of them. It was the feeling of belonging.

Part of it was the beer he'd drunk. A whole six-pack, and quick. It also gave him courage and fleetness. His clan was Antelope. Nothing could catch him. Nothing.

Howard rotated his head slowly and the light from the streetlamp turned the eyeholes into binoculars as he searched for her. He squinted. His glasses would not fit under the mask, so some things were blurry.

She was over there, with those other cops. Not other cops. The others weren't cops. One of them was from his class at high school. Savannah Analla. She'd always been nice to him. But she was nice to everybody. She walked away with that Chishe—Apache—kid. That guy had never been nice to him.

The drums and rattles sounded and tingles ran over his skin. It was time for the blessing. It was time to fool the fools, but he had to be careful. The war chiefs had spies everywhere.

As he hurried through the crowd, he took one more opportunity to brush Sergeant Matthews's clothes with his hand. The blue powder and paint would leave the mark of the Sky Clan on her. His own blessing? Maybe.

He'd marked her car, too, when she'd parked, so he would know where to leave his gift for her. His payback for the Flamin' Hot Fritos she'd pinned on the door of the adobe. His payback for finding him.

Howard wrinkled his forehead and his skin rubbed against little bumps on the interior of the mask. Sergeant Matthews found him—even though he'd swept—which meant she was not evil. Because sweeping keeps away the evil spirits.

The drums and rattles were louder now and he shivered. He'd hidden his gift underneath the first car to be blessed and he knelt on the rough concrete to retrieve it. The elemental Sky war chief and his attendants were ahead of him. Box clutched to his chest, Howard danced into the group unnoticed. They moved to the lady cop's truck. He waited as the war chief pressed his mudded hands against the hood. Waited as the war chief's attendants pulled out the cop's gift—he squinted—bags of roasted coffee, and handed it away. Waited as gifts were given in return, placed in the back and front seats. Drums thrummed in his head. The flood of Sky-masks moved to the next car. More footsteps and singing behind him as the next war chief came.

It was time.

He shuffled his feet to the beat, the blessing chant humming from his mouth, and leaned into the backseat. The rattles shirred loud and hollow and drowned out all else.

Howard wavered in despair. This could have been him. He could have been a war chief. He could have stopped the sacrifices. Dizzy from the scent of coffee, he stared, vision blurred with tears, as the other gifts started to shake and move. Sourness rose from his stomach to coat his throat. He closed his eyes, swallowed, and placed his box.

There. It was done. Drained, he pressed his hands against the cold metal skin of the truck and left his mark. He took a deep breath of his ancestors again and absorbed the strength he needed. The drums still pounded in his head, but the rattling dropped to a whisper as he backed away and melted into the crowd.

Howard looked for the cop. She stood there, along with the big man. He would stay a little longer, make sure she drove away. Once she opened his gift, she would try to find him again. He sniffed against tears. He must be strong.

On knees that felt like they were filled with water, he stumbled across the road.

And waited.

CHAPTER TWENTY-EIGHT

"Now, how did I know to get four cups of coffee?" Nicky asked as she walked toward Ryan, Savannah, and Frank. "Cream and sugar's in the middle."

Frank's gaze roved over her face. His lips tightened momentarily, but quickly relaxed into a grin. "Coffee, huh? Getting right back up on the horse that threw you." He took the tray from her and looked pointedly at her bandages. "How are they?"

Nicky held out her hand, now covered by a large flesh-colored pad. "Better." She tilted her head and smiled sweetly at Savannah. "So, did you catch them up on all the juicy gossip?"

"Don't you take that tone with me, young lady." The lenses of Savannah's glasses flashed in the streetlamp. "You were supposed to take yesterday off and rest, and you didn't. Admit it," she said. "And then you arrive at my house last night, and wouldn't tell me anything, and I'm your best friend. *And* I even let you sleep in this morning, left you breakfast, and didn't bother you all day." She tugged her sweater closer and shivered in the unseasonably cold night air. Ryan pulled her into his chest. Lips compressed, she glared at Nicky.

"We're all worried about you, Nicky," Ryan murmured. He looped his arms around Savannah's waist as she tried to burrow under his uniform jacket.

Nicky raised her eyebrows. "All of you, huh? Even you, Frank?"

"Yup." He stirred a tiny cup of cream into his coffee. "I got my partner's back."

Nicky relaxed. "Thanks." She looked around. "Where's your real partner?"

"PJ? He was in this morning. We extracted a big snake out of a bathroom in Tambora Park." Nicky shuddered and screwed up her face. Frank laughed. "But he only worked half a day. Said he felt sick, so he went home. I brought in the conservation truck for the blessing."

Drums echoed around them. The ceremony would start soon.

"So this is your first blessing?" Nicky asked. "Say, has anyone explained—"

"Don't try to change the subject, Nicky. And stop being so nice to her, Frank," Savannah demanded. "Tell us what happened. *Now.*"

Nicky pursed her lips and scanned the milling crowd. "Not much to tell, really. When I got home last night, the gate to my property was open and the windows along the front of the house smashed with, I assume, a crowbar left in the courtyard. Luckily, the inside of the house wasn't touched." She shrugged. "Took some pictures, made a call."

"To Dax," Savannah finished flatly. "Janet did this, didn't she?"

Nicky swallowed, throat tight. "Yes." She took a quick sip of coffee. "Dax was very apologetic. Said she'd gone off her meds and promised nothing like this would happen again. He sent a couple of guys over immediately to take measurements and board everything up. The windows are standard size. They've already been replaced." She swirled her cup. "There was blood. Janet cut herself on the glass. That was probably why she didn't try to get inside. I kept the crowbar and had it dusted for prints."

"You have evidence this time," Ryan said.

"There was evidence last time. It didn't mean much, did it?" She couldn't keep the bitter edge from her voice.

The silence between the four of them was heavy.

Finally, Savannah sighed. "Where did you go yesterday? I mean, thank goodness you weren't at home when she came, but you were supposed to be resting."

"Well, I had to get the blessing gifts, so I went to Costco in

Albuquerque. Then I was at OMI for an hour or so. I went home after that, but ended up back on the rez trying to find Howard Kie. I didn't."

"Was OMI about Sandra?" Ryan asked.

Nicky took in a long, deep breath. "This isn't a good place to talk. I know it'll be late, but can we meet at your place after the ceremony, Savannah?"

"Sure. I'm really cold. I'll go home now and make some snacks." Her brows puckered and she licked her lips. "Nicky, um, I need to tell you . . ." Her gaze zipped from face to face and she seemed to force a smile. "Never mind. We can talk later. There's too much going on. Anyway, you have my permission to take Frank around and explain the blessing. Walk me to my car, Ryan." He shrugged off his jacket and draped it over her shoulders. "Nicky, I'll see you in an hour or so. You, too, Frank," she called.

As Savannah and Ryan walked away, Frank asked, "Are those two—?"

"Not really, but . . ." Nicky rolled her eyes. "It's complicated."

She and Frank headed toward the bulk of the crowd. Neither spoke, but it was a comfortable silence and Nicky left it alone. Instead, she studied people as they moved in and out of the darkness. There were only a few booths, mostly selling hot drinks. She nodded to a knot of rescue and police personnel, who stood and talked in a circle. Over by the plaza, drums thumped and gourd rattles shirred.

Unlike Feast Day, this gathering didn't have as many tourists. It was easy to tell the outsiders from Natives because tribal members wore traditional clothing and masks or painted their faces. Even the children had masks on, but theirs were made of paper with a string tied behind their head. Nicky smiled at a little boy whose eyes stared out of a purple-crayon-colored raccoon face.

Nicky and Frank wove in and out of the crowd that gathered alongside the twenty-five or so vehicles to be blessed. Torches, racked high over large metal barrels, gave off the acrid scent of *turpentina*. Orange and yellow flames cast eerie shadows across the people all around them, the flickering light hiding their eyes and making the masks more ominous. Many of the painted faces resembled skulls—skin coated stark white with a thick black band across the eyes. Thin lines of red or blue outlined the black.

"Man, I don't like this," Frank said under his breath. "It'll be hard to identify anyone and easy to lose troublemakers in this crowd."

The drums pounded louder and dancers chanted a rhythmic song, the *chuckah-chuckah* of the rattles so fast they hissed. Nicky and Frank stopped in front of a crackling torch. Heat radiated and warmed the exposed skin of her neck. It felt good. The crowd was quieter here, more serious as they watched the ritual.

"They had the private blessings earlier today," Nicky explained. "Requests to bless homes and cars—even pets—in exchange for gifts. Tonight is the blessing for public safety personnel. It's done to give the guardians of the Fire-Sky Pueblo the protection of the tribe's ancestors."

"Who does the blessing? Priests?" Frank gestured toward the adobe church. Lights outlined its steeple against the dark sky.

"No. The war chiefs. They represent the elemental clans: Fire, Sky, Water, and Earth. Wait till you see their masks. Most are extremely old and very elaborate. When the Spanish first came, tribal elders hid the masks in caves up on Scalding Peak so they wouldn't be destroyed. Now the masks are kept in their homes and treated like honored guests, given food and light at night because the spirits of ancestral war chiefs are housed inside them." Nicky nodded toward the street. "Watch."

The row of cars parked down the middle of the lane included police sedans and trucks, conservation SUVs, a couple ambulances, even a fire truck. Their doors and trunks stood open to the night air. A group of traditionally dressed men moved along the line of vehicles. One wore a mask and headdress that stretched at least two feet above him. He dipped his hands in a bowl held by an attendant and placed them palms-down on the hood of a truck. His chant resonated from the round openings of the mouth, eyes, and nose of his mask.

"The bowl holds a special mud they mix and bless in a kiva ceremony," Nicky said. "That's why we wash our units beforehand, to cleanse them so the handprints will stand out. Don't wipe or wash off the prints. They have to come off naturally." She nodded her head toward the tall mask. "That's the Sky Clan war chief. All four war chiefs leave their marks."

When the man finished, he extracted a bulging grocery bag from the backseat, handed it off, and moved to the next vehicle.

"When these men are elected to be war chief, that's the only thing they do for the year. Most take a leave of absence from their jobs, without pay. The tribe supports them with offerings and gifts in ceremonies, just like they would support a priest. I left four extra-large bags of roasted coffee beans for them. How about you?"

When he didn't answer right away, Nicky glanced at him. Frank stared at her, an odd half smile on his face. The flickering torchlight caught in his sky-blue eyes and her heart rate quickened.

His voice was husky when he replied. "I was told to buy laundry baskets and boxes of detergent." He cleared his throat. "But there are way more than four guys—guys, right?—out there."

"Uh, yeah." Nicky tore her gaze away. "Past chiefs and other attendants. See that short one with the rattle? That's the governor. He's wearing his ancestral family mask. The color of the stripes on his shoulder-blanket designate his elemental clan." The noise of the drums and rattles became louder and she shifted closer so she could speak without shouting. His warm, coffee-scented breath whispered over her face. "Attendants carry the mud, take away the gifts, shake the rattles. . . . Another one comes at the end and leaves a boxed token in each vehicle. Little hand-formed pots, a piece of polished deer antler, stuff like that. At the very end, someone else closes the doors, so the blessings stay inside. And yes, they are always men. Women have their own sacred roles."

She met his eyes again, but this time Frank took a deep breath and stepped back from her. He crossed his arms over his chest, his gaze now firmly on the ceremony. "How are they elected? Can anyone in the tribe become a war chief?"

Nicky shoved her hands in her pockets, unexpectedly hurt by his sudden withdrawal. She straightened and stared ahead of her. "I've never asked. But I know all boys on the pueblo start training very young and that some of them are eliminated each year. To become a war chief is a huge honor. They can also be elected more than once."

"The war chiefs are the ones who go up to the off-limit areas on Scalding Peak, right? They perform ceremonies there, too."

"Yes. There are days when no one is allowed up on the mountain. They usually send out an email to tell us so we won't patrol. The rituals are so private and sacred, these and past war chiefs are the only men who know them. They're passed down orally, nothing written. I've heard it's forbidden for anyone who's not a war chief even to look into the face of the masks they use, or they'll be cursed."

Frank grunted, but asked no more questions. They watched a little longer, then wandered through the crowd. It wasn't until Nicky's gaze swept over the same masked figure for a third time that she realized they were being stalked. Above medium height, slim to medium build, dark clothing, and black stained moccasins. The mask fit over his whole head like a helmet and sprouted antlers. But it wasn't a deer. More like a bear with horns. The holes cut for the eyes were large ovals, the man's skin painted black underneath. A short brown snout jutted out above the nose and mouth. He stood in place now, but pivoted to follow them as they walked.

"Nicky." Frank's voice held a note of warning.

"I see him," she said. "He's been tracking us for a while, using the crowd for cover. I think he was part of the Sky war chief's attendants."

"I don't like his attitude," Frank growled.

"He's probably someone I've arrested in the past. I've noticed the masks always seem to give the wearers courage."

Nicky stopped and met the deer-bear-man's stare. She kept her face expressionless.

If anything, her acknowledgment of his existence made him bolder. From across the street, he took two steps toward them and shook a gourd rattle in sharp jerks, faster and faster until the sound was a continuous buzzing. Then he stopped, dropped the rattle down to his side, and stepped back. A large group of laughing teens passed in front of him. Nicky craned her neck to keep him in her sight, but when the kids were gone, the man had vanished into the blackness of the night.

"Should we follow?" Frank asked.

"Other than acting creepy, he's done nothing wrong." Nicky's radio crackled and she answered. "Two-one-three, over." She listened to the message as Frank walked across the road.

"See anything?" She joined him and stared down the slope. It fell steeply into a large, marshy arroyo. Scuttling clouds allowed the moonlight to shine forth and darken the shadows. A chill, wet breeze swept upward, heavy with the sulfur smell of rotting vegetation and stagnant water.

Frank shook his head. "We should have confronted the guy, asked him some questions."

Nicky looked around one last time, every instinct telling her they were still being watched, but saw no movement, no nothing.

"I guess." She pressed her lips together. "Too late now. Come on. They want us to retrieve our units. Ceremony's over."

CHAPTER TWENTY-NINE

Nicky kneaded the knot of pain in the back of her neck as she sat in her truck. God, she was tired.

It had taken almost everything she had not to blurt out the new information on Sandra Deering at the blessing. With her lack of allies at the police department, Savannah and Ryan were the only people she could talk to. To admit the awful facts of Sandra's murder and its link to a potential serial killer would expose her friends to the guilt and anxiety that hung over her head. It wasn't the right thing to do and she wouldn't drag them down with her. She'd wait for more information.

She glanced at her phone—almost ten o'clock. Lack of sleep the night before and the long Blessing Day had drained her. Although she hated to admit it, she was at the edge of her stamina and her frustrations about the case and personal life interfered with her ability to think clearly.

The cold inside her truck made her shiver. She turned the ignition, flipped the heater to high and pointed the output to her chilled hands and face. The air was loud in the confined space of the cab, but it was white noise. Nicky gazed at the ragged adobes built hodgepodge around the old church. It was quiet now. Few porch lights shone and the festival-goers were gone or driven indoors by the cold. Shifting into reverse, she maneuvered her truck to weave around the few vehicles left in the blessing row. Frank's truck was already gone.

Frank Martin. On some level, she trusted him. When they were partnered, she could relax because of an equality between the two of them, a subconscious knowledge that he had her back. She liked him a lot, maybe too much. But she wasn't sure what to do with that guy. If he was FBI, he wasn't like most of those arrogant jack-holes who showed up on the rez, ignoring the sovereign laws of the pueblo and wanting to do things their own way. He blended in. She'd decided to talk about the case when she got to Savannah's, trickle out information, test him. Would her revelations tonight spur Frank into his own confession? Could she convince him to allow her to be a part of whatever the Bureau was investigating at Fire-Sky? Damn it all, but she wanted to trust him on every level.

Her cell phone rang. Julie. She sucked in a long breath and her finger flexed on the wheel.

"I didn't expect to hear from you so soon. What's up?"

"Um . . . not Julie. Actually, she's in the shower. This is Lio Meloni. I didn't want to call you on my phone because I wasn't sure you'd recognize and pick up. In fact, let me send you my contact information. That way if you have any questions about our conversation, you can call me directly. I'll do it now." A couple seconds later her phone buzzed and an unknown number came up on her screen. "Done. Make sure you accept it."

Nicky frowned and glanced down at her phone. "What's this about, Dr. Meloni?"

"Lio, please. We've figured out the DNA database we found on Saunders's computer. Do you need to pull over to take notes?"

There was a faint, frenetic edge to his voice. And how did he know she was driving? Must be the background rush of air through the vents. Since the interior of her unit was now pleasantly toasty, she turned down the heater and directed the output to her legs and feet.

"No. Go ahead. I'm listening."

"We cross-checked the files against the OMI DNA database. Saunders kept all Indian blood information, as well as info on people he'd selected and grouped by race for comparison."

"Comparison? To what?"

"Ethnic genetic variability. The basis for the database was autopsy blood samples that OMI sent to the FBI for CODIS identification. You're familiar with CODIS? But probably not at a very detailed level, given your background. Criminal justice major, right?" he said. "I don't mean to be patronizing, but let me explain. It's important you understand, so I'll keep it relatively simple."

Nicky rolled her eyes and decided not to tell him she'd taken four weeks of FLETC forensic training. Julie had warned her about his quirks.

"The FBI developed the CODIS—Combined DNA Index System—back in the late 1990s. They built it around thirteen core genetic loci called STRs—short tandem repeats—every person inherits from their parents, or, if you think about it, from their ancestors. Each of these thirteen sites in our DNA is polymorphic, which means there are many, many alleles found across individuals at those locations—loci. Now, by alleles I mean a variety of different DNA codes can reside at the same position on the chromosome. An individual inherits only two of these codes for that particular site, one from each parent. Okay so far? Stop me if I go too fast."

"I'm fine." Nicky turned onto the main highway to Savannah's.

"So CODIS really looks at a total of twenty-six pieces of DNA—two for each of the thirteen sites for each person tested. The exact combination of DNA is almost completely unique to every person on earth, which is pretty cool. Your family, ethnic group—or ancestors—have the closest combinations. This is especially true if a population was isolated at some point, or inbred. Let me see if I can give you an example . . . Oh! Cheetahs are like that. You know, the big cat? They went through a bottleneck of very few individuals about ten thousand years ago. Each animal is so alike genetically they can graft skin from any cheetah to another and it won't be rejected. Amazing, huh? Since the introduction of CODIS, scientists have gathered genetic information from different human ethnic groups around the globe. So, if you send your DNA for testing, you can get an ancestral profile."

"I've done that," Nicky said.

"No kidding? Great." Yeah. He wasn't interested. "Now, back to what I was saying. Ethnic testing. There are exceptions. Some populations, because of religious or cultural practices, or some other reason, refuse to participate, so they're underrepresented in genetic databases. American Indians fall into that category pretty much as a whole. I really don't understand why. Do you have any idea?"

"Maybe because they've been exploited so much in the past, they decided their genetics would be off-limits."

He sighed. "I guess, but that's very shortsighted, especially in terms of medicine."

Nicky bit her tongue. A lot of outsiders didn't understand. They only scratched at the complexity of Native American cultures, extracted what was easy, what made them feel good, and discarded the rest as quaint or archaic.

"So . . . what? David Saunders used the CODIS markers to ethnically group Native Americans?" she asked.

"With your lack of background, that's a pretty good guess, but no," he said. "CODIS markers aren't definitive enough to tease out that degree of specific tribal ethnicity, even with the hugely expanded number of individuals he tested."

Nicky stiffened. "What?"

"In fact, Saunders selected another cadre of genetic loci. HLA markers. Human leukocytic antigens. It was brilliant! I swear he must have been collaborating with someone, because this guy was pretty workaday. I mean, he left his passwords taped inside a drawer."

"Wait. You said *hugely* expanded number of individuals." Eyes wide, she stared at the console before she shifted her gaze back to the darkened road. "How big is his database?"

"Well, the dates go back almost fifteen years. So far we've found three or four thousand profiles. It looks like most are from Indians and added in the last few years, so I doubt they were all from autopsies. I bet someone fed him samples from the different reservations in the state. He built a tremendous database. I'd say he's reached the level where he could actually come up with a specific percentage of Native American ancestry, and I mean down to the thousandth degree. He could even— for some individuals—tell from which tribe."

Nicky almost sputtered in disbelief. *Thousands* of samples? Her mind raced.

"Listen carefully, Sergeant, because what I'm about to tell you is very advanced. It turns out the HLA markers were the perfect target for this population. They're associated with the body's immunity and recognition of disease. Unlike the STRs, these genes are expressed as proteins and decorate all the cells in the body as a marker that identifies 'self.' Turns out that Fire-Sky Indians have a very, *very* unique set of HLA markers, probably because of the bottleneck effect. Like cheetahs, remember? After their migration to the Americas and before European discovery of the continent, Native populations were completely cut off by both time and distance from other people—thousands of miles, thousands of years—so they interbred. This narrowed their number of unique genes. Their isolation protected them from disease exposure and their immune systems got lazy." He chuckled. "So their HLA genes shifted to null alleles and Fire-Sky Indians have the highest number of null HLA alleles I have ever *seen* in a population. Since they were never *exposed* to deadly illnesses, there was no pressure to *keep* alleles that could help them fight off deadly illnesses. Of course, with the European and African migration to the Americas a few hundred years ago, that all changed." The excitement drained out of his voice. "Tens of thousands to millions of indigenous people died from disease, most likely *because* of their genetics. Questions?"

"The ones that survived, the ancestors of the present Fire-Sky population. Did their markers change back?" Nicky asked.

"No," he said. "Population genetics can't shift that rapidly—especially null alleles, which are essentially nonworking genes. Breeding with outsiders—in this case Old World peoples or other Indians—mixes up the pool of HLA markers. That's the only way to add foreign alleles to a population. Saunders found the purer the Fire-Sky blood ancestry, the higher the number of HLA null alleles they have. The purest specimens, er, individuals, contain almost one hundred percent nulls."

"But you said their genetics caused people to die when they were exposed to diseases. Why didn't the hundred percent nulls all die?"

"I don't know. Maybe there are other, unidentified genes that let them survive. Maybe *that's* why they should allow their DNA to be studied."

"Why did Saunders do this?" Nicky asked. "Do you think he was going to sell this information to these ancestry DNA companies as a way to genetically identify Indians?"

"Maybe. He had access to more dead Indians than most people. That might have given him the idea."

Nicky compressed her lips. That answer was plain ugly.

She shifted her body to relieve some of the tension in her neck and back as she turned off the main road to Savannah's, and moved her left foot back to the underside of the seat.

Her heel bumped into something firm, smooth, and unexpected. Curious, she pushed at the object. It jerked, contracted, and slid sickeningly along the back of her boot. A loud, brittle rattling came from under her seat and filled the inside of her unit with stomach-churning vibrations. Nicky snatched her foot away. Gooseflesh rose on her body. The hair on the back of her neck prickled painfully. Her heart thrummed so loudly, she had trouble focusing on Meloni's voice.

"Do you have any more questions, Sergeant?"

Fear stronger than she'd ever known cleaved her tongue to the roof of her mouth. Her eyes watered with it.

"Sergeant? Are you still there? Is something wrong?"

"No." Her reply came out as a dry whisper. She cleared her throat. "No," in a louder voice. "I'll call if . . . I have anything . . . else."

"Okeydokey. You've got my number. Call me with any questions at all." He hung up.

She drove down the darkened road, desperate to stay as still as possible, foot steady on the gas pedal. The fingers of her right hand slowly uncurled from the death grip she had on the steering wheel. She flipped a switch above her. The interior flooded with light.

The rattling sound intensified. Buzzing pulsations ran through the driver's seat.

Slowly, she leaned forward, parting her thighs to look down at the floor.

Half under the seat, inches from her feet and legs and coiled in a tense spiral, lay a large, agitated rattlesnake.

CHAPTER THIRTY

Nicky pressed her head against her knees and kept her breathing deep and slow so she wouldn't throw up.

"You sure it didn't bite you?" Frank knelt beside her. His hand rubbed back and forth over her back. Savannah sat in the sand next to her and clutched her fingers tightly. "Did she tell you it bit her, Savannah? Nicky, we have to be sure. I need you to go with Savannah to the house and show her your legs, honey."

"Just as soon as I can stand up without falling down." One more deep breath. She lifted her head. "Where is it?"

"Conservation Boy Scout had a five-gallon snake container in his truck," Ryan said. "Along with the snake lasso and hook."

"I'll take it out someplace tomorrow and release it. That was my original plan anyway," Frank said grimly.

Savannah gasped.

"So it was . . ." Nicky gulped and closed her eyes.

"Yeah. The same rattlesnake PJ and I pulled from the park today and left at the fire station. Same size, same markings, same broken rattle."

Ryan stuck his hands in his back pockets. "I called the firehouse. Snake's gone. Caused quite a panic for a few minutes." He smiled. "No one believed me when I told them Nicky got 'blessed' with it."

"Funny," Nicky said and extended her hand to Frank.

He helped her up and steadied her when she wobbled, hands curled around her waist above her belt. Eyes closed, she laid her forehead on his shoulder for a moment, before she pulled back and searched his face.

"Thanks, partner."

"Anytime. Partner." He smiled. "Now go and have Savannah check to make sure you didn't get bitten," he ordered gruffly.

"I didn't get bitten. I'd know by now," Nicky said. Frank's mouth flattened, but before he could speak, she turned to Ryan. "What'd you find?" She walked to her unit. The doors were open and the interior light fell harshly onto the ground.

"See the large container in the backseat? The snake was there. It's just a crudely painted boot box, but it did the trick." Ryan dangled a length of twine from his fingers. "Whoever did this probably wrapped the box up, untied it after delivery. The lid wasn't tight or anything. The snake pushed it open and dropped to the floor."

"It could have been buzzing like crazy, but with all the noise of the ceremony, especially the gourd rattles, no one would have been suspicious," Frank said. "The cold settled it for a while. But when the truck warmed up . . ."

Nicky shuddered and Savannah slid an arm around her waist. She leaned into her.

"Anything else?" Frank asked.

"You mean like a written confession?" Ryan said. "Nah. That would be too easy. As to who did it, my first guess would be Janet Stone. That woman's sick in the head and she hates Nicky because her husband still wants her." Frank scowled. "There were other gifts from each of the war chiefs. A couple of small pots, a corn husk doll, a bear fetish. But . . ." He reached into the truck and pulled out a small black and white clay box. "You were obviously *very* blessed tonight, and not only because Frank here expertly extracted the rattlesnake." Ryan opened the box with a flourish. "Looks like someone left you a flash drive, Nicky."

Nicky's mouth dropped open. "You're kidding."

Frank's jaw clenched. He held out his hand. "I'll take it."

Ryan's lips twisted into a smile, but his eyes were cool. He curled his fingers around the drive, dropped his arm to his side, and shook his head. "Nicky?"

"No, Frank. Not unless—"

Her phone buzzed in her pocket and she jerked, heart hammering. She'd change that to something less rattlesnake-like as soon as she could. Nicky tugged it out and stared at the screen. "Son of a—Would you look at this?" She handed her phone to Frank.

"'Saw you at the blessing, but you didn't see me,'" he read out loud. "'Touched you at the blessing, but you didn't touch me. Left you a gift in your car.' There's a happy face icon followed by . . ." His brow creased. "Flamin' Hot Fritos?"

Savannah let Nicky go and stepped behind her back. "Ugh. You have powder all over your jacket." She lifted her arm. "And it's rubbed off on me."

Nicky yanked her jacket off and held it up to the light. Handprints and blue streaks decorated the waist.

"Who sent this?" Frank held out the phone.

"Hot Fritos," Nicky said, "is Howard Kie."

CHAPTER THIRTY-ONE

Nicky cradled the mug in her hands, eyes gritty with tiredness, even after a shower. At least she had fresh clothes. After the excitement of last night, she'd ended up staying at Savannah's, secretly glad they'd agreed to wait until morning to open the flash drive. Nothing had kept her from sleep—she was out when her head hit the pillow.

All her good intentions about protecting her friends had been erased by the presence of the snake in her truck. Maybe it had been some kind of sick joke, but she couldn't take that chance. She'd come to a decision.

Savannah sat with her laptop open, the *Albuquerque Journal*'s banner across the top of her screen. Nicky breathed in the fragrant scent of coffee and took a sip, hoping it would settle the knot in her stomach.

The men arrived together as the sky pinkened with dawn. Frank had stayed at Ryan's place down the street and looked rough. He rubbed his stubbled jaw. "Ryan doesn't own a razor."

"Don't need one." Ryan shrugged. "Indian blood."

"Snake?" asked Nicky. She shuddered dramatically and tucked her bare feet onto the couch.

"We let it loose earlier, far away from here," Frank replied with a half smile. At the counter, he stacked a fresh biscuit-and-sausage sandwich. He took a bite as he poured his coffee. "Savannah, how come some man hasn't taken you off the market yet? These biscuits are amazing." His eyes glinted teasingly.

Ryan munched his food and looked away.

Savannah peeked over the screen with a smile. "Stop being so sexist, Frank. Everyone ready?" They gathered around the computer and she pushed the drive into the USB port. "Look. It's labeled 'Sandra's stuff,'" she said. "You know, I've been thinking a lot about that Hot Fritos message from last night. The flash drive has to be Howard's gift—not the snake. He knew Sandra, right?"

"I used his message to text him back about it. He hasn't replied." Nicky stared down at her coffee and let out a long breath. "Look, I didn't want to tell you, didn't want to burden you. But if that snake was a threat..." She raised her face. "Whoever did that might go after you next, if only because of me. You know I asked Julie Knuteson to review Sandra Deering's autopsy." Her gaze flickered to Frank. He watched her closely. "Well, she found something. Turns out, Sandra didn't commit suicide. She was murdered."

Savannah gasped. "Oh, dear God. Poor Sandra." Tears started in her eyes. Ryan clasped her hand, his jaw tight, his gaze riveted on Nicky.

"How was she murdered?" Frank's voice was flat.

"Her heart was removed before she was placed on the tracks." Savannah sucked in another gasp and Ryan went gray. "David Saunders altered the autopsy and, most likely, the toxicology report. And now he's disappeared. Until I actually speak with him, I can't rule him out as a suspect in Sandra's death."

"This is why you received the visit from the ancient one," Ryan murmured. "If Sandra's heart was taken, her spirit is lost."

Frank's head jerked to look at him.

"Lost," Nicky repeated. "That might also have been why she was murdered. She was doing a senior project on the lost or missing here at Fire-Sky for a journalism class at UNM."

"About the ones you think are related to the per capita distribution checks," Ryan said.

"What about the per capita distribution?" Frank asked.

"Fire-Sky Tribe members have to sign in every year to receive it." Savannah slid her finger under her glasses to wipe her eye. "For many, on or off the reservation, it saves them financially. For the transients—the alcoholics or drug-addicted—it's free blood money to feed their habits. When they don't come back, no one ever thinks to ask why. No one ever wants to look for them or find them." Her voice was strained. "Because we are ashamed of them. They perpetuate the stereotype." She dropped her head.

Nicky laid a hand on her arm. It was obviously a difficult confession to make.

"That's why I asked Savannah to find who had signed and picked up their checks the last few years. And who hasn't," Nicky said. "It would give us a place to start. But my captain and lieutenant made me close Sandra's case." She twisted her lips. "They know nothing about any of this and if they find out I'm still poking around, I could get suspended or even fired. Besides the fact that I have no hard evidence." She pointed to the computer. "Unless Sandra gives us some clues."

Frank crossed his arms over his chest. "Then open it. Maybe we'll get the evidence we need."

"Frank, any information in this flash drive is already compromised," Nicky said softly.

He kept his gaze on the screen, his face blank. Finally, he gave a curt nod.

Savannah clicked on the icon and dozens of files came up. "Sandra had the distribution lists, too, but she scanned them in, along with the actual signatures."

Nicky pointed to a file titled "Lost." "Open that one."

A list popped up with a couple dozen names. There were annotations beside each.

"She's eliminated some of them. See?" Savannah tapped the screen. "'Henry Melendrez—66. d. 12/14 home.'"

"I worked that case. He wasn't sixty-six, though. He was ninety-seven years old and died of natural causes," Nicky said.

"I don't think that number is their age. See? 'Jeremy Alonzo—90. d.' It must mean something else," Ryan said.

Savannah scrolled down the list. "There are still close to twenty people here who are unaccounted for."

"Did you get the PCD spreadsheets from the tribal database? Can you cross-check Sandra's list and look for new names?" Nicky pulled out her phone and grimaced at the time. "I have to leave for work in less than an hour. What else do you see?"

Savannah opened the other folders. "There's nothing else here."

Nicky took a deep breath. "I have something more you need to know. A couple of things, really. The first is something Dax told me last week when I met him in Santa Fe." She flashed Frank a quick glance. His face darkened before his expression went blank again. "He gave me some very disturbing information. He said the reason the FBI is undercover on the rez is because they think Fire-Sky Natives are being targeted by a serial killer."

They all stared at her in stunned silence.

"*Dammit*, Nicky! How could you withhold that information from us?" Savannah fumed.

"Do you believe him?" Ryan asked.

"Yes. He's been a reliable source in the past," she admitted. "The Bureau thinks there's a connection between Sandra's death and the murders of Maryellen K'aishuni and Vernon Cheromiah."

"So the FBI knows Sandra was murdered? How?" Ryan asked.

"David Saunders may have been on the lookout for suspicious deaths. A missing heart would qualify," Nicky replied dryly. "My timeline shows the undercover agents were in place within two weeks of her murder."

"How do you know all this?" Frank asked.

Nicky shot him another glance. "Sources. Dax only confirmed it." She would give nothing more away unless he confessed to his role. She was deeply disappointed he hadn't already.

"So are these missing tribal members on Sandra's list the killer's victims? Have they been murdered, too?" Savannah's voice rose. "Why? Why were they chosen? I don't understand any of this."

"I don't know yet," Nicky replied. She dragged a hand through her hair. "Maybe they were easy victims because of their lifestyle. Like you said, no one really worries about them. They could go missing for a long time before their families notice or care." She walked to the sink to rinse out her cup and collect her thoughts. "It goes without saying this information can't get out." She looked at each one of them. "I'm very sorry to burden you with this. Very sorry. But I have no one else to tell who would believe me. Especially without evidence."

"Who do you think put the rattlesnake in your car? Janet Stone?" Ryan asked.

"I don't think it was actually her. If she hired someone to harass me, maybe. But it must have been spur-of-the-moment, because the only people who knew about the snake were police, Conservation, and fire personnel. I think we saw who did it, didn't we, Frank? The guy with the shaking rattle. It was a direct taunt, a challenge. I hate it when criminals think they're smarter than us. It's like—"

"A puzzle you have to solve to prove them wrong," Savannah finished.

Frank went to the sink to wash his mug. "You said you needed to tell us two things, Nicky. What was the other?"

"It's also about David Saunders. Julie found an unusual database on his computer. It contains thousands of DNA profiles, including a large number of tribal members from Fire-Sky." She pulled a second flash drive out of her pocket and held it up, frustration coloring her voice. "I just don't understand why."

CHAPTER THIRTY-TWO

Nicky tossed her keys on the desk and dropped into her chair. Work was slow. It always was after the Blessing Day. The traditional cops speculated the sacred dances and chants reminded tribe members that spirits watched their every move, so behaviors changed—at least for a few days. The nontraditional cops countered everyone was exhausted after weeks of preparation for both the DAP day fiesta and the blessing. Nicky figured it was a mix of both. She jiggled her mouse and waited for her computer to boot up. Might as well get some paperwork out of the way.

When the call for the domestic came in, she was tying up loose ends in the mini-mart break-in. She'd found the perps with good old-fashioned police work, interviewing friends and family of the teens who'd taken the bat to the plate-glass window. The boys didn't have a record, so fingerprints and blood evidence had been a bust, but that wasn't unusual. Indians didn't do DNA. Her thoughts flashed to David Saunders's database, wondering if the boys were included in it.

She'd picked up the signed arrest warrants at the courthouse and was driving out to one of the teen's address when Dispatch called.

"Fire-Sky Dispatch to two-one-three, clear to copy. Received a call from a child reporting her parents are fighting, Mount St. Helens Subdivision."

"Dispatch, I'm direct and en route." Nicky flipped a U-turn and hit her lights, siren, and the accelerator.

"Address is 2311 South Mount Rainier. Robert and Veronica Koyona."

Nicky knew the house. She'd been there the other night, delivering food and diapers. "Who's the reporting party?"

"One of the kids. Venetia Vernon. Said her stepdad is drunk and beating up on her mom. She asked for you by name. Unknown weapons."

"On my way. Start another unit."

She arrived at the house within ten minutes. Hearing shouts and crashes inside, she decided to approach.

The lock was splintered on the front door. It was cracked open about six inches. She sidled up beside it, knocked loudly, and yelled, "Fire-Sky police! Come to the door! Come to the door! I can hear you fighting. We're coming in the house!" she lied. She didn't want to let the combatants think she was alone. There was a thump and the sound of glass shattering.

"Help! You have to help! He's gone crazy!" an adult female screamed.

"Just shut up! How could you do this to me?" a male moaned. Robert Koyona. Venetia and Valeriena had called him Bobby.

"Bobby? Hey, Bobby, calm down. What's going on? Come talk to me. Let's not make this any worse. We're here to help."

"You can't help! No one can help." His voice degenerated into sobs.

"We're coming in!" Hand on her sidearm, adrenaline high, Nicky pushed the door open farther. It creaked on broken hinges. She sidestepped inside, scanning the house. It was in shambles.

"Veronica? Are there any guns?" Nicky asked.

The woman was crying. "No. Nothing. He just hit me. Bobby, I'm so sorry. I didn't know—I wasn't sure—"

"Shut up! I *loved* him! He was my son! *My son!* And now he's not," Bobby wailed, his voice slurred.

A movement caught Nicky's eye and she swung around. Venetia, holding Victor, stood in the doorway on her right, Valeriena behind her. Nicky put her finger to her lips, beckoned to them, and hustled them outside. A siren wailed in the distance. Backup.

Her gaze ran over the children. They were dressed in T-shirts and leggings, no shoes. The baby was in a shirt and diaper, his chubby legs and feet bare. The girls cried softly, their faces streaked with tears, but

Victor was stoic, the nipple of a bottle tight between his teeth. He twitched his little toes.

"Are you hurt?" They shook their heads. "Where are your mom and stepdad? What part of the house?"

"In the kitchen. It's through the archway and on this side." Venetia motioned right with her shoulder and said, "Bobby's more drunk than I've ever seen him. He opened that letter today."

Valeriena sniffled. "Yeah, and he gets no distribution 'cause of it. Turns out he's not Victor's dad. Probably Victor's dad isn't even Fire-Sky, so Victor's not worth nothing anymore." She shook her head at the baby and wiped tears from her eyes.

"Does your stepdad have a gun or knife?"

"No. Veni hides the rifles under the bed in our room when they get drunk, like teacher told her in school. Bobby was just using his hands. They're pretty good for hitting," Valeriena offered. Her voice wobbled. "Can you help our mom?"

"Yes, honey. But you have to stay right here. Don't move from behind the truck."

Her backup pulled their car up to the curb, its siren cut abruptly, but the lights still flashed. Two uniformed officers jumped out and jogged toward them. Valentine and Aguilar. She gave them a quick update and left Valentine with the children—he had a couple of kids—while she and Aguilar hurried to the house.

"Veronica, Bobby? I've got the kids outside! They're safe! Officer Aguilar and I are coming in now!"

They stepped through the home's threshold into the darkened hall and trod silently to the arched opening. Nicky peeked around the wall. The furniture in the family room had been overturned. A lamp without a shade lay on its side, bulb shattered. Colorful baby toys were strewn about and a naked Barbie doll sat on the fireplace hearth. Broken glass and empty beer cans littered the floor.

"Veronica? Where's Bobby?"

"No! Don't take him! It's my fault he got so mad. I deserved it!" she sobbed. Her voice came from behind a long counter that blocked the view of the kitchen floor.

Glass crunched under Nicky's feet as she stepped toward the voice. She rounded the counter and found the two of them huddled together on the floor. Veronica looked up and Nicky grimaced internally. Her left eye was almost swollen shut, her lips puffy and bloody, and red marks circled her neck. Bobby leaned against her, eyes closed, mouth open. Veronica tightened one arm around him when she met Nicky's eyes, but the other wrist dangled limply in her lap.

"Call EMT and another car," Nicky ordered Aguilar and holstered her weapon. "Hey, Veronica, the kids are outside. They're really worried about you. I'm going to come closer and help you up so we can go outside to see them. They're so worried." She kept up the quiet, one-sided conversation as she slid her cuffs out and clicked the first one onto Bobby's wrist.

"No! Don't touch him!" Veronica lunged to her feet and Bobby's head thunked on the floor. She swung her fist. Nicky blocked the blow, grabbed Veronica's arm, and twisted it. The woman howled and squirmed as they grappled along the island counter. The toaster banged to the floor with a metallic clang.

Bobby moaned and woke up. "*No!* Vronnnie!" He rammed his body against Nicky's and she fell hard into Veronica. Her breath whooshed out of her. Aguilar dove in to help.

Nicky sucked air. "Cuff him! I got her." Aguilar pulled Bobby away.

"Leave him alone!" Veronica flung her head back, hit Nicky's cheek. She flipped and jabbed an elbow, but Nicky had had enough. She squeezed Veronica's damaged wrist, eliciting an earsplitting scream of pain, and Veronica went limp.

Nicky was snapping the second cuff on the woman's swollen wrist when Valeriena's voice yelled, "Mommy! Don't hurt her!" She plowed into their legs. Her skinny arms snaked around her mother's knees. Officer Valentine ran into the kitchen and snatched the struggling girl away, his eyes wide as they met Nicky's.

Veronica suddenly revived and screamed, "Let her go! My baby!"

"Dammit, Valentine! Get her out of here," Nicky said, absolutely furious. "Carry her. There's glass all over the floor." He swung Valeriena's feet up. They were bloody with cuts and his face went white.

Nicky sat the sobbing woman on the only upright chair at the kitchen table. Shoulders shaking, Veronica slumped forward.

"Aguilar. You good?" Nicky asked. They both were breathing hard from the fight.

"Yes. The husband passed out. Should I try to wake him up?"

From a distance came the high-pitched whine of sirens. "EMTs should arrive soon. Leave him," she answered.

Veronica rocked and cried. "My fault. He didn't mean to. My fault. I won't press charges."

It wouldn't matter if Veronica refused to press charges. The law allowed authorities to do it anyway. Nicky sucked in one more large breath and let it out slowly. She touched her cheek. It was tender. She'd have a good bruise.

The siren cut off abruptly. Car doors slammed and a voice yelled, "Emergency medical coming in!"

It was quiet. Nicky stood in the broken house, cheek throbbing. She stared impassively at the letter open on the kitchen table.

Even in all the devastation, it remained pristine. Two precise folds were pressed into fine creamy paper. She could see the faint watermark. The large, colorful seal of the pueblo was prominent, centered at the top on the page. A blood-red oval surrounded the top of a dark brown volcano that billowed thick, stylized gray smoke. The sky to the left of the smoke was a bright turquoise. On the right side, the smoke transformed into rain clouds, slanting perfect drops falling like tears. A masked face stared from the middle of the smoke, eyes red with fire. All Tsiba'ashi D'yini elemental clans were represented: Fire, Water, Sky, Earth.

Nicky silently read the contents.

Dear Mrs. Koyona,

This letter is to inform you that your child, Victor Koyona, will not receive the annual Per Capita Distribution. Our investigators have discovered he is not the child of Tribal member Robert Koyona as claimed on his birth certificate, and is in fact, only 0.1242 degree Tsiba'ashi D'yini ancestry. As you know, Fire-Sky tribal code Section 1-1-1. F [Membership in the tribe], requires individuals to have one-eighth degree or 12.5% (0.125 degree) Tsiba'ashi D'yini Blood quantum to receive minimum benefits.

Valeriena's statement about Victor being worth "nothing" made sense now.

The child has been disenrolled from tribal membership pursuant to tribal Code 1-3.1. D [Fraudulent Misrepresentation] and 1-1.5. A [Blood Quantum].

If you have any further questions, please call 555-4363. However, be advised that this determination is final.

Sincerely,

Peter Santibanez

CEO, Tsiba'ashi D'yini Tribal Enrollment Office

Santibanez's signature was scrawled elegantly across the bottom.

Victor was not the biological child of Bobby Koyona. Only a direct comparison of DNA profiles could make that determination. And he was only 0.1242 degree Fire-Sky blood. How precise.

Indians didn't do DNA.

Or so she'd been led to believe.

Nicky let out a humorless laugh. She now knew the significance of David Saunders's database.

CHAPTER THIRTY-THREE

"Excuse me. Excuse me! You can't go in there without an appointment. Stop right there!"

Nicky ignored the woman who hurried around her desk to bar her entrance into Peter Santibanez's office atop the Fire-Sky Hotel, Casino, and Spa. The Tsiba'ashi D'yini logo was carved into the center of the wooden double doors, the same one on the letterhead sent to Veronica Koyona. Nicky squared her shoulders and grabbed the iron handle.

A wall of glass greeted her with a magnificent view of Scalding Peak in the distance, the whole of the reservation splayed like a supplicant before the mountain.

Or maybe the reservation bowed low before the all-powerful Peter Santibanez.

He stood silhouetted against a clear blue sky, on his cell phone, face wreathed in a smile that disappeared when he swiveled toward her. He murmured something in the phone and a frown deepened on his face.

"What's all this, Joy?" His gaze shifted to the woman behind her.

"I'm so sorry, sir. I tried to stop her."

His brown eyes focused back on Nicky. They stopped briefly on three spots: her badge and sidearm clipped to her belt, the pink scald burn on her neck, and the darkening bruise and scratches on her cheek. Blood and dust from her earlier encounter with Veronica and Robert Koyona stained her clothes.

Nicky stared back impassively, even though her insides churned with anger. She needed some answers.

Now.

"Bill? Let me call you back," Santibanez said in his phone and hung up before he retreated behind his desk. He must have seen something of her roiling emotion, because he gave her a placating smile. "Rough week?" he murmured. "It's all right, Joy. I'll see Sergeant Matthews. Why don't you bring in some coffee?"

The doors behind Nicky closed with a discreet click. She stared at the man before her.

Peter Santibanez possessed a square and handsome face with a bold Roman nose, and his black hair—shot through with silver—fell in a braid down his back. In his early sixties, he looked a decade younger. He was close to six feet tall, but his stocky, powerful body made him appear shorter.

He waved a hand toward a chair. "Please, Sergeant, take a seat." Nicky tipped her head to the side and widened her stance. "No? All right. Then maybe you'd like to explain what precipitated this rather, uh, un-expected visit." His voice was almost jovial, but his posture was stiff. He reached up to tug at the inlaid turquoise clasp of his bolo tie.

Since the tension worked in her favor, Nicky stayed silent and let it simmer before she pulled the letter from a pocket in her jacket and tossed it onto the desk that separated them.

Santibanez's manicured hand spread the page open. "I heard there was a problem today." He stared again at her cheek. "You took the call? And bore the brunt of it, eh?" He tsked and shook his head. "The little girls are okay?"

"I need to ask you some questions, Mr. Santibanez, about this letter and its contents."

He sucked a hissed breath through his teeth and smiled. "I'm afraid all I do is sign these. You'll have to talk to my investigators if you need more information."

"Your investigators? Like David Saunders at OMI?"

His smile slipped.

"Saunders has been compiling a DNA database of Fire-Sky Pueblo tribal members for quite some time, hasn't he, Mr. Santibanez? But his collection really accelerated in the last few years, ever since the per capita distribution has been under your direct supervision. Is that when he first contacted you?"

Santibanez stared at her unblinkingly, a single eyebrow raised and his upper lip curled the tiniest bit. "You sure you don't want to sit down, Sergeant?"

Realization hit her. Nicky sucked in a breath, eyes so wide they burned. "No. *You* contacted *him*. He'd have been easy to manipulate, wouldn't he? After the debacle at OMI with Alicia Waseta's heart, if someone found out he was keeping an *illegal* DNA database of Indian blood, he'd be fired on the spot. Probably never to work again anywhere in the country. A huge incentive for blackmail."

"*Blackmail* is such a strong term, Sergeant. I prefer *motivated cooperation*." He sat and settled back in his chair, hands folded on his stomach. "Please. Sit down and I'll explain, although I doubt you'll understand, being an outsider." The door opened. "Ah! Joy with the coffee. Black with sweetener, am I correct?" he asked Nicky.

Peter Santibanez, all-seeing, all-knowing. It was his reputation on the rez. He had spies everywhere and a finger in every pie.

"Yes." She slid into a chair.

The door closed behind his assistant.

"Now, of what were we speaking? Oh, yes. David Saunders. You see, he made the mistake of trying to bribe a phlebotomist at the Fire-Sky Clinic. Of course, she came to me immediately. But that's not quite the place the story needs to start. This might take a while. Are you sure you have the time?"

Nicky leaned forward in her chair, neck and jaw rigid. "I just came from a domestic where a man beat his wife's face to a pulp because of this letter, Mr. Santibanez. I have nothing but time."

He stared at her, his body still. "All right. Then the best place for me to start is before the Spanish conquistadores and Catholic Church came to our lands. Of all the People, Tsiba'ashi D'yini has been here the longest. Each tribe has their own origin myth"—he waved his hand dismissively—"but we have stories of the last eruption of Scalding Peak.

Scientists say that was over fifteen thousand years ago, predating archae-
ological evidence of human occupation in this region of the Americas."
Santibanez sipped his coffee. "Of course, oral tradition doesn't equal hard
evidence, but what those stories tell me is that the Fire-Sky People are
very unique. And part of that uniqueness has to do with our genetics."

Nicky sat back and released a slow breath. Santibanez's statements
paralleled those of Emilio Meloni.

"Did you know I initially studied to be a physical anthropologist? I
took classes for over a year at Stanford, before I came to the realization
that proving to an uncaring world the Tsiba'ashi D'yini tribe settled this
ground before all others would get us nothing. It wouldn't solve our pov-
erty, or our alcoholism, or addictions. It wouldn't give us back our ancestral lands, or our water rights. It would give us no more power than
we already had, which was very little. Only money would do that.

"But I digress. With the arrival of Europeans and Africans, all of the
People went through a terrible time. There's still a lingering belief that
war killed off a majority of the indigenous populations of this continent,
a belief perpetuated by Hollywood and their testosterone-filled, Euro-
centric movies." He leaned forward and rested his elbows on the desk,
fingers steepled. Though he gazed at her face, she could see he really
wasn't focused on her. "Soldiers slaughtering peaceful camps full of
women and children, or the cavalry heroically charging into murder-
ous hordes of painted braves. Don't get me wrong. That did happen, but
by that time, millions were already dead of pestilence and disease. But
that does not a good story make."

He appeared to be in his own head right now, so Nicky didn't ask
the questions that circled in her mind. This was her time to learn what
he knew.

"Measles, smallpox, influenza killed us, brought and spread by the
earliest of conquerors, priests and settlers. We lived in a paradise, were
genetically *adapted* to that paradise. We couldn't fight disease. Populations collapsed. Cultures that had prospered for thousands of years gone
in a generation. Those left behind, remnants. But they had been forged
in fire. They adapted and survived. They married across tribes, across
cultures, muddying their DNA. But Fire-Sky tradition is endogamous. We

only married within our tribe. We resisted integration into the surrounding populations.

"Still, when the U.S. government paid us guilt money—paid us to be Indians—we took in anyone who had the slightest connection to our pueblo to swell our rolls, to get back some of what they stole. Now the additional money from our tribal businesses have made those benefits truly substantial. Per capita distribution is exploding." He blinked and his gaze focused back on hers. "Did you know outside applications for enrollment here at Fire-Sky go up every year? Non-Natives 'self-identifying' as Indians because they want our money, faking ancestry documents. And, of course, now it's popular to be a Native American. *My grandmother was one-fourth Cherokee* popular." Santibanez's voice was sarcastically singsong. "So many people say they are related to Pocahontas, they could start their own tribe," he mocked.

He leaned forward and tapped the wood of his desk, his eyes glittering. "What David Saunders found was that Fire-Sky clan members have distinct genetic profiles I can use to identify *our* People, to preserve *our* traditions and culture without the genetic pollution of outsiders. Soon it will be time to purge. To rid ourselves of the hangers-on, the genetically impure. To establish true blood quantum, controlled by the tribe, not some bureaucrat in Washington, D.C."

He was right. She didn't understand, especially when it tore families apart like he'd done with Robert and Veronica Koyona. And little Victor. Would Victor be raised in a culture that ultimately rejected him because of his *genetics*?

"*Soon* it will be time to purge?" Nicky gestured at the letter on the desk. "Haven't you already started?"

Santibanez's face shuttered. "No. I'm not completely ready."

"You haven't told the tribal council, have you? There are religious and traditional customs forbidding the use of DNA—"

He slashed his hand through the air. "Don't you talk to me about my culture. My position and influence are such that the council will agree with me once everything is in place. I'll make them see the utility of DNA tests, because our *culture* and *tradition* demand it."

Nicky stood. "Then why, if you aren't ready, did you send this letter and tear this family apart?" She picked up the paper and tucked it away. She couldn't stay in the room any longer or she'd be sick.

"Because a man deserves to know the paternity of his son before he wastes his time, his hard-earned money, and his love on a child that isn't his."

The bitterness in his voice was severe. And extremely personal.

DNA giveth and DNA taketh away.

Slowly, Nicky sat back down in the chair and tried to integrate Santibanez's statement. PJ—Peter Santibanez's only child—wasn't his biological son?

Santibanez stood stiffly and stared out the floor-to-ceiling windows, across the stark and beautiful land of his ancestors. David Saunders's database had certainly served him up a nasty surprise.

"Where is Saunders?" she finally asked. "He's missing."

"I don't know. He called me and said he'd been asked to speak at a conference. And after, he said he was going on a long-delayed vacation. I haven't heard from him since." Santibanez's voice was clipped.

"When did Sandra Deering contact you about the per capita distribution lists?" She switched topics, hoping he was still shaken and off guard.

No such luck.

"Sandra Deering? The train suicide? I've never spoken to her. I only know of her because my publicity team wanted to use her grandmother as part of the Distribution Day ceremony." He picked up his cup of coffee and took a sip, only to grimace. "Regardless of what you think of me, or even what I think of me, I don't know everything or everyone on the pueblo." He smiled.

"The FBI is undercover on the reservation. Why?" As soon as the question left her mouth, she wanted to take it back. She'd pushed too far.

His eyes flickered coldly, but the smile stayed in place. "There are . . . elements at the police department with whom you do not jibe well. And you have friends employed on the reservation? You seem to be a very smart lady. If I were you, I'd halt this line of inquiry. Do you understand?"

Her breath caught and a sudden coldness pierced her core. She held his stare for a long time. "Yes. I understand."

"Now, if that's all, Sergeant, I'm a very busy man—"

"One last question." This was a total shot in the dark. "What do you know about the death of Maryellen K'aishuni in the Chiricahua Wilderness two years ago?"

Santibanez's expression hardened, but not before she saw a flash of unease in his eyes.

"I was part of the search team. And I have read the official tribal file. Sergeant Matthews, that is all. We are done here." He turned to the view again. "You can show yourself out."

Phone pressed to his ear, Peter Santibanez traced a thin contrail—colored pink by the setting sun—across the dusky sky. "I don't know how I can make myself any clearer," he said. "Matthews is a loose cannon. Neutralize her or I will withdraw my support for your operation."

The silence stretched on the other end of the line.

"Sir, I don't think it would be in your tribe's best interest—"

Santibanez swiveled his chair and slammed the flat of his hand on the desk. "No. *I* don't think it would be in *your* best interest if she compromises this investigation. Where would the Bureau station you then? I hear there are some nifty openings in the depths of Alaska. I can make sure they save a spot for you."

"I have a man on her now. Though she doesn't know it, she's been very valuable to us. It's been difficult to earn the trust of the people—"

Santibanez scoffed. "I told you that when the Bureau approached me, didn't I? You Feds never listen. It takes years for outsiders to be accepted on the pueblo. Sergeant Matthews has earned that trust. She's very good at what she does," he added grudgingly. "But the protection of my people comes first. I'll burn you—without regret—if you don't get her off my back. And your undercover op to bring down the Coahuilan drug cartel will dissipate like so many smoke signals." With the sleeve of his shirt, he dabbed sweat from his brow. His hand tightened on the phone as he waited for a response.

Finally. "All right. I'll see what we can do." The phone disconnected.

Santibanez slumped in his chair and dropped his head into his hands. He'd made multiple missteps today. Hopefully they could be mitigated.

But in his heart, he knew his biggest mistake had been made almost two years ago when he let PJ return home.

CHAPTER THIRTY-FOUR

Nicky slunk into the police department early the next morning. She'd hardly slept, the repercussions of her rash confrontation with Peter Santibanez haunting her night, and her muscles ached with tension and exhaustion. The captain's office was still dark. Gut roiling, she braced herself for his arrival. Would he chew her out and suspend her for reckless behavior? Or was she looking at the loss of her job? Santibanez had that power.

Captain Richards arrived ten minutes later, but other than his normal contemptuous glance in her direction, he left her alone.

Santibanez obviously hadn't reported her. Yet. If anything, the knife-edged anticipation twisted her emotions tighter. He valued his control on the reservation and she'd dangled a sword over his head with her knowledge of the illicit DNA database. But that sword kept her safe—for now. All she had to do was place a discreet whisper into the ear of a traditional tribal councilman and she could completely derail Santibanez's plans for the future of tribal membership and disrupt the power he held on the pueblo.

That made her a threat to him. She pressed the heels of her hands to her eyes. Just like she'd been a threat to Janet and the Randals five years ago. She'd have to sell her home for sure if she lost her job, because no way Santibanez would let her even work in the state. On top of this, she'd put her friends and their livelihoods in danger, too. But how much, she didn't know.

Her meeting with Santibanez added even more pieces to the fractured puzzle of the murdered and missing on the reservation. And her tentative conclusions chilled her.

Peter Santibanez had a lot at stake. But was it enough that he'd kill for it? And kill so viciously? Was he behind the missing in Sandra's list? Had he already initiated a purge of the genetically undesirable?

And how did Maryellen K'aishuni and Vernon Cheromiah's murders fit into *any* of this?

Nicky squeezed her eyes shut. She couldn't sit in front of her computer and work. She had to get out, clear her head so she could—

"Sergeant Matthews?"

Nicky jumped to her feet. Her chair rocked back and she grabbed it before it crashed over.

Shanice, one of the Fire-Sky dispatchers, stood by her desk. "You okay? You look like you ate a bumblebee." She stared, eyebrows raised, at the bruise and scratches on Nicky's cheek. "Got a call from Grandmother O'Callaghan over on the north side of Scalding Peak. She specifically requested *you* to come out to her place. You saved her grandson from drowning in that arroyo, remember? Said someone vandalized her house and a barn last night. I bet it's those kids who hang out at Big Red Dog Cliff. Little derelicts." She shoved a note into Nicky's hands. "She also told me there's a bear or deer or whatever—I don't know what, my Keres is terrible—tearing up her garden or something, so I called Conservation. They're sending an officer to drive out with you. He'll meet you by your unit."

A frisson of panic trickled up Nicky's spine. Please let it not be PJ Santibanez.

Frank stood next to her truck—Nicky sent up a silent prayer of thanks—AR-15 slung over his shoulder and a long black case propped up against the back tire.

When he saw her cheek, he unslung the rifle and stepped toward her to touch her face.

"You okay?" His look was intent and searching.

She resisted a powerful urge to lean into his palm. "Yeah. Hazards of the job."

"Want to talk about it?"

Nicky turned her head so he wouldn't see her blink furiously against the burn of tears. "Maybe later," she said gruffly. "Where's PJ?"

"Called in sick again."

"You driving with me?"

"Yup. Might as well save a little gas. Global warming and all." He smiled and lifted the rifle case. "Tranquilizer rifle and vials of ketamine in case that bear or deer or whatever at the O'Callaghan place is still lurking around." He stowed the firearms in the backseat and climbed in beside her.

There was only spotty radio and cell phone coverage on the north side of the mountain. Nicky let Dispatch know they were leaving on the call and started the long drive, still stuck in her head. Frank stayed silent, his presence a surprising comfort, and she finally relaxed.

After about fifteen minutes, he asked, "The ranch is owned by a Native family called O'Callaghan, huh? Bet there's a good story behind that."

She humphed a laugh. "How does a handsome Catholic priest falling for a beautiful Indian maiden and giving up the Church sound?"

"Like a movie. We got time?"

"About forty-five miles' worth." She glanced at him. "Which is good, because it's a long and complicated tale."

At his half smile, she took a deep breath, the last of her tension leaving her shoulders, and launched into her story.

"Father O'Callaghan was young, brash, handsome, redheaded, and from the depths of Ireland when he arrived at Fire-Sky back in the 1870s."

"Redheaded? How do you know he was redheaded? Is there a color picture?"

Nicky chuckled. "And freckle-faced. You'll see. Now stop interrupting. He came here on a painted pony, two six-guns strapped across his chest—"

"A priest?"

"Frank," she chided. "Shush."

Her voice meandered as they drove. She slowed her unit near half a dozen battered mailboxes posted into the ground and turned off the highway onto the gravel logging road that snaked around Scalding Peak. The truck bumped through low meadows dotted with piñon and rabbitbrush, but as they climbed, up and around, the forest thickened, and tall, straight pines grew along the slopes. Nicky spun her tale, keeping a close eye on landmarks. A decaying stone house. A coil of barbed wire looped over a wooden post decades ago. A few miles later, a flat, cleared expanse that on one side dropped down a gentle bank to a tumbling stream and on the other climbed up a rocky red cliff.

As she came to the priest and maiden's declaration of undying love, she saw the wagon wheels that marked the narrow road to the O'Callaghan place. Trees and thick bushes lined the rutted lane. It wound another mile before it topped out and dropped into a large meadow tightly surrounded by a pine forest.

It was a place where time had stopped. A rectangular house built of smooth river rock, with weathered, hand-cut-timber barns and outbuildings set behind. Split-rail fences bordered the dirt road, and two black-and-white-spotted ponies lifted their heads from lush native grasses, tails switching lazily. The windmill spun with a squeak and grind, and the water in an oval corrugated tank reflected towering white clouds in a blue sky. A hawk flew overhead, its wings still as it rode an unseen wind current that swept up Scalding Peak. The mountain rose close and dark, gradually, then more steeply about half a mile to the south of the homestead. To the north, the Jemez loomed against the sky, another line of rugged mountains that seemed to go on forever.

Nicky parked her unit between an oxidized-red Datsun pickup and a shiny black side-by-side four-wheeler. When she stepped out of the truck, a breeze rippled through her ponytail. She breathed in the damp, pine-scented air with a hint of wood fire, and walked toward the open front door of the house, avoiding half-filled mud puddles. A thumbnail-sized toad hopped into the water and disappeared beneath the surface.

Grandmother O'Callaghan stood in the doorway, her long gray braid still shot with rusty red strands of hair, the skin of her face and neck covered in freckles. Her bright red-brown eyes were narrow slits under the fallen creases of her eyelids. Nicky sent Frank a grin as he blinked his surprise.

"After the stagecoach robbery, the buried gold, the buffalo stampede, and the sharpshooting contest and puppy, I was pretty sure you were spinning me a tall tale. I apologize profusely," he said.

The old woman licked her lips and stared at Frank before she looked at Nicky. Her face crinkled into a tense smile that showed a number of gold-capped teeth. She held out a warm hand to clasp Nicky's tightly and broke into a spate of Keres, gesturing behind the house in an agitated fashion.

As Nicky asked her to slow down in the same language, she caught Frank's raised brows out of the corner of her eye. His mouth dropped open when Grandmother O'Callaghan pulled out a large iPhone from a pocket in her black skirt. With crooked fingers, she scrolled through pictures. Finally, she pointed to the screen and handed it to Nicky.

Nicky looked at the phone and stiffened on an indrawn breath.

A man stood against the dark backdrop of trees. Above medium height, slim to medium build, dark traditional clothing, and black stained moccasins. A mask fit over his whole head like a helmet, and sprouted antlers, but it wasn't a deer. More like a bear with horns. He stared directly into the camera, a can of spray paint in one hand and a rifle slung across his back.

It was the stalker from the blessing. Silently, she gave the phone to Frank.

He stared at the screen, his face darkening with a scowl before he pressed the phone back into her hand. "You need to get in the house," he ordered. "I'm going to take a look around." He pivoted and scanned the trees. "Dammit! This guy could be hiding anywhere, and now he has a gun."

Nicky grabbed his arm. "If he's out there watching, he already knows *we* know. He let Grandmother take his picture, for God's sake." She tightened her grip. "And I'm not going to hide. *Ever.* Besides, I don't think this is a trap. I think it's another taunt. Look." This time the picture was of a spray-painted heart, the outline of a knife stabbed through it. "It's on the back of the barn. Come on."

He leaned in close to her face. "Not till I get my AR."

Nicky slammed the truck door and jammed the keys into the ignition. She was boiling over with frustration and a sick foreboding, and Frank wasn't helping. Waves of anger rolled off him.

"What's your problem? It's not my fault—"

"Really?" he interrupted flatly. He yanked off his sunglasses and shoved them into his front pocket. Lip curled, he gave her a hard stare.

She tore her gaze away and glared through the front windshield, her hands clamped tightly on the steering wheel.

"Who told you, Frank? Who told you I visited Peter Santibanez yesterday? Your partner?" She didn't mean PJ.

"Does it matter?" He looked away from her and crossed his arms over his chest.

She started the truck and accelerated up the road. The wind had picked up and thunder rumbled behind them. An afternoon storm—common on this side of the mountain—built over the trees. The moisture gave the surroundings a green lushness, but it came at a cost. In winter, snow made the roads impassable.

The truck slithered onto the logging road, gravel spitting behind her. Nicky took a deep breath and slowed to a reasonable speed.

"What did you find?" she asked.

When Grandmother O'Callaghan showed them her wrecked garden, Frank had slipped into the forest for a perimeter search. The affable, quiet man had morphed into a skilled warrior and she'd been chilled by how quickly and silently he'd disappeared into the shadows. That warrior was with her now, and she didn't know what to do with him.

"He came in on a four-wheeler, and parked about a hundred yards from the house." His voice was clipped, mouth hard. "Camp sign says he didn't sleep there and left before dawn. There was no reason to follow the tracks out. I figure he picked up this road. He wasn't there for very long, but he still made a fire."

"To purify the mask," she said. His brow furrowed. "Something to do with confusing evil spirits with the smoke, so they don't subjugate the wearer and guide his actions."

Frank snorted. "Well, then I think this guy needed a bigger fire."

A gust of wind sent a shower of pine needles pinging against the truck. They were approaching the open area by Big Red Dog Cliff, though everyone called it Clifford, after the children's books. It was a hangout for local teens, and fire pits littered the ground. A path wound steeply up through the rocks on one side. She'd worked an accidental death there a couple of years ago when a high, drunken high schooler had fallen the thirty feet from the top.

Nicky negotiated the corner into the clearing and the wind hit her truck so hard, the steering wheel jerked in her hands. She slowed again and sliced a sideways look at Frank's grim face. He'd somehow found out she met with Santibanez. What other information did he hold? She needed something, *anything*, to fill in the gaps.

Her stomach twisted and the words wouldn't come. Why was she having such a hard time broaching the subject with him? She'd had no trouble barging into Santibanez's office yesterday.

Nicky shifted in her seat and pressed forward. "Frank. We have to— *need* to—talk about—"

"Jeez, this storm's coming in fast," he said.

"Yeah, I guess," Nicky answered automatically and glanced into her side mirror at the ominous clouds obscuring the sky behind them.

She gasped and clamped the wheel.

Wind Mother's face cleaved through the clouds and hurtled toward the truck. Her graying hair snaked wildly around her head, mouth open in a silent scream. She vanished in a bright flash of light that emanated from the top of the cliff.

Sunlight caught on the glass of a scope.

Nicky's eyes widened. She wrenched the truck to the right. "*Gun!*"

The driver's side-view mirror exploded.

Adrenaline pumped through her. She punched the accelerator and angled the truck over the edge of the road as a second shot disintegrated the back window. The vehicle slid down the bank, narrowly missed a tree, and ended up half in the stream. Nicky yanked the door open and dove out. She scrambled around to the front of the truck and crouched next to Frank. They both pulled their sidearms and checked the magazines.

"You hit?" he asked.

"No. You?"

"No. Only a taunt, huh?"

"A taunt that has morphed into a trap. Don't rub it in, Frank." Her blood surged through her body, every muscle and fiber focused and ready.

"Actually, it's Franco. Francisco, really, but I go by Franco." He captured her gaze in a steady stare. "Where is he?"

"On top of the cliff. It plateaus out. There's a sheltered area between some of the rocks."

He hunched forward, using the trees and bank for cover. She followed closely and dropped in beside him when he stopped.

"There's a trail to the right, but it's pretty open."

He gestured to a sharp tumble of boulders on the left. "How about there?"

"Maybe. If you're a mountain goat."

He grinned wolfishly. "Afghanistan, baby. Cover me."

She jerked, eyes wide. "Frank—o! No!"

He spun away and jumped back down the slope to run along the edge of the stream until he surged upward where the road opened into the clearing. Nicky followed him out of the corner of her eye, her sidearm and gaze aimed at the top of the cliff.

The wind shrieked through the pines, whipping up dust and debris, and thunder cracked and growled above them. Scalding Peak loomed overhead, its jagged edges ripping gouges in the storm clouds.

Frank—Franco—sprang over the bank of the stream and hit the bottom of the rocky slope at a dead run. Muscles bunched, he bounded powerfully up the tumbled boulders. She kept her focus above him, ready to put a bullet in the sniper's ear if he so much as twitched into view. It took Frank—*Franco*—seconds to reach the top. Once there, he crouched low, then slithered over rocks on his belly. She lost sight of him.

Nicky counted in her head. Seconds stretched to one minute, then two, the only sound the howling wind and thunder. The sky darkened and black clouds covered the sun. Her palms grew slick with sweat. If anything was happening up there—a fight or struggle—she couldn't hear it. She searched the top—pulse hammering in her throat—and formulated her own run up the hill.

"Clear! I'll cover you!" Franco. Thank God.

She darted out from behind her tree and sprinted over open ground to the path on the right, her weapon still trained on the cliff. Movement stopped her to draw a bead, but it was Franco. She yanked her muzzle away and continued her run.

Nicky hit the top, not even remembering her climb, panting hard. A flat red-dust field stretched to a wall of trees deep with shadows.

"He's gone." Franco holstered his weapon. "I heard the four-wheeler start up. Found the tracks."

"His . . . tracks? What . . . about . . . shell casings?" Her heart banged in her chest and her leg muscles burned. Hands on her knees, Nicky sucked in great gulps of air.

"None. He policed his brass. But you need to see this." They walked side by side to the shooter's box. The first drop of rain hit her back. "Look."

There was a circle of rocks, perfect for a couple to lie on a blanket for a quick bout of outdoor sex. Or for someone to set up a sniper's nest.

Nicky went down on her haunches. "What am I looking at?"

Franco turned on his flashlight and played the beam over the dirt. There were no footprints, no scuff marks, no . . . nothing. The area looked like it had been swept clean—with a broom.

"I've seen this before," Franco said. "Two years ago."

She pressed to her feet. "Me, too. A couple of times." At Howard's adobe and in a Wind Mother dream about Scalding Peak. She looked up at the mountain, black against a blacker sky. The wind died down as the rain started in earnest. At least it was warm.

"Do you know why?" Franco gestured to the ground.

"So spirits of the dead can't find your tracks and follow you."

He pulled a small plastic evidence bag from a shirt pocket. It held half a dozen cigarette butts. "These were in the dirt. Probably another taunt. I'll get them processed ASAP," he said. "You know, Nicky, I don't think he was shooting to kill. I think this was a very serious warning. We're getting close."

"Yes." She stood, hands on her hips. "But close to what?"

The rain fell harder. It ran down her face and darkened her shirt. It would wash away any evidence.

Franco glanced at the face of his phone. "How far do we have to walk before we get cell service?"

"If we stay on the road? Three or four miles. I have slickers in the truck."

"Will that be long enough for you to finish the O'Callaghan story?"

They trudged down the slope.

She quirked a half smile. "Maybe. Did I get to the kidnapping part yet?"

He grinned back at her, blinking away the rain beading his eyelashes. The old, familiar Frank—*Franco*—was back. She wouldn't press him now for his story. But soon.

"No, not yet. Let's go get the guns and secure the truck. So, you speak Keres?"

She shot him another smile. "No."

CHAPTER THIRTY-FIVE

They found cell service sooner than expected and Nicky reported the incident. When Franco asked for a few minutes of privacy, she pressed her lips together and nodded. He walked down the road to make his call. On their way back to her vehicle, he requested they keep silent about the potential connection to the stalker at the blessing and the cigarette butts.

"I'm asking you to trust me," he said.

Because of the weapon discharge and damage to a police vehicle, Fire-Sky alerted both the FBI and BIA stationed in Albuquerque. When they arrived on scene, tribal police and Conservation had already combed the cliff and surrounding forest and found the four-wheeler tire tracks. Further exploration turned up the carcass of a deer shot within the last twenty-four hours. The downpour destroyed any other evidence. Everything pointed to a poacher who fired at their vehicle in panic and fled without his kill. The case would remain open, but might never be resolved. Nicky's unit was towed out of the streambed for processing and repair, and Conservation hauled away the deer carcass.

It was late by the time they finished and arrived back at the police station. Nicky was wet, tired, and hungry. They were told to report to the captain's office immediately.

Funny what a difference the day made. That morning, Nicky dreaded a confrontation with Captain. But now, settled and confident, she knew her investigation was on track. Her meeting with Santibanez had not been a mistake, but a good hunch and good police work, and the afternoon's adventure couldn't have been a coincidence; now they knew that somehow Deer-Bear man and Santibanez were linked.

She knocked on Captain's door and he barked for them to enter. He directed Franco to stand next to Lieutenant Pinkett and pinned her with a glare.

Nicky stood at ease, hands clasped behind her back. Franco and Pinkett watched from across the room. Richards stalked around his desk, stopped too close, and leaned into her personal space. She straightened her shoulders and refused to step back.

"First, that embarrassing arrest of Janet Stone at the fiesta—splashed all over the papers, I might add—then the accusation that Mrs. Stone broke out the windows of your home. Oh? Didn't you think I knew about that? Then you also don't know I received a phone call from her *father* the next day about your vendetta against his daughter. You're gathering enemies at every turn, aren't you, Sergeant? Now you've wrecked an expensive police vehicle because some *poacher* deliberately shot at you? Do you seriously expect me to believe that? Or was Janet Stone behind this, too?" he asked, upper lip curled. "Are you working with the FBI and DEA on their undercover drug operation?" Jealousy and envy permeated his voice.

Drugs? Nicky's breath skidded. That was information she didn't have.

"Yes, I have my sources too." Captain sneered. "You'd better tell me what the *hell* is going on. Because—besides being a thorn in my side—you're quickly becoming a liability to my police department, Matthews."

Her arms went limp and her hands dropped to her side. "I'm a . . . *what*? Do I have to point out, sir, that none of this is my fault? I didn't ask for the windows of my home to be broken, nor did I ask to be shot at."

She swept a quick glance to Franco and her lieutenant. Both stood stoically, their expressions neutral. No help from either of those men. She clenched her teeth. Nicky looked back at Captain Richards. The lieutenant was the captain's man anyway. But Franco . . . she'd given him her trust a few hours ago. Why wasn't he helping her, defending her? She brushed away the unexpected hurt.

Richards gave a sharp bark of laughter. "None of this is your fault." His tone dripped with sarcasm. "Off the record, Matthews?"

It was a taunt, a dare.

Lieutenant Pinkett shifted. "Captain, are you sure—"

"Off the record, Captain." Nicky challenged him with everything she had: her look, her stance, her tone of voice. She allowed her disrespect for the man in front of her—for the men in the room—to shine like a warning flare.

"It's only what you deserve," Richards said. "Lifting your tail to a married man. Women like you have no shame, whoring your way to the top. I've had to deal with your type my whole career. Promoted over good *men* because you can't get off your back and keep your knees together."

Blood burned across her cheeks, her anger so intense, a red haze crept into her vision. It circled the ugly, leering face in front of her. Fists and jaw tight, she counted backward from ten and did it again as the captain half sat on the edge of his desk, arms crossed loosely over his chest. Smirking, he looked her directly in the eye. He thought he'd won.

Through stiff lips she asked, "Off the record, sir?"

He shrugged.

"And I've dealt with men like you all my life. Brown-nosing their way up the ladder, looking for the next ass to kiss, until they can go no further because their incompetence and stupidity finally catches up to them, then blaming it on someone else. The world thinks they decided to retire at forty-five because they've got their twenty, but everyone on the job really knows they've been pushed out because no one can stand them. So, they find a job on a reservation or in a small town, given the power that somehow eluded them their whole life because some guy's dick was always longer and they never could measure up. They become spoiled tyrants who never have to take responsibility in their kingdom, because they think no one cares about Indians. And because there are no checks and balances, they fuck everything up royally."

The captain's face purpled with rage. "*Why, you cu—*"

"That's enough, Richards." Franco's voice was quiet, but the command was deep and serious.

Captain stabbed his finger at Nicky. "*She* can't say things like that to me! This is totally out of line."

Franco placed a small recording device on the desk. Richards's eyes opened wide as he stared down at it.

"What?"

"There were a number of things that shouldn't have been said, things that could ruin careers," Franco said. "Luckily, they were off the record."

Nicky paced the hallway outside Captain's office, hands pressed against the butterflies that filled her stomach. Through the closed door came muffled voices, sometimes raised in anger. She couldn't make out the words.

Franco was still in there, along with the lieutenant. She checked her phone. Twelve minutes since Captain had dismissed her. He'd told her to stay in the hall.

She pressed the heels of her hands against her eyes. Her head throbbed dully, but a smile stretched over her face. It had been so *stupid* to say the things she said. She'd probably poisoned any chance of promotion at the department, or at least while Richards was her superior.

But it felt so good, she didn't care. Off the record. Captain's order. Still, if Franco hadn't pulled out that recorder, she'd be looking for another job. She was almost ashamed she'd doubted him.

He'd invited her to dinner during the fiesta. It seemed so long ago. Maybe tomorrow night—instead of gathering at Savannah's—she'd invite him to her house and cook for him. Nothing fancy, and nothing more. But—

The door opened and Franco stepped out. She caught a brief glimpse of the stern faces of the captain and the lieutenant, before he closed it behind him. Nicky grinned.

He met her gaze, only to slide his away. "Two-week suspension. Effective immediately."

She jerked back like she'd been slapped and the blood drained from her head. Dizzy, she grabbed the wall.

"But . . . it was off the record. The recording—" she whispered. Nicky straightened, shook her head. "No. This is wrong. I need to speak—" She reached for the door.

"Stop." Franco grabbed her arm. "You've busted into enough offices uninvited lately."

Her gaze flew to his.

He dropped his hand. "I'm sorry, Nicky. I did my best."

She was numb, couldn't think. What happened when a cop was suspended? Why couldn't she remember? She knuckled her eyes. Her headache went from a dull throb to a sick pounding.

"My duty weapons . . . I need to turn them in."

"No. You keep your firearms and you will be assigned another unit. Part of the negotiations."

"But standard operating procedures—"

"Don't apply. The only stipulation is they want you off the pueblo for the duration," he said. "Nicky, when this is finished, I want you to appeal. You've done nothing wrong."

She searched his eyes. What was going on? Nothing made sense. Except . . . she owed Franco an apology.

Nicky laid an unsteady hand on his arm and squeezed. "I thought— in there—I'd made a mistake giving you my trust. I was wrong. I'm sorry I doubted you. Thank you for supporting me against him," she said. "Not many people around here have my back. It's comforting to know you do." The muscles under her hands tensed, and for a second she thought he would pull away.

"Richards is having someone bring around another unit. Go home, Nicky. Get some rest." His voice sounded strained.

Tears clogged her throat. She gave a jerky nod. Ignoring the speculative looks from the night shift personnel, she retrieved her jacket and bag.

The keys to her substitute unit were in the ignition.

From the shadows, Franco watched Nicky climb into the SUV. Headlights reflected brightly off the glass wall of the foyer as she backed the truck out and left.

He activated his cell phone. His partner's thread popped up immediately.

Is it done?

Franco texted his answer.

Yes. Matthews has been neutralized.

CHAPTER THIRTY-SIX

Nicky drove.

In a show of defiance, she stayed on the reservation. But it wasn't really defiance. It was where she wanted to be. Needed to be. Where she'd found purpose and confidence and a sense of peace.

She tuned the radio to a country music station. It wasn't late. Only nine-thirty. She wandered without direction, skimming along the roads, past open fields and scrub brush, double-wides, their yellow porch lights switched on against the night, and villages with a single streetlamp shining near the plazas.

Unthinking, she drove for over an hour and scanned the headlight-bleached land in front of her unit. It soothed her, let her mind rest and settle.

When she finally stopped the truck, she was in a familiar place. The Kuwami K'uuti overlook at the base of Scalding Peak. Hands thrust in her pockets, she walked to the edge to survey the vista laid quiet before her. Funny how she'd sneered at Peter Santibanez in his window-framed office, high over the pueblo. Had been filled with contempt because of the way he lorded over the land.

But was she any different? Wasn't that why she came to this lookout? In the mesas and arroyos below lay her domain, her own little kingdom. She was an outsider, but such had power over these people. They called to her when they wanted help. She controlled them when they broke the law. They needed her.

But she didn't realize how much she needed them, until now.

Nicky pulled the badge from her belt and held it up. It glinted in the moonlight, but the details were hidden by the darkness. Wind swept over her, warming her skin, tickling her neck. Reflexively, she stared at the piñon and chamisa along the edge of the overlook, braced to see Wind Mother. The vision had saved her from a bullet today.

But there was nothing—she was alone.

A sob welled up in her chest. Ruthlessly, she suppressed it. It would do her little good. She walked back to her car, unclipped her duty belt, and laid it on the passenger seat. Her shirt was still damp from the rain, so she stripped it and her vest off, leaving on only her long-sleeved black Under Armour and sports bra.

Inside the truck, she rolled the windows down. There was a door holster for her Glock. She secured it, set the alarm on her phone for one A.M., and leaned the seat back. It would be two in the morning before she got home, but there was no work to get up for the next day. The piñon-and-sage-tinged breeze wrapped like a blanket around her.

Exhausted, she closed her eyes and slept.

A scrabbling sound prickled the hair on her neck.

She stood in a narrow cylinder of light, darkness all around her, the patch of gritty dirt under her feet swept clean. Head tipped back, Nicky searched the heavens for stars, but there was only black. She stretched out a hand to touch the darkness, and her arm disappeared into the murk as if she'd pushed it through a curtain.

On her left, the shuffling slid closer. Head cocked, she strained to see. Slowly, she slipped her hand out of the darkness to retrieve her weapon, but when it reappeared, glimmering crimson covered her arm to the elbow. She drew it completely into the circle of light, lost focus on the noise inching toward her, and sucked in a breath. Palm and fingers lifted in front of her, Nicky rotated her hand back and forth in the bright, penetrating beam.

Her skin was completely coated in blood.

From beside her in the darkness, a whisper of breath touched her ear.

Nicky jackknifed up, gun in hand, its muzzle a scant inch from the painted man's forehead. He squeaked.

"Back away. Now!" she said. Her heartbeat drummed in her breast. "I want to see your hands." She opened the door of her unit and the interior light flooded the surrounding area. The man shuffled backward, but he clutched something against his chest. A helmet.

No. A round mask. With antlers. The hair on her arms tingled. "Drop it. Hands in the air."

He squeaked again and clamped the mask closer to his chest, cradling it tightly. "I . . . I can't. They wouldn't like it to be dropped in the dirt."

"Who?" Body tense, blood pumping through her, muzzle trained on his heart. Her back to the truck, Nicky glanced around quickly, looking for others. "Who wouldn't like it? Where are they?" It was still dark, but she could see the stars and the moon.

A dream. It had been a dream.

"My ancestors. They live here." He jerked the mask. "They are with me now for protection. I can smell them inside."

Nicky's brows lowered. She stared hard at the skinny man before her. His face and neck were painted white and he'd daubed a sloppy black bar across his wide, blinking eyes. Short dark hair stuck up untidily from his head. He was dressed in traditional Fire-Sky garments, down to dark moccasins. Black-rimmed glasses perched on his nose.

"Howard?"

He nodded and gave her a smile. "Hey."

Howard shifted on his feet, flinched. "They are here," he told the lady cop. "We must hurry."

"Stop squirming, Howard. I have to search you for weapons." She slid and pressed her hands over his body, down and up his legs. He widened his eyes and clenched his butt cheeks as she checked his crotch. Already she'd taken his knife. He fretted about that because he needed it for protection against the evil war chiefs.

His mask balanced on the hood of the cop's truck, the black eye holes staring at him as he stood splayed for Sergeant Matthews.

"I followed them up here but my car gave out down there." Howard's face heated under the paint and his voice rose high at the end. His ancestors were seeing this lady cop feel him up.

She finished and reached for the mask.

"*Dza!* Nah!" He snatched it into his arms and held it like a baby.

"I need to check it, Howard. Make sure it's safe. Can you hold it so I can see inside?" Her voice had gentled.

He pursed his lips. "Well . . . okay. But don't touch! These are *my* ancestors. They don't like to be touched by an outsider. Especially their junk," he grumbled as he tipped the opening toward her.

With the beam of her light, she lit up the empty interior. Then she retrieved his knife and weighed it in her hand.

"This is some weapon, Howard. Its tip is broken off and it's dull as wood." She shook her head. "What were you gonna do with it?"

He scratched his neck but the white paint got stuck under his fingernails. He picked at it. "Maybe it's for symbolic protection." Howard sniffed. He didn't really need it because he had his ancestors backing him up. Maybe.

Suddenly he remembered his purpose again.

"The war chiefs. They are on Scalding Peak, doing the ritual tonight. Three of them." He notched his chin at the dark mountain. "They have their sacrifice. I saw it. Wrapped up in a white cloth. They put it in the truck of that rich guy from the casino."

"Peter Santibanez?" Her tone was harsh.

Howard sagged. Finally, the cop listened to him. "*Haa'a.* Yeah. He was a war chief last year. He knows the rituals. He knows how to cut out the hearts and scatter our enemies. He's their leader, you know?" Actually, Howard wasn't sure about that, but it made the cop move.

She clipped on her belt, all business now. No more crotch-grabbing.

"I'll need my knife?" he said.

"No. Where on the mountain are they?"

Howard hunched in disappointment, but she was a warrior now.

Between the cop and his ancestors, power would soon fill him. He didn't need his knife. He'd expose the war chiefs' evil and win. Maybe.

Tipping up his chin, he peered into the darkness. A light flickered weakly above them, partially shielded by the trees and rocks. Abruptly, the low thumping of drums resonated in the atmosphere.

"They are in the First Sacred Caves. They have started."

CHAPTER THIRTY-SEVEN

Nicky dialed Franco's number. He picked up immediately.

"Nicky."

Her lips pinched in anger at the sound of his voice. She wasn't sure if it was because of him, the whole situation, or both. "I need you and your team up on Scalding Peak now. I'm at the Kuwami K'uuti lookout with Howard Kie. He's been tracking the war chiefs and Peter Santibanez. They're the killers, Franco. They're performing a ritual tonight. They may have a victim. I'm going up now."

"Dammit, Nicky, no! You wait for us."

"I can't. It might be too late. Howard says they're at the First Sacred Caves."

"Keep the line open, then."

"Sorry, Franco, no service." She hung up. "Get in the truck, Howard." The phone rang again. She switched the sound off.

The engine started with a growl. She punched the accelerator and pulled out of the lookout and onto the blacktop, tires squealing, and headed up the peak. The darkness of the forested slopes enveloped the vehicle, headlamps barely penetrating into the thick brush.

"You gonna call the Fire-Sky cops?" Howard asked, his helmet-mask in his lap. He'd calmed considerably from the jittery mess he'd been at the lookout.

"Nope."

"The war chiefs. From up there they'll see your headlights."

"Then I need you to hold the flashlight out the window." She tugged it from her belt and handed it to him. "You're my partner tonight."

He puffed up, a goofy grin on his face, and nodded.

She stopped her unit and switched the lights off and shadows invaded the interior of her truck. Howard pointed the flashlight out the window and Nicky directed him to find the edge of the road. They crawled along the blacktop but within a few hundred yards hit gravel.

"Where have you been, Howard? Where are you staying?" Nicky asked. Might as well get a little interrogation done while he was cooperating.

"After you found me at the adobe house, I stayed with Walker from the mini-mart."

The faux-hawk guy with the sleepy eyes.

"You gave me Flamin' Hot Fritos," he said. "That was a good deed. But the others who came to find me were bad."

"What others?"

"In the black truck and in the Conservation vehicle."

Franco and his partner.

"So you weren't mad at me?" she asked. "Did you follow me at the blessing on Tuesday?"

The road switched back.

Howard grinned, his painted face eerie in the low light. "You didn't see me. I touched your jacket." He lifted the hand holding the mask to show her his palm and the mask rolled forward. He lunged to grab it and dropped the flashlight. Everything in front of the truck went black. She stopped the vehicle with a jerk.

"Don't worry, I'll get it," he said in a singsong voice. He hopped out, carefully placed the mask on the seat, and disappeared under her unit. After he brushed himself off and climbed back inside, he pointed the light forward and they continued upward. The faint sound of drums pulsed through the trees, muffled behind a bend in the road.

"You weren't angry at me?" She thought about the snake with a shudder.

He was half out the window now, kind of like a puppy, and talking to the mask under his breath. "No. You gave me Hot Fritos." He shook his head and huffed.

"You left me a gift at the blessing."

"Sandra's flash drive." He nodded and made the mask nod, too. "No one else listened. Sandra was my friend. She listened."

Nicky swallowed the knot in her throat. Tonight she would have her answers. "Listened about what?"

"The war chiefs. They are the only ones who could do it. They know the sacred rituals."

"I don't understand, Howard. Do what?"

"Sandra thought it was about money. But it's about who belongs. The war chiefs are powerful. They choose who belongs to Fire-Sky." He sighed heavily. "I want to belong. I want to be a war chief. They won't let me because of the beer. And the ones they choose for their rituals are sick. Beer or drugs, other stuff. No good for the tribe alive or dead, so they make them lost."

Cold sweat popped out on Nicky's brow. She licked her lips. A purge. Peter Santibanez and the DNA database. It fit. They crawled up the road, rocks crunching and popping under the tires. In her head, loose threads swirled in a hundred directions.

"Howard? After Sandra died, we couldn't find any information about the war chiefs, or the missing Fire-Sky tribal members, or any of her emails," Nicky said.

"Because they swept everything clean so no one could find it." He pressed his lips into a pooch and slanted her a glance, the whites of his eyes shining in the black painted stripe. "They control your phone, you know."

"What?" Nicky hit the brakes. Howard jerked forward and the flashlight went flying.

"I'll get it!" He hopped out of the truck again.

"What do you mean, they control my phone?"

He jumped back in and sniffed. "I have a filter on my phone. Your message on blessing night had the same evil spirit in it as Sandra's phone and email." Although what he said was crazy, he sounded competent and coherent.

"I have a virus on my phone?" Nicky's mind raced. When and how had her phone been compromised?

"Uh-huh." He trained the light to the edge of the road. The trees towered above them and the terrain was rockier. "I can sweep it clean for you, but only when it's safe. After we stop these guys," he said and gestured with his chin up the road. "I should have stopped them years ago, but I was weak." He turned his head toward her and gulped. "It was the beer. I have decided to stop drinking. I can help better now."

Something he said made her drag in a quick breath. The phone would have to wait till later.

"You said years ago. Do you mean Maryellen K'aishuni?"

The mask nodded at her.

Her hands constricted almost painfully on the steering wheel. "How is she related to all this, Howard?" she asked.

"She was nice, but she . . ." He straightened and said firmly, "Maryellen did not fit what they want. She was their first victim, you know? They killed her like they killed Sandra."

Nicky's jaw clenched so hard her teeth ground. She wanted to scream at him to explain.

"Howard, how did they kill Maryellen?" Her voice crawled out of her throat as slowly as the truck crawled up the road.

"They cut her heart out," he said matter-of-factly. "She is lost. Stop!" He flashed the beam of light on a large extended-cab black truck tucked under some pines. Nicky recognized it. Peter Santibanez's.

Howard clicked off the flashlight, handed it back to her, and climbed out.

"Wait!" Nicky heard the thinness of her voice. "How do you know that? About her heart?"

He stood by the door, the mask under his arm, shifting anxiously from one foot to the other. "I shouldn't tell you. You are not Fire-Sky. It's a sacred and secret ritual, only known to the war chiefs. I should have been a war chief."

"Howard. Please."

She didn't think he was going to speak when he suddenly blurted, "It's a sacrifice! If our enemy loses his heart, his organs, he is lost. He cannot harm the Fire-Sky People forever again because he wanders. The Enemy's Heart Ceremony. Our ancestors did it to protect us. It's a sacred act. But today, the war chiefs are using it against Fire-Sky People who don't belong. They used Maryellen. Then I told Sandra and they killed her, too. I want to belong, yet they stalk me!" Howard hit his chest. "It's my fault," he sobbed.

He pulled off his glasses, jammed on his helmet, and marched toward the black truck. Nicky ran in front of him and pressed the flashlight against his chest.

"Howard, how do you know someone took Maryellen's heart?"

The black holes of the mask swiveled. "The FBI told me." His voice echoed hollowly. "After she died, they visited me and asked me about the rabbits. I emailed rabbits to Maryellen's mom, for comfort, you know? Maryellen loved rabbits more than anything. When they told me, I *knew* it was the war chiefs because I *trained* to be a war chief and know some of the rituals. But they rejected me because they didn't want me to know. I didn't understand then, but now I do. They were the only ones who knew the ceremonies. I tried to tell the agents, but they wouldn't believe me."

"What?" His logic confused her. Since the war chiefs wouldn't let Howard be a war chief, they must have cut out Maryellen's heart? But his next statement exploded that thought.

"I told *you* because you saw a white rabbit. The white rabbit leads the lost souls."

Mike Kapur, her cyber expert, said the FBI targeted Howard because of his weird emails with hearts and knives and rabbits, but they'd cleared him as a suspect. With Sandra's death, Howard had sent *her* bizarre emails with hearts and knives and rabbits. Nicky pressed a hand against her brow. Was *that* the connection? Was that why the FBI were on the reservation? They'd linked Maryellen and Sandra's murders because their *hearts had been cut from them.*

And thus, a murderer had graduated to a serial killer.

She pushed away a sudden uneasiness and focused on what she understood right now.

Peter Santibanez was using Fire-Sky Indians for some kind of sick, traditional protection ritual, to eliminate tribe members whose DNA and blood quantum he considered less pure. Wannabes Santibanez deemed enemies of the tribe because they drained the pueblo of resources.

And when Sandra Deering found out, he'd killed her to shut her up and had taken her heart, too. Sandra was lost. They all were lost. Almost everything fit. Almost.

The Spirit's Heart pendant seemed to burn the skin of her chest. Nicky pulled her Glock, cold anger flowing through her.

"Stay by the truck," she ordered Howard. "When the FBI get here, send them up. I'm ending this now."

CHAPTER THIRTY-EIGHT

Nicky left Howard standing in the darkness and approached the black truck. She angled her flashlight inside the bed. A bloody canvas tarp rested in the back, along with sleeping bags and camping equipment. The windows were opened and the drumming blasted out of the stereo, throbbing so loud it seemed to penetrate her skin and beat in time with her heart. Underneath the thrum, a low humming song accompanied it, almost soothing. A cooler sat on the ground near the front tire. She lifted the lid. It was filled with ice, food, and drinks, enough for a couple of days. Some of the rituals lasted that long.

The sound of laughter and talking echoed off the rocky slopes. Howard said three men had driven up in the truck. She crept forward and searched for a safe way to approach and observe. A narrow path disappeared in the shrubs, fresh boot tracks in the dirt. The mountain towered above her, jagged lava rocks strewn in the foliage and trees. Light glowed around the thin branches and leaves that shivered in a warm breeze. The cave lay back there, one used for some of the Fire-Sky sacred ceremonies. As an outsider, she'd never been inside.

Howard Kie believed the war chiefs came to sacrifice a human. But everything seemed too casual, too relaxed.

Something was off.

The drumming song ended. The next song was . . . *Adele*? What the . . . ? Nicky strode down the path. It ended in a small clearing near the arched entrance of the cave, which was lit brightly with Coleman lanterns. The cloying stink of blood and death hung in the air.

One of the men walked toward her, head turned away to throw a laughing remark to someone behind him. Nicky pulled her sidearm up, its muzzle pointed at the man's chest. When he finally saw her, he froze, eyes wide and jaw slack.

In his right hand he gripped a large curved bowie knife. Spattered blood covered him from head to toe.

She recognized him as a village elder from Ruby Crest—Brian Serachin'e—a Methodist pastor and the father of four kids.

A lump formed in her stomach. Something was *definitely* wrong with this scene.

"Drop the knife," she yelled. "Now! Lay down on the ground! Lay down! Legs spread, hands above your head!" He complied.

At the sound of her voice, two other bloodied men ran from the opening of the cave. Howard burst out of the bushes behind her, mask still on his head.

"What the hell? What's going on here?" Peter Santibanez. His expression quickly morphed from openmouthed shock to a glowering scowl.

"Get down on your knees! Hands on your head! Do it now! Howard, go kick that knife away." The second man obeyed her command and dropped to his knees. Santibanez kept coming.

"I said get down!" She slotted her sidearm in its holster and slipped out her Taser. "Sir, if you don't comply and get on your knees, I will tase you," she informed him loudly and firmly, and pointed it in his direction.

He halted, his whole face in a deep frown, and put his hands on his head. Control the leader and you control the followers. She cuffed him first.

With his hands behind his back, she patted him down, and helped him lie on his stomach. She yanked out a second pair of handcuffs and secured Brian Serachin'e in the same way. Eyes wide, he looked at her in confusion. Gore spotted his traditional shirt, jeans, and boots. His stench turned her stomach, but underneath it a tiny note of wintergreen oil sifted through. She stared at the sheen under his nose.

"Sergeant Matthews? What's going on? Why are you here? We're practicing a rit—"

"Shut up." Santibanez glared at him and he broke off.

Nicky pulled out her last set of cuffs and gestured to the third man. "Hands behind your back." Ed Jackberry, tribal enrollment manager. When he was on his stomach, Nicky retrieved the bloody knife and sternly warned the men not to move.

Howard faced the cave, his mask under his arm again. "He's there. The lost one. The sacrifice. We are too late." He took off running toward the cave and disappeared inside. Nicky groaned and chased after him. The closer she came to the entrance of the cave, the worse the stink.

Howard darted back out, a shining mass of bloody purple tissue in his hand, arm covered in putrid gore. He'd left his mask somewhere.

"See, see? I was right! It's the Enemy's Heart ritual!" he crowed and promptly threw up.

She'd paled at the sight of the fist-shaped heart in his hands. Nicky pulled her sidearm again and walked around Howard, who still heaved noisily in the bushes.

Putting the back of her hand against her nose, Nicky stood at the entrance to the cave. Inside was shaped into a room, the rock walls smoothed. A large stone against the far wall acted as an altar, and an archway in the back opened into a long, darkened tunnel that led deeper into the mountain. But she didn't need to go that far to see why the men were bloody.

Body parts decorated the walls, and blood, glistening in the harsh lantern light, had been used to paint symbols—swirls and arrows—on the rocks.

Howard's mask tilted on top of a flat rock, next to a severed head.

A severed deer head.

The men had performed their ritual on a dead deer.

And she'd bet dollars to donuts it was the one found poached yesterday after the shooting on Big Red Dog Cliff.

Crap.

CHAPTER THIRTY-NINE

Nicky stared dully at a bulky silhouette backlit at the cave's entrance. Franco stepped through the arch, but his movements were tentative, even shaky. He scrubbed a palm over a very gray face and closed his eyes. Hands clenched into fists at his side. With a sigh, she turned her head away and played with her flashlight. She'd been waiting for him.

"Don't like caves?" she asked, her voice quiet. The rock she sat on jutted out of the floor of the cave at the far end of the ritual room, a perfect chair. The Coleman lanterns hissed all around her, their lights turned to high.

Franco cleared his throat, paused as if to speak, and cleared it again. "No," he replied. "When I was deployed—the last time—I was part of a demolition team that cleared caves. A booby trap we tried to—to disarm triggered. I was trapped by falling rock, my partner buried. Killed."

"Your partner, huh? That's tough. I wanted to ask once, but . . . Anyway, sorry." She didn't look at him; instead she tracked the beam of her light across the dirt floor near her feet.

He took another step, boot crunching on pebbles. "You should have waited," he said.

Gaze on the dirt, she slowly twisted the flashlight's head to broaden the beam. "So how did—do—you deal with your problem? With caves? I mean, you came in here."

"I need to visualize the space. Walls, ceiling. Light helps."

"It's pretty bright in here." She trained her beam upward. "There's the ceiling. Better?" she asked, and dropped her light again, continuing to trace the floor, this time into the tunnel.

"Nicky. I know you heard—"

"Yep. I heard." Her glance sliced through him. "I heard Dr. Laughton tell Peter Santibanez that—on Santibanez's orders—DEA Agent Franco *Martinez* tried his *very, very* best to neutralize me. I heard him tell Santibanez that Agent Martinez talked my captain into giving me a two-week suspension, even though I could have walked away, my job intact. Thanks, *partner*. Second one you've buried, I guess," she muttered. Nicky twisted on her rock seat, her body and heart chilled, her face as stiff as Howard's mask. "Was I getting too close, Franco? To solving this case? Taking away the Feds' glory? What?" Shoulders hunched, she turned away to again study the ground, trailing the beam of her flashlight back and forth in the dirt. "Never mind. I don't care anymore."

"It was a direct order, Sergeant."

"And a good soldier never disobeys a direct order." Her voice was flat. She couldn't even work up any credible sarcasm. "And what are your orders now?" Nicky's gaze followed the light into the tunnel and—

She stiffened and bent lower. What the . . . ? Her heart began to pound out of her chest. Rising slowly, she took one, then another step into the tunnel, flashlight bright in the dirt.

Franco sighed. "Sergeant Matthews, my order now is to retrieve your person and make sure you leave the reservation. If you come with me, you might be able to save your job. Peter Santibanez wants your head on a platter."

Nicky's gaze jerked in Franco's direction. "He's still here? Do not let him go yet!"

"What? Why?" he asked, brows drawn down sharply.

"The tunnel. Look at the floor." Her voice held surprised excitement. She took another step. "It's been swept. Like the sniper's nest. He was here, Franco. He was here!" She examined the dirt as she walked into the narrow passage, following the path as it curved away from her. "Are you all right to come?" She beckoned before taking off into the hollow darkness.

Franco didn't reply and she didn't look back to see if he followed, but her beam was soon joined by a second. Nicky jogged down the rocky corridor, deeper into the mountain. The stink of death thickened in the tunnel. Her light flashed and dipped in front of her as she scanned the dirt floor with arcing sweeps.

"No prints, Franco. No boots, no moccasins."

"Just like the Chiricahua," he said.

"You were there? Two years ago?" A harsh combination of excitement and fear rushed through her.

"I was on a team that found Maryellen K'aishuni. And Vernon Cheromiah." He sounded stronger. "That's why I'm here. I wanted to be part of this operation because I couldn't—

Nicky skid to a halt, Franco at her back. Their way was blocked by a black and gray barrier of smooth flowing rock.

"I couldn't forget," he said. "Dead end. There's nothing here." Franco brought his sleeve up to cover his nose.

She'd expected the intense reek of the dead deer to dissipate this far away from the ritual cave, but if anything, it was oppressively worse here. Nicky dry-heaved but stared intently at the wall of stone in front of her. She blinked and sucked in a breath.

"No. There is," she whispered. Nicky stretched her hand, splayed wide, to the rock. It sank in and her fingers curled. "Not rock." She tucked her flashlight under her arm, grabbed with her second hand, and yanked hard. A large curtain, painted to disguise the opening of another room, fell to the floor.

The stench rose to smother them. But this time, it was not from a deer or animal. It was human. There was no other smell like it.

Franco stepped around her, but Nicky followed close, fingers clutched on his arm.

She shone her light over a killing room. Franco flinched and recoiled. Like the ritual deer sacrifice, blood painted the walls, congealed and black. Body parts were scattered as if the killer had been in a rage. At the center of the space stood another rock altar. On it was a human heart, centered within the rays of a sun drawn in blood.

Nicky swept her beam of light to one side and whimpered. She pressed a hand over her lips. Impaled on a thick, listing stake was a man's severed head, wire-rimmed glasses balanced drunkenly on his nose. A scruffy beard sprouted from the chin and jaw. Inside the gaping mouth sat a flat, rectangular piece of plastic.

"What is this? Who is that?" She stood rooted to the ground, her arm tight around her stomach. Her flashlight beam jittered.

"It's a murder room. In the Chiricahua, we found—" He heaved and she rubbed his back. "We found one like this after we discovered Maryellen's body." He inched closer to the severed head.

Careful to touch only a corner, he extracted the plastic card and held it up to Nicky's light. Blood washed it in a thin pink transparent splatter, barely obscuring the gold seal and name stamped across one side.

It was a New Mexico Office of the Medical Investigator's security ID.

"David Saunders," he read. "It says David Saunders."

CHAPTER FORTY

Nicky sat on the sofa, her legs curled underneath, a large towel wrapped around her wet hair. She'd showered when she got to Savannah's, but the stench of death stayed in her nostrils, so after she slept, she took a second one. Yawning hugely, she rubbed her head with the towel in a desultory fashion. Savannah bustled around the kitchen and Nicky found comfort in the domesticity. The smell of green chile mac and cheese wafted into the quiet den. She wasn't hungry, but needed something in her stomach. Other than coffee, she hadn't eaten since yesterday's breakfast.

Dressed in cozy sweats left at Savannah's just in case, Nicky leaned her head back against the soft cushions. She could sleep for another twelve hours, but instead had settled for a restless five. Now the sun was about to set and a warm breeze whooshed gently through the screen door, bringing in the scents of cedar and dust.

She was chilled and unsettled by what she'd seen. It didn't take an expert to know whoever killed David Saunders acted out of psychotic rage. That the Feds kept everything under wraps made her want to punch something. Specifically, Special Agent Adonis Laughton, M.D., Franco's superior and lead in the undercover operation. Last night, he'd laid into her about her interference, had her and Franco debriefed by FBI agents from Arizona, and sent her home with strict instructions to keep her mouth shut or she'd be detained as a material witness.

Well, she didn't care what Laughton wanted, and she wasn't going home. Nicky smiled grimly. The whole case was too hot, too dangerous. Tomorrow morning she'd head straight to the Fire-Sky governor's office with everything. Peter Santibanez and the FBI could go hang.

That meant tonight's job was to clear up a few loose threads and, most important, get a good night's sleep. Assuming she could get the images from the cave out of her head. Her sleep deficit was starting to take its toll, and the last thing she needed was to lose control of her emotions tomorrow. It would do no good to burst into tears in front of the governor.

And, if just to salvage her pride, it would be doubly important to suppress her emotions when he fired her from the job she loved. She couldn't see any way around that, but she was almost resigned to it.

Almost.

A bowl appeared in front of her. "Hey. Earth to Nicky. Dinner," Savannah said. "I asked if you wanted iced tea."

"Water's fine." She took a bite and forced a smile. "This is delicious."

Savannah sat across from her in a patterned armchair, bowl cradled in her hands. They ate silently for a few minutes. Her friend's gaze darted toward her periodically, but she kept her questions to herself. Nicky hadn't told Savannah any details about the night before, but she needed information, and Savannah knew almost everyone and everything that happened on the rez.

"What can you tell me about the Santibanez family?" Nicky asked.

Savannah's gaze sharpened. "Like in Peter Santibanez? Does all this have to do with him?"

"The FBI picked up him and two other war chiefs tonight on Scalding Peak. For murder. We found a body in the First Sacred Caves."

Savannah gasped and clunked her bowl onto the side table, eyes wide. "Oh, my God. Who?"

"They think it might be David Saunders from OMI."

"What? I don't understand. Why would Santibanez target David Saunders?"

Nicky put her barely touched bowl of food down. "Saunders and Santibanez collaborated on the illegal DNA database. I think Santibanez used the information to target his victims."

"Peter Santibanez? He's the serial killer the FBI is tracking?" Savannah's voice spiraled up almost as high as her eyebrows.

"It would explain a lot of things. Like Sandra Deering's missing pueblo members. Even her murder, if she found out what he was doing. David Saunders might have been targeted if he figured out what was going on when he examined Sandra's body." Nicky exhaled a long, deep breath. "Santibanez said we interrupted a practice ritual on the mountain last night, one supposedly done for the protection of the tribe against its enemies. It involved the removal of the heart from a deer." She swallowed a lump in her throat. "We found Saunders in a second cave. His heart had been cut out, too." Among other things.

Savannah's face tinged green. "Just like the removal of Sandra's heart. That's sick."

Nicky's brows knit. The *surgical* removal of Sandra's heart. David Saunders's heart had been hacked out of his body. It was a discordant point.

Savannah's glasses caught the lamplight. "Who is 'we'?"

"The FBI. Franco—Frank—and Adonis Laughton. He's the summer doctor working at the pueblo health center. I called Franco when I . . ." She described the events leading to her suspension and the reason she was on the mountain, then explained about Howard Kie and her cell phone. Howard had disappeared before the FBI showed up.

"So Frank *is* one of the undercover agents."

Nicky nodded.

"And he got you *suspended*?" Savannah's voice rose indignantly, but then her eyes widened. "Wait. I thought this all started with Maryellen K'aishuni. How is she connected to Sandra and David Saunders?"

Nicky hedged. "It doesn't fit, but it appears to be the instigating event." She adjusted the towel over her damp hair and wouldn't meet Savannah's eyes. "There's no clear motive for Maryellen's murder." She returned to her earlier question. "Tell me about Peter Santibanez."

"Married, one son—PJ—Stanford-educated. Before all this, I would have said he was completely dedicated to the pueblo and his people. Powerful, super-intelligent, knows everybody. He's done a lot for Fire-Sky. Jump-started Tribal Enterprises, increased PCD. Some of the tribe weren't too happy when he got the casino resort built, but it's one of the most successful—if not the most successful—in the region. It rivals the East Coast Indian casinos in revenue."

"What do you know about his wife and why don't you like his son?"

"PJ had a less-than-savory reputation in high school. Drugs, alcohol, sex—"

"So did Ryan."

Savannah sighed. "Yeah. There's no good excuse, but . . . Ryan was like that out of anger. He resented he couldn't be part of the Fire-Sky culture and tradition because of blood. PJ . . . well, PJ did it out of privilege. And when he got into any real trouble, his daddy bailed him out. You know"—she dropped her voice—"he even got a couple of girls pregnant during high school."

"PJ has kids on the rez?"

"Not that I know of. I heard any of PJ's little problems were settled by Family Meetings. Rumor was Peter Senior paid for the girls to have abortions."

Nicky frowned. Family Meetings to settle disputes or crimes were a tradition on the reservation and a scourge to police. Instead of involving authorities, the two parties met and the elders came to a fitting punishment and decided on reparations. Not only had Santibanez paid for the abortions, but he probably gave the families of the girls something else—money, property, a plum job. And then the shame was hidden.

Hidden . . .

The puzzle pieces in her head suddenly cleared, pressed to the borders of her mind. Something didn't fit. Something was out of place. Motionless, Nicky sifted through—

"Marica—his wife—is fragile," Savannah said. Nicky's thoughts scattered. "She was a classmate of my mom's. Really beautiful. She was the tribe's only Miss Indian World. She and Peter got married in between Stanford and his MBA."

"What do you mean, *fragile*?"

"Healthwise. And mindwise, I guess. She had a lot of miscarriages before she got pregnant with PJ. According to my mom, it made her desperate for kids."

"I paid a visit to Santibanez at the casino Wednesday," Nicky said. "He used information from the DNA database to alert Bobby Koyona that Victor—Veronica Koyona's youngest child—wasn't his son. That's the reason Bobby beat his wife to a pulp."

Savannah stared at her, openmouthed. "But . . . but . . . that means a paternity test was done. How else could Santibanez know that? How did he get the DNA? Why does he—"

"Want the information? Because he wants to purge the pueblo of genetically impure members. Now that the per capita distribution is rising so rapidly, more and more outsiders are trying to register as Fire-Sky Indians—even faking ancestry documents."

"But Nicky." Savannah's voice was tentative. "That doesn't make sense. Why would Peter Santibanez need to murder anyone as part of a tribal purge when he has a DNA test that could do the same thing bloodlessly?"

"Because tribal law states DNA tests are unacceptable as a tool to determine ancestry and membership."

"If Santibanez was persuasive enough to convince the tribe to embrace a casino, he could do the same thing with the database."

Nicky pulled the towel off her head and ran her fingers through her damp hair. "I know," she said. Santibanez had boasted as much.

"You said Santibanez wanted to remove those with impure blood from Fire-Sky. I have the list. We can check." She jumped to her feet and padded to a notebook on the breakfast bar. "I accessed the ancestral database with Sandra's list of the missing, cross-checked tribe members who didn't pick up their PCD check because they'd died. I also deleted people who skipped a year and showed up the next to sign out their money. That leaves twelve missing over the past two years." She handed Nicky a numbered list.

Nicky read through it, recognizing a few of the surnames. Twelve people potentially murdered because of their genetics.

She put her bowl down and trailed Savannah to the laptop.

Fifteen minutes later, Nicky sat back, hands pressed to her thighs. "This doesn't make any sense."

"What doesn't make sense?" Ryan's voice came from the back patio. He slid the screen door open and stepped inside.

Nicky swiveled and took in his blue jeans and faded red T-shirt. But the fierce scowl on his face captured her attention.

Savannah threw, "Chile mac and cheese on the stove," over her shoulder, like it was a normal Friday night at her place. He didn't respond. She finally turned her head to look him over. Her brow creased. "Why are you wearing mocs? And what's with that big-ass knife?"

He'd sheathed a large bowie knife at his waist, leather thongs wrapped around his muscular thigh to hold it in place. His dark brown moccasins came up to his knees.

"There are two men watching your house, Savannah."

"What?"

"The FBI. They're probably watching me." Nicky sighed. "Where are they?"

"In a black truck, out in the desert. They didn't see me. I didn't recognize either of them." Ryan stalked into the kitchen and dished a bowl of food.

"They brought in guys from Arizona to process the murder scene. They want to keep it hush-hush for now," Nicky said.

"Murder. You'd better explain." Ryan pinned her with stony eyes.

She recapped the situation, Savannah adding details.

"I heard about the shooting yesterday and rumors of your suspension. I tried to call and text. You didn't answer."

"My cell phone's been compromised. Franco and I met for coffee Sunday morning before our shift at the fiesta. When I came back from the ladies' room, he had it in his hand. My assumption is he put a tag on it." Her lips twisted. "I turned it off when I found out about the tag and haven't used it since." Swallowing the tightness in her throat, she said, "Before that, I needed time to process everything."

"Franco? You mean Frank Martin?"

"Agent Franco Martinez. DEA. Yeah. He's one of the two Feds undercover on the rez."

"You didn't answer my question," he said. "What doesn't make sense?"

The change of subject was almost a relief. Franco's duplicity made her heartsick. She didn't want to think about him any more right now.

"The list of the missing Fire-Sky tribal members. Peter Santibanez was compiling the DNA database so he could eliminate people from pueblo membership. Ones with low blood quantum. But every individual on Sandra Deering's list has a high blood quantum. Most are close to full degree. Remember the numbers Sandra put beside the names? Sixty-six means two-thirds degree; greater than ninety, almost full blood."

They gathered around the computer and the list and studied Nicky's notes.

"Then, based on your theory, Peter Santibanez isn't the killer. Isn't that right, Frank?" Ryan called out the back door.

Nicky whipped around and stared stiffly at the large figure on the patio. "Jeez, Ryan, how did you know—?" she whispered.

"I'd be a pretty damn poor Apache if a couple of white guys could sneak up on me," he said in a low voice. "Besides, I heard the gate latch open. Isn't that right, *Franco*?" he said again.

"That's right. Peter Santibanez didn't do this." Franco's deep voice drifted through the screen. "He's been thoroughly investigated, has alibis for the times of the murders. And he's cooperating with us on the undercover operation and David Saunders. He's pretty shaken up." He paused. "Can we come in and talk?"

Nicky folded her arms over her chest. Glancing at her, Savannah gave an exasperated sigh and nodded.

"I thought I gave you strict orders not to speak about this case, Sergeant Matthews," Agent Laughton said. He was right behind Franco and followed him into the room.

Nicky stared at the hard planes of his face and arched an eyebrow.

The addition of two more large men in the room seemed to shrink the space. Ryan stepped forward, ever the protector, aggression in every line of his body, and the testosterone-fueled tension in the air made Nicky want to roll her eyes.

Savannah thrust him out of her way and marched up to Agent Laughton.

"Seriously? You're berating *her* when you jack-holes hid the fact that a serial killer was running loose on the rez?" She punctuated her words with pokes of her finger to his chest. Laughton blinked with each stab and stared down at the woman in front of him. Savannah scowled and held out her hand. "Ryan, *'i'u hi'iska*," she demanded in Keres.

Nicky barked out a laugh as Ryan gently pulled Savannah back to his chest. "No, babe. No knives for you."

Laughton's eyes opened wide. Hands raised, he stepped back.

"She's right, Donny," Franco said. "We both originally objected to the operation's secrecy. And how far would we be on this case without Sergeant Matthews's help?"

He flashed Nicky a look, his smile more like a grimace. She turned her shoulder and her gaze to Savannah instead of meeting his eyes.

Savannah's face softened at Franco's statement. She extricated herself from Ryan's arms. "You'd better take a seat and explain. Frank, do you want something to eat?"

He nodded and his smile relaxed. "Thanks. I haven't really eaten since yesterday's breakfast and you are the best cook—"

Savannah pinched his arm. "Stop sucking up. It won't help."

Agent Laughton raised his eyebrows at the mention of food.

"Not you," Savannah snapped. "You can eat—"

"Savannah!" Lip quivering, Ryan shook his head.

She humphed and went in the kitchen, warmed two bowls of pasta in the microwave, and filled glasses with cold sweet tea as they settled on sofa and chairs.

The tension abated somewhat as the two agents ate, but Nicky itched with impatience at the delay. It was a relief when Agent Laughton put down his empty bowl.

"DEA Agent Martinez was one of the original men, two years ago, who found Maryellen K'aishuni and Vernon Cheromiah's bodies. He's been working the case ever since, but there were no good leads until the Sandra Deering murder."

"I was stationed in the southern Arizona sector," Franco said. "We received an anonymous tip drugs were being stored in a series of mines and caves in the Chiricahua Wilderness. The Coahuilan drug cartel operated in that area. We searched the cavern, but all we found were two buried bodies and . . . and a killing room, like the one last night." He flicked another glance at Nicky.

"That's only one link between the Chiricahua deaths and the murder tonight, but it's recent. So, besides their tribal affiliation, what else do these murders—two years apart and in different states—have in common?" Nicky asked. Would they admit the truth?

When Franco and Laughton exchanged looks and didn't answer immediately, Nicky snapped impatiently, "Why are you here on the reservation?"

"David Saunders called the FBI about Deering's autopsy. At first he was afraid he was being set up by the Fire-Sky police, but we think whoever murdered Sandra Deering is connected to the Chiricahua deaths," Laughton replied. "We believe Sandra was killed because she found out something. What that was, we don't know yet."

Franco picked up where Laughton left off. "At about the same time, we intercepted chatter from Mexico and Mariano Salas, the Coahuilan cartel leader, to Albuquerque. One message contained the word *corazón*. Heart. Another link."

"The cartel recently sent human assets into Albuquerque," Laughton added. "This convergence of clues triggered the undercover operation."

"Explain how Maryellen and Vernon are connected to Sandra and Saunders," Nicky demanded.

Franco's blue eyes shadowed. "Hearts, Nicky. It all comes back to hearts," he replied, his voice somber. "The two men we found in the Chiricahua killing room had their hearts ripped out and placed on an altar, like David Saunders. They were mutilated, also like Saunders. Both Maryellen and Vernon had been held alive for weeks, there in the caves. It was a perfect hiding spot. But a few hours before we searched, their hearts were surgically removed while they were still alive."

"Still alive?" whispered Savannah.

"As far as we know," Franco said.

Nicky knew about the removal of Maryellen's heart. Howard had told her. But hearing it confirmed by Franco left her shaken. And to have the hearts taken while they were alive . . . She pressed a hand against her chest and struggled to divorce herself from her emotions. She needed her mind clear. Needed to be a cop right now, because one thing Franco said really stood out: there was a big difference between "ripped out" and "surgically removed."

Franco leaned forward, hands clasped loosely between his knees. "The ground was swept in both caves—tonight and in the Chiricahua. Just like in the sniper's nest. Those cigarette butts we found? The DNA matched David Saunders and five other unknowns. We think they may be from Sandra's list of the missing. Nicky," he pressed, "David Saunders's murder was a taunt. Just like the anonymous phone call drawing us to the Chiricahua caves two years ago."

"Who were the other men, the ones in the killing room in the Chiricahua?" The question came from Ryan.

Franco answered. "They were identified as a couple of Mexican nationals, probably hired to help abduct and guard the captives. The killer . . . disposed of them once he took what he wanted. No witnesses. We think that's why he went after Saunders. Because he'd discovered Sandra Deering's heart was missing.

"We believed whoever killed Sandra knew David Saunders received any and all train-pedestrian fatalities from Fire-Sky," Franco said. "In the past, he'd almost lost his job over the harvest and removal of a heart from a Native American. It was a good bet he'd keep quiet. I think his paranoia got the best of him. He wasn't supposed to report the missing heart. But he did. And now he's dead."

A chill swept over her. That meant whoever was involved in the murders was familiar with both Fire-Sky and Albuquerque OMI procedures.

"He? You think only one man is involved?" Nicky let the skepticism show plainly on her face.

Laughton shifted, obviously uncomfortable with the question. "The profilers call it a Jekyll-and-Hyde personality. One thing's for sure, though. If these missing tribe members on Deering's list have been murdered, this guy is targeting Fire-Sky tribal members. He seems to have an animosity—"

"Animosity, Agent Laughton? *Animosity?* No. He has a deep and abiding *hatred* for my culture and people." Savannah sat up straight, her mouth a taut line. "The heart is the seat of our soul. To take it away from our bodies is to exile us. We become *los perdidos*. Lost ones. It's worse than death, for we wander and cannot ever join our family, our ancestors, our future. Can't protect or help the living. Your murderer knows this. He knows the rituals. He must be a member of Fire-Sky."

Ryan reached for Savannah's hand, his expression at once proud and desolate as he looked at her. Nicky blinked back tears. Now she understood Ryan's fears about Savannah and his future. Savannah was Fire-Sky. Ryan was not.

There was a tense silence.

Laughton sighed. "We believe that now."

Nicky cleared away her emotions. There were still too many unanswered questions. She addressed Laughton. "Howard Kie and Sandra thought the war chiefs were involved. They would know the secret rituals."

"No. Not so secret," Ryan said. "All young Tsiba'ashi D'yini men are trained and brought partially into the circle of war chiefs. They learn things, and they talk. Even I know something about the Enemy's Heart Ceremony."

"Great. That just expanded our pool of suspects," Laughton said, jaw tight.

Nicky pushed forward with her loose threads. "You had Saunders alter Sandra Deering's autopsy report. Her toxicology report showed marijuana, heroin, alcohol. Was it fake, too?"

"Yes." Franco held her gaze. "We only found traces of ketamine in her tissues and there was a needle mark on her thigh. It's another link to Maryellen and Vernon. They were injected with ketamine, too. It would have immobilized them for the taking of their hearts."

"Witched," Savannah whispered.

Hair prickled on Nicky's neck. All of the victims had been witched, just like Juanita Benami had told her.

"Ketamine. That tranquilizer is used at the pueblo's veterinary clinic, the animal shelter, and at Conservation. It wouldn't be hard to steal," Ryan murmured.

"No. It's also very easy to get in Mexico. And the Coahuilan cartel was experimenting with ketamine-methamphetamine mixtures two years ago. That was another connection," Franco said. His mouth thinned. "But we still don't fully understand how the cartel is connected to the taking of the hearts, or Fire-Sky."

Yeah, Nicky thought. Neither did she. It seemed for every piece of the puzzle she placed, another ten were thrown on the table.

"Did Sandra have other sources for her story? Or a boyfriend?" Franco asked Nicky.

She snorted. "You do realize I only found out she was murdered *four days ago*." He gazed at her steadily. She sighed. "Not that I know of. It looks like she did most of her project's legwork on her own. And no one mentioned a guy in her life. Why?"

"When she left her dorm the night she disappeared, she was dressed up. Heels, skirt, makeup."

"You took the UNM dorm videos, too? No wonder they wouldn't give me access." Nicky glared, her gaze swinging between the two agents.

Both Franco and Laughton had the grace to drop their eyes.

"Her murder would have generated too much publicity. The Coahuilan cartel case is huge. We couldn't let them think we were on to them. The FBI thought, by virtue of us being undercover on the reservation, we could ask around and get information that people might be reluctant to share with authorities. But that really hasn't worked," Laughton admitted.

"You're outsiders. It takes years for our people to trust." Savannah's voice was hard.

"That's why we decided to speak to you now," Laughton said.

"Really? Not because your case is collapsing around your heads and you're just about to be outed?" Nicky asked.

"Yeah, well, that might have something to do with it, along with Franco here hammering on me for the last week to bring you in on the operation," Laughton said.

Nicky shot Franco a glance, but looked away when she realized he was staring at her.

"We could use your help interviewing Dinah K'aishuni, Maryellen's mother. At the time, brass didn't think the K'aishunis told the whole truth about their daughter's disappearance. They see Dinah K'aishuni as a weak link. They think she's hiding something, or held something back." Agent Laughton gave a rueful laugh. "Right now anything she has might help. We're pretty desperate."

That was a nice touch. Laughton was good at his job, but she didn't believe him for a minute. He was right about the K'aishunis, though. They'd held something back.

"It was on my list of things to do, but they live in Omaha now," Nicky said. "Out of respect, I refuse to speak to her over the phone."

"That won't be necessary. The K'aishunis have been on the pueblo for the past week visiting relatives," Laughton said. "They fly out tomorrow. We need to go tonight."

Nicky's breath caught in her chest. She exchanged a sharp glance with Savannah, who bit her lip and slid her eyes away.

So much for a good night's sleep.

CHAPTER FORTY-ONE

Nicky fumed in the front passenger seat of Savannah's car, professional in black slacks and a bright blue top. Her service weapon lay hidden at her back, holstered in her waistband. Ryan was crammed in behind her, long legs stretched across the length of the seat. He refused to leave Nicky and Savannah alone, even though Laughton had assured him they were in no danger.

Franco, though, hadn't added his assurances, only pressed his lips together grimly as the agents climbed into a large black pickup.

"The K'aishunis were here on the reservation and you hid it from me," Nicky said flatly. She sent Savannah a narrow-eyed glance.

"They came for the fiesta. I almost told you at the blessing, but I felt like I was betraying Dinah." Savannah opened and closed her hands on the wheel of the car as she drove. "The K'aishunis kept the information hidden for so long and this will dredge up so much pain. I couldn't see how another interview would help."

"But she agreed to talk to me when you called her," Nicky said.

"Yes."

Savannah slowed to negotiate a turn, her headlights cutting through the darkness. The car slipped off the paved road onto a wide gravel street leading to the jumble of adobe buildings—some hundreds of years old—that constituted Chirio'ce. The village stood on the flattened top of a broad hill, low-profile dwellings dotting the edge. With no yards or fences, trucks and cars were parked close to front doors and *horno* ovens. The few feeble lights that shone from cracks in curtained windows hinted at occupation, but the streets were deserted. The village was known to be haunted. No one went outside at night.

Larger structures occupied the center of the town, including an adobe church with a small tree-filled courtyard surrounded by a wall. One of a couple of streetlights spotlighted the sanctuary's elaborately carved wooden doors.

Savannah pulled her car up to a sprawling house that rose two stories at one section. Its silhouette against the star-bright sky showed a tumbled outline, like a series of large muddy blocks thrown on the ground and carelessly pushed together—additions built over decades and centuries to accommodate children and extended family.

As Nicky stepped from the car, thunder rumbled in the distance. An incoming summer storm shrouded the top of Scalding Peak and the intermittent breeze that swept through the village carried the dusty, metallic scent of rain. Lightning flickered, illuminating a dark cloud above pine-covered mountain slopes. The Sacred Caves were up there. David Saunders and the killing room flashed in her mind. She wanted to crawl back in the car and scream for Savannah to drive somewhere, anyplace, where the gruesome images couldn't find her.

Instead, she stiffened her spine. What had happened in those caves had happened in the Chiricahua two years ago. Maryellen was part of it and Dinah K'aishuni might have withheld vital information. It was up to her to try to tease it out, see if it had any bearing on the murders.

Truck doors slammed behind her. Franco and Laughton crunched through the gravel as they walked toward Nicky, Savannah, and Ryan.

"It's only nine-thirty. Why is this place so quiet?" Laughton asked, voice low as his gaze swept the area.

"Ghosts." Ryan's long hair flowed loose around his shoulders and his hazel eyes gleamed. "They are all around us. In this village, the Stone Warrior is seen the most."

"The Stone Warrior?" Laughton's voice was sharp.

"The Fire-Sky boogeyman. Cut it out, Ryan," Savannah said. "What's the plan?"

"Okay. The plan. Franco, I need you inside because you know the case," Nicky said. "Savannah will introduce us to Mrs. K'aishuni. Ryan and Agent Laughton will stay outside." When Laughton opened his mouth, Nicky cut him off. "No. You are an outsider, even more than Franco and me. Savannah, after a few minutes, excuse yourself. Franco, under no circumstances do you tell Mrs. K'aishuni Maryellen's heart is missing, do you understand? It would devastate her."

He nodded, his face a lifeline she latched on to.

"And only speak on my cues." Nicky tugged down her top with trembling fingers. "Ready."

Savannah walked to the house and raised her hand to the door. She hesitated a scant second before knocking. It opened immediately. Warm light and the lingering scent of savory cooking eddied outside.

"Savannah! So good to see you." A softly plump woman, curly black hair haloed around her head, pulled Savannah into a tight, emotional hug that left them both wiping their eyes when they disengaged. "Please, come in. The men are at kiva tonight, so it's just my sister and me. Savannah, you remember Alba?"

Dinah K'aishuni bustled into a narrow, low-ceilinged room made even smaller because sofas and chairs lined every inch of the perimeter. Colorful weavings decorated the walls and a library book was cracked open over the arm of a cushioned chair. At the end of the room, a door led into the kitchen.

"Can I offer you some coffee?" Dinah called to the kitchen. "Alba?"

A woman who could have been Dinah's twin peeked her head around the corner, smiled, and ran her gaze over the group. Her eyes widened appreciatively as they fell on Franco's large form.

"Coffee would be great. Dinah, Alba. This is Sergeant Matthews of the Fire-Sky police and Agent Frank Martin from Fire-Sky Conservation." Savannah perched on the edge of the sofa nearest the kitchen door. "They'd like to speak to you about Maryellen and her disappearance." Her voice trailed off, eyes sheened with moisture.

Nicky sat down next to Franco and kept her own expression sympathetic, but carefully watched Dinah K'aishuni's face. It fell into sorrowful lines at the mention of her daughter and Nicky wondered if the deep sadness in the woman's eyes ever went away.

"I don't think we ever had cause to meet before my husband and I left, but I know of you, Sergeant." Dinah gave Nicky an unsteady smile. "You are trusted on the pueblo by many people I trust, and you worry those who worry me." Her smile firmed and ticked up higher.

Alba came in with a tray of mismatched cups, steaming with coffee, accompanied by a plate of homemade *biscochitos*. Nicky added sweetener, wrapped her hands around the mug, and took a sip. Its welcome bitterness burst on her tongue.

"Thank you so much for agreeing to answer more questions. I know this is difficult." Nicky trailed off delicately, sympathetically. "Why don't you start by telling me about your daughter, Mrs. K'aishuni."

"Call me Dinah, please." She pressed a hand below her throat, fingers rubbing the skin. "Maryellen was such a sweet girl. Our only child. Most parents know their children will grow up and move away, but it was a comfort to me she would always be with us. So special."

"Did she have a lot of friends? Did she know Howard Kie?" Nicky asked her second question with a grin.

"Oh, yes." Dinah chuckled. "Even with her disability, she was very easy to have around. She had Down syndrome, you know. And Howard? They were the best of friends. He was such an odd young man. Maryellen would tell me *she* could look after *him*. But when he left for college, they lost touch."

Nicky nodded. She cast a quick glance at Savannah, who hurriedly excused herself to the kitchen with Alba.

"I have photos of Maryellen." Dinah touched the screen of her cell phone. She handed it to Nicky, who scrolled through a sequence of pictures showing Maryellen as a young child with a fringe of black hair above sleepy eyes, chubby cheeks, and a wide grin, to her as an adult, hair longer, parted in the middle, but face still smooth and round, innocence lighting her features. In a few of the pictures, she held a rabbit.

Nicky's focus sharpened. Rabbits. Excitement shimmered through her. The FBI file Mike Kapur had seen contained references to rabbits. Howard had also said Maryellen loved rabbits. They'd been prominent in his weird emails.

She handed the phone to Franco. "We were never introduced, but I remember seeing her at some of the festivals. Did you keep rabbits as pets?" she asked Dinah.

Franco stiffened beside her.

"Oh, yes. She loved her bunnies."

He handed the cell phone back to Dinah. It was an expensive item, as was Dinah's outfit and jewelry. Lots of gold.

"I had a rabbit as a child," Nicky lied. "A big white rabbit named—unoriginally—Thumper."

Dinah stilled. She squeezed the phone, knuckles white against her skin. "She always wanted a white rabbit. But our culture believes they're associated with death. Maryellen didn't understand that."

"My grandmother believed it was bad luck to plant a willow tree in the yard. She said when it died, the person who planted it would also die," Nicky explained.

Dinah gave her a strained smile before her gaze dropped to tightly laced fingers. "Silly superstitions and traditions," she murmured.

Ryan believed the white rabbit that ran away from the mini-mart break-in was a sign that Nicky would need to rescue someone who might already be dead. A lost spirit. Nicky assumed it was Sandra. But now . . .

"Did someone use a rabbit to lure her, to harm her, when she was in high school, Dinah?" Nicky asked, voice gentle. Franco leaned in, his gaze intent.

Dinah closed her eyes tightly. Tears welled through her lashes. "You know?"

"Not everything." Nicky squeezed Dinah's hand with one of her own. "Can you tell me what happened? It could be important."

Dinah dabbed the moisture from her eyes. "She was older than most of the kids at high school and didn't go for the whole day. I homeschooled her as best I could. But they had an FFA program. Future Farmers," she elaborated. "And a rabbitry. She was high-functioning for a Downs person, to the point where she could be left unattended for a . . . a while. The teacher would leave her in the barn. That's when we think it happened."

"She was raped."

"Yes. And I don't care what anyone else says, it was *rape*," Dinah said fiercely. She looked back and forth between Nicky and Franco. "A girl like Maryellen *cannot* consent. She didn't understand about love and sex." Dinah's shoulders seemed to shrink. "She got pregnant. We didn't realize for some time. She said she loved the father because he promised her a white rabbit."

"Who was the father?" Nicky asked.

"You must understand, we were trying to do what was best for our little girl." Dinah's voice was pleading. "We called a Family Meeting with the boy's parents. His mother denied it at first, insisted her son never touched Maryellen. When we told her Maryellen was pregnant and threatened to take it to the police, she said our daughter was too . . . too *damaged* to attract her boy to have sex. Like rape is about that," she said bitterly. She paused and licked her lips. "Then she threatened us. The family was—is—very powerful."

Nicky's stomach dropped.

"Said there was no proof. Said she would bring charges of false accusation. That Maryellen would be taken from us because we were bad parents, that we didn't supervise her properly. That's when we told them we would get a DNA test on the . . . aborted material and prove—" Tears dripped down her cheeks. "We couldn't let our child have that baby. I think that his mother agreed to a test because her son insisted he wouldn't have . . . have sex with a girl like Maryellen. Later, we learned he had a reputation—that this had happened with other girls on the pueblo." Dinah shuddered in a deep breath. "So we did the test. It was the boy's baby. And . . ." She played with a ring on her finger, turning it around and around.

"And you accepted payment for your silence." Nicky tried to keep the censure out of her voice, but didn't succeed.

Dinah's face burned red. "They gave my husband a job—a good job with good pay—and settled money on us every year. And we insisted they banish that boy so he could never do this again to our girls." She sat up straighter. "And they did. It was funny. Before the DNA test, I thought that boy would never get punished, not really. They were almost proud of his reputation, his . . . his wildness. But after, it was like his father couldn't stand the sight of him. It wasn't until after Maryellen died we realized her rapist was back on the reservation, for I don't know how long. With a job." She darted a glance at Franco. "You know, my husband confronted . . . him, after he came back. He just laughed. Said there was nothing we could do anymore. All the evidence was gone. Gone. That's when we realized we couldn't stay at Fire-Sky. So, we became *se fue*. We are gone from this place now, only to visit."

"Who was the father, Dinah?"

But Dinah was shaking her head even before Nicky finished her question. "This has nothing to do with Maryellen's death. It can only bring her shame if the information gets out."

"Dinah, please." Nicky could hear the edge of desperation in her voice.

"You don't understand. When we left, my husband could not get another job that paid so well. We depend on the extra money. If I tell you, it will be withdrawn because I broke the agreement. I can't do that."

Dinah stood, her arms wrapped protectively around her waist. She wouldn't look at them. "I don't want to answer any more questions. I'd like you to leave now."

Nicky burst out of the K'aishunis' home and strode past Laughton and Ryan and into the night.

"Nicky? Nicky!" Franco called after her.

She ignored him and barreled toward the walled plaza, mind and stomach churning. *Please, God, no. It couldn't be. It wasn't*—No. Hand pressed against her stomach, she marched and heaved in deep lungfuls of air.

"Nicky. Wait." Franco caught up to her, matched her pace. "Don't beat yourself up because Dinah wouldn't give you a name. You accomplished more in that interview than you think."

She shook her head and sped up. Franco lengthened his strides.

"The removal of Maryellen's heart wasn't the only thing that we didn't release to the family and public. There was something else," he said. His voice echoed eerily off the narrow alleys and walls. "We didn't know about Maryellen's fascination with white rabbits. Never asked. I'm embarrassed now. We thought we had it all figured out. Everything slotted into place. When we did our research, we learned Fire-Sky tradition associated them with spirits and death, so it made sense . . ." He trailed off.

"What made sense, Franco?" Nicky asked.

He grabbed her arm, pulled her to face him. Nicky stood rigid under his hand. She didn't want to stop. If she stopped, she'd have to face her suspicions.

"There was a white rabbit in the grave, tucked into Maryellen's side," Franco said. "We figured her killer knew the customs, that's all. But now . . . She must have known him. Known her murderer." Nicky's muscles shook under his hand. "He must have targeted her specifically, using the rabbit as bait, as a lure. Dinah said Maryellen loved this guy. It was the perfect setup. Her murder was for revenge, not because she'd stumbled onto the cartel's hiding place. And now he's back on the pueblo. Has a job here. All we need to do is find out who got Maryellen pregnant—"

Nicky jerked away from him and reeled back. "Dear God, Franco, don't you think I realize that?" She pressed the heels of her hands against her eyes, before she looked back at him and drew in a long breath.

"What?" He widened his stance then stilled.

"There are two men I know who fit perfectly into every aspect of this crime. Two men I know who could have done this. Men who have reason to hate, to . . . to *despise* the Fire-Sky culture, people, and traditions."

"Who?"

"PJ Santibanez. There's information you need to know about him, about his parentage." Nicky swallowed the burning in her throat.

"Okay." His voice was steady. "The second?"

She pressed trembling lips together and closed her eyes. A single tear slid hotly down her cheek. "Ryan," she whispered. "Ryan Bernal."

Franco stepped in front of her and slid his hands up her arms. He tugged her into his chest.

"Nicky," he said. "Tell me what you know. All of it."

CHAPTER FORTY-TWO

Laughton approached Ryan, cuffs in hand, when they arrived at Savannah's house.

"I'm taking you in for questioning, Bernal, for the murders of Maryellen K'aishuni, Vernon Cheromiah, and Sandra Deering. I'll need your weapons."

"No! He didn't kill anybody!" Savannah pushed Franco out of the way to stand in front of Ryan, her arms stretched out as if to block the FBI agent. "Are you crazy? Nicky, Frank. Tell him." She blinked at Franco's hard expression and pivoted to Nicky. "Tell him. Nicky? Please."

"I'm sorry, Savannah," was all Nicky could say. She felt sick to her stomach. "He had opportunity and . . . motive." Her gaze flashed to Ryan.

Ryan's brows knit. "Motive?"

"The killer is targeting the Fire-Sky culture and people. You have every reason to resent . . ." Nicky's throat constricted and she cleared it, her gaze skittering to Savannah.

Savannah's eyes widened and she sucked in a harsh breath. She spun on her heel and faced Ryan, shaking her head.

"No. Ryan. Not because of me. I can't—You have to understand—The pressure, my father—"

He pulled her toward him. Her arms snaked around his back and she buried her head in his chest. With a sigh, he laid his cheek against her forehead.

"It's okay, babe. There's nothing I would change about us." His lips quirked. "Well, almost nothing." He pressed a kiss to her hair and met Laughton's gaze.

"I need to know she'll be protected while we do this. Otherwise I won't cooperate." The planes of his face were hard, but his eyes were anguished.

"She will be," Laughton said. "I've already assigned men to her house. They should be here shortly."

The two men stared at each other. Finally, Ryan nodded. He whispered in Savannah's ear and she moved to the sidewalk, arms crossed high on her chest, hands on her own shoulders. He turned over his knife, his cell phone, and the handgun he'd slipped into his right moccasin. Agent Laughton cuffed him.

"When I'm done, I'll text you," Ryan said to Savannah. She nodded and wiped away a tear from her cheek.

Laughton tucked him in the backseat and they drove away.

Savannah turned on Nicky. "How could you?" Her voice fractured.

"He has to be completely cleared. And the FBI is pursuing another suspect." Nicky glanced at Franco, who shook his head. She couldn't reveal PJ Santibanez's connection yet. "That's where we're headed right now. This might all be over by tomorrow. Your phone is probably compromised, too, but keep it on. I'll contact you as soon as I know anything."

Savannah stared at her from eyes swimming with tears. "Don't come back tonight. You can't stay here." She turned away, let herself into her house, and closed the front door.

"She'll be all right, Nicky." Franco's voice was gruff. He laid a warm hand on her shoulder and nodded to a dark car pulling along the curb to park. "They'll see she stays safe."

Nicky frowned at the vehicle, her tired mind trying to tell her something, but the moment was lost when Franco beckoned her to her police unit.

CHAPTER FORTY-THREE

Would this night ever end?

Nicky and Franco stood in Peter Santibanez's office, high atop the Fire-Sky casino resort. Santibanez lounged against the thick glass window that framed the gathering storm around Scalding Peak. Lightning stabbed constantly at the night-black clouds. He swirled the amber liquid in his glass, ice tinkling, his expression pulled into a listing sneer.

Nicky blinked dry gritty eyes as they waited for a response from the most powerful man on the pueblo.

"More questions, Agent Martinez? When I told you I'd cooperate fully, I hoped first to get a good night's sleep." He took a sip of his drink, sucking on the ice. "Where is Agent Laughton? And why is she here?"

Nicky returned his dark look.

"Agent Laughton is pursuing another lead," Franco said. "And Sergeant Matthews has been an integral part of the Sandra Deering case from the start. We've just come from an interview of Dinah K'aishuni."

If Nicky hadn't been watching carefully, she would have missed the tiny start Santibanez gave at the mention of Dinah's name.

Franco must have seen it, too. "You were aware she and her husband were visiting the reservation? Her responses to some of Sergeant Matthews's questions led us back to you, sir."

While Franco's words were deferential, his tone was not. Internally, Nicky relaxed a fraction. He was here for answers, as was she.

"We won't take up much of your valuable time, sir. Sergeant Matthews has a few questions. Sergeant?"

"Well, if this won't take long," Santibanez interrupted, "I won't invite you to sit."

A couple of Santibanez's words slurred the slightest bit. Was he already drunk? Good. Nicky dove straight in.

"Dinah K'aishuni told us about a very disturbing event. When her daughter Maryellen was in high school, she was raped and became pregnant. The parents of the boy only acknowledged their son's involvement after a DNA test proved he was the father." She paused, then gave him one more piece of information. "FBI agents have been instructed to pick up your son, Mr. Santibanez."

He barked out a harsh laugh. "Well, good luck proving PJ raped that girl. All you have is the word of a grieving mother who wants someone to blame for her own failings."

Relief settled hard and fast inside Nicky, and she almost slumped with it. Santibanez's statement cleared Ryan.

"And Dinah K'aishuni negated the Family Meeting agreement when she told you. About time. I was tired of forever paying out money to keep PJ's past indiscretions hidden." Santibanez tipped his head back and with a long swallow finished his drink. He walked to the sideboard, using a hand against the wall to steady his steps. Crystal clinked as the decanter knocked against his glass. "Pick him up! See if I care. The statute of limitations expired years ago anyway. Now, if you're done—"

"Actually, the clock starts when the crime is first reported to law enforcement," Nicky informed him. "After you banned your son from the pueblo, where did he go?"

"My son." Santibanez made a rude noise. "His mother gave him money to travel around, drift for a year or two. When he showed up in Albuquerque, she made me get him a slot at Glynco in Conservation."

He waved his drink at Franco, who eyed him narrowly, his phone pressed to his ear.

"When PJ graduated, I pulled a few strings, got him a job in Oregon, on a reservation." Santibanez scratched his face and took another drink. "He ended up in Arizona, at San Carlos Apache. It made his mother happy he was so close." He stared blankly across the room. "I hadn't seen him for a long time, but he was there, volunteering for the Maryellen K'aishuni search."

Nicky sucked in a gasp and stilled. Franco's arm dropped to his side, his white-knuckled hand clutching the cell phone. He stared at Santibanez, eyes wide.

"You know what was so funny? When the FBI interviewed the volunteers about the murders, they thought I'd been accidentally put on both the New Mexico *and* the Arizona volunteer list. But that was Peter Santibanez *Junior*. They didn't even *speak* to PJ." His brows knit at their reactions and he swayed on his feet. "What?"

"Did it ever cross your mind your son had both motive and opportunity to murder Maryellen K'aishuni?" Nicky lashed out at him with her voice.

Santibanez pivoted and threw his glass against the wall. It shattered into a thousand pieces. "He's not my son!" he screamed and dropped his head into his hands.

"No. He's not, is he?" She let anger flow into her words as she marched toward him. "The DNA test done on Maryellen's aborted fetus showed that, didn't it? But that's not the only reason you rejected him. His real father wasn't Fire-Sky, was he? His blood quantum didn't qualify him as a member of the tribe, did it? So you banned him from the pueblo. Purged him, like you're trying to purge others because they don't live up to your ancestral standards."

Santibanez lifted his head and stared at her, brows in a straight line over his eyes. His voice shook as he answered. "Every living member of the Tsiba'ashi D'yini Pueblo is here only because of the bravery of our ancestors. Many of them sacrificed themselves—*died*—to maintain our culture and traditions. Purging this tribe of hangers-on is *my duty*."

"He was raised for years by you and his mother on this reservation, with all of your traditions and culture," Nicky said. "To what end? To be torn from the only family he knew? Now you're doing the same thing to Victor Koyona. Do you know what one of his sisters said about him when she found out about his blood quantum? *Now he is worth nothing*. How would you like to be raised and then rejected by a culture that believes, because of your DNA, you are worth *nothing*?"

"Maybe Victor's mother should have thought of that before she got pregnant and tried to pass him off as Tsiba'ashi D'yini," he said, a sneer twisting his face.

"Like your wife did with PJ." Nicky let the statement hang in the air. "PJ is murdering high-blood-quantum members of Fire-Sky, Mr. Santibanez," she said. "And he's using your DNA database to select his victims." Everything was falling into place. "Was he dating Sandra Deering?"

Santibanez blinked rapidly and licked his lips. "How did you know?"

"Did you tell him David Saunders found out about Sandra's missing heart?"

He pulled out his desk chair and sat with a thump. "PJ was with me when Saunders called and said he'd told the FBI about Sandra's autopsy. That he'd been advised to leave town for a couple weeks." Santibanez's face was a gray mask. He wiped a shaking hand over his eyes. "You think PJ did that? Mutilated Saunders on Scalding Peak?"

"Yes. And I also believe he tried to implicate you."

"My God."

"But we don't think he did it alone." Franco stood next to her. "That one-guy, Jekyll-and-Hyde thing is ridiculous," he said softly in her ear before he addressed Santibanez again. "Does he have any close friends? Who does he hang out with? Anything you can give us would help."

"Any friends?" Santibanez twisted up his face. "Yeah. One guy stands out. I thought it was weird PJ would ever get to know someone like this, but he said they met in Mexico. Said he did some work for him and they, uh, they became friends. This guy moved up to Albuquerque a couple of years ago." Santibanez shook his head, obviously trying to gather his thoughts. "He's a doctor. Actually, a transplant surgeon. Works around the state on an organ retrieval team. His name is—"

"Meloni," Nicky said. "Emilio Meloni."

CHAPTER FORTY-FOUR

It seemed like she'd just fallen into a restless sleep when the buzzing of her cell woke her. She snapped on the lamp beside her bed and winced at the bright light. Her hand fumbled to put her glasses on and she peered at the phone's screen. After midnight. Her gaze dropped—a text from Ryan.

I'm at the front door.

Savannah sank her head back on the pillow and exhaled. *Thank God.* Phone in hand, she kicked the bedcovers off her legs and, barefoot, hurried to the door, glad she'd worn leggings and a loose top instead of her baby-doll pajamas. She flipped the porch light on, disengaged the dead bolt, and swung open the door, ready to fling herself into Ryan's arms.

And stopped dead.

"Hello, Savannah." He smiled as his gaze slid down and back up her body. *Skeezy PJ* popped into her head.

"PJ? What are you doing here? How did you—?"

PJ Santibanez walked toward her. Savannah scuttled back. Her heart beat double-time.

"How did we get past the FBI agents out front? Yeah. About those guys." His head tipped to the side and he smiled. "Sorry."

She whirled and dashed to the kitchen. If she could get out into the desert behind her house, she could—

The French doors to her patio slammed open with a bang, the wood frame splintered. Savannah screamed as two men in black jeans and shirts surged into her house, grabbed her arms, and flipped her around. Her glasses went flying and the world blurred. Hollow terror shot to her core and her knees collapsed beneath her, but the men kept her on her feet.

PJ sauntered into the kitchen, turned on the overhead light, and wrested the cell phone out of her hand. He waggled his brows and waved it at her as another man walked in behind him.

"Your phone. It's infected, you know. Courtesy of your friend Nicky Matthews," the second man said. "I bet she thought the FBI did it."

Savannah tried to focus, but her body shook so badly, his face remained fuzzy. Medium height, slim. The skin of his head reflected the light above him. He stopped in front of her and she thought he smiled.

"You're right, PJ. She is perfect. Perfect size, perfect sex, young, healthy." The man pressed his palm over the top of her left breast. Savannah froze, voice trapped in her chest, tears burning. "Perfect heart." His hand slid up to circle her throat. She whimpered and fought with everything she had.

"Hold her," he commanded.

One of the men behind her grabbed a fistful of hair and yanked her head back. Pain made her gasp. The bald man's hand reached for her neck again, but this time two fingers pressed against her rapidly throbbing pulse.

"Strong heartbeat. Excellent. Mr. Salas will be very pleased. And you." He addressed Savannah. "Genetically, you are a one hundred percent HLA null. Did you know that? Thank goodness I found out about the database when I did. It *literally* saved my life." He touched her cheek with the tip of a finger. "Too bad it won't save yours."

"*Su corazón. ¿Funcionará?*" one of the men behind her ground out.

This time, Savannah knew the bald man smiled. She could hear it in his voice.

"*Si, mi amigo. Perfecta.*"

CHAPTER FORTY-FIVE

Nicky hardly noticed the flashing lights of the slot machines or the thick smell of stale cigarette smoke as she and Franco hurried through the dark casino. Even after midnight it was packed with people who drove up from Albuquerque or down from Santa Fe and all the cities in between. The discordant clang of jackpots and a local rock band playing in a disco that was curtained off from the casino scorched her ears.

"Call Laughton," she yelled to Franco. "Tell him we need the Albuquerque FBI here ASAP, and have him send a team to Meloni's home and lab at OMI. And he needs to alert Fire-Sky police. Have them put out an APB on PJ Santibanez."

Franco nodded and pressed his phone against his ear as they pushed through the bank of glass doors and into the heavy air of the coming storm. He relayed her requests as they jogged to her unit. When they arrived, he handed her the phone, lips pressed thin.

"He doesn't believe—He won't—" His teeth ground audibly. "He wants to talk to you."

"What is it?" Nicky didn't try to keep impatience out of her voice. She unlocked her truck and leaped inside.

"Bernal is with me now," Laughton said. "We checked his alibi for the Maryellen K'aishuni search. He's been cleared. I'm taking him back to Savannah's place."

"Martinez and I are headed that way, too."

Franco climbed into the passenger side of Nicky's unit and slammed his door. She handed the phone back to him. He hit speaker as they sped out of the parking lot and held the phone near her face.

"Before I proceed, I need more information," Laughton said. "You're saying there are two killers? Our profilers—"

"Listen," Nicky interrupted. "The Jekyll-and-Hyde part is correct, but your profilers were wrong about a single killer." She negotiated the turn onto the main highway through the pueblo. "There are two men, two killers. Hyde is PJ Santibanez. He uses his rage against the culture and traditions that rejected him. He's subverted the Enemy's Heart Ceremony, killing tribal members and taking their hearts so they become lost. In a way, it's the same thing that was done to him when he was rejected by his father. He's been torn from the heart of his culture and this is how he enacts his revenge. Emilio Meloni is Jekyll, precisely harvesting the hearts of selected individuals. I was at his lab. He experiments on human organs and hearts. He told me they were legally obtained, but I think he's as twisted as PJ. Secure his lab immediately. Those organs need to be DNA-tested to see if they match any missing Fire-Sky tribal members."

There was a heavy silence on the other end of the line.

"Meloni's not keeping those hearts for testing," Laughton said. "*He's our link to the Coahuilan drug cartel. I received a call tonight about Mariano Salas, the cartel boss. He's on the move again. Our sources put him in Juárez. With his family. With his daughter.*"

"What?" Franco said. Nicky flashed him a glance. His face was stiff with surprise. "I thought she was too sick to move. I thought her heart disease had progressed to the point where she was close to death." He sucked in a sharp breath. "Unless she gets a new heart. God. How did we miss it?"

His words froze Nicky's blood. She pulled her truck to the side of the road and took the phone.

"HLA, Laughton. Fire-Sky individuals with pure blood quantum can be genetically identified by a high number of null HLA alleles. That's what David Saunders showed with his DNA database. You're a doctor. What does that mean?"

"Null HLA. Human leukocyte antigen. The proteins made by the HLA genes identify self. If these proteins are not made—or null—tissue and organs aren't recognized as non-self or foreign once they're transplanted into another body. They don't get rejected."

"That means pure-blood Fire-Sky Indians are the perfect organ donors," Nicky said. "It's only a six-hour drive to Mexico from here. If Salas is in Juárez with his daughter, then Meloni and PJ Santibanez have probably identified or even taken a victim for the heart transplant. They could be on their way now."

Laughton cursed. "Put Franco back on," he said.

Nicky handed the phone back to Franco. He wrapped his fingers tightly around her hand. She pressed her forehead to his, taking and giving comfort.

The night was far from over.

"Let's get coordinated at Savannah's place. I'll call the agents watching her house," Laughton said, "and tell them we're on our way." He hung up.

Nicky accelerated back onto the road. Rain spattered the windshield and the bright beams of her headlights punched sharp circles out of the darkness. Suddenly an animal darted out in front of the truck, a white flash that zagged across the wet blacktop and into the rain- and wind-washed chamisa at the side of the road. She gasped, hit the brakes, and swerved. Franco braced his arm against the dash as the truck stopped.

"Did you see that? Did you see—?" Her voice shook and adrenaline pumped dizzily through her body.

"It was a rabbit, Nicky, that's all. Just a rabbit."

"No, Franco. It wasn't just a rabbit. It was a *white* rabbit." She looked at him, his face illuminated in the eerie green light of the dashboard. "They already have their victim," she whispered. "We don't have much time."

CHAPTER FORTY-SIX

Nicky hit her lights and fishtailed her unit onto the rain-slicked road. She gritted her teeth, hands tight on the steering wheel. Just a few more minutes.

About a mile from Savannah's home, the cell phone rang again. Franco hit speaker.

"The men I stationed at Savannah's house. They're not answering. Neither is Savannah." Laughton's voice was clipped.

Goose bumps peppered Nicky's arms. She punched the gas and the truck squealed on wet pavement as it sailed around the entrance to Savannah and Ryan's neighborhood.

"We parked at Bernal's. Come in quiet. Watch for us," Laughton said. The phone clicked off.

Nicky cut her lights and used her truck to block one end of the road. Savannah's home sat on the last street of the neighborhood, nothing but desert behind her. She and Franco would approach from the left. Ryan's duplex was situated to the right. A distant streetlight only dimly illuminated the car stationed in front of Savannah's house. There was no movement inside it.

The rain slowed to a gentle, steady shower. Thunder grumbled. Nicky stepped out of the truck and pulled her Glock. She slipped two more magazines into her back pocket. Weapon in hand, Franco motioned silently for her to move in behind him. Hunched, they ran forward, from parked car to parked car, until they stopped in Savannah's driveway and crouched behind her white compact. Shadowy blurs traveled up the street from the direction of Ryan's house. One man broke off and ran to the dark sedan parked at the curb. The other loped like a wolf around the back of the house next to Savannah's.

Nicky and Franco crept to the edge of the long porch. Laughton met them there.

"Silva and Lwowski are unresponsive. I think they've been drugged." He held out his hand. "With this."

Franco picked up the vial and syringe. "Ketamine."

Stomach hollow, Nicky forced herself to breathe evenly. She was no good to Savannah if she couldn't stay focused. "We need to find her. Two entrances. The back door into the den. Front door into the living room," she whispered.

Laughton motioned he'd go to the back.

She and Franco ducked low to avoid the curtained window. Then Franco stood, weapon in hand, Nicky at his shoulder. The door was cracked open and Franco pushed it hard, yelling, "DEA! Police!" as he rushed inside.

The room was dark except for the porch light shining in behind them and the kitchen light coming through the archway. They quickly surveyed and determined no one hid behind furniture or curtains, when the back door slammed open and Laughton shouted, "FBI!" Within seconds, he yelled, "Kitchen, den, clear. Back door lock broken."

She and Franco headed down the hall to the bedrooms and Nicky sealed herself against finding Savannah bleeding, broken—or dead. The rooms were empty, but that was almost as wrenching.

She hurried back to the kitchen in time to see Ryan pick up Savannah's glasses from the floor and place them gently on the kitchen counter.

"They took her." He choked and stared at Nicky. "Why?"

"Because of her DNA. Her blood quantum," she replied through stiff lips. The completed puzzle of evidence she'd been working on since Sandra Deering's death fell into place. "They can't have been gone long. We can catch them—"

Ryan pulled his knife and darted through the back door. The three of them jumped after him. Nicky yanked out her flashlight and spotlighted Ryan as he dove into a large chamisa. High-pitched shrieks and a frantic spate of Keres filled the night. Ryan dragged Howard Kie from of the bush and threw him to the sand.

"*Dza! Dza! Chishe diya!* Apache dog!" Howard screamed.

Ryan plucked Howard to his feet and pushed him hard toward the house. He fell to his hands and knees and Ryan stalked up to him, planted his foot in the middle of his behind, and shoved.

Howard landed flat on his stomach, his glasses slipping to the end of his nose. He scrambled to his feet and whipped out a butter knife. "You almost killed me, *Chishe diya!*"

Arm raised, he ran at Ryan, who simply grabbed his wrist and twisted. With a squeak, Howard dropped his knife. Ryan thrust him away again.

"I still may kill you, *dyeetya.*"

Howard faced Nicky, a scowl on his face. "You saw what the *Chishe diya* did. Arrest him."

Nicky grabbed Howard's arm and frog-marched him into Savannah's kitchen.

"Sit." She tossed him into a chair. "Howard, did you see who took Savannah?" The men gathered around and Howard shrank back.

"You will protect me from"—his head jerked up at the three men— "them," he whispered, blinking up at her.

Nicky nodded.

"I saw. I been following PJ. He was mean to me in school. Like that guy." He frowned and notched his chin at Ryan. "PJ Santibanez, he was up at the cave during the Enemy's Heart Ceremony, but he is no war chief. He was banished from the rez, like that guy." Again, at Ryan. "PJ slipped away when those guys came." He jerked his head at Franco and Laughton. "I followed him ever since. He was dating Sandra, too."

Nicky almost groaned as Howard relayed his information. If only she'd questioned him more closely. If only she'd known what to ask.

"I got my cousin's mini-bike, but I left it in the desert. PJ and some bald guy took Savannah. They had two big *Baasu'um'e* with them. They kicked in the back door and took her. I hid. I knew you would come," he said to Nicky. "You are her friend. Savannah was nice to me in school." He sneered at Ryan. "That *Chishe* wasn't nice to me."

"*Baasu'um'e.* Mexicans," Nicky interpreted, pulse racing. "They must be going to Juárez. You need to alert Border Patrol and put out a BOLO—"

"No." Both Howard and Ryan said at the same time.

"There are tire marks out back heading north," Ryan said. "That black truck in the desert, the one we thought was FBI and watched the house? It wasn't." He scowled at Laughton.

"Not Mexico." Howard shook his head. "The bald guy said they are going to the mountain. To the caves."

Franco's face was white and grim. "Like in the Chiricahua," he murmured.

"The Sacred Caves. Meloni said something about how he would rather have a lair than a lab," Nicky said. "He must have some place set up in the caves on Scalding Peak. That's where he takes his victims for organ harvest. Right under our nose. Taunting us."

She rushed to the door and looked up at the cloud-shrouded mountain. The lights—the souls of the victims—that streamed from Wind Mother's skull had flown up the side of Scalding Peak. To the Second Sacred Caves.

Nicky closed her eyes on a quick prayer, then turned to the men.

"Laughton, send the BOLO and call for Fire-Sky police to secure this scene. We have to go now." She gave Ryan and Franco a searing look. "I'm pretty sure I know where they took her. I hope to God I'm right."

CHAPTER FORTY-SEVEN

They ran to Nicky's truck.

Howard called, "Shotgun," and slapped at Ryan when he opened the passenger door to yank him out.

"No. Leave him," Nicky said and handed Howard her flashlight as he gave Ryan a smirk. Howard knew the drill. Hopefully, he wouldn't drop the light as they got closer to their destination.

With three very large men crowded in the backseat of her unit, she drove toward Scalding Peak. Laughton and Franco were on their phones, talking rapidly before they lost signal. One called a prosecutor for the search and arrest warrants, the other directed the FBI and police to secure Savannah's house and to pick up Peter Santibanez and Dinah K'aishuni as persons of interest. They sent teams to OMI and Meloni's lab and apartment. And to find Julie Knuteson. They needed to make sure she was okay.

There was a brief lull, Franco and Laughton speaking quietly to each other, when Ryan's phone rang.

He hissed, "It's Savannah's number." He pressed the icon to put it on speaker. "Savannah. Baby? Where are you?"

"Ryan?" Her voice shook piteously. "They told me I could make one phone call, to say goodbye—" She choked. "I couldn't call Mom and Dad. I knew I could trust you to . . . to . . . tell them—" Savannah was sobbing into the phone now.

"Savannah—"

Nicky glanced into the rearview. Franco had shoved his phone under Ryan's nose and his eyes scanned the screen.

"I'm still at the police station," he said. "Where are you? I'll come get you—"

Another voice came on speaker. "God*dammit*, PJ! This isn't a game. Turn the phone *off*." Meloni.

The phone call ended abruptly and a chime sounded within seconds.

"It's a picture of Savannah in the backseat of a truck," Ryan said flatly.

"That means they have signal. They're still on the mountain, not at the caves. We can't be that far behind," Nicky declared.

She wanted to go faster, but the road was slick with rain and beginning its wind up the mountain.

"If they believe Ryan is still at the station and that we don't know where they're headed, they might not be as prepared for us. Counting the Mexicans, there are at least four of them. They won't hesitate to kill. We need to devise a plan," Nicky said as she passed the Kuwami K'uuti lookout and headed to the second spur of the old gravel logging road. She nodded to Howard as she turned off her headlights and dimmed the interior.

Nicky described the area around the Second Sacred Caves, Ryan—and Howard—giving details, even as Howard hung out of the truck window, flashlight beam steady on the road. Fresh tire marks in the mud ahead made Nicky's limbs weak with relief. They were on the right track. A sense of calm settled over her.

They'd all slipped into a purposeful demeanor, resolution unwavering, fear and panic gone. Warrior mode, cop mode, whatever it was called, Nicky could feel it. There was a basic understanding of the dangers, and an acceptance. They had a job to do and God forbid anyone get in their way.

"How do you know so much about the caves, Nicky?" Franco asked. "I thought they were off-limits to anyone but Fire-Sky war chiefs." His voice was steady, unruffled, with a hint of a smile in it.

"This is *my* beat, Agent Martinez. *My* territory. I make it my business to know every inch." Nicky curved her lips up. "At least on the outside. I've never actually been in the caves." She dropped her smile. "Are you gonna be all right?"

He met her gaze in the mirror and answered simply, "Yes. I have to be."

They crept along for what seemed like an eternity before Nicky told Howard to turn off the flashlight. They were close now, just a couple of switchbacks until the parking area. The half-moon in the sky seemed to weave in and out of the dissipating rain clouds, giving scant illumination, but it was enough to move forward.

She maneuvered around a sharp corner. "Now." The door behind her clicked open and Franco and Ryan bailed out. On foot, they could move much faster up the rugged slope than she could drive along the winding road. They'd get in position and wait for her. She and her unit would act as a target, a decoy, in case the Mexican cartel members guarded the outside of the caves.

As she hit another switchback, Laughton slipped out of the truck and disappeared up the slope. He would come at any guards from above.

"Time for you to get out, Howard. Once I top that rise, they can see the truck. It's too dangerous for you," she whispered.

"You are brave and a girl. I am a man. If you stay, I'll stay and keep you company." He sniffed. "There are large rocks on either side of the road. We can duck behind those."

The truck crawled forward.

"Okay, but you bail on my command. Ready?" she whispered.

Chin high, lips and brow pooched in determination, Howard gave her the thumbs-up.

CHAPTER FORTY-EIGHT

Nicky hit the sirens and her brights, stomped down on the gas. Tires spun in the mud and gravel flew before they caught and the truck shot over the hill, front grille high, and bounced down. Her headlights lit up a black four-wheel drive vehicle, two men, and flashes of powder as they fired. A bullet pinged against metal, then another and another. There was no pop of gunfire. The guards used suppressors.

The windshield cracked into crazed patterns as the bullets hit. Nicky dipped her head down and zigzagged the truck on the road, swiping bushes, glancing off trees. The side-view mirror crunched against a branch with a discordant metallic scrape.

Her unit approached the rocks Howard had indicated and she stomped the brake, yelling, "Get out! Now!" Nicky whipped open the door and flung her feet to the ground, ducking as she ran behind the open door. She let the truck roll forward, her guiding hand on the steering wheel for as long as possible. The passenger seat was empty, door half open. Howard was out.

Shots barked and bullets still pinged, but not as thickly. She heard a scream of pain and smiled grimly. Her guys were there. She dove behind the rocks and scrambled to her feet, gun leveled at the scene. The unmanned vehicle sped up, its trajectory downhill. One man lunged out of the way as it slammed into the parked truck. The siren cut off. The guy rolled and came to his feet practically in the arms of Franco, who punched him in the temple, threw him to the ground, and straddled him from behind. The dark figure of a man stepped from behind a tree, gun pointed at Franco. Nicky squeezed the trigger and the Glock bucked in her hand. The figure jerked and spun into the darkness. Franco swiftly cuffed the guy on the ground and leaped down the slope after the second man.

She raced toward the vehicles, scanning for movement under the swirl of red and blue lights from her unit. There was a blur of motion up the hill, and a tree exploded behind her. She turned to shoot, only to wrench her weapon down as a shadow enveloped the gunman. His head jerked back and a knife glinted silver in the moonlight. Ryan bent close and whispered something into the man's ear before he dropped him. Another bad guy took off down the road. Laughton exploded out of the trees in pursuit.

Franco grabbed Nicky's arm when she would have followed. "No. Donny was black ops before med school and the FBI. He needs to catch and stop that guy before he can get to cell service and alert Salas. You'll distract him."

"The guy down the hill." She sucked in a breath. "The one I—"

"The one who would have killed me," Franco said. "He'll live." He drew her to the edge of the flat dirt lot. A low groan emanated from the undergrowth. "Trussed up good and tight, but he's a big fellow—well, he's got quite a gut—so I left him there. Didn't want to strain my back." He smiled at her before he turned his head. "That all, Ryan?"

"Yep." Ryan calmly wiped the blood from his knife onto his shirt, a gun stuck in his waistband. He leaned into Nicky's unit and turned off the lights.

"Him?" Nicky motioned to the guy Franco had taken down. He wasn't moving.

"He'll have quite a headache when he wakes up," Franco said matter-of-factly. "I count three here, plus the one Laughton went after. Everyone whole? That guy on the hill. The one who shot at Nicky. What'd you say to him?" Franco asked Ryan.

"A prayer for the dead so his spirit won't haunt me. Good practice opportunity. I wanted to make sure I remembered it when I use it for PJ."

Nicky stared, processing his words, then swallowed and dipped her head. Ryan smiled faintly and nodded back.

Franco pressed his open hand on the hood of the black SUV. "Engine's still warm. They haven't been here for long."

"No Meloni or PJ," Nicky said. She straightened her shoulders, refocused. "They must have taken Savannah to the cave. Unless there's another place to park, my guess is that these guys are it, as far as guards."

"Two of them were behind Savannah's house earlier today. She's here." Ryan's voice was hard.

"All right, then. We need to get her back." Nicky reached inside her truck and pulled out a small flashlight. She handed it to Ryan. Franco had one under the barrel of his gun. She opened the glove compartment and grabbed two baggies full of plastic sticks, each about the size of a match. Slipping one out, she snapped it between her fingers and dropped it at her feet. It glowed with an eerie green luminescence.

"Thought I'd never have a use for these," Nicky said with a half smile. She scooped a handful before giving a bag to each man. "They'll be our bread crumbs in the caves, so we can find our way out." She looked back and forth at Franco and Ryan's shadowed faces. "I wish I knew more about the layout. Ryan?"

He shook his head.

"I know. Something." Howard's voice piped up from a nearby thicket. He scuttled forward, brushed away leaves at Nicky's feet, and picked up the tiny glow-stick. "Used to come up here as a kid and play war chief. Inside, keep to the right. Always. The floor slopes down for two hundred and four steps. I counted them. At the end of the tunnel, it forks into a series of six interconnected rooms, each ten to twelve steps wide and long. Good places for ambush," he said and met their eyes. "They all connect to larger caverns. One of those is the sacred space. It has a bottomless pit. It is where our ancestors performed ceremonies." He held the little stick to his face, his lips pulled down into a frown. "I cannot go. I am not properly dressed. If you give me a gun . . ." His voice was expectant.

"No guns," Nicky said and fervently hoped she and Franco had secured all the bad guys' weapons. That's all they needed: Howard with a weapon more lethal than a butter knife. "But you can wait for Agent

Laughton. Tell him what you told us. Franco." She pressed a hand to his arm. "You have cave experience. You're up."

The three of them left Howard in the road and jogged to the edge of the clearing.

"Okay. We go in ten seconds apart, me first, then Nicky. You last," Franco said to Ryan. "Watch for traps and trip wires. In the cave, keep your light away from you, to the side. They'll shoot at the light. Keep your voices low. Sound travels. The goal of this mission is to find and extract Savannah, nothing more. Understood?"

Ryan grunted.

"Ryan, go left around the meadow. Check the perimeter. We'll head right and meet at the cave entrance," Franco said.

The storm had drifted south and the moon glowed. A cool, wet breeze soughed gently through the tall pines, scattering little pops of water on the pine-needle-covered ground. The dark side of the mountain rose jagged with shadows. Across the small meadow, the opening of the cave gaped blackly.

Ryan crept soft-footed into the forest and disappeared.

As Nicky and Franco traversed through the woods, he whispered, "You never confirmed, Matthews." He slowed and she stepped in close behind him. "Save Savannah, then get out. Understood?"

"Aye-aye, Captain," Nicky replied in a low voice, searching the trees. And if she was able to stop the bad guys, too—

She didn't expect Franco to grab her. He pushed her up against a tree and kissed her. Hard.

He eased away, his lips lingering, and said hoarsely, "That's for saving my life back there." He gave her a little shake and she gasped. He was so close, so warm. "Don't do anything stupid in there. Please. I still owe you dinner." Franco released her, let out a long breath, and pulled his gun. "Let's do this."

Nicky nodded, speechless.

They headed to the cave.

CHAPTER FORTY-NINE

Nicky stared at the cave entrance, a smoothed archway wide enough for two people. Entering could be dangerous. If PJ or Meloni had heard the firefight, they could be waiting in ambush. Ryan played his light down the passage, but it curved to the right within about twenty yards.

The dirt and sand around the opening was peppered with footprints—no one had made an effort to sweep. Maybe they were in too much of a hurry. She extended her hand. There was a strong wind, damp and warm, that blew straight out of the cave, its scent pungent enough to taste—herby, mildewy, dusty, but not unpleasant.

"Ancient Fire-Sky stories tell of the *k'uuti tsa'atsi*—mountain's breath—that originates from hidden lakes deep within," Ryan whispered.

Franco stood rigid next to her and she placed a hand on his back. "Hey. You all right?" He stared into the gloomy passageway, jaw set.

Ryan edged forward, knife in one hand, flashlight in the other. "I'll go first—"

"No," Franco said. He wiped his brow with his sleeve. "Go slow, stay low. Don't ever look directly at any light. Keep your own light down and away from your eyes. Use it as a weapon to blind your opponents, to give yourself a few seconds." He turned to Nicky. "Count to ten and follow. One-Mississippi, two-Mississippi . . ." His back disappeared in the darkness of the cave before he switched his light on. Nicky pressed a hand against the Spirit's Heart pendant and counted. At five-Mississippi,

Franco's light winked out as he turned the corner. By eight-Mississippi, her stomach was knotted. At ten-Mississippi, she squeezed Ryan's arm, took a deep breath, and stepped into the cave.

Keep to the right. She prayed Howard's info was good as she crept forward. Like Franco, she waited until all light evaporated before she turned on her flashlight. She held it away from her body, gun gripped in her right hand.

Nicky ran the beam around the walls of the cave, heart pounding with each step, and remembered what Franco had said about measuring the dimensions, how it calmed him. The walls and ceiling this close to the opening were hand-worked and smooth, a perfect arch. The floor was packed dirt, like an ancient lava tube that had been filled halfway.

She peered into the darkness, straining to see Franco's light ahead of her. Nothing. Swiveling around, she looked for Ryan's, but the cave snail-curved and dropped, hiding both men.

At fifty paces, she snapped and dropped a glow-stick. At one hundred paces, the tunnel divided. She stayed right and found one of Franco's sticks. Pressing her wrist against her mouth, she smiled and just stood for a moment. So far, so good.

The passage snaked left and the ceiling dropped. The wind—what had Ryan called it?—*k'uuti tsa'atsi* sped up and whistled faintly and her ponytail tickled the skin of her neck. Craggy walls with dark niches folded around her, perfect hiding places. Someone could be close enough to touch her and she wouldn't even know. She popped and dropped another stick. The tiny glow made her feel better. Nicky trained her light on the ground. It sloped dramatically as she continued her descent.

Another split, another of Franco's glow-sticks, this time tucked into the wall at knee-level. The floor flattened out, but the path narrowed. Her hand was clammy with sweat and she holstered her weapon to wipe her palm down her thigh. How much farther? She'd lost count of her steps. Gun in hand once again, she pushed forward. The blowing air around her hummed louder with each step. The hair on her head and arms stood on end.

Something was off.

She tensed and swept her flashlight frantically. Strong hands grabbed and pulled her into a shallow alcove. Franco's scent surrounded her and she slumped into his chest, heart pounding in her ears. He pressed her light against his side to hide it. With trembling fingers, she fumbled with the switch.

"Generators. We're close." His lips tickled her ear. A warm hand slid over her chin to tilt it higher. His other arm rotated her body until his scratchy cheek pressed against her temple. "Up there. Cable and closed-circuit cameras."

Her eyes adjusted and the tunnel rocks grayed. Lights on somewhere, their glow erasing a percentage of the darkness. She could just make out a thick bundle of cables tacked to the ceiling.

"We've probably been made, but I want Ryan to be a surprise. Stay here."

And he left her to stride back up the tunnel like he was strolling in the park on Sunday. Nicky laid her gun across her chest, straining to hear anything beyond the generator's underlying thump. She tipped her head. A low, undulating sound emerged behind it. Voices?

A rock clicked down the floor of the cave, like it had been kicked or thrown. She crouched, gripped her weapon, and stared into the darkness. Franco, his large body and face a gray blur, ambled toward her, nodding as he passed. His vague silhouette grabbed the cables, gave a powerful yank, and pulled down the wiring above him. The camera swung into the stone with a crunch.

A faint, "Dammit!" echoed from the end of the tunnel. Meloni? PJ?

Ryan silently tucked in beside her. Nicky frowned. "I could have shot you," she whispered.

"Nah. You're too good for that." His teeth flashed with a smile. "Franco says there are two openings, farther down, along either side of this wall. They lead to the interconnected rooms. He's our diversion. You right, me left. Be careful." He tugged her ponytail and slunk away.

Blood rushed hard through her veins. Go time.

Franco still crashed around somewhere ahead of her as she glided down the tunnel, stepping over the downed cables. An opening blacker than the walls lay about ten yards forward. She slid in, held her breath, and listened.

There was nothing. She switched on her flashlight, narrowed its beam, and ran the light around the chamber. Her flesh crawled as she cataloged the contents. Small white coolers painted with a thick red stripe lined the lowest rung of shelves stacked against the wall. A sticker on the side read: HUMAN ORGAN FOR TRANSPLANT. Boxed packages of saline drips and needles rested neatly above the coolers. Tubing, masks, and disinfectant in square brown bottles were lined up next to plastic-wrapped surgical drapes and cases of scalpels. Meloni and PJ were well stocked. It was obvious they'd been doing this for a while. She traversed the room and found a gap in the wall barred with a metal door. It wasn't locked. Did they keep their victims here until they were ready to harvest? She pushed the door and winced as the metal hinges groaned. Her light held away from her, she ran the beam around the second room. Empty but for a cot.

Inside, the scent of cigarettes, stale urine, and sweat was suffocating, and the walls closed in tightly. She could almost hear their sobs, feel their panic. Nicky squeezed her eyes shut and sagged against the cold stone. So many people—so many *spirits*—sacrificed by a pair of monsters masquerading as human beings. They had to be stopped.

Anger built and thrust away the despair that threatened to swamp her. She straightened. First Savannah. *Then* . . .

A second unlocked grate led to another connected room, brighter gray and brown walls inside. Light spilled in from somewhere. As Nicky stole toward the next room, the generator noises became louder. She peeked around the edge of the last opening and her eyes widened. The connecting cavern was huge. Tucked along the wall, lights illuminated a high, curved ceiling with mineralized water stains and fields of tiny stalactites. The floor was stone, with worn paths between bulging pillars of rock, and the air smelled of dust and bleach.

She detected no movement and stepped out from the door. A draped and curtained tent against the far wall drew her immediate gaze. Light from the interior cast shadows from what looked like a tall bed and metal instrument tables. Amassed beside it were a dozen chest-high canisters plastered with angry red COMPRESSED HYDROGEN GAS, HIGHLY FLAMMABLE, NO SMOKING stickers. They stood next to half a dozen smaller oxygen tanks.

PJ and Meloni harvested their hearts here.

At least three openings squared with stacked stone cut through the walls of the cavern. Nicky identified one that might lead back to the corridor out of this place. Another doorway, a dozen yards behind the surgical room, glowed with light and throbbed with generators. Electrical cords ran from it to the draped tent. Her gaze trailed back to a rounded hole, circled with crumbling rocks, that dropped through the middle of the floor. She sidled closer. Air blew out of it, hot and wet. Howard's bottomless pit.

The last opening was a dark, jagged gap to the right. She walked toward it, skirting the embedded rocks, some taller than her. The click of her flashlight was loud as she turned it on. Its beam glimmered against a black metal grate. It would be the perfect place to keep a victim.

Gun ready, she inched closer, her gaze darting all around her. She didn't know where Ryan or Franco were. Hadn't heard anything over the throbbing sound of the generator. How long had she been alone? Ten minutes? Fifteen?

"Savannah? Are you in there?" Another step. She leaned forward, searching the blackness. "Savannah?"

Movement flashed and Nicky jerked in pain. She brought her gun around, only to have her wrist whacked with a numbing strike. Her weapon went flying. It clattered off the rocks and fell into the bottomless hole. Swiveling, she leveled the flashlight's beam directly into her attacker's eyes and he scuttled back. With numb fingers, she yanked out a syringe stuck in her shoulder.

Suddenly her mind seemed to catch on a breath and whirl away. She wobbled and stopped herself from falling by grabbing a pillar of stone. It cut into her hand and the pain briefly cleared her head.

"God*dammit*! You almost blinded me!"

A voice ricocheted weirdly off the ceiling and ballooned behind her eyes. Human-shaped shadows stuttered in front of her, doubled and tripled, brilliant colors pulsating around them. She shook her head to make them go away, but it only became worse. A hand reached toward her—or maybe away—and spun wildly, like a kaleidoscope, and a giggle sounded. She belatedly realized it came from her.

"Ketamine acts so bizarrely. It's all dependent on the individual." Someone spoke but the sound came from all directions.

The shadows slid sideways. Nicky dragged a foot to follow, but her head lolled. She shook it again and her brain washed back and forth in her skull.

"Oh, by the way, your love interest is dead in the tunnel over there. PJ bashed his head in with a rock."

Franco. Nicky started to cry, but laughed instead. "No," she sang and stumbled to another large rock. Her knee slammed against it and her mind cleared again—for an instant. "Where is he? Where's PJ?" No. Not PJ. Franco. Meloni wavered in front of her. She swiped at him, staggered. Lights around his multiple heads popped and jumped.

"Around here somewhere. But I'm over here. Come and get me. You know, he's been a good partner, a good friend. He led me to Fire-Sky Indians as organ donors, although at first we didn't know what we had. We actually met in Mexico. I was a surgeon in a very professional, completely illegal black market organ transplant ring. He, shall we say, procured the donors. That's where he told me about the Enemy's Heart Ceremony and his desire for revenge against the Fire-Sky people. It seemed a match made in heaven. I got the organs I needed and, according to his culture and traditions, he destroyed their very souls as they'd destroyed his."

Nicky stopped her forward motion. The shadows had consolidated, but now the lights bounced like rubber balls.

"Come on. Almost there," Meloni coaxed, like he was calling a dog. He stepped closer to the operating tent. "PJ targeted that Downs woman. Lured her with a white rabbit, isolated her away from her family and all she knew. I thought it was kind of cruel, myself." He shrugged and his whole body rippled. "But he said she was the core of all his problems. Really a sick young man. I was disappointed, though. We couldn't use her heart because of her trisomy," he continued as Nicky scuffed forward. "But he told me to have patience. Said her parents would never give up on her, no matter how much her DNA was . . . wrong. And he was right. The scout they hired was surprised to see PJ, but trusted him. I don't remember his name." Nicky tried to tell him—Vernon—but couldn't work her lips. "I used his heart for a transplant and it was amazing. There was no rejection, no complications." He backed away and Nicky followed. "A little to the left, Nicky. May I call you Nicky?" He loomed larger. She swung a fist through air, noting her hand was long and black. Her flashlight. "Now, now. Behave. The job at OMI was brilliant. Made it much easier to select donors. We don't know how Sandra Deering found out about our— for lack of a better word—project. What wasn't so easy was to delete all of her electronic records. But we did."

Nicky stopped. Opened her mouth. "Howard was her friend. He knew."

"Howard Kie? Easy to divert. All PJ had to do was drop the hint the war chiefs were behind this, and that guy was off and running. But it made him hard to catch. He would have made a great donor. Keep walking, Sergeant." He continued his rambling conversation. It drew her, compelled her to follow. "And who would've thought Saunders would tattle about Sandra's missing heart? Did you know I used it to test my perfusate? Nothing like the real thing, baby. It'll be hell to publish, though." He grinned, and Nicky squinted. Both of his faces crinkled up. "PJ thought if we took Saunders, we'd have more time. When David *finally* figured out what we were doing, he tried to bargain for his life with the DNA database. Explained the HLA markers, everything. But we really didn't need him. Julie Knuteson had found his files, so it was easier to go through her."

"Why are you talking so much?" Nicky asked and leaned into a standing rock. She was so sleepy and he wouldn't shut up.

"Didn't Julie tell you I had quirks?" He snickered. "She kept me abreast of your progress, you know. And I used her phone to send you a dandy little virus when I called the night of the blessing. The night of the rattlesnake. That was PJ's idea. He hoped you'd get bitten while we chatted. And since I had to keep you on the line, I chatted away about Saunders's database, never thinking you were intelligent enough to understand the implications. But you realized why we took Savannah. It was the cheetahs, wasn't it?" Meloni sighed. "I've always been an over-sharer. Are you sleepy, Sergeant? Come lie down over here and you can close your eyes." He backed up again and she pursued. It felt like she was floating.

"Mariano Salas—the cartel boss—his daughter needs a new heart. Savannah was perfect. We had her prepped, ready, and now she's gone. Who took her?"

Nicky's relief was so profound, she almost dropped to her knees. Savannah was gone. Rescued. "Ryan . . ." Ryan must have, because Franco was—She sobbed.

"Ryan Bernal," Meloni muttered. "Figures. So, here's the problem. I need a heart, or I'm a dead man. Since yours is the only one available . . ."

She reared back, relief and sadness replaced with bone-chilling cold. Then she giggled and the cavern spun around her.

"I know. Hilarious. Into the operating room. Come on." He pulled back one of the curtains.

His voice coerced her shaking muscles into motion. Nicky zigzagged toward him. He patted the empty cot and turned away from her for a split second. She swung the flashlight like a club at the most solid set of fingers on the bed. His scream was high-pitched and agonized. She cracked the flashlight against his chin and his teeth snapped. Meloni toppled to the ground in slow motion, taking the instrument tables and draped sides of the tent with him.

Nicky lurched into the black interior of the tunnel and ran. She tripped over a large soft object a dozen feet in, coming down hard on her shoulder. Panting, she crabbed-walked back. PJ Santibanez, his neck twisted unnaturally, his gut a black glistening mass, lay on the blood-soaked dirt. Lungs frozen, she stared as his head rotated toward her. He blinked and grinned, exposing blood-stained fangs and a fluttering forked tongue. She catapulted to her feet, slammed blindly into the wall, and fell to her backside. A shock of pain jarred through her and her flashlight rolled away.

Hallucinations. Ryan said ketamine brings hallucinations.

Scrambling to her feet, Nicky sidestepped along the wall, looking back to see if PJ followed her.

"You broke my hand, oh, God, my hand," Meloni whimpered. "I will *eviscerate* you! Carve you into pieces!" His voice rose to a feverish wail.

But she didn't care. Savannah was safe. A wave of lassitude washed over her as she dragged her body into darkness. The tunnel opening telescoped madly, the light at the end pulsing like a heartbeat. Her eyes and nose stung with tears and a sob croaked from her throat. He would get her. No one would find her. She'd be lost. Like Sandra, Maryellen, Vernon . . . *Franco*—

"Nicky." A voice rasped out of the darkness.

She swayed. "Franco? He said you were dead."

Franco's body glided toward her, arms outstretched. "Not dead. PJ just knocked me silly. Keep talking. I need you to keep talking."

"I'm here. Come to me, Franco." She reached out a hand and they connected. Franco wilted against her and she hugged him tightly. "PJ's dead. Someone used a knife. Gutted like a fish." That was funny. Nicky snorted. "Savannah?"

"Ryan took her out. Had to carry her. They drugged her."

"Me, too. Ketamine. Like Sandra." There was something else . . . Meloni. "Do you still have your gun?" Her words slurred and Nicky squeezed her eyes tight. When she opened them, the lights at the end of the cave wavered and hopped around, like rabbits.

White rabbits.

Her mind blurred, then cleared. She still had to find the missing. Had to save their hearts, their souls, but her limbs were groggy, heavy.

"Meloni's down there. In the lights. You have to shoot him. Then we can go, we can escape. Do you have your gun?"

"Yes. In my ankle holster."

A fuzzy shadow at the end of the cave moved and the light winked. The shape tentatively walked into the open area.

"Oh, God." She wheezed in a hard breath. "He's there." Silhouetted against the lights—one black body that shivered into two. Meloni leaned over the lump on the ground. He gave a low moan that got louder and louder. She pressed her palms over her ears.

"PJ's dead, Sergeant Matthews." His arms swept around. "Poor PJ. He was *my* friend. You know what? I think I'll take your heart in his honor." He paused. "How are you feeling? Dizzy? Sleepy? You didn't get a full dose. Too bad, so sad." He said the last in a high voice, made all the more chilling by the echo. "That means it's going to hurt when I cut into you."

Franco slipped behind her and looped his arm tightly around her waist. He pressed completely against her, his strong body supporting her weakening limbs.

"Nicky, I—I can't see." He kept his wavering voice low. "PJ splashed something into my eyes before he hit me."

"Franco. No." She lost control of her voice. It bellowed out from her throat.

"Is Agent Martinez there, too? Well, hello, Franco. Were you the one who killed poor PJ? *Tsk, tsk.* Such violence." He stepped closer. Was he searching for them? Could he see where they were?

Nicky's eyesight cleared and, for a moment, the cave behind Meloni sharpened into focus.

"Tanks." Her voice rasped. "He has oxygen and hydrogen tanks, Franco. Hydrogen is famibel . . . flame-ibly . . ." Two sets of tanks wobbled drunkenly as her vision doubled again. "If we can't get Meloni, we have to shoot the tanks. Cause an explosion. Trap him, kill him. It's the only way. Your gun. Get your gun."

Franco slid down her body. He unsnapped the thumb break on his ankle holster, and the tiny sound rang loudly in her ears.

"How are you doing, Franco?" Meloni asked. He paced back and forth. "PJ told me about your little phobia. Cave crushing down on you? Or are you distracted by that head wound? So much blood. I thought you were dead. My mistake. But I'm sure it won't be long before you go down and I come for you, too."

Franco hissed as he straightened. The hard press of a revolver slid coldly along Nicky's arm. Fingers thick, she fumbled for the gun. She would have dropped it if Franco hadn't wrapped his hand around hers, closing her hand tightly around the grip.

He whispered into Nicky's ear, "Can you shoot Meloni instead of the tanks?"

"I don't think so. He's moving all over the place. Franco, he's the witch Juanita Benami told me about. He injected me with evil. He injected all of the missing with evil." She stopped on a shiver. "I'm having a hard time staying conscious."

"I've got you. I'll hold you up, help you keep steady. But you have to aim." He pulled in a shaky breath. "Nicky, an explosion could trap us. We could die." His whole body shuddered behind her and he clutched her tighter.

"If we don't stop him, he'll continue killing. More people will go missing, their souls lost. It's my job to protect these people." Her free hand covered the hand he'd wrapped around her waist. She laced their fingers and squeezed. "It's okay," she murmured. "Don't be afraid. You aren't alone." She closed her eyes again on a wave of dizziness. "It's getting bad, Franco. We have to do it. We have to," she said through gritted teeth. Nicky clutched the gun, finger on the trigger. Her arm felt like it weighed a ton and the lights quivered and jumped.

Meloni's shaved head shone at the end of the tunnel. "I'm actually feeling pretty good right now. Sergeant Matthews? You should go down soon. And Agent Martinez, you shouldn't be too much trouble after that. I have the Enemy's Heart planned for you both. Like the Fire-Sky war chiefs and their deer. Like PJ did to David Saunders. I'll have time. You think Savannah and Ryan Bernal can save you? Even if they make it out of the caves, it's a long way down the mountain."

It took every ounce of strength for Nicky to lift her arm. Franco's chin pressed against the side of her head, his hand around her wrist, his arm a brace to secure her aim. She sighted the gun on the stack of canisters, breathed out slowly.

Steady . . .

Meloni continued to talk, drawing out the seconds until they were incapacitated and he could get to them. "Actually, I'll probably be able to catch Savannah again, and use her—"

But his time was up.

"Now," Nicky said and squeezed the trigger.

CHAPTER FIFTY

The report of the shot was nothing compared to the noise of the explosion that followed.

Orange-red clouds the color of hellfire expanded and pushed air down the tunnel, hitting Nicky and Franco with a force of wind and noise that knocked them backward. She landed with a hard thud, Franco beside her. Nicky's absolute panic and will to live had her up on her feet in an instant, yanking at Franco and running.

But the heat and sound followed them, throwing balls of streaming, bouncing light past them as tiny superheated shrapnel blew down the tunnel. Pieces landed and sizzled on their clothes and exposed skin. She brushed them off with quick, frenetic movements as they stumbled and ran.

Her heart rate spiked and a slug of adrenaline mixed nastily with the ketamine that still pulsed through her. Nicky tugged and pulled at Franco and ran so fast she floated over the ground, anchored only by his large body. Lights streaked past her and she followed them, tempted to spread her arms and fly. To let go and flip in the air, free.

"Faster, Nicky! The cave—" Franco's voice choked. A rumble like the loudest thunder shuddered over the rocks and through her bones. "Left! Keep left! Look for the glow-sticks. Get us out!"

The lights zinged around her, off the walls, ceiling, and floor, bright, long tails that bent and arched and faded slowly. They bounced and hopped and she was suddenly running with bouncing, hopping rabbits that glowed green and white in front of and beside her.

Nicky grinned. They would know how to get out. "Don't worry. We'll follow the rabbits. They know the way," she said merrily as she ran and floated and dived through the wet, hot, dusty wind.

As they pounded up the tunnel, a tiny spot of light winked ahead of her, and the rabbits began to morph from animals into shimmering, running men and women.

Someone brushed her side and she turned to see Sandra Deering grin at her and speed past. Vernon Cheromiah's glowing face caught her eye before he hooked his arm through Franco's and helped them fly along. And Maryellen K'aishuni smiled sweetly as she ran in silence toward the mouth of the cave, her hand in Vernon's, pulling them forward. More faces, faces of the missing and lost, ran by, speeding out of the mountain as it rumbled and cracked behind them.

She and Franco burst from the cave and heaved in gasps of cool air, tripping on rocks and grass and shrubs. Nicky let Franco go and sailed forward, running and flying—

Only to jerk to a stop and stare around the meadow at the sentinels within the trees. Misty, glowing people—Fire-Sky Indians in traditional clothing—at least a dozen white shadows in a semicircle before her. Dawn was breaking, and the grays of the night transformed into the washed-out pastels of morning, then matured into dazzling colors as the brightness expanded with the rising of the sun.

Nicky stared at the People—no, their spirits—who beamed and nodded, until her dazzled gaze rested on an ancient figure in the center of their line, long gray hair flowing behind her in the breeze. The wrinkled skin of her face creased even tighter as she met Nicky's astonished eyes and smiled her thanks.

And the sun broke over the jagged rocks of Scalding Peak, dissipating the mists, the People. And Wind Mother vanished in a swirl of gray and gold.

Nicky dropped to her knees, openmouthed and blinking, before she fell forward and fainted spread-eagled across the moist soft grass.

CHAPTER FIFTY-ONE

Savannah skirted the rocks and ruts on the side of the road and smiled at Nicky in greeting. She picked up the Spirit's Heart pendant from Nicky's neck, its coral glowing blood-red in the afternoon sun.

"Hey! The empty slot's been filled." She touched the bright sky-blue turquoise as she spoke.

"Ryan did that for me. He chose turquoise because it represents Sandra's clan. Hummingbird."

Savannah made a noncommittal sound as she laid the pendant on Nicky's class A's. She leaned back against the Fire-Sky Police unit behind them.

"Have you two talked since . . ."

"Since PJ and the kidnapping and you, Franco, and Ryan rescued me? No," answered Savannah.

"It's been three weeks," Nicky commented.

A group of Fire-Sky and state police, FER, and Conservation officers milled about and talked in the dirt and grass in front of the house. Ryan wasn't there. He was already at the cemetery with Howard Kie. The rehab program Howard had entered for his alcohol problem had given him a two-day pass because he was doing so well. They would graveguard the first twenty-four hours.

Savannah shrugged. "Ryan's different now. Detached. Like he doesn't—"

"Doesn't love you anymore? He'll always love you, Savannah. It's just . . ." *Maybe he's finally realized he's chasing something he'll never catch.* Nicky didn't say it out loud.

"Yeah. Anyway, look at you with your hat and white gloves and all! You look badass." She tugged playfully at the brim of Nicky's peaked hat. "Even your hair is up." Her smile was back, but it had a poignant quality.

"It's only right, you know?"

Black sedans and Fire-Sky police and Conservation trucks were parked in a long line down the road. The black limousine behind her truck had been rented by the tribe for the family. Juanita Benami had asked Nicky to lead the procession to the cemetery.

"Dax Stone is here, dressed to the nines. He's in the same car as the chief and governor. He's watching your every move."

Nicky craned her neck to look. Dax smiled and talked to the chief and Captain Richards, devastatingly handsome in his dress uniform. As if feeling her eyes on him, he turned to stare. Captain followed his gaze and frowned before he looked away.

"They rescinded my suspension," Nicky said.

"Damn straight. I can't believe Franco and Laughton did that to you, especially with twenty-twenty hindsight." Savannah grinned. "You're kind of a big deal. A hero." She gave Nicky a quick hug. "Speaking of Special Agent Adonis Laughton, where is he?"

"Franco said he flew to D.C., trying to drum up support for another undercover operation against the black-market transplant ring. They didn't get Mariano Salas."

"I heard. Do you know what happened to his daughter?"

Savannah's voice was tentative. It must be hard to ask after the health of someone who had played such a prominent—if unknowing—role in her selection as victim of Meloni's organ-harvesting scheme.

Nicky shook her head.

"So will Laughton be back?" Savannah's voice was a bit too casual.

"Maybe. There are still a few loose threads to tie up. They haven't interviewed Julie Knuteson yet. I was pretty sure PJ and Meloni killed her. They got rid of everyone else associated with this case. I'm glad she was safe and sound at her sister's the whole time. And the FBI still have to get into the cave and see if they can find Meloni or any of his victims. I just don't see how."

The explosion had collapsed part of the large back cavern, opening up a hole that dropped seventy-five feet into a huge reservoir of water. One of the lakes Fire-Sky tradition said existed within Scalding Peak.

"Peter Santibanez is here, too, near the end of the procession, with some of the other war chiefs," Nicky said. "His wife didn't come." Neither had the K'aishunis. They'd held a private ceremony for Maryellen and went back to Nebraska. "The FBI said Santibanez is a cooperating witness. They won't file charges."

"Did you hear the tribal council is going to review his DNA database? They voted for money to hire an expert to study it. See if it can be used to help with membership."

"I can't believe it." Nicky shook her head.

Savannah tugged at her skirt, her gaze drifting to Scalding Peak. "It's weird how Meloni kept all those internal organs in his lab. But I'm glad, especially since one of them turned out to be Sandra's heart."

"Franco said they were trophies of his kills. Even though most of the organs he harvested were used for transplants, Meloni always kept something from his victims. The DNA testing the FBI did went a long way to give closure to the families, even if no bodies are ever found. Plus, Meloni said he was using them for experiments with his organ perfusate. He told us that when we were in the caves with him, monologuing while he waited for me and Franco—" Nicky stopped on a breath.

"Yeah. But you outsmarted him."

And had been in the hospital for two days. Franco was in even longer. He had a concussion from the rock-pounding, and whatever PJ had splashed on his face—some kind of caustic chemical—had done a number on his skin. Miraculously, the blue contact lenses he wore as part of his undercover persona had protected his sight.

She'd known something was off the first time she saw him.

Shifting, Nicky stared at the front door of the house. What was taking so long?

Savannah nudged her arm. "So Franco decided to stay on, keep his Conservation job?"

Nicky couldn't stop the slow smile that crept across her lips. "Yeah."

"When are you two going to dinner?"

"Next week. My house. Maybe." It was a start. There were still a lot of trust issues she had to deal with.

Savannah gasped. "But you *never* have anyone over to your house!"

"I said *maybe*," Nicky reiterated, but Savannah ignored her.

"*I've* never been over to your house. You like him better than you like me." Savannah humphed and crossed her arms, her lips quivering as she suppressed her grin.

Finally, the front door opened.

Nicky called, "Attention!"

The officers and agents in the yard quickly fell into two stiff columns that lined the walkway from the house. Squire Concho eased out of the door, eyes wide as he stared at the formal escort. Cyrus Aguilar followed and the two walked solemnly toward the latched front gate.

Nicky swung it open to allow them to pass through.

A few seconds later, Franco stepped out, gently guiding Juanita Benami. In her hands, she cradled a turquoise inlaid box.

Sandra's heart was inside, to be laid to rest beside her at the ceremony this afternoon. Nicky swallowed the thickness gathering in her throat.

Juanita hobbled toward her, Franco next to her, tall and handsome. The brim of his fawn-colored Stetson shadowed eyes and skin still sensitive to sunlight. As the two of them moved through the gate, his eyes, a warm, deep brown, smiled at Nicky.

The men in the yard assembled into a line behind Franco and Juanita and marched past Nicky to their vehicles. When the last one was through, Nicky swung the gate back into place and latched it securely.

She climbed into her unit and took one last look at the metal gateway in her rearview as she drove away. It was the one that wouldn't stay closed when Sandra Deering was lost. But, today, her Spirit's Heart would be returned to her. She and all the others weren't lost anymore.

They could finally come home.

ACKNOWLEDGMENTS

I'd like to thank Anne Hillerman, the Western Writers of America, and St. Martin's Press/Minotaur for the wonderful Tony Hillerman Prize they sponsor each year. I'd also like to thank LERA and my critique group members, BP, EK, and LR. I learned so much from you. I'm still learning.

ABOUT THE AUTHOR

CAROL POTENZA is an Assistant Professor of Chemistry and Biochemistry at New Mexico State University. She and her husband, Leos, live in Las Cruces, New Mexico. *Hearts of the Missing*, her debut novel, is the winner of the 2017 Tony Hillerman Prize.